"YOU BELONG HERE. YOU HAVE FROM THE MOMENT YOU SET FOOT ON THE ISLAND. . . ."

She moved her shoulders, his hands fell away, and she rose, facing him.

"Fiske, don't . . . I can't . . ." She didn't know what to say.

"You can." He pulled her to him and covered her lips with his. His arms held her tight against him and wouldn't let her go. Unable to resist, she found herself returning his kiss; her arms stole around his neck, and when he buried his head in her hair, she didn't move except to turn her head into his shoulder.

His voice was husky when he whispered, "You see?"

She was unable to answer.

"I think I'm falling in love with you, Caddy."

She wrenched herself away. "You mustn't. You can't love me."

He held her by the arm, not letting her escape entirely. "Why not, for God's sake? Why?"

"It could never work. We're too different. I can't give up—"

"I'm not asking you to give up anything in your life —only to add something wonderful. . . ."

Also by Carol Marsh

Mornings of Gold

Carol Marsh

A DELL BOOK

Published by
Dell Publishing
a division of
Bantam Doubleday Dell Publishing Group, Inc.
1540 Broadway
New York, New York 10036

ISBN: 0-440-21627-3

Printed in the United States of America

Published simultaneously in Canada

April 1995

10   9   8   7   6   5   4   3   2   1

RAD

If thou must love me, let it be for nought
Except for love's sake only.

Sonnets from the Portuguese
ELIZABETH BARRETT BROWNING

CHAPTER 1

"The mountain has come to Muhammad," Agatha announced from the doorway. She looked around Caddy's low-ceilinged top-floor room with interest. "Since you're apparently too busy to spend any time with your old aunt, you've forced me to visit a part of the house I haven't seen in years. It's really quite nice up here, isn't it?"

"Aunt Agatha." Caddy paused in the act of straightening the paisley cover on her brass bed. She smiled broadly at the portly octogenarian with dyed bright red hair and quickly swept a pile of manuscript paper from a low wicker chair. "Sit here and talk to me. I'm so glad to see you."

"Is this thing safe? Couldn't you find something

sturdier for yourself in the storeroom?" Still breathing heavily from the unusual exertion of having climbed three steep flights of brownstone stairs, Agatha gingerly lowered her bulk into the chair. She resumed her inspection of the tiny premises, scrutinizing in silence the photographs that covered one whole wall. A hint of a breeze scented by the clematis vine that covered the back of the house drifted in from a tiny terrace framed by French doors. Agatha sighed deeply.

"To what do I owe the honor of this unexpected visit? It's awfully early for you to be up, isn't it? Not that I'm not always happy to see you, darling," Caddy added hastily. She pulled the sash of her bathrobe around her waist more tightly.

"It *is* early," her aunt replied in an injured voice. Picking up a magazine, she fanned herself lightly. "You're never in for dinner anymore—or for breakfast, Mathilde tells me. We haven't had a chance to talk for weeks."

"Aunt Agatha," Caddy chided. "You've got something up your sleeve. What is it?" Ducking behind a tall folding screen, she stood for a moment contemplating her meager wardrobe.

"Do I have to have a reason to talk to my favorite niece?"

"You do if you get up in the middle of the night to do it. It's only twenty of ten, and you never stir out of your room before noon." Making up her mind, Caddy dressed swiftly, pulling on neatly pressed well-worn beige cord slacks, a man's plain white tailored shirt, and over it all a gold-braided navy officer's jacket she had unearthed in a nearby thrift shop.

Another deep sigh came from the other side of the screen. Caddy smiled to herself. Emerging from her makeshift dressing room, she dropped a kiss on top of the shockingly red head and perched cross-legged on the end of her bed facing Agatha.

Agatha looked at her with dismay. "You're not going out dressed like that, are you?"

"Of course. A free-lance interview and then lunch with Ward. I'm very trendy. Don't you like it?" Caddy looked down at her outfit with pleasure, admiring the faded gold stripes and the brass buttons on her jacket.

Agatha sniffed. "Are you meeting Ward dressed in that rig?"

"Right after my appointment." Caddy leaned forward eagerly. "I'm seeing the managing editor of *Nature's World* this morning. I'm pretty sure he's going to offer me a big assignment, and if he does I'm going to take it so fast it will make his head spin. God. Do I need the money." She grinned at her aunt.

Agatha frowned. "I wish you'd let me help you, but I know your idiotic pride won't allow it. Besides, I didn't climb all the way up here to get started on that old discussion."

Caddy leaned forward earnestly. "But you do help me, darling, just by letting me live up here in my penthouse without paying rent. I probably couldn't afford to live in New York, much less this neighborhood, if it weren't for you."

"Never mind. Never mind all that." Agatha forestalled any further expression of gratitude by holding up one plump hand, which glittered with several large diamond rings.

"Tell me why you've come to visit, then. Is it something nice?" Caddy drew her knees up beneath her chin and prepared herself to listen to a tale of the latest domestic crisis in the Gramercy Square house.

"I've come to discuss your future, young lady," Agatha replied ominously.

Caddy was both amused and surprised. Despite the warmth and charm with which she had been welcomed into Agatha's home, her aunt rarely commented on Caddy's life-style. Actually, Caddy thought affectionately, she wasn't a true aunt at all, since Agatha's first husband had been merely a cousin of Caddy's father. Married three times and a famous hostess on two continents in her youth, Agatha Dinsmore Wilcox Parnett DaSilva lived in near seclusion in the house on the Square, which she inherited from her last husband, Roland DaSilva. Despite the remoteness of their relation and the more than sixty years that separated them, the two entirely dissimilar women had forged a strong bond. "Why my future so early in the morning?" Caddy inquired with a chuckle.

"Because it's the only time you're here, child. Imagine. I had to have Mathilde wake me up just to talk to you. She was scandalized. But I simply told her, 'Mathilde, I must talk to that girl before she does something foolish, so stop your muttering and get me dressed because I'm going to the top of the house if it kills me.'" Agatha adjusted her silk shawl primly.

Caddy gave a shout of laughter. "You're outrageous. What on earth is so important? I can't have Mathilde giving me dark looks every time I pass her on the stairs because I've upset her darling madame. What *is* it?"

"I think it's high time you stopped having an affair with your young man and married him," Agatha replied bluntly.

"Married? To Ward?" Caddy flushed.

"Well? He's certainly proposed by now, hasn't he?" Agatha looked at her keenly.

Caddy nodded briefly in acknowledgment. She twisted the narrow silver bracelet around on her slender wrist, wishing Agatha wouldn't pry. Ward had been pushing her to get married for the past several weeks, ever since he'd decided to run for Congress from the silk-stocking district, and she was unsure herself why she was so reluctant to accept. He was her first lover, the only man she had ever thought she loved, but there were still moments when she felt as if she didn't completely know him.

"Well?"

"Well what?"

"Have you accepted? Are you going to become engaged to him?"

Disconcerted, Caddy rose from the bed and picked up the clothes she had discarded on the only other chair in the room. She folded them neatly and put them in the bottom drawer of a battered cherry chest. With her back to her aunt, she replied with assumed lightness, "We're fine the way we are. I like our relationship, Aunt. Besides, why are you worrying about all this now, this morning?"

"Because it's been on my mind. I know you think I'm a relic from another century, but I know this: If you don't marry Ward Abernathy, he'll find someone who will. He's handsome, wealthy, well connected, and ambitious. He loves you and wants to take care of you *and* your family. What more could you want? What more could you need? He's a catch, my girl, and you'll be foolish if you let him slip away because you have some silly, wild idea about having your own career."

Caddy wheeled around. "It's not a silly idea. I do have a career, one I've worked hard for. I'm finally beginning to get some real recognition for it."

Agatha made an exclamation of disgust. "Recognition. A long word that won't keep your feet warm on a cold night. *Or* put diamonds on your wrist."

"I don't want to give up everything for marriage.

Marriage would interfere with my work. I'll never let that happen to me," she continued crossly, entirely disregarding her aunt's homily.

"Ward can provide you with security for the rest of your life."

Caddy drew a deep breath. "Security isn't everything, Aunt Agatha. Besides, helping out at home is my responsibility. I won't marry Ward just because he has enough money to give Thad the things he needs. I can do that myself, and I will." She felt a surge of pride saying the words, pleased with herself that her modest success already allowed her to send money home to Philadelphia, money that made a difference in the small household there.

"Pshaw," Agatha snorted. "Even wrapped up in their work as they are, that father and mother of yours are perfectly capable of taking care of your brother. Multiple sclerosis isn't the end of the world."

"I know, but . . ." Caddy's words trailed off. What she couldn't bring herself to say was that from the time she was a young girl, she had found herself assuming the job of running the cramped Philadelphia row house as her anthropologist parents became more and more immersed in their life's collaboration, an exhaustive study of a tiny, obscure subspecies of an aboriginal tribe. It was Caddy who had supervised the small household, making sure the bill collectors were satisfied and food appeared on the table at regular intervals. Now that she had come to New York to further her career, she was driven by the need to send enough money home to pay for the daily worker who cared for Thad.

Agatha eyed Caddy shrewdly. "Let you run the house, did they? I always thought James and Louisa were fools."

Stung, Caddy replied quickly, "Don't say that. They're not fools at all. It's just that they're dedicated to their research."

"They never could think about anything but each other and those books they write together. Dull things, those books. I can't imagine who reads that dry research; I never could get beyond the first page of any of them."

Intrigued by the unexpected picture of her other-worldly parents as lovers, Caddy resumed her seat on the bed and asked, "Is that really true? About Ma and Pa only thinking about each other."

"I think the only time James Wilcox looked up from his studies was the day your mother walked into his class at the university. She didn't have a cent and neither did he, but they were determined to get married and work together. Your father was a very good-looking fellow in his time, and with the Wilcox name behind him he could have married any girl in Philadelphia, even though he was as poor as a church mouse. Love," Agatha snorted.

"You must believe in love, Aunt Agatha. After all, you've been married four times," Caddy teased.

"There's love and there's love. My mother told me it was just as easy to fall in love with a rich man as a poor one, something you might keep in mind, young lady. Look at your parents. They don't have the slightest interest in money; they never have and I doubt if they ever will."

Caddy leaned forward intently. "This is silly. You can't be serious that I should marry Ward just because he's wealthy. If I marry anyone, it will be as a partner I love, not just to be a wife."

"And what, may I ask, is wrong with being a wife?"

"Nothing, unless it means always giving up my career for his political needs, presiding over his household, and raising his children without any other interests of my own while he advances his career," Caddy burst out passionately.

"Is that what's holding you back? I thought there was something. He wants you to give up all this? You could take your pictures after you were married, couldn't you?" Agatha gestured toward the wall of photographs.

"It might be all right as a hobby, but I don't think Ward gives a damn about my professional life," Caddy confessed. She sat up very straight with her shoulders squared. It wasn't just the money for Thad that drove her, she thought fiercely; the work itself meant too much to give up for any man, even Ward. She wanted to be recognized, wanted to be known as a great photographer, wanted everything that went with it. Unlike her mother and father laboring away together in obscurity, she was going to be a success in life in her own right.

Silence filled the sunlit room as Agatha stared thoughtfully at Caddy. "I applaud your dedication, my dear, but don't let your ambition hamper your ability to compromise. Ward Abernathy is a catch and you'll regret it if you let him get away."

"Oh, Aunt Agatha," Caddy replied with a smothered sound somewhere between laughter and tears. "What a word, *catch*. It's antediluvian."

"It's common sense, Catherine. Common sense. If that mother of yours had done her job properly, you'd know it. Well, I've said my piece. Give me your hand and help me out of this absurd chair. Mathilde will think I've had a stroke up here."

Sure enough, after Caddy had gently helped her aunt to rise and kissed her rouged cheek, they found

Agatha's stern-faced maid waiting disapprovingly at the head of the stairs. Without a word to Caddy, Mathilde held out her arm as a crutch and the two elderly women carefully descended to the lower floors.

Left alone, Caddy closed the terrace doors and locked them securely, picked up her briefcase, and after a moment when she wondered soberly if her aunt's advice could possibly have some truth to it, walked slowly down the three narrow flights of stairs to the main floor.

Sunlight filtered in through the etched-glass windows on either side of the front door, touching the marble floor tiles in the small entryway. Pausing to check her appearance in the tall pier mirror backing the Victorian mahogany hat rack that took up part of one wall near the front door, Caddy hesitated, examining her reflection in the glass. Looking back at her was a tall, slender woman with dark brown hair pulled back into a French braid and wide, clear hazel eyes and a thin, rather serious face. She frowned. Then, quietly, she let herself out of the house and stood for a moment on the stoop, enjoying the view of Gramercy Park across the street. Inside the park, rows of tulips were unfurling their bright colors on the borders of the neat gravel path, while above them the trees sported proud new pale green leaves.

She was still deep in thought when she reached the sidewalk, turning over and over Aunt Agatha's admonitions in her mind. Her preoccupation was so great that she crossed Park Avenue without waiting for the signal to change.

Startled out of her reverie by the siren of a passing police car, she looked up and realized she had reached her destination: the dull brick building that housed *Nature's World*. She ducked into the doorway, checking her watch for the time. It was just ten o'clock. Deciding against the slow-moving elevator, she ran up two flights of stairs and arrived breathless at the office of the managing editor, Dave Barrish. Within minutes she was listening eagerly as he described the assignment he wanted her to accept.

"They've never let photographers on Kincade Island before," Dave instructed her soberly in his gravelly voice. "This is a one-shot deal, and I expect you to come back with your best work. We're going to give it the lead in the fall."

"Cover?" she asked, holding her breath. Her last assignment for *Nature's World* had been in Maine, exploring in pictures the shy, elusive ospreys that nested along the rocky coast. There had been some talk then of putting one of her shots on the cover, but much to her disappointment that dream had failed to materialize. It was her goal to be able to pick and choose her own assignments, and for that she needed more exposure.

"Maybe, maybe," Barrish conceded, lighting his third cigar of the morning; his partially buttoned vest was already covered with a thin layer of ashes from the previous ones. "That's up to you. The island is so private, it's not even on the charts and that's the way they want to keep it, so tread carefully."

She nodded. "How did you do it? To whom do we owe and what?"

Barrish pointed toward the ceiling of his office with his cigar and she nodded again. They smiled at each other. It was apparent to her that he was also thinking of the short, ruthless publisher who ruled the magazine like a despot and whose one weak spot seemed to be a bewildering passion for bird-watching. Besides sitting on the boards of both the Audubon Society and the National Wildlife Federation, Nathan Miller referred to himself proudly as a "birder" and vanished periodically to other continents to add to his list of sightings. "Nathan was at an Audubon meeting and one of the other board members, Nelson Lovering, the ornithologist, approached him about getting a photographer to record the white kite."

"White kite?"

"A bird that rarely comes this far north. Apparently he's got a small colony of them on the island that return year after year from their home in Chile. Lovering wants the phenomenon recorded professionally, and Nathan wanted to be the first to publish any photographs that were taken, so they made a deal."

"How come Nathan's not coming too? This sounds like something he'd kill to see."

Barrish rolled his eyes in mock horror. "The island families didn't want anyone on the island at all. Lovering managed to get them to agree to allow one *Nature's World* photographer on their hallowed land, but since Nathan doesn't know a lens from a viewfinder, that excluded him." They grinned at each other.

"How much?" she asked in a businesslike tone, bracing herself for a bargaining session. Her palms were damp with perspiration and her heart was pounding. She needed this job. The photography course she taught at the New School had just ended and with it the regular paycheck on which she lived, allowing her to send all her other income to Philadelphia; her second textbook of photographs for an educational science series was currently in production, but she wouldn't see any money from that for another six months; her next assignments for *National Geographic* were scheduled for August, and it was only the beginning of May now. She was never entirely free of worry that someday there wouldn't be enough money because she could have done even more, and Thad would suffer because of it.

"Three thousand," the managing editor said flatly in a voice that said "This is my best and final offer."

"Five."

"Out of the question."

"Try."

"Four?"

"Four five." She felt her heart skip a beat as she waited to see if she had pushed him too far.

"I'll try."

"Done."

Caddy let out a barely perceptible sigh of satisfaction. The muscles in her neck ached from the tension of holding out for a higher price, but she felt a spurt of exultation at the thought of the extra money she had achieved. "Thanks," she grinned, hoping her relief wasn't too obvious.

"No thanks needed. You're worth it. You've come a long way in six years. You've got your own niche now as one of the photographers of endangered wildlife we can count on."

"I wish it paid better. Not that I'm not thrilled with this fee," she added hastily.

"You sure work your tail off, Caddy. What the hell drives you? You photograph for textbooks, you teach, you do God-knows-what. Do you ever sleep?"

"Not much," she admitted with a short laugh.

There was silence between them, during which Dave relit his cigar and eyed her speculatively. "Thad doing all right?"

She closed her eyes briefly. In a weak moment during one of Thad's relapses, she had confided to Dave about her brother. She knew Dave was only being solicitous, but it hurt when she thought about Thad. The day Thad had been diagnosed with multiple sclerosis still remained in her memory as one of the darkest days of her life. "He's okay. The same," she replied sadly.

"Cortisone working better?"

"I think so. He's been in remission for almost eighteen months, and some of the worst of his symptoms have disappeared. No more vertigo or trembling."

"No more hospitals?"

She held up crossed fingers. Although she had never mentioned it, and Dave had never asked, she thought he probably guessed that sometimes she felt as if her whole life had been a constant worry over where the money was going to come from to cover the cost of all the care Thad needed.

Dave leaned sideways and tossed his crumpled cigar wrapper expertly into a battered wastepaper basket. "Two points," he announced with satisfaction. "You mind telling me something?" he asked almost shyly.

"What?"

"Why don't you get yourself a steady job that pays a real salary instead of all this running around? You could make more money that way, on one of the big magazines. *Life,* or *People* maybe, or the *National Enquirer.* They pay big dough."

Caddy considered his question for a second. She chose her words carefully. "Not right away they don't. I've got it all planned out, Dave. When I graduated from Bryn Mawr I knew I could get a job with a steady income, but it wouldn't be a very big one. I gambled that if I free-lanced and was willing to do other things at the same time, I'd make more money in the long run. And if you're a nice guy and give me the cover with this job, it will take me one step further."

"One step further to where? Where are you going?"

"Fame and fortune," she replied lightly, but she could feel the tension in her neck again. Her gamble just had to pay off. Not only for Thad's sake, but for her own.

When Dave smiled at her, she put her feet up on the desk with an audible sigh and prepared to listen to the background research the magazine had assembled.

The managing editor rustled through the messy pile of papers on his desk and unearthed a thin folder. Opening it, he cleared his throat and began to read aloud: "Almost two hundred years ago, a wealthy doctor from Hartford, Micah Kincade, bought a sixty-acre island off the Connecticut coast for his family, along with several lesser islands long since sold off by his heirs." With a grimace of distaste, he grunted and threw the folder back down on his desk. "It's too early in the morning for me to read this crap. One of our researchers used to work for *Town and Country* in an earlier, more unfortunate incarnation, and this is an unpublished article she managed to finagle for us from their files."

Retrieving the file, Caddy thumbed through the folder, looking for photographs. "Why didn't they publish it?"

"They never got to first base. No one would give them an interview. They sent a reporter across with a photographer, but their boat was turned away. They couldn't even land."

"Is it still owned by one family? Were they the ones who wouldn't talk to *Town and Country*?"

"Even the Kincades didn't have that much money. When the financial drain became too much to manage, the surviving family members divided the island into seven parcels of land and invited a few rich pals to join them as owners. By the turn of the century six or seven new families had joined them and each had built their own rambling, shingled summer home. Reportedly, each house is right smack in the middle of its own parcel of land, as if being on an island isn't privacy enough."

"Who were they?" she asked curiously.

"I'm not entirely sure," he admitted. "We could find out by searching land deeds, I suppose, but since you're not allowed to talk to them anyway, I figure it doesn't much matter."

She nodded her head. She had little interest in the people anyway; they would just interfere with her getting the job done.

Barrish paused in the act of relighting his cigar and, using the stub as a pointer to emphasize the gravity of his words, lectured her sternly. "Don't ever forget: You're absolutely prohibited from talking to the natives. Just photograph the birds and the marsh and get the hell off the island."

She grinned. "They'll never see me. I'll be on and off like a gray ghost. Anything else I should know?"

"There's not a hell of a lot more information to give you. Nothing much has changed up there in the last hundred years. There aren't any paved roads, no stores or churches. The electricity comes from private generators, and water comes from their own wells. What's left of the Kincade family still summers in the original house. That's it, pal." He watched as she carefully stowed the folder in her slim attaché case.

"I don't mind the restrictions, but why all the fuss?"

He smiled ironically. "Seems these folks have a highly developed sense of their own right to privacy. They hold all the land between them and they ain't about to share with anyone. They think if anyone finds out what they're sitting on, they'll want a piece of it."

"Sounds paranoid to me," she scoffed, rising to her feet.

He scratched his head and sighed. "What the hell. If you can't speak to them, you don't need to know who they are, right?"

"The hell with them," she said in mock ferocity.

"The hell with them," he agreed. "Good luck. Make me proud of you."

With a wave of her hand she made her way through the cluttered outer office, down two flights of steep stairs, and out into the bright sunlight.

The *Nature's World* building faced onto the east side of Union Square and, dodging the uptown traffic, she crossed the street and walked to the north end of the square where the Greenmarket was in full progress. Halting abruptly, she stared at the pyramids of radishes, carrots, and cabbages that were stacked side by side with early spring daisies and branches of yellow forsythia; the scent of herbs vied with early melons and homemade cheeses; the smell of freshly baked bread hung over it all. The scene blurred for a moment as she remembered where she was going next. Lunch with Ward. Her elation vanished and was replaced by a feeling of distress. How was she going to tell Ward she had accepted yet another assignment that would take her away from the city? He would be furious.

Walking slowly through the market, she evaded a shopper while she worried over how to coax her lover out of his certain anger. She narrowly escaped being hit by a shopper carrying a bottle of mineral water inside her Rollerblade, and she automatically circumnavigated another who was flower-coordinated from the print of her dress to the rose tattoo on her back.

Reaching Sixteenth Street, she paused on the corner, still thinking hard.

Ward had been her lover for almost three years, but their relationship went back much further than that, to the days when she was a scholarship student at Bryn Mawr and he the handsome, glamorous brother of one of her dorm mates. Even then he had made her laugh. It had been electrifying when he called her shortly after she arrived in Gramercy Park, and when he swept her up into a glamorous whirl of New York nightclubs and Broadway openings, she had been dazzled. He was her first lover, the only man she had ever loved. They were good together.

She remembered the feeling of inevitability she had had when they became lovers, his attentiveness matching her willingness, with the only surprise being Ward's when he discovered he was her first lover. Caught up in the thrill of her first real affair, it had been months before she realized how little her professional life meant to Ward. He would expect her to be a traditional housewife. Could Agatha be right? If she loved Ward, and she was sure she did, would the best thing be to put her career to one side and marry him?

The thought of losing him, as Agatha predicted, filled her with loneliness, and suddenly all she could think of was that she had to see Ward before another second went by.

Taking a deep breath, she almost ran the half block to the doorway of the tall, dignified building that housed the Union Square Café.

She was late, and the restaurant's three rooms were already filled with the literary agents, editors, and publishers who were its most loyal clientele. The bar was crowded with executives waiting for their tables, and she spotted a famous food journalist arguing with a well-known winemaker at a little table by the front window. She found Ward sitting at a table beneath a brilliant-colored Frank Stella oil, and she smiled at him apologetically as she slid into the chair the maître d' held for her.

"I'm late. I'm sorry," she said, kissing his ear before she slid into the seat opposite him. She reached across the table for his hand.

With a small smile that didn't reach his eyes, Ward Abernathy raised his eyebrows interrogatively. His blond hair was carefully combed, and his suit was tailored to make the most of his tall physique. She was sure his shoes were perfectly polished and that he probably had a spare fresh white shirt in the limousine waiting outside. He looked like the ambitious, up-and-coming politician he was.

When he didn't acknowledge her apology, she leaned back in her seat and picked up the long menu. "I got the assignment," she announced proudly, peering over the top to see his reaction.

"Which one is this?"

"I told you. To photograph the marsh on Kincade Island."

"Where's that?" His clear forehead was marred by a tiny frown.

"Ward, I told you about it before. It's off the coast of Connecticut, in Long Island Sound." Sometimes, she thought with a sigh, it seemed as if he barely listened to a word she said.

"Is that where the Dwights go?" Ward had the politician's knack for knowing someone everywhere.

"Who knows?" She shrugged her shoulders and leaned to her left as the waitress placed a fresh arugula salad in front of her.

"When do you leave?" He didn't look at her as he

asked the question, twirling the stem of his glass as if the answer didn't matter.

"Tomorrow morning from New London. There's only one ferry over—at ten o'clock—and I've got to be on it."

"I don't want you to leave right now, Caddy." He was frowning as he raised his eyes from his glass and looked directly at her. "I need you here. You know how important the meeting with the governor is for me, and he expects you to be there too."

She shifted uneasily in her seat, but her voice was firm when she replied, "You knew when you were asked to dinner that I would accept the assignment if it was offered to me. You should never have said I'd be there."

"But it's important. If Governor Lewis gives me his backing tomorrow night, I'm sure to get on the primary ballot in September. It's a once-in-a-lifetime chance, Caddy. I don't want to blow it."

"You don't need me there. *I'm* not a politician. It's you he's interested in, not me." And anyway, she reminded herself, Ward knew perfectly well how she loathed long, tedious evenings of political conversation.

"Come on, Caddy." Ward's voice was thin with barely concealed exasperation. "It's bad enough that we're not married, but if you don't show up at all it'll look like you don't give a damn." He spaced his words out for emphasis. "And if you can't support me enough to change your plans to show up for dinner with the governor, for Christ's sake, what will he think?"

"It doesn't matter what he thinks about me, Ward; you're the one who wants to run for Congress."

"We've been together for three years now. Every-

body thinks of us as a couple. It won't look right."
They stared at each other, and when she didn't reply,
Ward burst out angrily, "If you'd just marry me, we
wouldn't be having these arguments."

"Why? Because then you'd expect your wife to drop
everything and do what your career demanded? My
work's just as important to me as yours is to you. Besides, I told you right from the start, I was not the
marrying kind." Hearing the tremor in her own voice,
she took a deep, steadying breath. She just had to
make him understand how important her work was,
once and for all.

"You take pictures, Caddy. You can do that anytime.
It's not as if you have a nine-to-five job in an office or
anything like that."

"I don't just 'take pictures' as you call it. I'm a serious photographer with a serious career and responsibilities of my own. I need every cent I earn, and you
know it. I know you've heard it before, but I do mean
it. You just don't seem to remember." She spaced out
her words to give them emphasis, to underline their
enormous significance to her.

The smile faded from Ward's face as they looked at
each other wordlessly. "How long are you going to let
your life be controlled by your family?" he asked finally.

"As long as they need me. That's part of who I am,"
she replied levelly. She wondered why Ward could
never understand how much she minded the genteel
poverty in which her family lived, in a run-down neighborhood sandwiched between fashionable Rittenhouse
Square and Society Hill. She wanted them to have all
the comforts they lacked: Her dream was that one day
she would be able to buy them a new furnace to re-
place the old one that was always breaking down in the

dead of winter, perhaps even new bathrooms or, better yet, a new house in a safer part of Philadelphia.

"You could start by finding a better place for Thad, with other people like him where he'd get the care he needs."

"Put Thad in a home?" She stiffened up in anger, seeing Thad's pale, uncomplaining face in front of her. She couldn't imagine him somewhere without his beloved books and music, free at any hour of the day or night to play the violin that was never far from his side.

"Something like that," he admitted. "You can't go on like this forever, running down to Philadelphia every time there's a flap. You've got to get on with your own life. I could make that possible; you'd never have to worry about them again."

"I have my own life, Ward, and I won't just abandon my family. And I certainly don't plan on getting married to anyone just because they could assume my financial responsibilities."

"I seem to remember we planned on getting married sometime soon. Aren't we?"

"You're the one who wants to get married. I'm not as sure as I should be. I can't right now." She lowered her eyes. She didn't want to hurt him, but she couldn't lie. He was the first man she had ever cared for, finding in him a glamour and excitement that had been absent from her hard-working life until they had met, but she wasn't convinced that the public life of the wife of a New York politician could ever mesh with the career she had fought so hard to build.

They sat in a pool of silence surrounded by the clatter of the dining room while Ward signed the check and smiled automatically at the waitress.

He looked at her, assessing her mood. "It's obvious

you have no intention of coming," he said in a flat statement.

"Not this time." She made her voice soft, but Ward looked away.

His head was still turned from her as he spoke in a voice that was almost detached. "I'm fed up with this crap. I'm fed up with you running off all the time to take pictures of some fucking birds. You could get a job on the staff of any magazine in New York and earn more money than you do free-lancing and without always having to leave the city. It's time for us to get married and have a family. I've waited long enough." He looked at her, waiting for her response.

"Not right now," she repeated.

"Shit."

"I *have* to go tomorrow, Ward. Please." She saw the anger in his face and leaned forward, ready to explain all over again. But without waiting to hear what she was going to say, he pushed back his chair and started to rise. His face was flushed with resentment.

"If that's your final decision, I won't be here when you come back, Caddy. These damn birds mean more to you than I do, and I've had it." Without another word or a backward glance in her direction, he turned and walked across the dining room, up the steps, and out of the restaurant.

"Ward," she protested. But he was gone. She gasped, hoping it had all been some sort of surrealistic nightmare, but he really had left the room. She felt bruised, as if he had physically struck her across the face, and slowly she raised one hand to her cheek to ward off another phantom blow. Numbly, she turned her head and watched through the window as Ward entered his waiting car, her gaze automatically following the limousine's smooth progress as it pulled slowly away from the curb.

Should she have stopped him? Should she have given in? It would be so easy to marry Ward and be surrounded by all his wealth; she would never have to chase another job or spend another sleepless night worrying about the future. She tried to think calmly, but her thoughts were too scattered. She had put such single-minded effort into making a success of herself. Her work meant too much to her to give it up, even for Ward.

Wearily, she gathered her things. She felt battered and exhausted, and all she wanted to do was go back to the safety of her small apartment and lick her wounds in privacy. She couldn't think about the scene that had just ended, surrounded by strangers in a crowded restaurant. Still in shock, she rose and walked slowly, almost blindly, up the same stairs Ward had taken to the street and, without thinking, turned left toward Gramercy Square. Retracing her way through the crowded Greenmarket, she blinked back hot tears, realizing that Ward had actually discarded her; he had removed himself from her life as if their years together had meant nothing. She felt almost dizzy as the sting of his cool rejection washed over her, and she edged blindly through the throngs of noonday shoppers trying to reach the other side of the market.

Although her tears were coming faster now, beneath her pain there seemed to be a small, quiet voice of reason telling her that trading her freedom and career for his position and financial security would have been too great a price to pay.

CHAPTER 2

Leaning out over the wooden railing, Caddy stared down at the churning wake the creaking private ferry made as it pulled slowly away from the Connecticut mainland and plowed its way out of the harbor into Long Island Sound. Above her head sea gulls cried to each other as they circled the boat looking in vain for food. She watched through the lingering fog until the shore slowly receded and the New London houses became indistinguishable from the trees. She shivered and pulled the collar of her anorak tight around her throat as she made her way unsteadily to the front of the boat. The early May wind was biting, more like March than May; spring was going to be very late this year. She shivered and hugged her arms around her body for warmth, peering over the choppy waves for her first glimpse of Kincade Island.

Except for a burly man in a down parka who had parked his plumber's van next to her ancient Ford Mustang in the parking lot at the end of the dock on the mainland, she was the only passenger. Hoisting a large bag of tools easily to his shoulder, the plumber had nodded to her pleasantly and strode down the dock to join a white-haired man who turned out to be the captain. She was, the captain assured her as he showed her where to stow her luggage and her cameras, lucky the fog was lifting or they might not have made the run across the four miles that separated them from the island. Tipping his well-worn hat politely, he had left her to her own devices as he and the obliging plumber busied themselves with the lines and then disappeared into the tiny pilot's cabin for the rest of the voyage.

She was relieved not to have to talk to anyone. She was tired. She had barely closed her eyes the previous night, unable to stop going over and over in her mind the scene in the restaurant with Ward. Drifting into a fitful sleep just as dawn was breaking, she had been awakened after only an hour by the ring of her alarm clock, and determined not to have to spend the night in a motel in New London, she had hurriedly packed and left New York in order to catch the single daily ferry that left for the island. Now, with an uninterrupted ride stretching ahead of her, she took a deep breath and attempted to clear her mind, giving herself a chance to sort out the years she and Ward had spent together.

From the very start she had thought his life seemed so electrifying compared to hers. He was just starting his career as a politician, working in Washington as an

aide to the senior senator from New York, and she had
been captivated by the titillating bits of inside information and witty stories he told her about the horse-
trading that went on in the capital. Her face softened
and she almost smiled, remembering what a thrill it
had been for her at the beginning when she, a serious,
somewhat shy girl from an academic background,
would see his picture in the papers and realize she
actually knew him. He used to pick her out of the
crowd of undergraduates and tease her, telling her he
was going to show her New York when she was old
enough, but back then she had never taken him seriously.

Then, right from the first night, he had been a wonderful lover. He had been so gentle, so tender, that all
her apprehensions had vanished and she had been able
to meet his passion with an intensity of her own that
delighted them both. With an ache of loss, she thought
about how he loved to see her naked in the sunlight,
how he wanted to make love to her in every conceivable position, and how she had quickly learned to do
what pleased him most. The awe of having a lover who
brought her to such peaks of ecstasy had overwhelmed
her right up until the past year. If she had recently
come to wonder if there might be something missing in
their lovemaking, she had pushed the thought from
her mind and never mentioned it to him. She stared
blindly down at the water, seeing clearly at last what
she should have acknowledged then: when their ardor
for each other diminished, it was the signal that something larger was missing.

Startled by a short, imperative blast from the boat's
horn, she turned and looked back at the captain, who
pointed off to the left. A towering, double-tiered ferry
surged by them going in the opposite direction from

Orient Point to New London, its great wake making the smaller craft roll precipitously from side to side. Caddy grabbed the rail to keep her balance, watching absently as the larger boat beat its way across the sound like a stately ocean liner in comparison to the sturdy little *Kincade*.

What was there about Ward that she loved? After three years in New York she was no longer beguiled by flashy parties or trendy gatherings; she had been wondering for some time why the life of a politician had to be so much on the social circuit, and she had been conscious of the fact that she wanted more out of life. Or if not more, something different. She shivered, remembering the long evenings spent in the company of wealthy Park Avenue denizens who dabbled in politics, watching Ward flatter one socialite after another, or sitting uncomfortably in dark, trendy clubs while he wooed well-known entertainers for their support. Was it then she realized the life he led wasn't so exciting after all, merely rather superficial?

"But what about the homeless people, women who can't afford to feed their children, kids who grow up only knowing about drugs? You could make a difference, Ward," she had pled passionately on more than one occasion.

"These are my people, Caddy. They're the ones who will back me and pay for the campaign. It's who you know in this business that gets you elected."

"They don't care about making things better. All they want is to get their pictures in Suzy's column."

He laughed. "Did you see her there? With that designer?"

"The one in taffeta you were so cozy with in the library?"

"Watch. Bet she mentions us in her column tomorrow." He nuzzled her neck. Caddy shifted uncomfortably. No matter how many times Ward told her it wasn't true, she was sure the chauffeur watched them kissing in the rearview mirror.

"Is that what you want? To be in her column with the rest of those people?"

He pulled away. "What I want is to get the nomination and then I want to get elected. It's very simple, Caddy. And she, and our hostess tonight, and the rest of their friends can make that happen."

"And if you get elected? What then?"

"Then, my dearest little do-gooder, then I'll worry about all your lost souls."

"They're not lost souls. They're people who need help from their elected officials," she protested.

He moved closer again and smiled engagingly. With his fingers drifting across her neck, he whispered, "I know, darling. I know. And I promise you I want to change the world for the better as much as you do, but for now we have to politick. I need you, Caddy. I need you to help me. You're so lovely. We're good together, aren't we?"

When he kissed her she closed her eyes and sank back into his arms. At moments like this, they were good together, very good, she thought.

He nuzzled her hair with his chin. "You'd look terrific in a taffeta dress. You'd kill them. I'm going to buy you one—bright red so everyone can see what a smashing girl I've got."

Caddy hadn't responded, but she remembered feeling vaguely depressed that night and wondering, not for the first time, if she was important to him because she made him part of a couple or, worse, if his ideals were not quite as shining as she had assumed at first.

She lifted her face toward the spot in the sky where the sun was struggling to shine through the low clouds.

Was it that his life came to seem superficial to her? Or was it that her career came to be more fascinating by comparison as the possibility that she might become a success began to look like a faint reality? Certainly, he had openly resented the increasing time she spent working, time away from him and the public appearances he expected her to make with him. She blinked back quick tears. Why couldn't he have loved her as she was, career and all? Did loving someone always mean having to sacrifice so much? Would she have been the same person if she had given in to him? Who was she if she wasn't Caddy Wilcox, a woman who wanted to be a famous photographer and was willing to work hard for that goal?

Another short blast of the horn startled her into awareness of her surroundings, and she looked up. This time the captain was pointing beyond where the New London ferry had come from, toward the middle of the sound. Following his direction she peered straight ahead until she saw a small mound that became a longer mound, taller at one end, until finally it took shape as an island stretching six miles to either side of a long, wide dock waiting to receive them. At the high end of the island, a brown structure that looked like a lighthouse or a windmill stood guard, and at the lower end, a stand of short scrub pines. The trees had grown on a permanent right angle from the prevailing winds that blew down the coast from Canada. They were arriving at Kincade.

For a moment a wave of claustrophobia swept over her as she realized that once she got off the boat she would be stranded on the island, at the mercy of a ferry that arrived to take passengers off only once a day. She sighed, hoping the islanders wouldn't make her job too difficult. Clearing her mind resolutely, she watched the long dock come closer as the ferry navigated its way carefully through a short, narrow channel marked by buoys. Peals resounded across the water as a figure on the dock clanged a ship's bell. As if in response, a few people began to straggle down the path toward the water, some pulling empty wagons. A husky man came out on the dock carrying two large cartons, and behind him a tall man strolled unhurriedly to meet the arriving boat.

The plumber, who had moved up next to Caddy, said, "Not many people here today. You should see it in the summer when all the families are here. Everybody comes down to meet the boat."

She looked at him inquiringly. She opened her mouth to ask him about the residents, but remembering Dave Barrish's strict injunction against mixing in, she closed it without speaking. Don't be curious, she told herself firmly. You're only here to take pictures.

As if in answer to her unspoken question he continued, "This is the only way these folks have of getting their supplies and mail. Captain Hardy brings it over, and if they have anything to send or want to get off the island, this is their one chance a day to do it."

"What if someone's sick? Or what if there is a storm and the boat can't get here?" she asked without thinking.

"Well, there are telephones on the island, and most everybody has their own boat so's they can sail back and forth when the weather's good. If there's weather, that's a different story. Once old Mr. Jennings had a heart attack and the coast guard had to lift him off in a helicopter."

"Thank heavens for that," she said with a shiver.

"For a moment I felt as though I had left civilization forever." A fleeting image of her little apartment on the top floor of Aunt Agatha's house crossed her mind: she would give a lot to be home, safe and comfortable among her own things. I need this job, she scolded herself. I need this job. I'm not going to have to be lifted off in a helicopter. I'll take my pictures and leave on the ferry and one of those pictures will be the cover of *Nature's World,* damn it.

"This your first trip to the island?"

"Yes, it is."

"Which house are you visiting?"

Caddy pulled from the pocket of her anorak a piece of paper on which she had written the name Barrish had told her. She read aloud, "Manor House."

"Well, looks like someone's come to meet you. . . . There's Fiske Spencer." He pointed to the tall man who had come to the end of the dock and was standing a small distance away from the knot of people gathered with their wagons. He stood with his hands in his pockets, watching with interest as the captain docked the ferry.

"Who's he?"

"Lives at the Manor." With a nod the plumber moved from her side and went to uncoil the forward line; as the ferry bumped gently into the dock he threw it neatly over the piling and pulled the ferry even with a small square landing area. The captain turned off the engines and immediately began lifting various packages and cartons onto the dock, including a gray canvas bag with U.S. MAIL stenciled on the side. One of the women, a tall, spare, elegant figure in tailored slacks and a man's jacket, pulled her wagon up to the small pile, extracted two boxes labeled J. NORTHRUP, THE HALL, KINCADE ISLAND, and lifted them into her wagon, which had THE HALL painted on its side. Before she turned and began pulling her cargo up the path, she stared at Caddy, openly assessing her. After she had turned back to her wagon, Caddy looked at the small knot of remaining figures and saw that they, too, were looking at her, but when she assayed a tentative smile they averted their eyes and continued searching out their own parcels. Fine, she thought. I can be just as stand-offish as you are.

She climbed up the two steps from the ferry to the dock. In each hand she carried a canvas bag, while slung over her shoulder was a much heavier case that held all her neatly packed camera equipment.

She found herself face to face with a broad-shoul-dered man, fair and tall and unsmiling despite the laugh lines at the corners of his dark gray eyes. He didn't speak for a moment, but simply stared down.

"You're Catherine Wilcox?" he asked slowly.

"Caddy. If you're Fiske Spencer, I believe I'm sup-posed to be staying with you," she replied politely. She wished he would stop staring at her; his eyes never left her face.

He looked vaguely amused. "I'm Fiske. Welcome to Kincade."

Somewhat flustered, she glanced down at the small mound of luggage at her feet. She pointed down. "Thanks for meeting me. I think I'm going to need that wagon you've got."

"Sure this is all?" He looked at her inquiringly as he packed the bags into the wagon with the efficiency of someone used to making these trips.

"Isn't that enough?" She shook her head as he reached for her camera bag. "No, thanks. I carry this one myself." The bag held a 35mm camera, several long-distance lenses, and her treasured Leica, which she allowed no one but herself to touch.

"Then let's go." Fiske began pulling the wagon carefully. It was piled high with Caddy's belongings, two cartons of groceries, and a crate of wine carefully wedged between several parcels addressed to "The Manor House."

As she walked next to him she was aware that he glanced at her more than once, but she pretended not to notice. The last thing she needed was some island Romeo trying to make an impression on her. She kept her head down and avoided his eyes as they walked the length of the dock.

Leaving the dock area, the dirt road forked into three branches; Fiske took the one that led straight ahead. As they walked she ignored his silence.

"Where are we going?" Caddy asked. There were no houses in sight, the people from the ferry had vanished, and she suddenly felt nervous.

Striding ahead, Fiske replied briefly, "To my parents' house."

She quickened her step to catch up. "The Manor?"

"Yes."

"I was told originally I was staying with Nelson Lovering, who arranged for the shoot. He's my contact here."

"You were supposed to stay with Nelson and his sister, Eliza, at Grange II, but their housekeeper fell and broke her hip last week."

"I'm sorry," she said inadequately.

"So you're staying with us." He frowned and looked down at her. "Tired? Do you need to stop?"

"No." She had gotten up before dawn that morning and she was tired, but she'd be damned if she'd complain about anything while she was on this island. By her companion's cool welcome, it was evident she wasn't wanted on Kincade.

They walked in silence for almost a quarter mile, their steps matching, but their eyes straight ahead. Behind Fiske, the cart bumped noisily in the ruts of the narrow road.

Fiske finally broke their silence. Without looking at her he announced, "All the original houses on the island have names. Ours is the Manor, then there's the Hall, two Granges, big and little, a Priory, and a Manse. All the newer ones have newer names like Homestead or Crow's Nest, or the Bird's Nest."

She kept her eyes on the path, amused for the first time. "How many houses are there?" she asked, looking around for some signs of a roof. They still hadn't seen any people or houses since they left the pier.

"Thirty-one, all told." He clamped his lips shut as if he'd given away too much information.

Two can play this game, she thought. The hell with not asking questions. They invited me here; I didn't ask to come to their stupid island. Knowing the answer perfectly well from the research Dave had given her, she asked sweetly, "How long have there been people on Kincade?"

"The Kincades bought the island in seventeen ninety-eight, and six other families didn't arrive until after almost eighteen ninety."

"How nice," she purred. She ventured a look at Fiske and was surprised when she saw the flicker of a smile on his face. It disappeared as quickly as it had come, and she thought she must have imagined it. He looked down at her for an instant and caught her staring at him; he raised his eyebrows and she turned her head away, embarrassed to feel herself blushing.

She paused at the top of the rise where the path

turned left and looked back over the way they had come. The sky was a brilliant blue, below them the tiny harbor looked like a miniature setting, around them the trees grew tall and close together above bushes whose berries were just beginning to form. Everywhere the sound of birds filled the air. Slowly, she set her camera case down on the grass and took a deep breath. She felt she had traveled further than the hundred miles or so from the city; surveying the serene, untouched-by-time landscape below them, she felt far enough removed from the noise and confusion of New York that this spot on Kincade might be on a different planet.

Fiske watched her examine the panorama. When he spoke, his voice held a note of warning. "We value our privacy on Kincade."

Caddy felt a quick flash of irritation. She wasn't trying to invade his precious privacy, merely admiring the view. Picking up her case, she slung the strap over her shoulder and replied coolly, "I know all about your privacy. The magazine passed along all the restrictions."

"Good. Just so long as you understand." He smiled then, and once again she could have sworn he was amused by something.

In silence she continued up the narrow path behind him until it widened into a sunny clearing with a view of Long Island Sound. They stood for a moment, catching their breath from the climb. A sprawling gray-shingled house rose up in front of her, with three stone chimneys pointing toward the sky; the wraparound porch that surrounded it was partially obscured by overgrown lilac bushes, which seemed to grow everywhere. She felt a shock of surprise, as if she recognized the house sitting so unexpectedly in the middle of the glade, looking as if it had always been there, waiting for her to discover it. She felt as if she was being watched, and when she looked up Fiske was staring at her, his eyes intent.

"Welcome to the Manor," he said quietly.

CHAPTER 3

Fiske stood to one side of the French door leading onto the porch, looking out at a figure crossing the lawn toward the house. Despite her determined walk and her pleasant smile, his sister's forehead was creased in a frown; she looked as if she was having second thoughts about the visitor who was unpacking in the front bedroom above him. His fingers tightened on the handle of the mug of steaming coffee he held in his hand. He turned abruptly and walked across the wide room, letting himself down into a cushioned wicker chair with a sigh.

The two people sitting on either side of the fireplace were silent, but Fiske could feel the tension of their unspoken words filling the room.

"What's she like?" his mother asked. Dorothy Lattimer Spencer's thick blond hair was streaked with gray and pulled into a bun at the nape of her neck. Her long legs, encased in wool slacks, were stretched out in front of her toward the warmth of the small fire burning briskly in the tiled fireplace. Only the strong hands with long fingers and square-cut nails holding her own mug of coffee hinted at the accomplished concert pianist she was.

"I only met her for a moment," Fiske replied noncommittally.

"Fiske," his mother said warningly.

"All right," he laughed grudgingly. "She doesn't wear any makeup, she looks intelligent, and she's got enough luggage for a month."

"A month?" His father, who had been reading yesterday's *Wall Street Journal,* looked up in alarm over the top of his reading glasses and shot a severe look at his wife. "Dorothy, you promised no more than three days."

"Cameras, Dad, cameras." Fiske grinned at the elder man affectionately. "She's got a lot of equipment."

"Well, she'd better keep herself busy with it and keep the hell out of my way." Douglas Fiske Spencer returned to his paper, rustling the pages to show he had dismissed the intruder from his mind. Nearly as tall as his son but with a receding hairline, he wore an old plaid flannel shirt and paint-spattered khaki pants, his favorite uniform when he was working on one of the large, abstract canvases that hung around the otherwise traditionally furnished room. Amused, Fiske thought he looked a far cry from the philanthropic head of one of the country's wealthiest families—a man who annually distributed millions of dollars to the world's underprivileged—much less the chief executive officer of a multimillion-dollar factoring corporation that he had been until his recent retirement.

"What else, Fiske?" His mother put her empty cup down on the coffee table and leaned forward with interest. "Tell me what else you think about her. I can tell there's something more."

"Not really." He remembered the wide hazel eyes that wouldn't quite meet his, the capable way Caddy had shouldered her heavy camera bag, the way her face lit up when she smiled despite the smudges of weariness beneath her eyes. Momentarily baffled, he paused, thinking to himself how, while Caddy couldn't be described as overwhelmingly attractive, there had been something about her that disquieted him, something he couldn't describe.

The door opened and then closed with a bang, interrupting his thoughts. "Here I am," Barbara Spencer Davidson announced with a sigh of relief. She dropped the heavy canvas bag she was carrying on the floor. A slim, freckled woman in her late thirties, she had short blond hair that curled around her face, framing green eyes and a turned-up nose. She crossed the room and handed a small pile of mail to her mother and placed a stack of newspapers on the table next to her father, stooping to kiss the top of his head before she turned to the figure poised hesitantly in the doorway. "You must be Catherine Wilcox."

Fiske rose politely with his mother and father, but drew back into a shadow near the window, letting his mother cross the room to hospitably welcome the guest none of them had even wanted on the island. He wondered what Caddy would make of them all, how she would respond to the tightly knit group of people whose families had known each other for generations and who viewed any newcomer with distrust. He wished she would smile again, but she didn't, and he found himself searching her face intently as his mother, followed by his father and sister, went through the good-mannered motions of conversation. He was surprised by the way she affected him. She wasn't really beautiful, her face was too long and too thin, but she intrigued him. She seemed so businesslike about her Kincade assignment, and yet she had clearly been touched with more than professionalism by her first views of the island.

He watched her take a seat next to his father; her head was in profile as she listened to something Douglas was saying to his wife. He had an overwhelming desire to take her by the hand and lead her out of the house, into the garden.

His father, he knew, had never become reconciled to having a professional photographer, the first in the island's history, given free rein to wander the coves and inlets of Kincade, taking pictures of, as he put it, "God knows what." But Nelson Lovering had persisted, convincing them that the birds were too rare, their species too endangered, to leave their recorded history to an amateur such as himself. Fiske knew that if Nelson had been anything less than the noted ornithologist he was, the project would have been doomed, the isolationists among the islanders would have prevailed, and the birds would have gone unrecorded forever. In the face of the superficially polite, less-than-welcome reception Caddy had received, he gave her credit for remaining grave-faced and aloof even when Barbara announced she was going to help with lunch and his mother decided to give their guest a tour of the gardens. There was never a moment when Caddy met his gaze.

"I still don't like this," Douglas said when the women left them alone. "We've never let anyone photograph before and I don't see why we have to do it now. It's just going to cause trouble for everybody and set a bad precedent."

"She's photographing the birds, not us. Nelson made it very plain to *Nature's World* that all the people and houses are off-limits. After all, it's a well-respected nature periodical, Dad, not *House and Garden.*"

Douglas rose and stretched his arms over his head with a huge sigh; his glasses had fallen down on his nose and he peered over their tops at his son. "I don't want her nosing around, finding out what's going on here," he warned.

"No," Fiske agreed soberly.

They looked at each other bleakly. Fiske saw his own dismay reflected in his father's eyes. "Anything new?" he inquired soberly.

"Not a word. That son of a bitch better not call me again."

"Bruce Asher doesn't give up that easily, Dad. He usually gets what he goes after."

Douglas scowled. "Not this time, he doesn't. Kincade's not for sale, to him or anyone else."

"Has he been in touch with Hank and Babs?"

"Your sister won't talk to me about it. Hank's told me they will never give up their parcel though. The kids love it here."

Fiske grinned and his father shrugged, looking a bit embarrassed. When Barbara Spencer had become engaged to the young, aggressive bond trader a dozen years ago, Douglas had made every effort to stop the wedding. He thought Hank was too smooth, too solicitous, too eager to please to fit into the easy, affection-

ate, intellectual atmosphere of the family. But Hank
had kept a low profile, waiting his father-in-law out,
until Douglas had finally accepted him as a full member of the Spencer clan. Part of what made Fiske grin
was knowing that Barbara was her father's delight and
wondering how much of Douglas's initial aversion to
Hank had been the dislike he would have felt for anyone who married his precious daughter.

"Babs would never give up Kincade, Dad. Not for
herself or for the kids. Jared loves it here and so does
Allison. They'd be heartbroken if they couldn't run
wild here every summer. You're worrying too much.
It'll all blow over," Fiske reassured his father.

"I'm not so sure. For Christ's sake, even Clifford is
fascinated by the numbers."

"He is?" Fiske was startled. It seemed unthinkable
that his father's oldest and dearest friend could even
contemplate leaving Kincade's shores, much less sell it
to a developer who would destroy the land and ruin
the ecology. Like the rest of the original families, Clifford Ludlow was intensely committed to keeping the
ecology of the island intact. The few dozen people who
came to Kincade annually weren't the only ones who
valued Kincade's pristine environment; generations of
birds had made it their home at the end of migrations
that started as far away as South America. Perhaps,
Fiske mused, this was more serious than he had
thought.

"He is," Douglas snapped. "And so is Jake Lovering, and those fools who built Journey's End, and God
knows who else."

"Bess and Arthur Dwight. Jake's daughter. They're
the ones who built Journey's End," he said absently,
mentally reviewing the families who lived on the island.

"I don't care who they are. They think it's time we all got out from under these taxes."

Both men were silent, thinking about the real estate taxes that kept rising each year along with the crippling cost of liability insurance they were required to have.

"If this is at all serious—I mean, if you think there's a chance that this thing could possibly come to a vote —I can have the firm look into it. Maybe there's something in the original deeds that would prevent a sale."

As Fiske made the offer, his heart sank. He thought of the hours of work involved in looking through deeds a hundred years old, not to mention sorting out the legalities of the weighted votes spelled out in the corporation that governed them all. Each landowner had a vote based on their acreage, an easy system until the original families began selling off smaller parcels of land to their sons and daughters and they, in turn, to their children. There had never been a reason to have to figure out the effect of the land division on votes before.

The only other issue of any magnitude in the island's history had been whether or not to run a telephone line from the mainland, and that had been decided at the turn of the century by an elderly matriarch of the Peck family who banged her cane on the floor of Kincade House for attention and announced that the telephone was the only intelligent invention made in her lifetime and she, for one, wasn't going to do without it. The other islanders, as eager as she for the new invention, had agreed unanimously. Indeed, all the votes he could recollect or had been told about had been unanimous, but they were for far lesser things like ferry service, or rebuilding the windmill, or deciding who was going to be awarded the contract for garbage removal—not whether or not they were going to destroy their island.

Douglas turned away and began to walk toward the door, obviously headed for the shed where he painted. Fiske knew he would probably lose himself in his work until his wife went and got him for dinner. Before he left the room Douglas turned to his son and grinned, the smile reaching his eyes and making him look for a moment like the younger man Fiske had left five years earlier. "I'll take it under advisement, counselor. And I'm glad you're back. Damn glad." With a wave of his hand he disappeared, and Fiske was left alone.

I'm glad to be home, he thought as he stared out at the familiar view of the sound through the trees. The sun had finally emerged and glinted on the water in the distance, making it look almost silver. He had missed his father and, deep down, he had missed Kincade.

He looked around the high-ceilinged room and thought it looked exactly the same as it had the day he made his decision to join the New York law firm Johnson and Day rather than go into his father's business or the family foundation. It had been difficult for his father to accept at first, but Douglas had reluctantly come to admire his son's need to establish a track record of his own. At the age of twenty-five, having graduated third in his class at Harvard Law School, Fiske craved a challenge. When the opportunity arose to go to work in Johnson and Day's London office servicing their European corporate clients, it had proved irresistible. Johnson and Day, astounded and gratified by his achievements abroad, wanted to keep him in London, but when the head of the corporate department in New York suffered an unexpected heart attack, Fiske was given the nod to come home and head up the division, the youngest partner to have ever been accorded such authority.

Deeply troubled by the idea of anything threatening the serenity of the place they all took for granted, he went in search of his sister. He found her standing on a stool, pulling plates and glasses down from the cabinets in the large sunny kitchen at the back of the house overlooking a bare vegetable garden. Below her at the counter, Grace Byrne, their longtime housekeeper who came with the senior Spencers from their New York apartment every spring, was carving a small chicken with a lethal-looking knife. As he entered the room she turned, brandishing the knife like a weapon, and asked, "Did I see Mr. Spencer going into his studio? Did you let him get away so close to lunch? Shame on you, Fiske; now he won't eat anything until dinner."

"Am I my father's keeper?" Fiske responded blandly, reaching around her for a drumstick, which he munched while he backed out of her reach. "You really ought to be careful with that thing, Grace. You look like an ax murderer."

"Fiske, leave the food alone. We hardly have enough for lunch as it is." Barbara had descended from the stool and stood, a stack of plates in her hands, looking at the small fowl doubtfully. "I forgot about the photographer."

"She has a name, Babs," he admonished mildly.

"I know, I know. Here, take these into the dining room and tell Mother lunch is ready. She's eating with us, isn't she?"

"Mother always eats with us."

"No, you fool. The photographer." Barbara opened a drawer in a huge walnut corner cabinet, pulled out a handful of knives and forks, and piled them on top of the plates.

"What have you got against her besides the fact that Nelson's the only one who wants her on the island, we're stuck with her as a houseguest, and she's a professional photographer?" he asked cheerfully. He followed her into the long dining room that overlooked the water.

"Nothing. Who said I did?" Barbara walked primly around the table in front of him, setting a flowered place mat in front of each chair.

Fiske followed obediently behind her, laying a white china plate on each mat and placing a knife and fork on either side. "You keep calling her 'the photographer' in the same voice you used to call Roddy Banks 'junior.'"

"Well, he was. A junior, I mean." Barbara laughed. She shrugged her shoulders and shook her head. "I don't see why Uncle Nelson couldn't find somewhere else for her to stay though. It's just more work for Grace, and Pa doesn't like having her here."

"And?"

"And I don't think it's a good idea to have an outsider on the island."

"Calm down, Babs. Nelson asked Ma for a favor, and Ma said yes. Caddy will spend a few days wandering around the marsh and then she'll be gone." He fleetingly wondered what Caddy looked like when she smiled.

"I still don't like it," his sister burst out. She slammed a vase of flowers down in the center of the table. A few drops of water spilled on the polished board and she wiped them up furiously.

Fiske stood absolutely still and stared at his sister in surprise. He was startled by his sister's vehemence; it wasn't like her and it certainly seemed far harsher than the situation warranted. He looked down at her intently, but she lowered her eyes and wouldn't meet his gaze. "Babs, what's the matter?"

"Nothing." Her face was pale with tension and the freckles on her cheeks seemed darker than usual.

"Don't fudge the truth. What's wrong?"

"You haven't been here, Fiske. You don't know."

"Wait a minute, for Christ's sake. I was here for ten days last August and I came home for Christmas. You and Hank and the kids came over at Easter. I've been in London, not on the moon. What's going on with you that I don't know?"

She shook her head and tried to edge around him.

He barred her way and asked sternly, "The kids? Hank? You?"

"It's nothing, Fiske. Leave it alone," she snapped. Before he could apologize, she turned on her heel and left the room. The heavy kitchen door swung back and forth from the force of her exit. He stared at the doorway in astonishment. He and Barbara had always been close; it wasn't like her to evade him this way.

"Did I hear you and your sister arguing?" His mother entered the room from the long hall that stretched the length of the house. She had put on fresh lipstick and thrown a brilliant green shawl around her shoulders.

"Is Babs okay?" he asked, still caught off guard by his sister's unlikely anger.

"Fine, as far as I know. A little tired, perhaps. You know—the end of the children's school year, opening the house, entertaining for Hank." Dorothy paused in the act of rearranging the table flowers and looked up. "Why? Did she tell you something?"

"Not a thing, beautiful. Just checking," he evaded as

he pulled out her chair at the foot of the table. The kitchen door swung inward once more and Grace entered with the carved chicken on a platter, followed by Barbara carrying a large bowl of salad and a long loaf of French bread. Setting the platter on the table in front of Dorothy, Grace shot Fiske a dark look before she left the room. He sighed to himself and waited politely until his sister, still not looking at him, had taken her seat across the table from him before he sat down. Obviously, Grace thought he had been the one who upset her favorite Barbara, and now he would have to make amends or risk having the housekeeper glower at him for the rest of his visit home. He reached for the open bottle of wine in the middle of the table, then paused. "Where's Caddy?" he asked, looking behind him into the hall.

"She wanted to make a call, dear. I told her to take her time and join us when she could." His mother helped herself to chicken and passed the platter to her daughter. "Try and save some for your father, darling. I'll take a plate out to him later." She looked at the large platter and the small amount of chicken, frowning slightly. "You'd think we'd have gotten better at planning how much food to bring over after all these years."

"Well, there's always baked beans," Fiske consoled them cheerfully, and they all laughed. One memorable summer their grandfather had ordered several cases of mixed canned goods to be sent to the island, but when they opened them they found they had been sent sixty cans of nothing but baked beans, which they had eaten, can by can, throughout the season. They were still laughing when Caddy entered the room.

With a nod of thanks, she slid into the chair Fiske

pulled out next to his own. "I'm sorry I'm late," she apologized.

He poured some wine into her glass while Barbara passed the salad and bread across the table.

"Did your call go through all right?" Dorothy asked, clearly curious. "Our phones frequently have a life of their own, what with odd static and unexpected disconnects. We keep meaning to have another cable put down, but I don't know . . ." Her voice trailed off.

"What mother means is we're all too cheap to pay for a new one, so we have to put up with nineteen thirties equipment." Fiske turned his head so he could look at Caddy. She was wearing beige cord trousers and a man's tailored white silk shirt open at the throat. Her face was still bare of makeup, but her skin looked soft and her hazel eyes were ringed with thick, dark eyelashes. Unaccountably, he wanted to reach out and touch her skin.

"Yes, it did, thank you," she responded politely to Dorothy's question.

"How did you and Nelson Lovering happen to meet?" Dorothy asked in her most social voice, the one she had perfected in the years when she had acted as her husband's hostess all over the world. Brother and sister grinned at each other, their brief altercation forgotten in shared appreciation of their mother. No one could resist Dorothy Spencer when she wanted to extract information.

They all leaned forward with interest as Caddy told them how the publisher of *Nature's World* had been approached by Nelson Lovering at the annual dinner of the National Audubon Society and how she had been given the assignment to preserve in pictures the spring migration of the elusive white-tailed kite.

"It shouldn't take me more than three or four days," she finished, looking around the table.

"How nice." Dorothy leaned back in satisfaction, having found out what she wanted to know. "We're so pleased you'll be with us."

Fiske looked at his sister, and her expression was so startled at their mother's obvious untruth that his shoulders began to shake as he tried to conceal his laughter. Barbara saw his distress, knew its cause, and began laughing too. Their shared laughter reminded him poignantly of the years of their childhood, when they had been inseparable and Barbara had dogged his heels, wanting to be just like her older brother. Dorothy looked sternly at them both, but her eyes were twinkling as she said, "I apologize for my children, Miss Wilcox. Sometimes they don't seem much older than my grandchildren."

Fiske looked down at Caddy. Seemingly, she was intent on buttering a piece of bread, but when she looked up, her eyes were amused. Obviously she had understood exactly why he and his sister were laughing. He wondered if she knew her eyes gave away all her secrets.

"Miss Wilcox—" Dorothy began.

"Her name is Catherine, Mother." Holding the platter in his hand, Fiske looked around the table inquiringly. When he heard no objections, he speared the last piece of chicken onto his plate.

"It's really Caddy," she said, smiling at Dorothy.

"Caddy, then. How do you plan to do your photographing? Is there any help you need from us?"

Caddy shook her head, pushing away her empty plate. "No, thank you. I want to talk to Nelson Lovering, and then I'd like to walk around and get the feel of the island."

"He was supposed to lunch with us. I wonder what happened to him." Dorothy looked around vaguely as if she expected to see the noted ornithologist standing in a corner of the dining room.

"He's worse than Pa when he's painting. He probably got birding in the woodlands this morning and forgot to come in." Barbara emptied the remains of the bottle of wine into her glass and finished it with one long swallow.

Fiske exchanged looks of silent communion with his mother and sister as they signaled to each other their uncertainty what to do with their visitor next. He rose hastily from the table. "I'm off." He grinned at his sister. Though intrigued by Caddy, he had no intention of spending the afternoon stuck with tour-guide duty. Nothing was going to interfere with scraping the bottom of his small sailboat and getting it out of the boat house and into the water.

He walked with long strides through the house and down the porch steps to the path. One of the things he had missed most during his stay in England had been sailing.

His grin faded, remembering more about England than he wanted to.

Her name was Dierdre Carmody, and she had hated sailing. Their liaison had lasted for five reckless years, years filled with the hectic pursuit of pleasure she enjoyed, while he, besotted by their affair, had been perfectly happy to follow her to every house party in every shire in England and a few in Scotland. Until the night he returned to the flat unexpectedly from a trip to Hamburg and found her in the arms of the elder son of a baronet. The veil had dropped from his eyes and he had seen her for what she really was: a lovely, wanton fortune hunter. Without a second thought or a word to either Dierdre or her lover, he had thrown his keys on the floor and left the bedroom. His last memory of Dierdre was of her slanted, laughing eyes, her raven-black hair lying on the pillow, her mocking smile as she watched the expression on his face. Only Fiske knew how badly her betrayal had burned him. Never again, he promised himself darkly, never again would he allow himself to be made a fool of by any woman.

Rounding the corner of the house, he hurried down the incline to the boat house nestled at the edge of the water beneath a cluster of towering weeping willows. He had to kick at the base of the wooden door to free it from where it had swollen shut over the long, damp winter. Entering the boat house, he halted, looking through the long room, past the boats stacked up on both sides, to the water beyond. The wind coming off the sound was bitterly cold, and he shivered. On one side of the boat house a stack of three canoes rested in their racks, and on the other a small sailboat badly in need of paint, its bottom rusted, leaned against the wall. He pulled the boat upright, placed thick blocks beneath it to hold it steady, and picking up a thick wire brush began to patiently scrape a small corner of the hull. Soon he was oblivious to his surroundings as he became lost in his work.

Once he looked up, distracted by the sound of laughter in the distance, and for an instant Caddy's grave eyes and soft, pale skin appeared in his mind. He half-rose, thinking he might join her in the garden, but almost immediately knelt back down and resumed his scraping. No more Dierdres for him, no chasing after a woman because, just for a moment, she seemed intriguing; he was free and footloose and determined to stay that way. The world was filled with pretty companions able to amuse him for an evening or a weekend. His heart was once again intact and he was going to keep it that way.

CHAPTER 4

The dining room was very still after Fiske left the room. Sunlight shone through the large uncurtained windows; it touched briefly on the deep cherry wood of the cabinets, the remains of their lunch on the long oak table, and picked up the muted colors in the faded tapestry rug. Caddy was aware of the tensions floating between the members of the Spencer family, and she was uncomfortable being in the middle of them. Avoiding each other's eyes, the three women listened to Fiske's retreating footsteps without speaking. Deciding to make her escape, she folded her napkin and prepared to rise from the table.

"You mustn't mind Fiske, dear." Dorothy squared her shoulders and pushed back her chair with decision.

Turning to Barbara, she asked, "Do you think you could take our guest to Uncle Nelson's on the way to the cottage?"

"I can find my own way," Caddy said quickly. "If you just point me in the right direction, I'll be fine."

"No. I'll show you. I have to get back to work anyhow, and it's on my way." Barbara rose and began stacking the empty plates. "Ma, can I borrow Grace? I'm never going to get the house ready by tomorrow and I've got to be on that afternoon ferry come hell or high water." She looked at Caddy and smiled pleasantly. "My husband and I have a cottage on the property, about a quarter of a mile down the beach. We're all coming back this weekend, but I came up to get the place opened up for the season. It's easier to do without the two kids underfoot, but I can't leave them to fend for themselves in town for more than a few days." She moved toward the kitchen with the plates and stood with her back against the door, waiting for her mother's response.

"If Grace doesn't mind being borrowed, it's all right with me, darling. But you will be back for dinner, won't you?"

"Yup. What doesn't get done today won't get done, and we'll survive the weekend somehow."

"You know you're welcome to stay here. I'd love to have the children."

"That's a thought. Hank and I can stay at the cottage and you can have Allison and Jared. Sounds good to me." Barbara's voice grew faint as she disappeared into the kitchen.

"Oh, dear," Dorothy sighed. "That really wasn't what I meant. I mean, I love my grandchildren, but . . ." Her voice trailed off and Caddy smiled at her in commiseration. They walked slowly into the hall and back toward the living room.

She stood uncertainly in the doorway. She was anxious to leave the house and get started with her own work. Having to be a guest in a strange house among people she didn't know and would never see again once her assignment was completed was awkward, and she didn't like it at all. Fervently she wished that she had a nice, anonymous room of her own in a hotel where she could retreat and be alone to try and get over Ward's rejection and her own ambivalent reaction to it.

She looked up in relief as Barbara appeared, wearing a thick down vest and obviously ready to leave. Running lightly up the wide staircase, she went quickly to her room and gathered up her anorak and camera bag. A flash of sun on the water caught her eye and she paused for a moment at the window, looking out over the gardens at the back of the house to a small hill that inclined gently up to the horizon. An irregular pond surrounded by white and yellow daffodils lay nestled against the base of the hill, which was covered by more daffodils, growing singly and in clumps, like someone had stood at the base of the hill with hundreds of bulbs and thrown them in a wide, graceful arc, planting the bulbs where they fell. She made a mental note to photograph the enchanting sight before she left the island, then turned and quickly left the room.

"I don't want to talk about it."

Caddy stopped on the landing, unsure whether to retreat or continue down the stairs. The voice was Barbara's and it was raised in anger. She could hear Dorothy's low voice murmuring in return and then Barbara's again. "You're making a big deal out of nothing, Ma. Hank and I like parties. We like to go to them and we like to give them, and drinking is just part of the fun."

Caddy descended two more steps and stopped, wondering what to do. Obviously she had stumbled into the middle of a mother–daughter altercation, and she certainly didn't want Dorothy and Barbara to think she had been eavesdropping on a private conversation. With a sigh of relief she heard the ringing of the telephone, and when Dorothy approached the hall where the phone was, she continued down the stairs, putting each booted foot down loudly on the bare wood steps to announce her arrival. Entering the living room, she found Barbara standing at the window, her back to the room and her shoulders hunched. She didn't turn, and they stood in silence until her mother returned and said in a determinedly cheerful voice, "Nelson's on his way. You can meet him halfway and he'll take Caddy under his wing for the rest of the day. That's all right with you, dear, isn't it?" Caddy smiled politely and nodded; she couldn't wait to get out of the house.

The wind had died down and the sun glinted off trees whose trunks still glistened with spring damp and whose leaves were just beginning to turn from pale green to darker colors. Along the path Barbara took through the woods, dogwoods bloomed with creamy white blossoms among the oak and pine trees. Hardy wild lilac mingled with shrubs of pale pink peonies, and the remains of early-flowering forsythia added touches of yellow to the palette. Caddy felt exhilarated by the fresh scent of salt air mixed with the smell of damp earth. The woods around her teemed with the promise of a new growing cycle. They rounded a corner and she gasped with pleasure on being met with a wide patch of early violets, their white and blue blossoms nestled close to the ground like a velvet carpet.

Quickly she pulled her camera out of her canvas bag, unscrewed the lens cap, and crouching down, began shooting rapidly, afraid somehow that the fragile beauty of the violets would disappear forever if she didn't capture it on film. Turning her body sideways, she aimed the camera to her left and was startled to see an old pair of boots in her viewfinder. Looking up, she found they belonged to a very elderly, very thin man with white hair and a short, full beard; he was leaning on a malacca walking stick, binoculars slung around his neck. She was struck by the brilliance of his blue-gray eyes as he smiled down at her. She looked around in confusion and saw that Barbara had quietly disappeared.

"I'm Nelson Lovering," the stranger said. "Welcome to Kincade Island, Miss Wilcox."

She rose and held out her hand; his was gnarled and rough, but he shook hers warmly. She felt disoriented. Lost in the patterns of the delicate tracery of tiny, dark leaves nestled close to the ground, she had totally forgotten Barbara and the purpose of their walk, which was to meet the man standing serenely in front of her, looking as if he had all the time in the world to wait for her to notice him.

"I'm sorry," she said with genuine remorse. "I was afraid they'd disappear." She pointed down and he nodded understandingly.

"Don't stop," he said gently. "I'm in no hurry. In fact, I'm never in any hurry."

Despite his advanced years, his face was unlined and oddly innocent. Without thinking she raised her camera and clicked the shutter, framing his head against the silvery Russian olive behind him. As soon as she did, she realized her error and looked at him apologetically.

"That's all right. It will be our secret." He looked at her and there was a twinkle in his eyes as he confided, "You can't imagine the trouble I've gotten into insisting there be a proper photographic record of our little phenomenon. I've made an absolute pariah of myself with all my relatives, not to mention my neighbors." He paused reflectively. "Actually, they're pretty much the same. Neighbors and relatives, I mean. I think I'm related one way or another to damn near everybody on Kincade." As he went on more seriously, his voice was deep and had a natural courtesy of intonation. "I did give my word you would stay away from people and houses though, Miss Wilcox. I hope that won't pose too much of a problem for you?"

"Not at all," she assured him, screwing the lens cap back on her camera and slinging it behind her back. "I just couldn't resist, but I'll control myself from now on." They smiled conspiratorially at each other and walked slowly together along the path away from the Manor. She decided she liked Nelson Lovering very much, and for the first time since landing on the island, she began to relax.

"Do you know much about the white-tailed kite?" Nelson asked.

"Nothing," she admitted. "I hope that doesn't disqualify me. I've found that when I'm in the field the animals and birds I photograph become real to me in a way they never do when I read about them. It's as if I enter their world somehow."

"Splendid!" Clearly delighted with her answer, his words tripped over each other in his eagerness to instruct her about the project. "Our kites come from South America—Chile or Argentina. They usually migrate to California or southern Texas and they've been seen as far north as South Carolina, but ours are the only group ever spotted in the northeast. They've been coming for fifteen summers now, the same families each season. We've got quite a colony on the edge of the great marsh, and no one can understand why they're here." He looked around with satisfaction. They had crested the small ridge and were looking down at the other side of the island. The low woods stretched almost a quarter mile in front of them, giving way to open fields and then to lower wetlands where clumps of tangled trees leaned out over narrow canals. In the distance the ocean rolled in over a wide stretch of white, sandy beach; the hint of the Long Island coast touched the horizon. To the left, a large shingled house much in the style of the Manor sat on the edge of the woods.

"That's the Hall. Northrups live there. He's a doctor and she's an editor," Nelson said dismissively as he turned and continued walking along the path at the top of the ridge.

"Aren't we going down?" She hurried to keep up with him. His appearance was deceptive, she thought; he walked like a man of twenty.

"No, my no. We're going to the Great Marsh about a half mile further. You're not tired, are you?" Nelson asked anxiously. "Despite what you may have been told, there are Jeeps and some pickups on the island; every family has at least one. I hate the smelly things myself. I always walk."

"I'm fine. There's just so much to see. You're probably used to it all, but I'm still surprised to see so much unspoiled land and wetlands so close to Connecticut and New York, where every inch of shoreline has been developed beyond recognition."

"I never get used to it," Nelson said simply. "I've been coming here for eighty-three summers, and I learn something new every time I take my daily hike. Because the island's private, it acts as a natural wildlife preserve. We have raccoons, badgers, red foxes, deer, all kinds of snakes and waterfowl, pheasant, and every kind of wild turkey. But the real joy is the birds. I think it's why I decided to study ornithology when I was a boy; more varieties of birds migrate through here than almost anywhere outside of Gibraltar."

"I never knew that." She was awed.

"Not many people do. It would be a criminal act if the island was disturbed by anyone." Nelson stabbed his cane angrily into the ground for emphasis. "This island belongs to the wildlife, and if it's the last thing I do I'll protect it for them, no matter who I have to go up against."

She was taken aback by his vehemence. It made her wonder what she had stumbled into on the island. Nothing that was any of her business, she told herself firmly. She was on Kincade to photograph the white-tailed kite and that was all. Their walk had taken them along the ridge parallel to the Northrups', and she was able to look down at a gabled roof on a rambling brown-shingled house that was almost an identical match to the Manor. An eaved porch wrapped around the house, and on it she could see a woman on a stepladder; she looked like she was scraping the ceiling.

"Who built all these houses?" She was struck by how large the original homes were, and she wondered how they had managed to get doors and windows, giant mantelpieces, and curved banisters over the water from the mainland.

"They brought workmen over, had them build themselves a barracks to sleep and eat in, and kept them here until they'd built six houses. Paid them a fortune to do it too. That's why the houses look alike. Rufus

Kincade's great-grandfather drew a plan from memory of a house he'd stayed in during a visit to Maine, and the contractor just moved things around a little every time he built another. Some have more gables than others, some staircases have one landing and others have two, and all the windows are different. They made the window frames right here, and with each house the ornamentation got fancier and fancier until by the time they got to the last one, the Manse, it looks like a hodgepodge; it's got one of everything all the others have." They had passed the Hall and he gestured backward with his walking stick at the laboring woman. "You'll like Josie Northrup."

Caddy hurried to keep up with him. She was breathless from the effort of trying to talk and match his pace. She was about to remind him that she wasn't supposed to speak to the islanders when he stopped so short she nearly careened into his back.

"There," he said simply.

They had reached the end of the ridge. A large area of wetland, almost a half mile in diameter, stretched out in front of them, protected on all sides by pine and willow, oak and linden trees. In the center, birds of every conceivable description fed and roosted. Warblers and finches, cardinals, orioles, tanagers, and blackbirds swooped and soared in groups, pausing in concert to cover first a gnarled bayberry bush, then rising in a rush of wings to light on a nearby pine trunk. As she watched, a vee of mallards arched in a semicircle over the canal in front of her and lit in the water below, searching for food. Everywhere she looked she saw terns and waterfowl, brant and diving teals; she heard a loud, coarse honk and felt a shadow as a flight of Canadian geese dove raucously from behind them, scattering the smaller birds as they claimed their share of the territory.

Without removing her gaze from the panorama in front of her, she reached behind her for her camera and began trying to capture the infinite variety of the avian peaceable kingdom hidden in the middle of Kincade. For the first time she understood why the islanders wanted to defend the privacy of their island.

"Miss Wilcox?"

Startled out of her reverie by the unfamiliar voice, she looked around in surprise. The sun had shifted, long shadows were beginning to edge into the vast wetland, and she found herself in a crouch near the bottom of the ridge, her feet in cold, murky water. She realized her hands were cold, and blowing on them for warmth, she trudged up the incline to where Nelson was sitting patiently on a log, waiting for her to join him.

"I'm sorry." She felt repentant as she looked at the old man and realized that he had allowed her to become lost in the spectacle of the bird sanctuary without a thought for his own comfort. "I've never seen anything so wonderful."

He hoisted himself up with the aid of his stick and smiled kindly. "And you haven't even seen my kites yet."

"Are they here?" She looked eagerly back to where the birds were staking out their territorial claims for the evening.

"They are, but you can't see them from where we're standing. They're on the eastern edge of the marsh, in the low trees over there." He pointed and she followed his direction, but the trees he pointed to were too far away for her to see anything.

"It's too late this afternoon, isn't it?" She was unaccountably disappointed.

"Yes. We'll come back in the early morning tomorrow. I wanted you to see all this though." He swept his stick around in a proprietorial gesture. They stood shoulder to shoulder, reluctant to turn away, until Nelson said briskly, "Right. Home and tea."

Obediently she turned and once again followed him back along the ridge until he made an abrupt right turn, almost losing her, and plunged down a well-kept path through dense woods, emerging at last onto a bluff. The familiar shape of yet another shingled house was perched almost on the edge of the bluff overlooking the ocean. This one was painted gray and covered with silvery-green ivy that blew gently in the wind; a sundial surrounded by a bed of daylilies not yet in bloom stood in the middle of the path leading up to the porch. The front door swung open as they approached the steps, and a spare, gray-haired woman, obviously related to Nelson, waited for them grimly.

"You old fool," she said to Nelson, her bright blue eyes snapping with anger. "Do you have any idea how long you've been tramping around this island? You don't have any more sense than you were born with, and that's a fact."

"Afternoon, Liza. I've brought company home for tea." He smiled sweetly at her and turned to Caddy. "This is my big sister, Eliza, and she still thinks I'm in the nursery. Liza, this is Miss Wilcox who's come to photograph the kites. I hope you've made cake for tea."

"Don't I always? How do you do, Miss Wilcox, I'm glad to meet you." Eliza Lovering smiled down at Caddy, who was waiting uncertainly on the path.

Eliza's smile transformed her face into that of the

beautiful old woman she was; a glint of mischief in her eyes making her seem, like her brother, far younger than Caddy was sure she must be. Standing side by side, Nelson and Eliza could be taken for twins, she thought, or maybe it was just the look people get when they have lived together for years and like it.

"You come right up here and get warm. I've got a fire in the library, and after tea Andy will drive you back in the station wagon. Although, for the life of me, I don't know why you aren't staying here with us." She glared at her brother.

"Blame Dorothy, not me." Nelson beat a hasty retreat into the house.

"Our housekeeper fell and broke her hip the day before yesterday. We had to have the Coast Guard run her over to New London. You were supposed to stay with us, but Dorothy was adamant. Nelson and I are so disappointed," Eliza confided.

Following her up the steps and into the hall, Caddy found herself mentally agreeing. She, too, wished she were staying with the Loverings. Unlike the Spencers at the Manor, Nelson and Eliza certainly seemed as if they were united in their desire to be hospitable; for the first time she felt welcome on Kincade. "This is lovely," she exclaimed, admiring the wide hall that ran the width of the house and framed the ocean that lay beyond. She joined Nelson on a bench next to the door and began pulling off her muddy boots. Her socks were soaked too, and she looked down at them helplessly. All of a sudden she felt very tired and cold. It had been a long time since she had woken up in her room on Gramercy Square, and she felt as if she had traveled much further than the ninety miles between the two points.

"Take those off." Eliza pointed at the socks. "You

can borrow a pair of Nelson's and we'll put yours in front of the fire. By the time you leave they'll be dry."

"Stop fussing, Liza. We want our tea." Nelson led the way into the cheerful, overcrowded library and soon they were seated comfortably around the fireplace, drinking hot, reviving tea and eating dark-chocolate cake.

"Did you see the kites?" Eliza poured the last of the tea into Caddy's cup.

"She never got her nose out of her camera. We didn't have time." Nelson snorted in disgust.

"I've never seen anything as breathtaking as the Great Marsh," Caddy said apologetically.

"Is that right?" Eliza shot a sharp look at her brother. He nodded and they smiled at each other happily. She looked at Caddy, and her eyes were soft. "You've passed the test, my dear."

"Test?"

"Yes, of course. Nelson says he can tell everything he needs to know about a person by how they react to the marsh. You've made him extremely happy by keeping your nose in your camera and photographing his beloved birds, even though he'd never tell you that."

"Well, I don't have to, do I? I've got you to blab everything I think or feel to the whole world," he snapped disgustedly, helping himself to another thick slab of cake.

Caddy was speechless, wondering if the old man was mad at her. But seeing them nod at each other in such a congratulatory manner as if she was some aborigine who, having stumbled into their midst, was suddenly found to speak perfect English, she was unable to contain herself and she began to laugh.

The three of them talked easily after that, the hour stretching into two while Nelson pulled out old, yellowing maps of the island and charts of the surrounding waters. He pointed to a large open space on the map and said instructively, "This is where we were and here's where the kites are." He moved his bony finger further north. "This is the other Grange, where my brother Jake lives with Jake, Jr., and his family. They're some of the ones—"

"Nelson, you'll overexcite yourself," Eliza said warningly. "Don't start with all that now."

"I'm not excited," he answered testily. "I'm just saying they're some of the ones who want to sell the island to that God damned developer. Bruce Asher." He pronounced the name with venom. "It would ruin the whole ecological balance of the area. Some of these birds have been migrating here for hundreds of years, before there were houses, before there were people. There isn't a member of a family who lives here who shouldn't know better."

"Nelson. I won't have you talking about family that way. They'll see the error of their thinking, given time." A look of sadness shadowed Eliza's eyes, and Caddy felt sorry for her as the older woman confided, "I know we're not supposed to talk about it to outsiders, but it really is such a worry that it's hard to think about much else. You see, some of us want to sell our land and some don't. In our case, our family has had two houses since the beginning; our brother and his family live in Grange One and Nelson and I live here, in Grange Two. Our sister Mary left the island, but her children are landowners now and they have a vote too."

Caddy hesitated for only a moment. She knew she probably shouldn't pursue the subject, but despite her determination to remain aloof, her natural curiosity was aroused. With a mental apology to Dave, she asked, "What you're saying is, the people who live here aren't all in agreement about the future of Kincade. Is that it?"

"What she's trying to say is my brother and his family have lost their minds and want to sell out." Nelson rolled up the map and restored it to its place on the shelves. "He's a horse's ass. Always was and always will be. Why, anybody could sell him anything, and as for those Dwight kids, all they think about is money."

"Or the lack of it. Be fair, Nelson. The younger generation aren't all blessed with the same resources you and I have been given."

"Security." He snorted. "They have enough left in their trusts. They just want bigger cars, bigger boats, bigger everything. All they think about is buying new toys before they've even used up the ones they have."

"You're forgetting the children's education—and all the costs of Tina's special therapy so she can learn to speak properly, not to mention the taxes. It's not so easy for the young ones to keep up the property here when they have other homes and obligations raising their children on the mainland. Taxes . . ." Her voice trailed off.

"Taxes." Nelson said the word as if he hated its very sound. "Sure, they're bad, but we've always paid them and we always will. Why, Jake's got enough money to pay them for his whole family for the next hundred years."

"Nelson," his sister cautioned again. She turned to Caddy and said, "You see, we can't keep away from the subject. Everybody's on one side or the other, and it's all we talk about anymore. You must have had your fill at lunch."

"Not really," she replied. Her curiosity got the better of her again. "Do the Spencers want to sell too?"

Nelson chuckled. "Douglas never will. He says they're going to have to cart him off the island in a pine box. Young Fiske owns a third of their section now and he won't sell, and I know Dorothy won't vote for it. Hell, she's my favorite niece, she'd better not."

"And Barbara?" Caddy asked hesitantly.

Nelson frowned and drew his brows together. "She and that husband of hers, Hank Davidson. I just don't know."

"Barbara's a darling, Nelson, and she adores the island, always has. She wouldn't think of having her children summer anywhere else in the world." Eliza reached into a faded carpetbag and brought out knitting needles and a half-completed bright red sock.

"Well, he's no darling, that's for damn sure. Conceited windbag."

"Nonsense. Everybody else but you loves him," his sister silenced him firmly.

"Is Barbara's husband the one who owns the land their cottage is on?" Caddy asked, confused by who actually owned the land on the island.

"Barbara owns it. She's family, you see. Hank married into the Spencer family, but that doesn't entitle him to own land here on his own." Nelson rose and, picking up a long brass poker, began to stir the fire vigorously. The door opened and he looked up and smiled. A blond, husky young man with the well-muscled build of an athlete entered the room with his arms full of logs. "Where have you been, Andy? I ate all your cake. Come meet Miss Wilcox."

"This is our friend Andy Gleason. He keeps us together here and we couldn't do without him." Eliza stretched out her hand to touch Andy's sweatered back as he bent over next to her chair and neatly stacked the logs against the wall next to the fireplace.

Rising, he crossed to Caddy's chair and gripped her hand warmly in his. His face was pleasant and his smile of welcome was genuine.

"Don't let them kid you; they're slave drivers who keep me up on the roof, patching the gables."

"Andy's a graduate student doing a study program with me this summer. I teach him about the ecology around here, and he teaches me how to drive a straight nail."

"We love having him too."

She felt the undercurrents of affection flowing back and forth between the three people, and she wished she didn't have to leave. Looking at the ship's clock on the mantel, she saw it was almost six o'clock. With an exclamation of surprise she rose swiftly to her feet.

"I didn't realize it was so late. The Spencers will think I'm lost. Thank you—for everything." She smiled at the Loverings.

"Andy will drive you, won't you, Andy?" Eliza rose a little stiffly from her chair and looked anxiously at the younger man. "It's a long walk and she doesn't know the way." She turned to Caddy and said, her voice still anxious, "And you'll come back and see us, my dear, won't you? You won't let all our talk about the unpleasantness keep you away?"

Caddy took her hand and held it for a moment. "Of course. As often as you'll have me."

"She's not here to socialize with us, Liza. She's here to photograph my kites." Nelson put one hand in a courtly fashion under Caddy's elbow and they all walked into the hall. "You tell young Fiske I want him to have you here by seven tomorrow morning. That's not too early for you, is it?"

"No, of course not. I'm used to getting up before dawn to shoot. It's the best time, when the light is pure." She put her boots back on over her dried socks, and thanking them again she left them standing together on the porch. Caddy waved back at them from the station wagon, as they peered out into the dusk as if they were reluctant to have her leave. Or maybe, she thought as the trees closed in around them and the house and the ocean beyond disappeared from view, she was the one who was reluctant to leave their warmth and friendliness for the strained atmosphere that awaited her at the Manor.

CHAPTER 5

A pale gray falcon-shaped bird sat poised on a forked branch of a dense bayberry bush, turning its white head from side to side as it kept watch on the hidden nest Caddy was trying to locate. At first she had thought it was only a small gull, but the large black patches on the fore edges of its upper wings and its long white tail clearly signified that she had found the white-tailed kite she was searching for. With a sigh of relief she quietly began to photograph the elusive bird through her telescopic lens.

She had been the one who, awake and fully dressed shortly after dawn following another largely sleepless night, had answered the telephone when Eliza called the Spencer house to say that Nelson had indeed caught a chill in the marsh the previous evening. With dismay, she had listened to Eliza's tale of how Nelson had finally obeyed and agreed to remain in bed when Eliza told him she had no intention of allowing him to leave the house until he was quite well again.

"Fiske will drive you to the marsh today," she instructed firmly. "After all, he's been there a thousand times with Nelson. He can drop you off this morning and come back for you whenever you tell him."

"But I don't know anything about the kites, only what I read in the research folder, and that wasn't much. Perhaps we'd better wait until he's better," she protested.

"Nelson says you'll be fine. Just try and find the nest. He says it's there, he's seen it and you can too, if you persevere. Besides, my dear, you'll probably do just as well without Nelson talking a blue streak and telling you more than you want to know."

"But won't Fiske mind?" Despite the fact that she was alone in the dark hall, she instinctively lowered her voice. Flustered as she had been by being late for dinner the previous evening, she couldn't help being conscious that the little group that gathered around the dinner table was, despite Dorothy's best efforts, very somber.

"Of course not. You just tell him Uncle Nelson says he's to drive you to the marsh. He'll understand."

With a sinking heart she had hung up the receiver and followed the scent of freshly made coffee to the kitchen. To her relief she found that the coffee maker was Fiske, dressed in old clothes and wearing running shoes. He was standing by the stove watching the dark brew drip down into the pot.

"Good morning," she ventured hesitantly, unsure

how to tell him his services had been offered as her guide. "You're up early."

"Coffee?" Without turning, he pulled down two mugs and filled them with steaming black brew, swallowing a great gulp as he walked across the kitchen floor to hand her one. He smiled ruefully. "Sorry. I can't talk before I have my coffee."

She looked at him, considering. She really didn't want to talk to him, but she needed his help and, after all, she was a guest in his home. In an effort to make polite conversation before she passed along Eliza's instructions, she searched around for something to say and finally asked, "But you've been running, haven't you? Doesn't that wake you up?"

"Sometimes."

She sat at the large, round wooden kitchen table and watched as he opened the refrigerator door and stared glumly inside. He looked as if he was still in a daze, she thought. His hair was sticking up in the back and he hadn't shaved.

"Eggs? Cereal? Toast?" He pulled out a dish, smelled it, and returned it to its shelf. "What do photographers eat in the morning?"

"Nothing."

"Nothing?"

"Too busy."

"Orange juice. That's good for openers." He pulled out a large carton, poured some juice into two glasses, and lowering himself into a chair across from her, slid her glass across the table. He eyed her reflectively over the rim of his glass as he drank.

His eyes were a grayer green than his sister's, she decided, and she noticed again that there were nice laugh lines around their edges. Perhaps he wouldn't be too difficult about taking her to the marsh if she approached him very carefully.

"Who was that on the phone?" he asked.

"Eliza Lovering."

"What did she want? Ma?"

"Actually, she called to tell me Mr. Lovering can't take me to the marsh this morning." Caddy looked at him over the rim of her mug, assessing his mood. She was glad to see he looked more awake, almost human. Before she could give him Eliza's message, he began to smile; the smile turned into a grin that lit up his face and she thought he definitely looked human. More than human, she decided, smiling a little in relief; definitely approachable and even quite attractive.

"What's funny?" she asked.

"How are you going to do it?"

"Do what?"

"Tell me I have to give up my morning to drive up to the marsh and find the kites for you."

"How did you know?" She was surprised. Had he been listening in on an extension or did he have psychic powers? No, she thought, there was no extension and he looked too ordinary to be able to read minds.

"Logic. Uncle Nelson can't go. You have to photograph. I know where the kites are. Ergo, I'm it."

"Thank you." She breathed a sigh of relief. The vision she had of wandering around by herself in the shallow canals searching for a bird that didn't want to be found disappeared, and she smiled at him companionably. "You can just leave me there after you point me in the right direction. I'll be all right; I've done this before."

He yawned. "I saw your photo essay on the ospreys. I liked it."

Despite herself, she was flattered and she looked at him with renewed interest. The osprey spread had been her best work to date, the article that had won her an award from the Audubon Society, and she was very proud of it.

"Thanks. Not many people have. Ospreys aren't exactly in the mainstream of the cutting edge," she said reluctantly.

"Maybe you should photograph them covering Madonna next time—that would make you rich and famous," he mused. He refilled her cup without asking.

Without thinking she added, "Or swarming Michael Jackson in the middle of a Coke ad?"

"Ross Perot could start breeding ospreys, and you could shoot it live on *Good Morning America.*"

"Oprah with ospreys."

"There's really no end to it, if we put our minds to it." They looked at each other seriously for a moment, and she felt herself beginning to smile. Fiske's face still bore a trace of amusement as they slumped back over their mugs and quietly finished their coffee together.

The early morning sun began to break through the fog outside; it filtered in through the kitchen windows and moved across the wood floor to the table. From the depths of a dark shadow in the far corner, a large black cat uncoiled itself and walked slowly toward the center of the room. With one fluid motion it leapt to the center of the table and began lapping cream from a low pitcher.

"Farquehar. Stop that." Fiske slapped his hand sharply on the wooden table. Undisturbed, the cat continued to drink.

Caddy laughed involuntarily. "Farquehar?"

"It's a perfectly respectable name," Fiske replied stiffly, but beneath his tan his cheeks flushed.

"Farquehar," she said solemnly.

"An old island name."

"Of course. Farquehars been here for over a century, have they?"

"Longer. The first Farquehar was an Indian."

Their eyes met, the little lines around Fiske's eyes crinkled again, and Caddy found herself grinning at him across the table. He paused in the act of reaching for the coffeepot, and she was aware of his hand, of the bare skin of his wrist. He looked at her, his head cocked slightly to the left, his eyes suddenly intent. Feeling as if she was going to blush, she reached out and concentrated on smoothing the cat's fur. She heard Fiske pour the coffee, the sound of the pot being set down again, and then only the sound of the cat as it purred beneath her hand. She was acutely conscious of the presence of the man sitting across from her and she frowned, not wanting to acknowledge that she was aware of his very provocative aura of masculinity.

"Ready to go?" he asked.

"Ready."

"Let's do it." He rose.

Later, looking at her watch, she realized breakfast had been almost three hours ago. While she had carefully watched the single kite Fiske had found for her, photographing it in every conceivable pose as it soared and hovered around the same narrow area, she had still been unable to find the nest. There had to be a nest nearby. The kite wouldn't have been so territorial if there weren't. She sighed impatiently, but she knew her impatience was directed at more than the shy bird so intent on concealing the whereabouts of his sitting mate. While it was true that she worried there could be no story unless there was at least one family to explore with her lens, ever since she had set foot on the island she had felt that something in this particular job was different from any other. Perhaps it was the fairy-tale quality of the physical beauty of Kincade, which made her feel as if she had stepped into another world and contributed to her sense of disorientation; perhaps it was the undercurrent of tension among the interrelated islanders that, despite her promise to remain detached, was somehow drawing her into their lives. She frowned. Perhaps it was Fiske Spencer, but if that were the case she would just have to force herself to ignore him. Not given to premonitions, she tried to shake off the feeling that something was looming over her.

Looking up at the sun, which was directly overhead, she put her camera away and began to trudge back up the hill to the road. It must be her imagination: too little sleep last night and too little success at her work that morning had made her tired and fanciful. One way or another, she had to find the colony of kites; she needed the forty-five-hundred-dollar fee too badly to fail.

She reached the road and looked around for the Spencers' Jeep, but the road was empty. Fiske had said he would return for her at noon, and she looked at the spot where the road disappeared into the trees, hoping the Jeep would emerge if she wished hard enough. She didn't know whether to wait or start walking, if he had forgotten her or was merely late. Pangs of hunger made the decision for her, and she started the long walk back to the Manor, her camera bag getting heavier and heavier as she made her way along the ridge.

The faint sound of an engine made her smile with relief, but the vehicle that came toward her wasn't driven by Fiske. Instead, the elegant-looking blond woman she had seen at the ferry landing and later on her front porch, the one Nelson had told her was Josie Northrup, sat at the wheel of a shiny new red Land-Rover. Next to her sat Barbara Davidson with a small, blond boy asleep on her lap. Pulling even with Caddy, Josie leaned out and asked, "Lost?"

"I'm not sure. Fiske said he'd come back for me so I could have lunch at the house, but there's no sign of him. I really want to film some more this afternoon before the light goes, but I'm too hungry to work straight through. I guess I'm walking back for my lunch. I wish I'd thought to pack sandwiches this morning." She explained tentatively, hoping she would be offered a ride to the Manor; she was really very tired.

Josie conferred briefly with Barbara. "Get in. I'm Josie Northrup and you'd better come with us. I'm taking Barbara to my house for lunch before she catches the ferry. She says she hasn't seen her brother."

Barbara called languidly, "He's probably been delayed for a good reason; he's always reliable."

"I don't want to—"

"Nonsense," Josie interrupted briskly. "You look tired and thirsty. I'll drive you down to the house and we'll call from there. If Fiske's already left, he'll know where to find you."

Caddy climbed up into the backseat and held on as Josie let out the clutch and made an abrupt turn off the ridge down toward the Hall. Barbara didn't turn around. They bumped over a road that badly needed to be leveled, and for a moment she thought they'd broken an axle when the Land Rover bounced into a large hole. "How will he know?" she asked, trying to keep her eyes off the speedometer; she was sure they were going at least sixty on a road that was never meant for cars.

"No place else to go," Josie said simply. "We're the only other house on the ridge road. All the others are off the north shore road."

Turning her head sideways without moving her body, Barbara elaborated politely to the air. "There are three roads: north shore, middle, and south. Middle is the main highway; it stretches the whole length of the island." She faced forward again, smoothing the sleeping child's hair absently.

With an expert turn of the wheel, Josie swung the car around the back of the house and brought it to a halt in front of a pile of bicycles and wagons left haphazardly on the grass in front of the door. Climbing down, she lifted out a carton of groceries and said, "This is it. Grab that other box."

Inside the house, Barbara disappeared through the far door, carrying her burden gently while Josie set down the two-gallon cans of kerosene she was balancing. Caddy dumped the heavy box she was carrying next to Josie's on the kitchen counter and looked around.

The kitchen was a mess. Breakfast dishes were still on the table, small sneakers and dungarees littered the floor, and toys were everywhere. Obviously more than one child lived here, and Caddy waited with some trepidation for the onslaught. Except for growing up with Thad she had little experience with children. But Thad had been different than most. Even as a little boy he'd never been noisy or disruptive, just brave and affectionate, and full of wonderful stories he created especially for her. She never quite got over missing him between visits to Philadelphia.

Josie grunted. She was bent over, stowing cans into a baseboard cabinet.

"Do you get groceries like this every day?" Caddy asked.

"Every single day until the small island store opens."

"Your son didn't even open an eye when I put him down," Barbara announced to Josie. Obviously accustomed to treating Josie's house as her own, she opened the refrigerator door, pulled out a bottle of pale wine, and closed the door and leaned on it while she poured a glass for herself.

"Do you mind leaning somewhere else? I've got groceries to put away." When Barbara edged to one side, Josie arranged her load of groceries inside the refrigerator and slammed the door. With a sigh of relief she retrieved a wineglass from the dish drainer for herself and, after only the most minute of pauses, held up an empty glass inquiringly in Caddy's direction. Caddy shook her head.

Josie looked around the kitchen with a sigh. "God, I'll be glad when the shack opens and we don't have to meet the ferry for our food every day."

"When the shack opens *and* the au pairs arrive, you mean."

"Definitely the au pairs. Who's running the shack this year?"

"The Landers kid."

Neither woman really looked at Caddy while they sipped at their wine and finished unpacking the food. She felt acutely unwelcome and, attempting to hasten her departure, looked around the kitchen for a telephone. "Is there somewhere I could call?" she finally asked.

"Shit. I'm sorry. It's out there, in the little hall to the

left of the door. Just dial three for the Manor." Josie pointed with her glass.

"Thanks." Relieved to have escaped the kitchen, Caddy followed the instructions. Her heart sank when all she got was a series of unanswered rings from the Manor. Obviously no one was at the house and Fiske had forgotten all about her. Somehow or other she had just assumed he would do what he said, and she was surprised at how disappointed she felt that Fiske had forgotten her so easily. She replaced the receiver carefully. From the other side of the kitchen door she heard Josie chuckle in response to something Barbara murmured in a low voice, and she leaned against the wall, wondering what to do next. The hot bath and nap she had been longing for began to seem a long way away.

"No answer?" Carrying her wineglass, Josie came through the swinging door followed by Barbara bearing the wine bottle.

Caddy shook her head.

Barbara and Josie exchanged a quick glance. "Fiske will probably be along any minute now," Josie offered briskly. "Better change your mind and have a drink while you wait." She led the way through the house to a vast living room that ran the length of the house, overlooking the lower wetlands and the ocean beyond. The view was breathtaking, made more so by an uninterrupted sweep of glass on the south wall. The room itself was just as cluttered as the kitchen; books and magazines covered the couches and chairs, which were brightly upholstered in sturdy patterned linen, games were balanced on almost every surface, and a complicated structure of hundreds of blocks rose up in a corner behind a Ping-Pong table. A golden retriever jumped down from a wing chair and went to Josie to be petted.

"Nice boy, nice boy," Josie crooned.

"God. What a mess." Barbara shoved aside a stack of magazines so she could lay full length on the couch, setting her glass and the wine bottle conveniently on the coffee table next to her. Sensing that the other two women had counted on being alone to talk privately and acutely aware that she was in Josie's house on sufferance, Caddy perched uncomfortably on the edge of a scarred Windsor chair.

"What's wrong with this room?" Josie demanded.

"It's a mess. Don't you ever pick anything up?"

"It's either neatness or family, kiddo, and family won without a second thought." Josie dismissed the condition of the room with an airy wave.

"Speaking of which, where are the other kids?"

"At their cousins'."

Barbara smiled at the ceiling. "Peace. Blessed, blessed peace."

"How many children do you have?" Caddy interjected. Josie and Barbara looked at her as if they had forgotten she was in the room, and she flushed, wishing she had remained silent.

"Three. All boys. The oldest is five and the twins are three," Josie responded briefly.

Barbara giggled, a gurgling sound that dissolved the chilly air of remoteness she had worn ever since Caddy's arrival. Charmed by the sound, Caddy smiled involuntarily. Barbara rolled over on her side and, propping her head on her hand, elaborated, "Mickey's the eldest and should be in school now, but Jonno and Josie figure he's so brilliant he can miss a little kindergarten and survive. The twins are terrors. Absolute terrors."

"They are not," Josie denied indignantly, but she laughed. Caddy was struck by how lovely she looked when she smiled, almost like a model.

"Child abuse. Total disregard for the kids' welfare and intellectual development. They'll never get into Harvard," Barbara teased.

"Getting island sand in their sneakers is better for the kids than anything they can learn at Montessori School any day. You wait: Your kids will turn into over-achievers if you aren't careful. Besides, is it child abuse if the only time Jonno and I can get away from work at the same time is before the season starts?" When Josie grinned this time, it was straight at Caddy and Caddy returned the smile gratefully. She decided she liked the loose-limbed, tall blonde very much. The contrast between Josie's elegant appearance and the chaos of her house was captivating, and she liked the ease and humor with which she described her household. The smile swiftly faded from Josie's face as a thin wail pierced the air. "Damn. Jonno's crying. His ear must be bothering him again." She disappeared from the room in the direction of the sound.

Left alone, Caddy and Barbara sat in silence. Barbara refilled her glass and drank in a preoccupied fashion. After a moment's deliberation Caddy made up her mind. "I think I'll walk back to the Manor. If your mother gets back she might think I'm lost," she announced.

"Mmmm. I don't think so." Barbara yawned.

Caddy rose. "I think I should. Will you tell Josie thanks for the lift?"

Barbara turned her head and looked at Caddy, but something about her gaze made Caddy feel her mind was really busy thinking about something else. She took a tentative step forward. With an abrupt movement Barbara sat up and smiled brightly. "Stay for a while. Josie has to drive me to the ferry soon anyway; she'll drop you off on the way. It's a short drive but a long walk. You haven't finished your wine."

Caught off guard by the almost coaxing invitation, Caddy sank back down. She eyed her companion warily, wondering what had caused the sudden thaw in the other woman's chilly reception.

Barbara turned her head and asked, "How's your work going?"

"Fine," she replied cautiously.

The other woman looked down at her hand, took a sip of wine, and cleared her throat. "Nelson and Eliza are wonderful, aren't they?"

"Yes."

"Nelson doesn't usually spend so much time socializing. Eliza's really sweet to everyone, but sometimes he can be a pain if you don't understand him." Barbara's laugh was artificial; only her lips smiled, not her eyes.

Puzzled, Caddy remained silent. She couldn't imagine Nelson being anything other than the charming, garrulous host he had been the day before.

"What on earth did you two find to talk about all that time in the marsh? And you were at their house for hours having tea," Barbara persisted.

"Birds. The scenery. Kincade." Caddy carefully left out any mention of the fact that Nelson had let the cat out of the bag about the issue of the developer. Ashford? Ashman? She couldn't remember his name and she frowned.

"What about Kincade? What did he say?" Barbara asked quickly. She leaned forward and searched Caddy's face.

Taken aback by Barbara's persistence, Caddy shrugged. "He just showed me some old maps."

"Ahhh. Then he did tell you." Satisfied, Barbara leaned back. She picked up her glass and drained it. "He wasn't supposed to talk about the island. If he had the maps out, he was talking about the land, and if he was talking about the land he wouldn't have been able to stop himself from losing his temper at the idea that anyone could conceivably want to sell their shares in Kincade. I bet Eliza shut him up pretty fast." She giggled again, but this time the sound was shrill.

Confused, but not wanting to get Nelson in trouble, Caddy tried to laugh the whole thing off. "You make us sound like something from the French Resistance. I'm not interested in anything but finishing my shoot and getting back to New York."

"Giving her the third degree, Babs?" Josie asked from the doorway as she returned to the room. She picked up the nearly empty wine bottle and winked in an almost friendly fashion at Caddy. "We better eat something."

"Young Jonno okay?" Ignoring the warning look Josie directed at her, Babs stood up and stretched.

"Fine. Back to sleep, thank God. Tell you what: Let's divide the last of this and throw some food together. Then I'll drop Caddy off on the way to the ferry." She parceled out the small amount of wine between their three glasses. With a grin at Barbara, she raised her glass to Caddy. "Welcome to Kincade," she intoned solemnly in a deep voice.

"Oh, God. Must we?" Barbara groaned theatrically.

" 'Welcome to Kincade' is what every islander says to anyone on their first day here, even if you've been coming over all your life. It drives us all crazy at the beginning of the season," Josie explained.

Caddy finished her wine with one swallow. "Thank you. You know, I saw you yesterday when I was getting off the ferry."

Josie grinned. "I know. We were all giving you the once-over, pretending to pick up our mail, but really wondering what the interloper looked like."

"Did I pass inspection?" Caddy couldn't resist seeing what kind of an answer she would get.

"Who knows?" Josie shrugged her shoulders. "The ones who didn't mind having a stranger photograph here probably thought you looked fine, and the ones who did probably thought you looked like the devil."

Barbara perched on the back of the couch. "And which did you think, Jose?" she needled.

"She's here, isn't she?" Josie laugh shortly. "You'll get used to it, Caddy."

"We're all always on one side or the other of some hot issue up here," Barbara drawled.

"Right. Do we hire someone to take the garbage to New London, or do we recycle it on the island? Should we have two ferries instead of one? Should we paint the ferry we have blue rather than off-white? There's no end to issues on Kincade."

Barbara sighed. "Yeah, but . . ."

"But nothing, Babs. Don't start."

"Girls, girls, don't bicker."

"Fiske," Josie cried. Crossing the room at a run she threw her arms around the man standing in the doorway and hugged him fiercely. She was almost as tall as he was, but he picked her up and swung her around effortlessly like a child; Barbara dove for his knees and they were all laughing when they reeled to a halt. It was clear to Caddy they were fond of each other, and she felt a little pang of envy; she hadn't had time to make many friends of her own. At first her life had

been full of work and study and responsibility for
Thad, and later, with Ward, she had been too busy
leading his life to have time to make friends of her
own. It wasn't often that she minded, but sensing the
easy camaraderie among the three other people, she
wished she had more close companions.

"I'm sorry I was late," Fiske apologized to Caddy. "I
didn't forget you, I just got diverted. Ma got worried
when she came home and you hadn't shown for lunch,
and she made me come looking for you."

"I'm okay. You shouldn't have bothered; I could get
back to the house on my own," she replied coolly,
feeling somewhat offended that he could so easily have
left her alone in the marsh.

Despite the smile that lingered at the corner of his
eyes, he replied just as coolly, "I knew you couldn't get
lost. I was trapped. I'm sorry."

Barbara coughed to cover a laugh. Fiske shot her an
irritated glance, which silenced her. With a concerned
look at Fiske, Josie hastily clapped her hands. "Lunch?
We've finished off the rest of last night's wine, but
there's more, and there's beer, and we have plenty of
food."

"Beer sounds like a good idea," Barbara said
quickly.

"I could eat," Fiske acknowledged tiredly.

"I really should get back to the house, I think,"
Caddy looked at the doorway with longing. The feeling
that she was on sufferance had returned with a ven-
geance, and the last thing she wanted to do was sit
through a meal with these people with their private
jokes and their shared secrets.

Fiske drew his eyebrows together in a frown. "I've
got the car, remember. You can't go until I drive you."

"I'm perfectly capable of walking," Caddy responded hotly. Any pleasure left over from their breakfast together vanished. He was just another good-looking rich man, as selfish as all the others. She stood up very straight, determined not to let her exhaustion show.

"Let's have lunch. Come on." Briskly, Josie led the way back to the kitchen. Looking around the room she scooped up an armful of plates and hid them in the dishwasher.

Barbara pulled a new loaf of bread from one of the cartons and looked around vaguely for something to put on it. "Ham and cheese all right?"

"Fine by me." Fiske pulled out a chair and straddled it backward, resting his arms on the back. He looked appraisingly at Caddy and whistled tunelessly through his lips.

"We've got Brie and leftover steak. Caddy, sit down." Josie piled Brie and the steak on a large plate, pulled mustard and tiny pickles out of the refrigerator, and spilled strawberries from a basket into a blue bowl. Barbara slid a package of sliced ham onto the table and added a loaf of dark bread to the collection.

Caddy eased into a seat across from Fiske without speaking. Fiske was so different from this morning. Then he had been funny, almost vulnerable, not at all the unfriendly, preoccupied person he seemed now or that he had been when he met her at the ferry. She liked him better this morning. Without looking at him she began to make sandwiches.

Barbara pulled four cold bottles of beer from the still-open refrigerator, slamming the door closed with her foot as she put them on the table.

With a sigh Josie settled into a chair and patted the one next to her for Barbara to take. "So, why were you so late?"

"Business." Fiske spoke with his mouth full, reaching across the table for a beer.

"What kind of business?" Barbara nibbled at the end of a small pickle.

"Business that's none of your business, big sister." He reached over and tweaked a lock of her hair.

"Damn it, Fiske. Don't do that."

"Well, what kind of business? I want to know too. And I'm sure Caddy wouldn't mind an explanation," Josie said.

Fiske frowned at her sharply. His face was serious, and he stared at her as if he were trying to telegraph a message. "Cliff Ludlow came to see us this morning."

"So? Cliff Ludlow comes to see your father every morning. Or your father goes over there. What's the big deal?"

"I didn't even know the Ludlows were here yet," Barbara commented without much interest.

Caddy toyed with her strawberries and wondered how soon the meal would be over. She looked at Fiske, trying to gauge how near he was to the end of his sandwich, and caught him looking at her with an expression of extreme distaste. Startled and wondering why he disliked her so much, she looked quickly away, her heart pounding.

"They've been here for a few days."

"So? What's the big deal? Why were you late?"

"Jose, for Christ's sake," he said in a threatening voice. Caddy saw him look meaningfully at Josie; she saw that Josie looked directly at him, and saw, too, when the color drained from her cheeks and her smile vanished.

"My God, Cliff too?" she whispered.

"Not now, Josie," he instructed her in a quiet voice that silenced her as effectively as Barbara had been earlier by his look. What a bully he is, ordering every-one around, Caddy thought. He really thinks he's King Tut.

"You don't have to be quite so mysterious, Fiske. Caddy's heard," Barbara informed him. There was res-ignation in her voice.

Three faces turned toward Caddy and then looked at each other in consternation. She sensed they were suddenly remembering she was an outsider.

"I won't say anything," she reassured them quickly.

"Nelson," Fiske stated flatly. He stared at her coldly.

"Yes. It was when he was telling me about the is-land. I think he wanted me to love it the way he does and just got carried away."

"He shouldn't have said anything. It's a private is-land matter."

Josie sighed. "Poor Nelson. He can't accept the fact that anyone, especially people he knows and cares about, would ever violate this place." She made a ges-ture that encompassed more than the room in which they were sitting. Her voice faltered as she looked at Fiske.

Fiske covered Josie's hand with his in a gesture that was so natural, so tender that Caddy suddenly won-dered with a pang if they had ever been lovers. She held her breath, curious all over again about what mo-tivated these people to care so possessively about an island in the middle of Long Island Sound.

"Never mind Nelson. Tell us what happened with Cliff." Barbara looked at her brother as she reached absentmindedly for a piece of ham.

"He wants to bring the issue to a vote."

"My God," Josie breathed.

Barbara leaned forward, the ham forgotten. "Could that happen?"

"Dad refused to sign the call for a vote." Caddy saw that the lines of worry had deepened on his face, and he looked the way he had when she first saw him that morning, standing alone, watching the coffee boil. His face was expressionless when he looked first at his sister and then at Josie, but Caddy saw something she thought was pain deep in his gray eyes.

She held her breath, fascinated by the byplay and surprised they had revealed as much as they had in front of her. Still trying to avoid drawing attention to herself, she sipped her beer cautiously. She knew she was in the middle of a story that would make headlines in the mainland newspapers. She didn't want to remind them she was there, a representative from the media who could, if she chose, take their story to the world and effectively end their privacy.

As if he could read her mind, Fiske looked directly at her. He frowned slightly. She lowered her eyes quickly, but it was too late. She heard the sound of his chair as he rose and it scraped on the floor.

"Time to go, Babbo. The ferry won't wait." He tossed his beer can into the garbage bucket by the back door and pulled out his car keys.

Barbara finished her beer with a gulp and stood up. She looked down at the table. "Shit. The dishes."

"I'll do them. Go." Carrying used glasses to the sink, Josie blew her a kiss.

Without looking at Caddy, Fiske asked Josie, "You'll drop her at the marsh? I can pick her up at three."

"Yes. You'll call later?" While Caddy watched, they looked at each other in silent communion. Then Fiske leaned down and put his arms around her waist and hugged her tightly before he left without another word.

Bastard, Caddy thought.

As Barbara, with a careless backward wave, followed him, Caddy could hear her demanding of Fiske, "Now I want to hear everything that happened." So do I, she thought in surprise. So do I. The sound of an engine dwindled away and she and Josie stared at each other.

"I'll drive you to the marsh."

"I'll help with the dishes."

They spoke simultaneously. Josie smiled briefly, a rather wintery smile. "That's okay. I can do them."

Caddy shook her head. Rising, she began to clear the table, stacking plates on top of one another, replacing the tops on the jars, and crumpling up their used napkins. With a shrug, Josie turned around again and began to scrub the serving bowls. The two women worked quietly and efficiently without speaking until the large kitchen was completely in order, the counters wiped and the dishes all put away in the cabinets.

"Never looked so good, and it probably won't again. Thanks," Josie said, looking around with satisfaction. "Thanks a lot."

"Thanks for lunch," Caddy replied honestly.

Josie attempted a smile, which didn't quite cover her face. "We weren't very amusing, I'm afraid."

"It's a difficult time for you," Caddy commented carefully.

Josie moved slowly toward the hall to the front porch. Picking up her heavy camera bag, Caddy followed, pleased that at least one of the younger generation appeared to be offering some sort of appearance of civility. On the walls of the wide center hall were a series of prints, pastel pictures of animals deep in a forest.

"These are lovely," Caddy exclaimed, stopping to examine one. "Are they yours?"

"No. They're illustrations from one of my books."

"You're an author?" Caddy looked at her hostess curiously. It was difficult to imagine the elegant woman next to her as the writer of children's stories.

Josie smiled and shook her head. "No. An editor."

"They really are wonderful. I wish my brother could see them."

Josie swung open the screen door that led to a wide porch overlooking the dunes and walked to the edge of the porch. Caddy joined her and they stood side by side, looking out over the low grasses to the dunes.

Swarms of gulls and terns were circling along the shoreline, diving for fish; above them, low clouds were forming and it looked like rain. The retriever padded over to Caddy and rubbed against her leg; his eyes begged to be petted and she obliged him, enjoying the feel of his soft coat beneath her hand. She and Thad had never had a pet, but if they had, she would have liked a dog just like this one. In fact, she thought, she liked everything about the Hall, including its mistress.

"How much did Nelson tell you?" Josie asked, gazing straight ahead.

"Not much. Just about someone making an offer for Kincade."

"Bruce Asher."

"Yes. And that there's a good deal of disagreement over the offer."

"You could call it that," Josie admitted dryly. "Seems you came at a bad time." Josie's face was very soft as she looked east, and her voice was almost friendly.

"I should get going."

"Mmmm. I'll get the car keys."

"No. Really, I'd like to walk."

Josie looked at her. She seemed startled. "You sure? You sure you want to walk? It's almost a mile."

"I like walking here. It's lovely."

"It is that. It would be hell . . ." She halted herself in the middle of a sentence.

Caddy sensed Josie was worried and preoccupied over what was happening on the island. "I'm sorry," Caddy said inadequately. She wasn't sure what she was sorry for, but there was something about the people she had met that intrigued her, something besides their obvious wealth. Perhaps it was that they were so remote and reclusive, yet at the same time she kept being made aware of a deep bond of loyalty and affection between them that she almost envied. Who or what could possibly threaten such apparent allegiance and fidelity?

"Thanks again," she said as she started down the broad front steps.

"You're welcome," Josie replied. She seemed to hesitate and Caddy paused, waiting for her to continue.

With a smile both apologetic and amused that seemed to light up her face, Josie looked down and said with a little laugh, "Come back sometime, if you like. We're not all horrible all the time."

Caddy felt a spurt of pleasure. She nodded. "I will," she replied with a grin.

Skirting a child's red truck, she made her way across a small patch of grass to the lane and started up the incline to the road. She walked briskly, the weight of her cameras forgotten as she tried to put together in her mind the people she had met so far: Dorothy,

Douglas, Nelson and Eliza, Barbara and Josie, and Fiske. He was the real mystery. At first he had seemed so standoffish, then at breakfast that morning almost human, but just now over the lunch table he had treated her as if she wasn't to be trusted, almost as if he actively disliked her. She shivered and quickened her pace. It had seemed a simple thing to follow Dave's instructions not to become involved with the islanders, but now she wasn't so sure.

CHAPTER 6

Fiske pulled his Jeep to a halt in front of Clifford and Marcy Ludlow's yellow bungalow, which nestled in the hollow of a large meadow surrounded by woods that stretched north of the Manse. Except for the smell of salt in the air and an occasional gull blown away from the shore, it was almost like being back on the mainland. The house itself was a neat ranch with shutters, surrounded by a split-rail fence and with an incongruous-looking wagon wheel positioned to the right of the front door.

The Ludlows' marriage was unlike any other he had seen, Fiske mused as he turned off the engine. The cerebral Clifford and the fey Marcy shouldn't have had anything in common, but they had managed to live together for almost forty years and still appear perfectly delighted with one another. The story of how Marcy, when she married Clifford in the fifties, had flatly refused to live in the Manse—describing it to her husband as a gothic horror—had always amused Fiske. The only way Clifford had been able to keep his young bride on the island had been to allow her to erect the small modern house that now faced Fiske. The house was complete with a sparkling, modern kitchen, with a self-cleaning stove that rarely worked, and a swimming pool whose filter system was broken more often than not, but Marcy loved it, declaring that anyone who preferred the vast spaces and winding stairs of those old original houses must be mad.

Letting himself in the front door without knocking, Fiske dropped the pile of books he had brought for Marcy on a table and walked through the L-shaped living room to the patio.

On the back lawn Clifford was practicing his fly casting, while Marcy, a blanket over her knees, was stretched out on a chaise longue with a stack of catalogs on her lap that she wasn't reading.

"Fiske," she cried with pleasure. The magazines slid to the ground as she raised her arms to hug him. Her hair was tinted a bright yellow and she wore too much makeup, but she was still a pretty woman and there was no mistaking the warmth of her welcome. Fiske liked Marcy: she was gay and frivolous, the life of every party, and she worshiped her husband with a passion that belied her artless manner. She and Clifford were his parents' oldest friends, and he and Babs had grown up with their two sons, spending their summers running wild with the Ludlow boys.

"Aunt Marcy, you look radiant as always." He bent down and took her hand.

"Darling boy."

"Ah, not a boy anymore." He kissed her hand and held it.

"Flirt." She pulled her hand away and patted his head.

"Cruel woman. You're breaking my heart." He pulled up a wrought-iron chair and sat next to her, and together they watched Clifford cast once or twice until Fiske began clapping his hands rhythmically. "More wrist, more wrist, more wrist," he chanted like a football fan. "Come on, Uncle Cliff, you can do it. Let that line go."

"Fool." Clifford stumped up to the patio. He leaned his rod carefully against the side of the house before offering Fiske his hand. "What do you know? You couldn't catch a trout with a trawling net."

"Just trying to be helpful," he replied blandly.

"You wish," Clifford snorted. He wore baggy, grass-stained pants and a loud purple checked shirt; when Clifford was on the island and wrapped up in his fishing, he looked anything but one of the world's foremost theoreticians in abstract mathematics that he actually was.

"I could give you a few pointers," Fiske teased.

"Don't mess with the master, my boy. Don't forget, I taught you everything you know." The older man pulled up a chair and let himself down into it, leaning over to pat his wife's wrapped-up legs. "Warm enough?" he asked her.

"Fine, dear."

His smile faded and a frown creased Clifford's normally pleasant face. "I didn't expect to see you again after this morning."

"Whoa, Uncle Cliff. You and I go back a long way."

"Your father and I go back a hell of a lot longer."

"I know," Fiske agreed sadly.

"Clifford, darling . . ." With a worried look, Marcy reached out and took her husband's hand.

"Don't 'Clifford darling' me, Marcy. Douglas made his views perfectly clear, we said things neither one of us can ever forget, and I'm not going to talk about it anymore." As he looked out over the lawn his face was set in angry lines, but the expression in his eyes was bleak. He swiveled and looked at Fiske. "If you think you can make me change my mind, you've got another think coming, young man."

"Clifford, darling, don't. Fiske is as dear to us as our own boys." This time Marcy removed her hand from her husband's and spoke quite firmly, in a no-nonsense tone of voice. With a sigh Clifford finally nodded his head.

Leaning forward, Fiske told them earnestly, "I wanted to see you both. And I wanted to talk to you, Uncle Clifford. I feel like hell about the way things ended up this morning."

Maybe he had been wrong in coming over here so impulsively. It was just that the aftermath of Clifford and Douglas's argument that morning had been so devastating, he felt he had to try to repair the damages. Despite Dorothy's entreaties and his own pounding on the closed door, Douglas still hadn't emerged from his studio. They had been able to see him through the shed window, standing at his easel, but neither of them had believed he was really painting. When Fiske had turned the Jeep around and driven back the length of the island to the Ludlows' home, it was because he had suddenly thought perhaps he could talk some sense into Clifford. Now he wondered if he was straying into territory that wasn't his; Douglas and Clifford's friendship stretched back to their childhood, and perhaps he shouldn't butt in on their quarrel. Fiske looked at Clifford watching him with an unfamiliar guardedness and thought that it was more than a friendship that had suffered a blow, it was the whole island that was at stake. He just had to try and change the older man's mind.

Trying to buy himself time while he felt his way into a discussion of Clifford's fight with his father, Fiske asked, "Have you heard from Ford and Bill lately?"

"They're coming up Memorial Day and we're having a party," Marcy said with delight.

Relieved to have her pick up the conversational ball, Fiske grinned at Marcy gratefully. "When aren't you having a party? That's great. Is it your turn this year?" The islanders only got together three times a season: once on Memorial Day, on the Fourth of July, and again on Labor Day. The first and last parties were rotated so no one family bore the brunt of entertaining the seventy or so owners plus their hordes of children, but Fourth of July was always held at Kincade House. If it was Marcy's turn for Memorial Day this year, the party was certain to be especially lively, with music and dancing into the night.

"As always, I'm counting on you to bring a pretty girl, Fiske. Ford and Claire are coming for a week with the children, which is bliss, and Bill will be up for the weekend."

There was a small lull as they all thought about the slender boy who had grown into a willowy man who designed stage sets. Neither of the Ludlows ever spoke about it, but it was evident their younger son was homosexual. Fiske knew that even though they loved and supported Bill, his life among his gay companions was a heavy burden for the Ludlows to bear.

"You didn't come to talk about the boys, you see

them in New York, and you didn't come to apologize for your father, so why don't you just come out and say what's on your mind." Clifford's voice was dry and professorial.

"You're right, I didn't come to apologize for Pa."

"Well?"

"Can we talk about this morning, Uncle Clifford?" he asked softly.

"There's nothing to talk about," the older man growled. He looked intractable and Fiske sighed to himself; Clifford was going to make this as difficult as he could.

"I'm going to leave you two men alone and go inside where it's warm." Gathering her magazines together, Marcy dropped a kiss on the top of her husband's head, gave him a warning look, and retreated to the house. The two men rose politely and didn't resume their seats until the door closed behind her. Her discarded blue blanket lay like a pool on the terrace, and Clifford leaned down and picked it up, folding it carefully in sections without a word.

"Can't we talk about the offer, Uncle Cliff?" Fiske asked again. He leaned forward, his elbows on his knees.

"What about it?"

"Do you really want to sell?"

"It's a hell of a lot of money, boy."

Fiske was startled. "You don't really need it, though, do you? That's not a good enough reason."

"No, you're right, I don't."

"Who approached you?"

"Bruce Asher."

"Himself?"

"Yup. Sent me a letter saying he'd been in touch with Rufus and then called me himself."

"That's what he did with us too. He actually called Babs and invited her to lunch without Hank."

Looking interested for the first time, Clifford asked, "She go?"

"No, not yet, but she says she's going to, just to see what he's got to say."

"She's right. Listen, Fiske, we'll never have a deal as good as this again. I met with him myself."

"Jesus." The word escaped Fiske before he could halt himself; for some reason the idea that Clifford had actually met with the developer made the whole situation more threatening. If it had gone that far, it meant the offer was not a speculative one.

Clifford rose and began pacing up and down the terrace. He passed one hand over his bald head in the way he did whenever he was trying to think through a difficult problem, and then he waved toward the trees at the south end of the meadow, beyond which, Fiske knew, lay the Manse. His voice was angry and he didn't look at Fiske as he elaborated. "Who's going to use that?" he asked rhetorically. "I'm the last of my generation and Marcy hates the big house. Ford and Claire don't want the damn thing. And Bill . . ." His voice trailed off as he turned away.

Fiske was startled. Seeing the revulsion the older man was trying unsuccessfully to hide, he realized for the first time how violently upset Cliff was by his son's homosexuality. Cliff had always acted so proud of his two sons, with no apparent difference in the overt affection he showed the boys, but suddenly it became painfully clear that Bill's homosexuality was more than a burden for his father, it was eating him alive. Instinctively, Fiske rose and began to pace too, allowing his shoulder to touch the other man's as they walked slowly back and forth. He began to understand that

Cliff's true reason for deciding to leave the island might lie in his distaste for Bill's life-style and his own inability to face his oldest friends with it, rather than with any need for money.

A wave of sadness swept over him. He wanted to embrace Cliff but he was afraid of embarrassing him. He thought of all the time Cliff had spent teaching them all to fish when they were young, applauding their successes and dismissing their failures with a joke; he remembered when Bill had won the Block Island race and Cliff had been the proudest man on the island. He wondered if Bill had told his father or if Cliff had merely guessed.

"I saw a lot of Bill in London last winter when they brought his show over," he offered hesitantly, picking his words carefully. "He's well-liked, you know, and the reviewers all said he was the coming man in the field."

"I know, I know." Clifford still wouldn't look at him.

"The sets were brilliant, even I could see that."

"I know, we saw the show when it opened here." They turned and retraced their steps.

"I don't know what to say," Fiske burst out. "I love the guy."

"For Christ's sake, don't you think I do? He's my son." Clifford faced him angrily. His voice was harsh, but there were tears in his eyes. "I don't want to talk about it, Fiske."

"And that's why you think you want to sell? Could you really give up the island because of Bill? What about Ford's kids? Don't you want them to have a chance to grow up here? And their kids? That's not fair," he protested, incredulous that Clifford could do anything inequitable.

"Balls. If we sell, the families that are here can stay

for their lifetime; they'll develop around the big houses. That's enough time."

"But what about the island?"

"What about it? Why should I be the one to keep it up? Whether your father likes it or not, it's a damn good thing there's going to be a vote—you can't stop it, you know. Rufus Kincade and I aren't the only ones by a long shot."

"Regardless of how you feel on this issue, can't you and Dad at least talk to each other? He's been locked up in his studio ever since you left."

"Christ, Fiske. He threatened to clean my clock," Clifford answered in outrage.

Despite the gravity of the situation, Fiske couldn't help grinning. "I've never seen him so pissed off."

"And your mother, pshaw." Clifford smiled a little reluctantly. "All smiley and trying to get us to quit yelling at each other. She looked like a ruffled hen with her hair in her eyes."

"It's no joke."

"No, son. It isn't. I'm calling for a vote and that's all there is to it. Your father can take it or leave it."

"You know he won't leave it. Besides, most of the islanders don't get here until Memorial Day, and we don't even know which ones aren't coming at all this year. Hell, young Rufus is in Madagascar, and he's got a vote."

"It's gonna happen, Fiske."

"Shit," Fiske responded glumly. It seemed impossible that a man he had loved like a second father could ever be instrumental in breaking up Kincade. It would ruin it.

He felt a little ill, afraid there was no reaching Clifford, as if in spite of his arguments he had just lost the biggest case of his life. Sensing there was nothing further he could say, he put his arm around the older man and hugged him. Clifford tried to smile, but the effect was more of a grimace, and he turned away, walking toward the house and his wife, his hands in his pockets and his shoulders hunched.

Fiske looked at his watch. He'd promised Caddy he'd pick her up at three and that was twenty minutes ago. Not wanting to be further delayed by a long farewell with Marcy, he quickly skirted the house and drove away without looking back. He had left Caddy waiting once and it had obviously made her think badly of him. She had been so remote at lunch, almost cold, completely unlike the intriguing girl with whom he traded jokes at breakfast. He gunned the engine, determined not to let her down again.

He steered the Jeep up onto the middle road and began driving fast back toward the marsh, his hands automatically turning the wheel over the familiar terrain while his mind went back and forth over the coming vote. The issue had come to a head so quickly. When he had arrived on the island he thought it was just a vague rumor that would blow over. It wasn't the first offer that had been made for Kincade, and when his father had told him about Asher's offer that first evening, he had just laughed it off, expecting that the islanders would rebuff this developer the way they had all the others. But Asher seemed to have made contact with more than one resident: Rufus, Clifford, the Spencers, the Davidsons, and certainly Nelson and Jake; he didn't know how many others had been approached, but he had to assume the other families had been solicited too.

He rounded a bend and saw the ocean glimmering through the trees; the larches made a silvery screen in front of it. As he slowed the car to savor the moment, a young deer, startled by the noise of his engine, broke cover and bounded across the road. He felt a bubble of delight at the scene. How could anyone spoil the purity of Kincade's own special kind of natural beauty? Accelerating again, he wondered what he could do to slow down the process of the vote. He felt it was all going too fast. If he could somehow delay a confrontation and give the islanders time to think, they would have to realize what they were putting in jeopardy and certainly reconsider. His brow furrowed as he turned over names in his mind, trying to figure out who might want to sell and who was on the fence. Fiske grinned when he thought of Josie's husband, Jonno Northrup, and his brother, Randy. The three of them, along with the Ludlow boys, made five who wouldn't want to give up the island no matter how much money was offered or what Clifford thought his sons might do. That was a start. Maybe he could gather the rest of his generation together, make them a solid pack like they were when they were kids pretending they were taking over the island, only this time they'd take it over for real.

He almost laughed out loud. What the hell, it would be fun to beat some hotshot developer at his own game; he'd beaten tougher adversaries before and he could do it again. The smile faded from his face and was replaced by a hard glint of determination. He had no intention of giving up without a fight.

A slim figure rose up in the road ahead of him. He slammed on the brakes, swerving to the left and narrowly avoiding going into a ditch. With a leap of pleasure he recognized Caddy and pulled the Jeep to a screeching stop.

She regarded him calmly from outside the passenger window. Her hair had come loose from its braid, there was mud on her nose, and she was carrying her camera bag in her hand as if it had gotten too heavy to sling over her shoulder. This was the second time in the same day he had gotten involved in island problems and neglected to pick her up when he promised. She was probably ready to kill him.

"I'm sorry," he apologized contritely. He leaned over and opened the passenger door for her. "I got delayed."

"That's all right." There was no rancor in her voice. She sighed with relief as she climbed up into the Jeep and into the seat. "You're here now."

"You look all done in. How did it go?" He reversed the Jeep and turned it around, driving slowly back the way he had just come. He looked over at her. She was leaning back, her head resting on the edge of the door. Her eyes were closed and dark lashes softened her thin face. She looked very young.

"Watch the road." A smile lurked at the corners of her mouth. She opened her eyes and sat up straight. "Where are we?"

"On the way home. This is the same road we came out on, don't you remember?"

"It looked different this morning. I think more leaves came out today." She reached an arm out the window and touched a pale dogwood that grew too close to the road. "This is my favorite time of year, when everything's just beginning."

"And this is my favorite time of day, when the sun is just starting its final descent and gleams white on the water."

"Mmmm."

"You should see more of Kincade than the Great Marsh then. The whole place is coming alive. I saw a deer today," he offered.

"I saw two of them, twins I think," she countered.

"Braggart."

"Really," she insisted. "They came down to the edge of the marsh and I kept hoping their mother would come too, but she never did. I took pictures."

"No kites?"

She shook her head tiredly. "No family. Just the same one I saw this morning. I think he's laughing at me. I've wasted more rolls of film on him than I could ever hope to need, just to get him used to me." She sighed despondently. She looked about twelve.

He concentrated on making his voice sound indifferent. "Then you'll be staying longer?"

"I have to," she replied worriedly.

A shadow crossed her face and he wondered why. Maybe she didn't like the island after all, he thought. It often affected people that way. It was too unpopulated, too wild, too remote from civilization for some. Perhaps she was the sort of person who needed a town and bright lights to be comfortable.

"If I don't get the pictures, I don't get paid," she said simply.

He was ashamed of himself. He hadn't even considered that she might really need the money. He had just assumed that even though she was a professional photographer, because she came to them through Nelson she was another one of his wealthy acolytes.

"Tomorrow I'll go down with you in the morning. We'll find the nest," he promised, without a thought for the boat he had been so anxious to get into the water.

"Thanks, you don't have to do that. I'll be okay. And maybe Nelson will be better and come with me." She cheered up visibly. "Isn't that the turn?" she asked as they went by the road to the Manor.

"You like spring. I want to show you something." He

drove faster until they reached the intersection where the island roads came together.

"Where are we going?" Caddy held on to the dashboard as the Jeep swayed over the dirt road.

"Wait." He gunned the engine up an incline, through a copse, over a small one-lane wooden bridge, and through an opening in a low stone wall. He brought the Jeep to a fast stop and turned off the engine. "Here," he said quietly, offering her one of his favorite scenes.

The road ahead of them wound through an old wild-cherry orchard in full bloom. The gnarled trunks held boughs laden with sweet-smelling pale pink blossoms. Beneath the trees a carpet of fallen petals covered the ground, and the whole effect was as if they were surrounded by a cloud of soft satin. It was one of his favorite sights each spring.

"Oh." Caddy acknowledged the gift with a sigh of pleasure.

"Want to walk?" He got out of the car without waiting for her answer and went around to her side of the Jeep. He looked at her rapt face as she studied the trees and remembered she had spent the day working. "Unless you're too tired?" He didn't want her to feel she had to get out of the car just to be polite.

Caddy climbed down and looked up at him. She looked as if someone had given her a birthday present. "Thank you," she said.

He felt unaccountably flustered. He hadn't expected her to be so moved by something he took for granted. A picture of Dierdre appeared quickly in his mind and just as quickly disappeared: her thanks were limited to gifts that came in small boxes. "You're welcome." He stood to one side, allowing her to walk in front of him. She was almost as tall as he was and she walked easily, as if she was used to being outdoors. Her shoulder brushed his and he was swept with an urge to pull her close to him, to hold her against him so their bodies fit together like the pieces of a puzzle. She was so lovely, so seemingly unapproachable, he wanted to kiss her and make that calm face of hers come alive. *Fool,* he told himself fiercely. You barely know her and she's bound to be involved with another man; there must be a man somewhere in her life. The idea made him feel unaccountably cross.

They wandered through the small orchard in silence, looking up at the branches and stepping softly on the petals. At the far side the ground sloped gently on both sides, forming a crater with a house on one side and on the other, a towering windmill.

"I saw that from the boat," Caddy exclaimed with delight. "We're on the very north end of the island."

"We are indeed, and this is Mill House. The windmill actually works, and they get all their power from it."

"Who are they?"

"The Pecks. He's a poet and she's the curator of Byzantine coins and seals at the Fogg."

He looked up at the house as if Madeline Peck might appear on the porch, thumping her cane on the wooden floor to get his attention, but the house was dark and unoccupied. He wondered which way they would vote, promising himself to call them as soon as he got back to the city.

He turned to speak to Caddy, but she was already far ahead of him, scrambling down the steep path that wound from the top of the bluff to the sand below. He stood for a moment, savoring the smell of the ocean and assessing the size of waves lapping against the thin strip of beach. Caddy had reached the bottom and was jogging to the water's edge. As he watched her, she stooped and unlaced her boots, pulled them off with her socks, and then, rolling up the cuffs of her slacks, proceeded to wade into the water. He laughed out loud as the icy water covered her ankles and forced her to turn. Now she looked like a carefree child, and he liked that; it fascinated him the way she changed from moment to moment. She ran back like a sandpiper to the safety of dry sand, and he slid down the bank to the beach.

"Didn't anybody ever tell you the water doesn't warm up until late June?" he asked as he arrived next to her. She was still hopping around, trying to get some feeling back into her numb feet.

"No," she moaned. "My God, it's cold. I'm used to lakes, and lakes have ice on them to warn you away. It looked so pretty."

"Here. Put these back on. You'll catch pneumonia. Come on. We'll walk up the beach—that'll warm you up." He handed her her socks and she pulled them on hastily.

As she began to walk east on the beach, her hands tucked into her pockets and the collar of her anorak turned up around her face. Fiske fell in beside her. The wind was at their backs, and as far as they could see ahead of them, the beach was empty.

"Will you tell me about Nelson?" she asked after they had walked about a quarter mile.

"What about him?"

"Anything. All I know is that he was the person who arranged for the shoot."

Fiske drew his eyebrows together. Curious as he was about Caddy, he still didn't know how much he wanted to tell her about the islanders, or himself, for that matter. "And got himself in hot water for it, I might add."

"Sorry I asked," she said stiffly.

Fiske sighed. It would be downright rude not to respond. "He's an ornithologist, a highly respected one, who goes around lecturing to universities and colleges. He has a seat at Yale, but he doesn't spend much time there. Most of the time he's here, on Kincade."

"I've never met anyone quite like him."

"Because he's feisty?"

"Because he cares so deeply about the island."

"Why should that surprise you?" As soon as he had snapped out the question, he regretted it; he hadn't meant to be curt.

Sure enough, she frowned and half-turned away from him. He was afraid she was about to go back. Hastily, he elaborated in order to divert her from leaving. "He seems to have some sort of communion with the seasons here."

Her face lit up. "That's it. That's it exactly."

"He's possessed by the migrations in the spring and fall, the nesting seasons, the birth and death of the whole ecology of the island each year."

"The cycle of life?" she asked slowly.

"It's as if it was a kind of religion for him."

She hesitated, color that wasn't from the wind rose in her cheeks, and she asked shyly, "Is that how you feel too?"

Fiske nodded, unable to tell her how deeply he felt about Kincade. There were no words to express it, even to himself; it was part of his soul.

He looked down at Caddy's ringless finger. "You're not married, are you?" he asked abruptly.

"No."

"No man in your life?" He felt as if a lot hung on

her answer, and it made him angry. He wished he could retract the question; after Dierdre, he wasn't about to get involved with another woman for a long, long time.

"No."

"Why not?"

She frowned. "Because there isn't."

He knew he should leave it at that, but he persisted, knowing full well he shouldn't. There was something about this woman—the way her lips moved and the way she looked at him so gravely—that stirred him. Watching the way the wind blew through her hair, he asked absently, "Was there?"

Caddy halted and looked at him with steely eyes. "I thought I wasn't supposed to speak to the natives on the island. Isn't that a two-way street?"

Unrepentant, he hunched his shoulders against the wind and grinned nonchalantly down at her. "Sorry, just making conversation."

"I'd prefer not to discuss my love life," she informed him in a level voice.

"Or lack of it?" he asked. Feeling ridiculously hopeful, he bent his head to look more closely into her face.

"That's really enough."

Abashed, he saw tears in her eyes. "I didn't mean to . . . I was just . . ."

She waved her hand as if to brush away a fly and blinked furiously. "It doesn't matter. I've been going with someone for almost three years and we've just ended the relationship."

"I was just teasing." For someone who dealt with precise language on a daily basis and who had never found himself at a loss for words with a pretty woman, he suddenly found himself tongue-tied.

"It was a mistake. I simply prefer not to talk about

it." Leaving him to follow, she began to walk again, her head turned toward the horizon.

He matched his stride to hers and they proceeded in silence. Fiske frowned, searching for a safe topic to make Caddy talk about herself; despite the way she kept retreating back into her shell, he wanted to know more about her.

Searching for a topic that wouldn't offend her, he asked, "Did you always know you wanted to be a photographer?" He was pleased with the harmless question.

She looked at him judiciously for a moment. "Yes."

"And?" he asked. He knew he could make her answer if he didn't give up.

She shrugged. "My aunt gave me an Instamatic camera for Christmas when I was twelve."

He kicked at a piece of sea wood and persisted. "So you became a photographer at the age of twelve?"

Reluctantly, she smiled a little. "Not really. I just thought it was fun. It wasn't until I was in high school, at Friends, that I began taking pictures at school events. The school had a small darkroom, and one of the teachers showed me how to develop my film."

"And you liked that, developing your own film?" Her face became animated and he wanted to reach out and touch her lips gently with his fingertips.

"That's the exciting part, watching the images take shape and being able to lighten and darken the prints to add your own emphasis." She gave a little laugh, as if she was slightly embarrassed to have revealed so much about her craft.

"It sounds like you got hooked, like any artist." He turned around and walked backward, his back hunched against the wind so he could see her face better. When she stumbled slightly, he put out one hand to steady her, but she pulled away sharply. They stared at each other.

"We should go back," she said slowly.

The desire to kiss her returned, and he had to put his hands in his pockets to keep from pulling her into his arms. He frowned, wondering why she affected him so much. "When we get to the point, then we'll turn around."

After a second she nodded. Skirting around him, she walked more quickly, her heels crunching in the sand as she made for the point of land jutting into the sea up ahead.

"Tell me the rest."

"There isn't much to tell. I got a job one summer on the *Philadelphia Inquirer,* not as anything important, just doing clerical work, but there was a staff photographer there who let me go out with him and he taught me a lot. He helped me buy my first real camera, the first Leica I ever owned. After that summer I knew I wanted to be a photographer."

A flash of movement caught his eye. He pointed overhead. "Look," he exclaimed with pleasure. A hawk was soaring above them, its wings casting a shadow on the sand. They watched until the bird disappeared over the bluff. "You don't see that often, this close to the shore. He must have come out for you."

"Even the birds have to check out the newcomers?" She smiled faintly, cocked her head to one side.

Again Fiske wanted to cover her lips with his. Instinctively, he stepped closer, but then, overcome with a sensation that this wasn't a girl who could ever simply be flirted with, he turned away abruptly. "Are you feeling a little noidy?" he asked gruffly.

"Noidy? What kind of a word is that?"

"A kid's word for paranoid."

"A little noidy then, yes," she admitted. "I'm here to work though, so it doesn't matter." She hesitated for a second, then asked impulsively, "Doesn't it ever bother you?"

"A little. I've been living and working in London for five years."

"How long have you been back?"

"Just a week. I've got one more week before I start a new job at the firm." He sighed to himself at the thought of the office he had only spent a day in before leaving New York for a well-earned vacation. There was so much work waiting for him. All the cartons from London would have arrived, his new secretary would be waiting for him with a load of messages and appointments, and his partners would be chomping at the bit for him to pitch in and get the department reorganized.

"Don't you like your job?" Caddy looked curious.

"I love it," he answered without thinking. Even though there was a mess waiting for him, he knew he loved the practice of law. He loved his job even when it was difficult, which was most of the time; he loved having been named the youngest partner the firm had ever had; and he couldn't wait to take over his own department, even though he was replacing a man who had run it as his own personal fiefdom for years and whom everybody loved. He felt torn between impatience and anxiety at the work lying ahead of him.

"That's the way I feel when I'm behind my camera. It's my life." When she looked up at him so soberly, as if she was confiding the greatest secret she had, he wanted to sweep her into his arms. He could only stare at her. Uncertainly, she stared back.

The sun was low on the water and the shadow of the bluff covered the sand. Their eyes continued to lock until, without speaking, they turned and began walking back to the windmill path. She shivered and began to walk faster, wrapping her arms around herself for greater warmth. The breeze had turned into a chill wind and they had to bend slightly to meet it; the temperature must have dropped ten degrees in the short time they had been on the beach.

"Can you run in those things?" Fiske looked down at her boots.

She raised her eyebrows in mock surprise and then, before he could say anything more, took off down the beach, her hair blowing free behind her. Her boots kicked up spurts of sand as she covered the ground with long, even strides. He was caught off guard by her speed, but he recovered himself quickly and set off, running flat out to catch her.

"You're good," he panted as they reached the foot of the path together.

"You're not bad yourself." Her face was flushed with exertion and she was laughing. Impulsively, she held out her hand to shake his.

When he took her hand in his, it was warm and fit into his perfectly; he held it an instant too long. "Come on, I'll give you a tour of the windmill."

Caddy looked up at the path they had to climb to reach the top. "We're so late now. I don't want to be late for dinner two nights in a row." She turned her head away.

"I'll show it to you the next time," he said without thinking. He knew for certain that there had to be a next time. He found himself waiting anxiously for her to say something in response.

She began climbing up, not looking back. He wondered if she had heard him.

"Next time." The words floated down, and he smiled to himself.

CHAPTER 7

Caddy zipped up the last canvas bag and put it on top of the small heap by her bedroom door. She looked around the room, making sure she hadn't forgotten anything, and then, with one swift motion, she stripped the used sheets off the bed and piled them on a straight-backed chair. After she pulled the bedspread up and smoothed it neatly over the pillows, she looked around again, but there was nothing left to do. She still had two hours left to fill before the ferry left for the mainland. The Manor was quiet, and she wondered if she was alone in the house. Douglas would probably be in his shed, she figured. She had heard Grace Byrne making plans with Dorothy to go over and finish cleaning Barbara's cottage, and she knew

Fiske had gone off before breakfast to find the Northrup men. She paused, wondering again why she had been so disappointed when he didn't appear at the table that morning. She had actually lingered over her coffee, expecting he would walk in, still preoccupied from his run, the way he had been the other morning. She felt as if their conversation on the beach was unfinished, as if there was more to be said, and she frowned, unclear as to what she meant, even to herself. She rubbed her hand reflectively, remembering how hard and firm his grasp had been and how he had held her hand a moment too long, and how he had looked right into her eyes as if he wanted to kiss her. She wondered what it would be like to be kissed by Fiske. She shivered. She had to stop imagining things. He was reticent, almost cool to her, and she barely knew the man. Still, there was something about him that was different, something that both disquieted her and drew her to him.

She wandered over to the window and stared down at the profusion of daffodils waving gently in the garden. The patterns they made in the morning sun were as beguiling as they had been the first afternoon she arrived. With a spurt of excitement, she realized this was the only opportunity she would ever get to photograph them, and she was smiling as she grabbed her camera and took the stairs, two at a time, to the ground floor.

When she stood in the doorway overlooking the garden, her smile broadened to a grin; the sunlight dappled the trees and vines into designs of dark and light, and the breeze ruffled the leaves, turning dark green into gold and silver and the daffodils into a cloud of waving white and pale lemon yellow.

She sighed with sheer pleasure at the vision and

almost laughed at herself: It seemed she had spent the
past three days being enraptured by the insidious
beauty of spring overtaking the island. She walked out
and sat on the top step of the porch, enjoying the
sensation of the sun warming her body; her camera lay
forgotten by her side as she drank in the view. Except
for when she had been photographing in the marsh by
herself, this was the first time she had been alone since
landing on Kincade. It was a wonderful moment and
she savored the feeling.

Part of her sense of well-being came from the en-
chantment of the garden, and part from the triumph
she still felt from having found the kite nest the previous day with Nelson. Most of all, however, she felt
newly released from the shock of Ward's abrupt departure. It wasn't losing Ward that had caused her the
pain she felt, but the sense of abandonment his leaving
had aroused in her, and regret for the end of their
affair, which, she admitted to herself, had really been
over for months.

She thought with relish about the hen she had
found. As Nelson had promised, she was sitting on her
eggs. The hen had been so deeply concealed in the
underbrush that only Nelson could have found the
nest, but she was sure her feeling of accomplishment
had been no less than his when he gently pulled aside a
leafy branch and pointed to the nest with his cane. He
had left her soon after that, but she had stayed on
photographing for most of the afternoon, until the
pale shadows fell over the marsh and all her film was
gone. And this time—she smiled at the remembrance
—Fiske had dutifully come for her promptly.

Even dinner the past two nights had been less con-
strained than the first night probably, she mused, because Barbara had gone back to the city, taking most

of the tension with her. Certainly there had been no discussion either night of the land vote or which islanders might or might not want to sell, and for that she was relieved. Instead, Dorothy had played the piano last night after supper, and the firelight had glowed softly on Douglas's face as he watched his wife with a gentle, proud look in his eyes. From her seat on the couch in front of the fire, Caddy had been acutely conscious of Fiske, seated in the shadows next to the fireplace. Every time she looked in his direction he seemed to be studying her, his eyes hooded and his expression unfathomable. Once, when she raised her chin and stared straight back at him, he had leaned forward slightly and she had felt a drop in the pit of her stomach, as if she were standing in a high place looking directly down. Fiske had leaned back, and the moment had passed, but the mere remembrance of it made her tremble slightly.

The rumble of a cart roused her, and she looked for the source of the sound. Dorothy was coming around the corner of the house pushing a small empty wheelbarrow. She was wrapped in one of Douglas's heavy wool shirts and wore a battered gray fedora pulled down over her hair. A professional-looking metal gardening fork stuck up from her shirt pocket, and there was a determined look on her face.

"May I help?" Caddy asked quietly, not wanting to startle her.

"Oh, my dear." Dorothy looked surprised and not entirely pleased to see her house guest. "I didn't see you sitting there."

"I came out to shoot the daffodils, but I got waylaid by the sun."

"Yes, it is nice, isn't it?" Dorothy looked up dubiously as if she had just noticed the weather. "I know I should be helping Grace at Barbara's, but I just had to get into the garden."

The older woman was having difficulty hiding her impatience. Clearly she was eager to get to work. Caddy empathized. She knew just how Dorothy felt; she hated it when anyone interrupted her when she was shooting or developing.

Caddy joined her and took hold of the handles of the wheelbarrow. "Here. Let me do that."

"Lovely," Dorothy sighed with relief. "I want to start over there, in the herb garden." She pointed to a corner of the garden near the house in front of a low brick forcing wall. "I have it all laid out in my mind, and I want to clear the beds. Last year it came up all wrong. Such a disappointment."

They stared down at the brown earth where just a few shoots of green were forcing themselves up through the dead leaves. It didn't look like much, Caddy thought, but she didn't know much about gardens.

"It doesn't look like much now," Dorothy echoed her thoughts, "but when you see it later it will be lovely." She pulled an old piece of carpet from the barrow and threw it on the ground, kneeling on it awkwardly. "I want to clean all this out and stake out the lines. I've made a diagram this year and I'm going to follow it absolutely. It doesn't pay to get creative in midplanting; everything comes out looking a muddle."

Caddy squatted next to Dorothy and began gently brushing the leaves into small piles. "What will you plant?"

"Wild thyme in the back, next to the wall—it's tall and yellow and will look pretty. Johnny-jump-ups in front of that, I think, then lavender, rosemary, yarrow, and sage over here. On the other side of the path I'm going to have primroses, marjoram, miniature peonies, and dill. Some feverfew and basil, perhaps, just over there." Dorothy's voice was dreamy as she pointed around the bare patch, and Caddy thought she probably could see it all in bloom, a riot of low color and small buds, filling the beds with sweet-smelling plants.

They bent over and began to clear the bed, pulling out the dead stalks and loosening the still-hard sandy soil. She imitated everything Dorothy did, using the extra trowel in the same fashion and pulling up the same kinds of dead-looking plants as the older woman. Living in Philadelphia, the Wilcoxes had never had a garden; she found she liked the feeling of the sun on her back and plunging her hands into the chilly dirt. They worked in silence until Dorothy exclaimed sharply and sat up looking angrily at something in her hand.

"What's wrong?" Caddy had moved farther down the bed and she looked back in alarm.

"The deer have eaten my bulbs again. Damn," she swore softly.

"Will that ruin anything?"

"Probably. The island deer are adorable to look at, but there are too many of them now and they're so destructive. The men talk about thinning the herd, but no one really wants to shoot them, so they're left to multiply and we get more and more of them every year. They're very audacious." She threw the stump of the bulb into the barrow and sat back on her heels with a sigh. "I'm getting tired. My back isn't what it used to be. I can't do this as long as I did when I was your age."

"Have you always gardened?" She thought Dorothy looked perfectly natural, as at ease in her garden as she was playing the piano in the big house.

"Always. Doesn't your mother have a garden?"

"No, we live in a little house in the middle of Philadelphia. My parents are both professors of anthropology. I can't imagine either one of them getting far enough away from their books to do anything else."

She thought of her mother's sweet, distracted smile and grinned to herself. Louisa Wilcox could research everything there was to know about a garden and thereby make herself an expert, but it wouldn't occur to her to then turn that knowledge into a reality by actually planting anything. Having read about it would be enough for her; she would already be on to the next topic. Caddy looked around and wished Thad could see this though; he would love it.

"You must be very proud, with both your mother and father professors."

"I am." And she was. Despite the constant lack of money and the times when her parents were so deep into writing their books they might as well have not been there at all, she had always been proud of them.

"It's odd." Dorothy reached for a trowel and resumed turning over the earth. "We know so many interesting people, but I don't think we know any anthropologists. Nelson is an ornithologist, of course, but I don't imagine that's quite the same thing, is it?"

Caddy laughed out loud. "Not really, unless you think of all the 'gists' as studying behavior of one kind or the other. My parents are much more academic than Nelson, I think. They'd be perfectly happy to closet themselves with their research and books and never have to teach again."

"And yet you chose not to become a teacher."

"I teach a course at the New School, but that's just another way to make money. I don't have the patience to be the kind of teacher I would want to be."

"Yet you can spend hours photographing in a freezing marsh. That takes more patience than I can imagine."

"As much as practicing, I expect."

The two women paused in their weeding and smiled at each other, acknowledging the truth of her statement.

They had reached the halfway point in the herb bed, leaving behind them neat rows of freshly turned earth. The wheelbarrow was nearly filled with dead leaves and small stones they had cleared from the ground; ahead of them, two small beds on the other side of the path remained to be cleared.

"Are you an only child?" Dorothy asked gently, pulling the piece of carpet with her as she moved to a new spot.

"I have one brother, Thad. He's twenty-two."

"Would he like to follow in your parents' footsteps?"

"Not really. He has multiple sclerosis," Caddy said in a low voice.

"I'm sorry, my dear."

"He can only walk with canes." Caddy shivered, feeling as if the sun had just gone behind a dark cloud.

"That must be very difficult for you all. For him, of course, but for you and your mother and father too. Seeing someone you love in distress is one of life's most hurtful things, I think," Dorothy commented gently.

"He does a lot of things, really," Caddy continued defensively, with the tone of voice she always seemed to adopt whenever she discussed Thad, which was rarely. "He plays the violin beautifully and he writes poetry. He's funny too. He tells fantastic stories, full of life and wit—he always makes me laugh." Her smile had returned, but this time it was soft and reminiscent.

"You're very close, aren't you?"

"Ever since he was born. You see, our parents are wonderful, but they're so immersed in their work together, they're almost oblivious to what goes on around them, so I wound up taking care of Thad when he was little. It made us very close, and then, when he began to get sick, I was the one he turned to."

"It must have been hard for you." Dorothy looked over at her with compassion. Intercepting the look on her face, Caddy turned abruptly and wrenched a weed out of the earth with unnecessary force.

"Harder on him," she said shortly. "He's the one who has to live with it."

Dorothy thought for a moment. "But he could still teach, couldn't he?"

"Not really. He doesn't have the stamina. Some days, the really bad ones, he can't leave his room."

"I don't know much about multiple sclerosis. Some people do get better, don't they?"

Dorothy sounded so concerned that the wall of control Caddy kept tightly around her crumbled a little, and tears pricked her eyes. Although she tried not to show it, it was wrenching for her to watch Thad struggle so bravely with the disease that wasted his body.

She kept her head lowered and made an effort to steady her voice, not wanting Dorothy to pity her, but before she could speak, the older woman went on briskly, "It's such a shame. He's too young to be so unwell, but fate has a way of giving us gifts to compensate for the things we lack in life. It sounds as if your brother has his own talents, and that must be a blessing."

"His stories really *are* wonderful, I'm not just saying

that. It's not always easy for him to write either, but one of his tutors wrote a few of them down one year and actually had them printed in a little literary magazine where he worked," she confided, smiling as she always did whenever she thought about the sagas Thad constructed. "One of my dreams is to get his stories published someday."

"Doesn't he have a word processor?" Dorothy asked in surprise. "He ought to be able to use one of those; even I can manage and I'm the least mechanical human being I've ever met."

"It's on the agenda," she confided. "As soon as I get the money I'm going to get him one of his own. Then we'll see."

"Good girl," Dorothy said with approval. "He's lucky to have you taking care of him."

"I don't really," she confessed. "I feel guilty that I'm in New York and he's in Philadelphia. I should be closer so I could oversee the household better."

"And yet you came to New York?"

They had given up all pretense of gardening and were sitting up. Dorothy was leaning against the low brick wall and Caddy faced her from a spot on the warm gravel of the tiny path.

"Right from the start I wanted to be a photographer. I always knew I could make more money in New York than at home. I thought if I lived simply, I would be able to make a good career for myself and at the same time send most of my earnings back there to help with Thad's expenses."

"Has it been successful?"

"As far as the money goes? Yes, most of the time, but I still feel torn—driven, actually. Sometimes I think about the time when I'm really successful, when I'm famous enough so I can command my own price, and then I'll be able to afford my own apartment. I'll be able to make a home for him—that's my dream."

"Oh, my dear. You've set a hard path for yourself. But I admire your ambition."

"I am ambitious, I suppose. I love my work and I want to be the best photographer around. Being able to do what I love and have it support Thad, too, doesn't seem too difficult at all. I mean, when what you want to do and what you have to do are the same thing, then you're lucky, aren't you?"

"Absolutely. You and I are both lucky: I with my piano and my family, and you with your photographing —your career, really—and your brother."

"And the garden. Thank you for letting me help you today." Caddy stretched luxuriously and breathed deeply.

Dorothy stuck the gardening fork deep into the earth and, using it as a crutch, pulled herself up to her feet. She looked down at the ground with satisfaction.

"We've done good work here this morning. Now you'll have to come back and see it when it's in bloom."

"I'd like that," Caddy answered, but she didn't think she would be back, and the thought suddenly made her wistful. Quickly, she rose and took the handles of the wheelbarrow again and, following Dorothy's instructions, pushed it around the side of the house to the toolshed, leaving the garden empty in the sun.

The memory of her time in the garden with Dorothy stayed with her all the way to the ferry and beyond, like an oasis of serenity in her mind. By the time she reached the mainland and had retrieved her car, it seemed to her as if the three and a half days she had spent on Kincade were like a dream of a magical king-

dom where beautiful, wild things grew unspoiled by
the trappings of modern-day life. She felt she had been
very far away and, despite the undercurrents of tension
between the islanders, she had been renewed in some
way, made more whole. She seemed stronger, as if she
had been given fresh strength to go on. More than ever
she was determined to make a success of her life. As
she left the parking lot in New London, she looked
back once, straining her eyes as she tried to see the
island, but it lay too far beyond the horizon and all she
could see was water stretching out to meet the sky.
She let her breath out and squared her shoulders as
she stepped on the gas. It was time to return to the real
world.

CHAPTER 8

Fiske dodged a fast-moving taxi and gained the curb. After the quiet of Kincade he always forgot how dirty and clamorous New York was. Every time he returned to the city he wondered again if he would ever get used to it. He ducked into the doorway of 55 Wall Street with a grunt of relief. He squeezed into the crowded elevator between two overly perfumed secretaries.

As he rode up to the twenty-first floor he mentally reviewed the things he planned to do on his first day at the new job: make sure to touch base with each partner, if possible; review the corporate client files he hadn't had sent to him on Kincade; somehow try to meet all the members of the new department, not just the associates. With his mind fully occupied with work, it came as a shock to find a slip on his desk with a message to call Bruce Asher. Staring down at the unfamiliar telephone number, he lowered himself slowly into his chair. Should he call or throw the slip of paper away?

He reached into his briefcase and pulled out the letter he had received from the Asher Development Company asking him to contact Bruce Asher; he had never done so. He put the letter squarely next to the slip of paper and stared at them both. Perhaps it was just as well to confront Asher now and find out just what his gambit was.

His mind made up, he dialed quickly.

"Mr. Spencer, thank you for calling." Bruce Asher's voice on the other end of the line was brisk and cordial.

"You called me, Mr. Asher," Fiske reminded him pleasantly. He thumbed mechanically through his other messages, organizing them in order of importance. There was one from Nelson, which he slipped to the bottom of the pile.

"I was hoping we could get together sometime soon, perhaps within the next few days. I've been looking forward to talking with you," Asher said smoothly, as if there were no question Fiske would be eager to agree. But Fiske had no wish to meet Bruce Asher in person.

"I'm pretty busy, Mr. Asher. I'm not sure that's possible right now."

"Call me Bruce, please." The voice on the other end chuckled, as if they were already friends. "Perhaps a drink? My club's the Metropolitan. We could meet at the end of the day."

Fiske swiveled around and peered out his new windows. "I'm really quite busy, Mr. Asher. What did you want to talk about? Perhaps we could discuss it now."

Bruce Asher's voice immediately lost some of its pleasantness as he replied bluntly, "You've received our letter of inquiry and probably heard from some of the other owners on Kincade that Asher Development has an interest in acquiring part of the island. I'd like to talk to you about your family's property."

"Kincade land isn't for sale." Fiske drew a legal pad closer, uncapped his fountain pen, and began to take notes on the conversation.

"That's not quite true, Spencer. Several of your fellow islanders have shown great interest in hearing what we have to say. I have every reason to believe they are quite receptive to an offer."

"Well, that's always possible, but hardly probable in the long run," Fiske replied casually, but he could feel the tension between his shoulder blades. Carefully, he drew a numeral one and put a dash next to it.

There was a thin edge to Bruce Asher's voice. "Oh, we feel quite sanguine about the project. It's a good one, sound ecologically, and with a handsome return. Those who decide to participate will come away very content, I'm sure."

Fiske clenched his teeth. "By content, who do you mean? Your investors or the people who sell their land to you?"

"Both, of course, Spencer. A man like you could do both and win twice: Sell your land for a healthy sum, and come aboard as an investor."

"Supposing I *was* interested, what kind of investment are you planning?" Fiske swiveled his chair around and took in the full sweep of his freshly painted office. There was a conference table with four chairs in one corner, a brown leather couch and two comfortable chairs in another; at right angles to his desk, a computer screen blinked. His cartons from England had arrived and the prints he had collected overseas were stacked neatly against the walls.

"The project we're thinking of would be something like Mystic Harbor, a natural village in a natural setting, except this one for well-heeled vacationers. Town houses, docks, a marina, tennis courts, riding trails, the whole nine yards. A small airport for private planes and maybe even a golf course if we can fill in the marsh."

Christ, Fiske thought in horror. The man's insane. Even worse, he's done more than think about this; it appears he's already got a fully developed plan. He hunched over his desk and spoke almost intimately into the telephone. "Sounds like a money-maker, and I like deals. Do you think you could get enough of us to sell? I mean, I wouldn't want to proceed any further without knowing who else is on board." He scored a heavy line beneath the numeral one he had written on the page.

"Well, my friend, I wouldn't want to show my hand completely, but I can tell you that at least one of your neighbors has signed, and a mighty important one at that." Again the chuckle.

Fiske was stunned. He felt a surge of adrenaline. Who could have agreed without all the others knowing? "Signed what?" he asked, purposefully allowing his honest disbelief to show in the intonation of his voice.

"An intention to sell pending a title search," Asher replied with obvious satisfaction.

"Well, that's fine, assuming it's binding," Fiske acknowledged slowly. Hastily, he wrote down the words *title search* and underlined them twice. His first act as department head would be to shanghai some young associate into going up to New London and checking out all the island deeds. He tightened the muscles in his jaw. It would take hours of work at the courthouse in New London to search out and copy down all the information from the original deeds of land sale.

"It's binding, you can be sure."

"What kind of money are you talking about?" Fiske stared blankly at the closed door to his office. He hoped his voice didn't sound as shaken as he felt.

"Hundreds of millions," Bruce Asher replied simply.

"I need to think about this, Mr. Asher. Perhaps if I knew who has already signed it would help me make up my mind whether we have anything further to talk about."

"I'm glad to hear you thinking so positively, Fiske. You don't mind if I call you Fiske, do you? But for now the party wants to keep in the background, so to speak. Not reveal himself. You understand, don't you?"

You bet your ass, I do, Fiske thought. You want to lure each property owner to the altar one by one and then spring it on the entire island that Kincade's going to be turned into a cement playground. Not on your life. "Let me think it over, Mr. Asher."

"You do that, Fiske. Let me buy you that drink, or better yet, come up to my place in Westchester next weekend. We'll talk the whole thing over in a civilized fashion like the gentlemen we are."

Bullshit. Fiske scrawled the word on his pad in capital letters. But all he said was "I'll get back to you." Carefully he replaced the receiver and stared worriedly out the window. Between the thin towers of the buildings across the street he could see the glint of

New York Harbor. Somehow, the idea that he could see open water from his office made him feel better.

"Welcome home, Fiske." One of his partners waved to him from the doorway. Fiske half-rose from his seat to shake hands with him over the desk top and, in doing so, made a conscious effort to clear his mind of Kincade and its problems.

It was six o'clock that evening before he had a chance to think about Kincade again. The entire day had passed in a whirl of meetings and planning sessions. To his dismay, he found the department in worse shape than he had anticipated: His predecessor had managed to lead by the force of his considerable charm, but with little regard to procedure, with the result that several of the firm's major corporate accounts were in disarray and needed his personal attention. He figured by the wary way in which the two partners and half dozen associates in the corporate division greeted him that they were waiting to see which way the wind blew with the new head. He knew he had a long road ahead of him to pull them together into a team. The secretaries and clerks had left at six and the office was quieting down; only the other attorneys working in their offices and a small night steno pool remained.

He pulled the telephone closer and dialed Nelson Lovering's number on the island. Swiveling around, he looked out at the sun descending behind the buildings and thought about the way night fell on Kincade: not with the brightness diffused by pollution into a palette of secondary colors, but clearly and crisply, with streaks of red staining the ocean.

"Uncle Nelson?" He smiled into the receiver and sat up straight as if Nelson could see him.

"My boy, thank you for calling. I've got a job for you, if you would be so kind."

For the second time that day, Fiske's heart sank. How could he possibly fit one of Nelson's jobs into his already overcrowded schedule? He had planned on working far into the night, and he could only hope Nelson didn't want him to go on some wild goose chase. His shoulders sagged as he listened to his island mentor continue.

"I've been trying to raise Caddy Wilcox on the phone, but there's no answer at the number she gave me. I wonder if you would drop a note off for her—I'll tell you what I want to say, and if you would just write it down and make sure she gets it, that would solve my problem."

All of a sudden it seemed like a very good idea to do the favor for Nelson, since it presented an opportunity to see Caddy again. There was a note of enthusiasm in Fiske's voice that hadn't been there before as he pretended to tease his uncle. "I'll be glad to help, Nelson, but what's wrong with the U.S. Mail? You know, fire, wind, sleet, and all that."

"No. No." Nelson's voice was testy. It grew faint and then came back loud and vigorous. "My fault, my boy. Liza says how could you know what the problem is when I haven't told you. I found a whole colony of kites, Fiske, and I want her to come back and photograph them. I knew there were at least three other families, but I've found almost a hundred. You've never seen anything like it."

Despite his weariness, Fiske was excited. He could see the marsh in his mind and the corner where Nelson had found the kites originally. He wanted very much to be the one to tell Caddy.

"Are they by the big stump?" he asked eagerly.

"Exactly." Nelson answered with satisfaction. "I always knew you were wasted on the law, my boy. You should have thrown your lot in with me."

"I can do both, can't I?" He pretended affront, knowing his answer would drive Nelson crazy.

"Fiske," Nelson roared. "You know God damned well you can't." He sighed audibly over the line and Fiske chuckled into the receiver.

"Don't get yourself into a twit. I could never be the birder you are and we both know it. Now tell me, why do I have to get a message to Caddy so fast? Not that I won't, mind you, but I always like to know what I'm doing and why."

"Lawyer." Nelson snorted. "Because it takes three days for a letter to get to New York by the time it sits around on the ferry and they lose it once or twice in New London, and I want her here now."

"Why not after the eggs hatch? I would think that would make for a better record." He gave a friendly wave to one of the associates passing by his door on her way to the elevator.

"Of course it would, you fool. I want her back then too. But I want her here now, to photograph them now." His voice lowered and he sounded almost embarrassed. "I've never seen so many so far north, Fiske. What if they leave? What if it's a stopover and they aren't here to nest? I need to have those pictures, boy. I want a record of the whole colony in our marsh."

"Right. You got it." He pulled a yellow legal pad toward him and ripped off the top page so that he had a fresh sheet to write on. "I'm ready to take it down. Shoot."

"Here goes: 'Dear Miss Wilcox: A colony of approximately one hundred white kites has arrived on Kincade. Will you return as soon as possible to photograph them either for *Nature's World* or on commission for me? Eliza and I would be pleased to have you stay with us and look forward to hearing from you by telephone as soon as you receive this letter. Yours, etcetera, etcetera.' How does that sound?"

"Brief and to the point. Have you got her address?"

"Somewhere. Wait. Ah, here it is: Forty-three Gramercy Square. That's on your way home, isn't it?"

"In a direct line. I must pass by the house every evening." Fiske snorted and they both laughed. His office was on Wall Street and he lived on upper Park Avenue—nowhere near Gramercy Park, as Nelson knew full well.

Nelson grew confidential. "Listen, my boy, there's something else: That little girl wants to get a picture of hers on the cover of her magazine, and this will do it for her. Eliza says to tell you to get in touch with her as soon as you can and tell her to come on the first ferry she can get."

"I'll do it tonight," he promised. "How's everything else up there?"

"You just left yesterday, nothing's changed. Now you go and find that little girl and get her up here pronto." With a curt good-bye, Nelson hung up the phone, but Fiske was used to that. Nelson didn't believe in prolonged farewells; when he was finished talking, that was that.

After a second's hesitation Fiske quickly flipped through a small, well-worn leather address book and dialed the number of his sister's Park Avenue apartment, making a mental note to himself to have his secretary program all his personal numbers into the instrument's automatic dial. He had to touch base with someone he could trust about his conversation with

Bruce Asher, and who better than his brother-in-law, Hank. He was throwing piles of paper into a large, leather briefcase when the phone was answered by a machine. Disappointed, he shrugged into his suit jacket while he left a message for Hank to call him and, looking at the piles of paper needing attention that he hadn't been able to cram into his case, he hung up the receiver. Whistling to himself, he left the office on his way to Gramercy Square.

Fifteen minutes later Fiske alit from a taxi and ran up the steps of the Gramercy address, feeling light-hearted with anticipation at the idea of seeing Caddy again. As he rang the old-fashioned iron bell, he peered through the narrow window at the side of the tall door. The glass was covered with a tidy lace curtain, and all he could see inside was a light glowing softly from somewhere in the hall. His heart sank. Perhaps he should have called first; perhaps there was nobody home. He rang once more and turned around, admiring the way the trees growing inside the park across the street were unfolding their blossoms. It was so quiet here; it didn't seem like he was in the middle of a bustling city.

The door behind him opened and he turned with a smile that grew into a grin of appreciation. An elderly woman with dyed bright red hair stood facing him in the doorway. She was wrapped in what appeared to be several beaded shawls, all of them fringed, and the hand that held them had a large jeweled ring on every finger as well as her thumb. Her face had more makeup on it than he had ever seen on one face before, but the eyes behind the mascara were shrewd and her voice, when she spoke, was decisive. She was clearly a woman to be reckoned with, and he greeted her with the deference she obviously expected.

"Does my niece know you?" the old woman demanded when he had modestly stated his name and his
business.

"She stayed with my family on Kincade," he answered as persuasively as possible. He wondered if he
was going to be allowed into the house or if he was
going to be kept on the stoop like the delivery boy she
seemed to think he was. The idea amused him and he
had trouble keeping a straight face.

"You may come in. I am Agatha Dinsmore Wilcox
Parnett DaSilva," she intoned, leading the way down
the hall into the back parlor. As he followed her, Fiske
examined with appreciation the wall sconces that
dimly lit the marble floor tiles in the hall and which
had obviously been there from before the house was
converted from gas to electricity. When they passed
wide doors flung open onto a formal front parlor, he
was unsurprised to see windows shrouded in dusky velvet, dark mahogany formal Victorian furniture placed
stiffly around the room, and walls crowded with oil-
painted ancestors peering somberly down. Every
great-aunt he had had a parlor just like this one, and
he felt right at home.

Agatha settled herself on a small horsehair love seat
surrounded by a matching set of horsehair chairs, each
with its own footstool, and waved him to a chair. He
seated himself gingerly on a wobbly chair and looked
around the room. Every surface was covered with
memorabilia. Vases with dried-grass arrangements
were on every table, china bibelots were arranged in
tiers on a small corner shelf, and antique petit point
pillows were piled on each chair. One table held stacks
of old leather volumes, another a gleaming brass sam-
ovar, a third was covered incongruously with city telephone books. On the mantel, rows and rows of photo-

graphs in every conceivable kind of Victorian frame marched from left to right in front of a mirror with the silver back showing through. Even the ceiling was covered. Looking up, he saw naked cherubs twined around each other surrounded by impossibly blue clouds, and he made no effort to hide his delight as he looked down from the ceiling to his hostess.

"Lovely, isn't it," she said complacently, waving a plump hand at all the clutter.

"Lovely," he agreed, drawing his feet up as an ancient King Charles spaniel squeezed out from beneath the love seat and waddled across the rug to sniff at the cuff of his trouser. The dog was drooling, and even from a distance Fiske could tell he needed a bath. "Have you lived here long?" he asked unnecessarily, wondering how long he would last in the room if he gave the dog a swift kick.

"Behave yourself, Eddie." Agatha DaSilva scolded her pet in an unconvincing voice. "He's named after my second husband, Eddie Parnett. He was a famous equestrian, you know." She shot him an arch look. He decided she was probably testing him.

He pretended he didn't know Eddie Parnett had been a famous jockey of thirty years ago who rose from the gutter and returned there when he grew too old to entice rich women. His picture had been all over the papers when Fiske was a little boy, and his admiration was unfeigned as he nodded pleasantly to his hostess. She must be quite a woman, he thought. She seemed to be well into her eighties, so she had to have been approaching fifty when Parnett married her, not to mention the fact that she must have been an armful to have caught the jockey at all. Not only had Parnett been renowned for the ferocious way he rode the inside rail, he had been even more famous for his penchant for tall, extravagant, party-loving women. How in hell, he wondered, did she happen to be related to Caddy? He had never met two more dissimilar people in his life: the colorful, almost bizarre redheaded lady sitting across from him, and the pale, composed girl he had last seen by firelight and who kept creeping into his thoughts. The dog sneezed and he drew his foot hastily away from the damp spray, hoping there wasn't another dog around, named DaSilva for her third husband.

"And why do you want to see my niece?" She settled herself more comfortably and pulled a box of marzipan from behind a pillow. When he refused the proffered box with a polite shake of his head, she popped a garishly colored red strawberry into her mouth and held out a blue rose to the dog who, much to Fiske's relief, waddled back to his mistress for his reward.

"I have a message for her from my uncle."

"He is?"

"Nelson Lovering, the ornithologist." He threw that in, with a mental apology to his uncle, hoping she would be suitably impressed.

"Quite right. Caddy mentioned him. If you would be so kind . . ." She waved her hand at an instrument hung on the wall, and her voice trailed off as she stared down into the half-empty box, torn between another strawberry and a lemon-colored triangle.

He rose and crossed the room. He found himself looking at a wooden box with an old-fashioned cylindrical receiver hanging at one side; on the top of the box were numbered buttons, one for each room in the house. He examined the numbers carefully, but could see nothing that indicated where Caddy might be.

"Top. She's on the top."

"Thank you," he murmured. He punched the button

that had *top* scrawled over the number fourteen and held the receiver to his ear.

"Yes, Aunt Agatha?" Unaccountably, his heart skipped a beat when he heard Caddy's voice come tinnily over the line. He frowned, wanting to conceal his excitement from the old woman.

"It's Fiske Spencer," he shouted into the square mouthpiece set into the middle of the box. "Could you come down? I have a message for you."

"You needn't raise your voice, Mr. Spencer. We're not deaf in this house. She'll be down."

He shook the receiver as if he could make it answer and, when there was no response, returned it to its hook. He was loath to return to his lumpy seat, so he stood next to the door, watching Agatha and the spaniel warily. Eddie had finished his treat and was looking around for something else. Since he didn't want the dog to spot him, he edged behind a library table piled high with outdated *Tatler*s and old photograph albums with split spines; it was there Caddy discovered him when she entered the room.

"Fiske!" she exclaimed. "What are you doing here?" All he could do was stare at her, marveling at this new, elegant Caddy. She was wearing a topaz-colored silk blouse, and her hair hung loosely down her back. She looked sophisticated and very lovely, not at all like the rumpled, frozen girl in muddy boots he had raced down the beach a week ago.

Involuntarily, he took a step forward, just to be closer to her. "Nelson sent me with a message for you."

"Manners, Catherine, manners." Agatha yawned, turning on the tasseled lamp next to her. "Say hello prettily and offer your guest a drink."

They both looked at Agatha as if they had forgotten

she was in the room. At last Caddy nodded her head. Smiling back at Fiske, she moved gracefully to a glass-topped tea cart turned into a drinks table and held up a bottle of pale sherry.

"Good heavens, girl. Give the man a proper drink. There should be some gin left in the decanter."

Fiske placed himself next to Caddy as she competently mixed a pale martini, stirring the mixture gently and pouring it evenly into three crystal glasses. He presented Agatha with her glass and then took a swallow of his own drink, barely managing to keep a straight face when the strongest mixture of gin and vermouth he had ever had burned its way down his throat. He saw them watching for his reaction and with difficulty managed to keep his voice bland, remarking only "Very pleasant."

Agatha snorted, but her eyes twinkled with amusement as she emptied half her glass with one swallow. "Sit by me, Mr. Spencer. I'm beginning to approve of you. You don't happen to know any good gossip, do you?"

Obediently, he settled himself comfortably on the love seat. He nudged Eddie away from his ankles with a surreptitious movement of his foot and leaned forward confidentially. "I've just returned from London and I'm a bit out of touch, but I did hear that the Anglican Bishop of Washington has been seen with the wife of the Ambassador of New Guinea. Will that do?" he asked with an intimate chuckle.

He dared a glance at Caddy and caught an expression of puzzlement on her face. He returned her stare levelly for a moment, hoping he had made her laugh. Just when he was about to give up he realized her shoulders were quivering with suppressed laughter. Pleased with himself, he racked his brain for any bits of news that had passed back and forth across the dinner tables while he was on Kincade.

"I understand Queen Elizabeth is publicly contemplating reducing the income she gets from the state, but the royals are dead set against it so the betting is that she won't in the end." He finished his drink and thought some more. "The President is said to be keeping a mistress in Georgetown." He turned his head and smiled directly into Agatha's eyes. "I'm afraid that's all I can think of." Naming a famous doyenne of New York society, he continued smoothly, "Oh, yes. Toddy Wayminister has diabetes, but you probably know that."

"She used to live across the square when she was first married. A pretty girl, but so busy all the time." Agatha yawned again. "I liked her husband though. So attractive. He died young and there were those who said he died to get away from her. I don't think that's true though, do you?" She looked at him expectantly.

"Probably not." He nodded his head sagely as if he was privy to all sorts of confidential knowledge he wasn't allowed to share.

Agatha tapped him playfully on the arm. She began to chuckle and then to laugh. The sound was infectious and he began to laugh with her, and then Caddy joined in. The sound of Eddie yapping made them all laugh even more.

"Oh, my," Agatha said, wiping her eyes with a flowered silk handkerchief she had fished from somewhere beneath her shawls. "How foolish. How amusing. You must come and see us often, Mr. Spencer. You're very entertaining." She looked at him almost flirtatiously. Amused, he grinned back, liking her enormously and relishing their mock flirtation.

Fiske rose. "I've still got more work to do tonight. I

don't like to leave when I'm enjoying myself so much, but I should go."

He fished in his pocket and brought out the piece of paper on which he had neatly rewritten Nelson's message and handed it to Caddy. He wished he could stay. He would have been perfectly happy to stand in one spot if he could make Caddy smile at him again. She looked so different: not as reserved as she had on the island. He decided it must be the pale pink lipstick she was wearing, or perhaps it was the light shining on her long hair that made her seem softer. Whatever it was, he liked it. *I like her whenever I see her,* he admitted to himself; *I could get to like her too much.*

Caddy read the note and looked up with unabashed delight. His heart skipped a beat when he saw the smile he had been hoping for. "How wonderful. He must be so excited. He was sure there were more, at least five families, but a whole colony. That's unbelievable." She waved the paper in exultation. "I'm so glad you told me. It's wonderful news."

He had been right. It was worth the trip to see the pleasure in her face. "Then you'll go up?" he asked hopefully.

Her face fell and she twisted the paper in her hands. "I can't. I've got to finish the work I have." She pointed to the ceiling and he thought she must be referring to her darkroom. "I just can't leave now."

"But the cover. Nelson says this will guarantee you a cover," he persisted gently. He remembered how calm and serious she had been during their walk on the beach when she confided that she needed the money she earned. He wanted her to return to Kincade very much; if he could convince her to make the trip, he'd have another chance to see her. He knew, too, how disappointed the old man would be if she didn't come back to record his discovery.

Her face was closed, as if she was considering all she had to do. "I know. I need that cover. It would make all the difference for my bookings next year."

"Then do it," he urged.

They were standing close together in the middle of the room, both of them with their heads down as if they were discussing the faded pattern on the old oriental rug. He could smell the faint scent of her cologne. If he leaned forward, he thought, he might be able to touch her hair. Behind them, Agatha and Eddie snored softly. Except for that gentle sound the tall house was quiet around them. He could sense her struggle and he held his breath, not wanting to say the wrong thing; he could see she wanted to return to the island. The urge to touch her was almost irresistible, but before he had a chance to act on it, she looked up at him and her eyes were filled with misery.

"I've accepted money for the work I've done. There's all the developing to finish. A deadline to meet. I want to see the kites, I really do, but I've promised." Their faces were very near each other, and she halted, her eyes widening at something she saw in his face.

"What are we talking about here?" he asked gently in the soft, reassuring tone he used with his young nephew when he was trying to teach him something new. "How many hours?"

"Not hours, days. If I worked without stopping, it would still take me over a week," she replied slowly. Her gaze traveled slowly across his face and she looked suddenly very thoughtful.

He felt the beginnings of elation. "A week. That's

not too bad. If you don't mind pushing yourself you can finish your work and I'll see you get up to the island."

"But you've just started a new job," she protested almost automatically. She had nervously torn the note he had given her into shreds, and she dropped the pieces in a tarnished silver dish on a table next to them. "You can't just leave to make sure I get back there."

He felt exultant, as if he had been given a huge prize. "No, I can't. What I can do is see you get up there in a hurry as soon as you're ready. I'll fly you up."

"Fly me?" Her voice was incredulous and her eyes were wide with surprise. They were a lovely hazel, he noticed. "What does that mean?"

"It means I have a plane out at MacArthur. As soon as you're ready to leave I can put you in a car here, have you driven out, and have the pilot take you over." And the hell with all my appointments, he swore to himself.

"The pilot? What pilot?"

"You sound like an echo." He wanted to tease her, just to prolong her puzzlement, but she looked too worried, so he kept his voice low and reasoned while he explained. "I own a small two-seater. Randy Northrup has been using it while I've been in England. We keep it at MacArthur, and if someone needs to be flown over and we can't do it ourselves, we hire a pilot from the airport to do the ferrying."

She shifted her weight, but the distance between them remained the same. "But where can you land? There can't be a strip on the island."

"I must have forgotten to drive you by Kincade International when we were coming back from the windmill."

"Kincade International? You're kidding." She looked at him dubiously, as if she was reconsidering whatever good opinion of him she might have previously held.

"I'm not, I promise. There's a long strip of grass between the middle road and the north shore, where we land the plane. There's an official wind sock and a proper sign that says 'Kincade International.' Randy and I call it an international airport because we sometimes fly up to Canada and back during duck season."

"My God." Caddy dropped down on a small Victorian chair that creaked alarmingly when she moved. She started to laugh.

This time he did reach out and touch her shoulder lightly, just for an instant. "That's better. There isn't anything here we can't solve if you're willing to overwork yourself and go without food and sleep to the point of exhaustion for a week." He looked down at her and asked soberly, "Are you? It'll be hard on you."

"I don't mind. I will." Her face lit up with excitement.

"Then Nelson will be pleased," he said with satisfaction. And so will I, he thought. "The kites will be officially recorded, you'll get your cover, and . . ." He almost added, "And I'll get to see you again," but he stopped short of saying it out loud.

For the first time in his life he felt unsure of himself and unable to say the cheerful, matter-of-fact words of flirtation. There was something about Caddy that was different from all the other women he had known; she touched him in a way that made him uncharacteristically hesitant. He had felt the moment he met her that he knew her, and that never-before-felt sensation made him proceed very cautiously.

Agatha, rousing from her nap, peered at them from across the room and, apparently satisfied with what she saw, closed her eyes again and pretended to snore.

CHAPTER 9

Caddy knelt back on her heels, studying the prints circled around her on the floor. The doors to her little terrace were wide open and the early morning sun streamed into the room; it shone on the photographs with a glint that obscured the composition. Groaning with irritation and tiredness, she gathered them together and rose to her feet. She had been up most of the night working in the darkroom, pausing only to eat the food Agatha sent up and to nap for a few hours on the sofa; she hadn't dared lie on her bed for fear she would fall into too deep a sleep and lose precious hours she needed to meet her deadline.

It had been three days since Fiske had left, promising to call Nelson for her and extracting a promise from her in return that she would call him the instant she was ready to leave New York for the island. She swayed unsteadily on her feet. Exhaustion swept over her in waves and she sat down on the sofa, the prints still in her arms, and let her head fall back against the cushion. If she could just work through one more night, she could finish in time to leave Saturday morning.

There was so much to do. She still had to crop the prints she had in her arms, finish developing the last of the negatives still in the darkroom, and print the negatives out as final proofs. If she could do that she could deliver the proofs on the way to the airport and be on Kincade Saturday night, ready to photograph in the marsh on Sunday morning. It could work, but not, she thought, if she sat on the sofa all morning. Thank God Dave Barrish had understood the importance of locating a colony of kites so far north and had agreed to hold the space in the fall issue for an enlarged photo essay. If she could get the pictures, she was guaranteed the cover.

The house phone clanged and she rose and crossed to a smaller version of the instrument in the parlor, juggling the prints to pick up the receiver and hold it to her ear.

"Catherine," Agatha's voice ordered her peremptorily, "pick up your telephone. Thad wants to speak with you." Her aunt disconnected before she could agree. What could be wrong? Hastily she reached for her own telephone, which was attached to an answering machine on the desk; the red message light was flickering. With a frown of worry she realized she had turned the sound off while she was working and hours must have elapsed since she had listened to her messages.

"Caddy?" Thad's voice sounded strong and healthy, and she felt her body flood with relief. If anything had been wrong she would have known it in an instant by the sound of his voice.

"Thaddeus. How are you? I miss you." She dropped the prints in a pile on the desk and settled herself into the antique wooden office chair she had found in the basement. No matter how much work she had to do, she was anxious for a chat with her brother.

"Listen. When are you coming down? I've something new. It's another Max story, but I've put Aunt Agatha in too. It's funny as hell."

His voice was deep and vibrant and she could picture him leaning forward in his chair, resting his elbows on the board that served as a table on his wheelchair. He had told her three Max stories before. Max was a debonair balloonist, who sailed into impossible situations with all sorts of wonderful, quirky characters and managed to extricate himself by using his prodigious wit rather than his brawn.

She loved the tales because they were inventive and colorful and because they allowed Thad to escape the monotony of his invalidism into a world of high adventure. Mostly she liked them, she realized, because they were just plain good, original adventure stories.

"Tell me," she ordered.

"You sound like Aunt Agatha."

"I feel like Aunt Agatha this morning—about a million years old." Now that she had let herself actually sit in a chair for what felt like the first time in days, she feared she might never move again.

"Are you all right?" There was quick concern in his voice, and she felt a sharp twinge of guilt for upsetting him.

"I'm fine, darling, just working hard and sleepy. Now tell me your story."

She reached out and took an orange from a small arrangement of fruit in a white china bowl and began to peel it, balancing the receiver between her ear and her shoulder. Thad launched into his newest fantasy, his voice going up and down as he assumed all the roles in the saga. Her orange had long been eaten by the time he finished, and she had stretched the cord of the telephone so that she could move to her one over-stuffed chair and make herself more comfortable while, totally rapt, she listened to the tale of Max and Agatha finding uranium in a small town in Bolivia.

"It's perfect, Thad. The best Max story yet. I love it."

"Really?"

She remembered Dorothy's advice. "I do," she assured him solemnly. "Thad, I want you to write it down. I don't want these stories to get lost."

"I've never written any of them down," he responded dubiously.

"That doesn't mean you can't," she replied with a touch of asperity.

"Shit." Thad's voice faded and grew loud again. She pictured him lying in bed and felt the frustration that came whenever she thought of him that way, trapped in his room by his illness.

"Stop that, Thad. There's no reason why you can't write the stories out. I didn't want to tell you, but I'm saving up to buy you a word processor. Until then I want you to promise me you'll try and write the stories on a pad. You can do that, can't you?"

"I can try, but I don't see why the hell I should. The stories are just for you and me."

"Well, I want them on paper, so do it for your big sister."

"Maybe," he conceded grudgingly. "Are you coming down soon?" he prodded once more. She longed to see him; it had been weeks since she had been able to leave her various jobs and go to Philadelphia. She knew how much her visits meant to Thad—almost as much as they meant to her. The two of them would stay up for hours and, after Thad told her the latest installment of his newest Max story, she would tell him about New York and all the places she had been. To Thad, imprisoned by his wheelchair and frustrated by his inability to lead a normal life, New York was the promised land, a place full of glitter and shining promise where everything was possible. She promised herself she would get down to Philadelphia as soon as she returned from Kincade, and she told him so.

"Great, great, great. How long can you stay?"

"As long as I can," she replied truthfully. "But you know . . ."

". . . you have to work. I know." His voice was determinedly cheerful and she felt a pang. She wanted so fiercely to have him near her, to get him away from the four walls of his room. She worried that their parents sometimes forgot to spend as much time with him as he needed; his world was so small.

"How are the parents?"

"Annotating away. The next volume's almost ready for the printer," he replied, referring to the Wilcoxes' several-volume study of twentieth-century anthropology, which was being published over the course of two decades. She sighed. That meant her mother and father would be more distracted than usual, if that was possible.

"I'll be down soon. Probably the weekend after this."

"Deal. Bye, Cad."

She listened to the sound of the dial tone and replaced the receiver reluctantly. If she wasn't careful she would turn out just like her parents, forgetting there was a life outside her work. She rose from her chair and looked around the room.

Purposefully, she swept the prints back into her arms. An opened letter on heavy stationary that had been under the pile fluttered from the desk to the floor, and she looked down at it blankly. It was the letter Ward had delivered to the house while she was away on the island. She stooped and picked it up, re-reading it for the first time since Nelson's invitation had plunged her into a daze of work Monday evening. It all seemed so long ago. There was no endearment at the top of the page, only her name.

Caddy,
Despite our unpleasant scene in the restaurant, I had hoped you would reconsider and stay with me this weekend after all; you knew how important your being here was for me. Since you don't seem to understand that, I stand by my decision—I won't be seeing you again.
        Good luck,
        Ward

The prints cascaded from her arms one last time and she stood staring down at the letter. All the energy she had gotten from Thad's phone call disappeared, and she felt more tired than she had ever been before. Wrenching her sweatshirt up over her head with both hands, she headed for the tiny shower in the hall bathroom where she stood, her eyes closed while the warm water cascaded over her shoulders and down her body. At last she turned off the spray and reached for a towel, glad to wrap herself in its warmth. Standing in front of the little oval mirror propped over the sink, she looked at her reflection without seeing it.

How could she have even considered giving up her entire career to become the wife of a junior congressman in Washington, playing the role of acolyte? She pulled on a clean flannel shirt and a pair of faded dungarees and ran a comb through her damp hair. Looking back, she wondered how she could have been so blind to the real Ward, the Ward that loved her as an appendage to himself, not for the woman she was. Not for the first time she faced the fact that Ward lacked the principles he should have had to be a public servant. After all, shouldn't a public servant truly serve the public and care about things like housing and day care? Shouldn't he be involved in the problems of drugs in the city and the homeless? She thought so, but Ward never had. All he cared about was being elected.

She looked down at the discarded prints and realized she would never give up her career for any man. What would she be without her work? Would she still be Caddy Wilcox or simply some man's wife? Wanting to have sex with a man wasn't the same as loving him enough to marry him. She supposed she should feel something more, something that would make up her mind for her, but she knew she hadn't felt that with Ward. She'd invested so much of herself in becoming the photographer she was. She had plans for her future. No man was going to take that away from her, and while it might be satisfying to share her life with someone, she just couldn't see it happening to her. She rubbed her shoulder absently, remembering the way

Fiske had reached out to touch her, as if he wanted to touch more than her shoulder. His face had been expressionless, but she thought she had seen something stirring, deep in his eyes. She shook her head impatiently. It was her imagination again, she lectured herself, leading her astray when the last thing she wanted was another man in her life. Fiske Spencer was one of those powerful men who had a way with women, from Josie Northrup to Aunt Agatha, and she was looking for trouble if she thought for a second that his touch meant anything at all to him.

She sighed deeply. She should stop thinking about Ward and the whole unsettling question of love. She should certainly never think about Fiske—she had too much work to do. Shivering with cold, she walked slowly to the end of the room and closed the terrace door. She half-turned, thinking she might go down and talk the whole thing over with Agatha, but she paused, remembering her the night the two of them had sat up late, drinking wine. Her aunt had banged her glass down on the table with authority and declaimed in a voice full of conviction, "You always know when you're in love. If you have to wonder, then you aren't." She sighed. Not much help there.

She picked up the fallen letter, folded it carefully, and put it in the top drawer of the desk. She closed the drawer softly and, with that act, closed the door on her affair with Ward. Her feeling of distress was quickly replaced by one of such relief she almost laughed out loud. What if she was one of those women who were happiest when they were single? After all, she was determined to make herself famous, and she was determined to give Thad the life he deserved; there was little room in her life for a lover, much less a husband. Single. She turned the word over on her tongue, liking the feel of it. After all, Margaret Bourke-White had remained single all her life, and look at her. Lots of women never married and had full, rich lives without caving in to some man who tried to change them. Perhaps marriage simply wasn't for her, at least not now and maybe never.

She looked at the door of her darkroom with pleasure and determination. Right now she had to meet her deadline, and then she was going to Kincade.

CHAPTER 10

Caddy closed her eyes as they taxied down the runway. The wheels of the Cessna two-seater lifted from the ground heading north, into the wind, and the cabin creaked as the plane banked to the right. She opened her eyes, then closed them again quickly as her stomach lurched; it looked as if they were flying right into the ground.

"You can look now. We're up." Fiske sounded amused.

Cautiously, she peeked out the window and was relieved to see the ground beneath them, where it belonged, and the Long Island coast stretching ahead on their right. She looked at Fiske apologetically.

"I hate to fly, I'm sorry."

"I thought you'd been in far-off places, shooting those ospreys for instance."

"But I've never been in a two-seater before," she explained patiently, trying not to look out the window.

"There's nothing like a small plane to really get the feeling you're truly flying. It's like nothing else in the world."

"Mmmm." She wondered if it was too late to pray.

"Most people are afraid to fly, they just don't admit it. Try and relax, you may find you like it."

She sneaked a peek at him, to see if he was serious, but his gaze was focused on checking the dials and he didn't turn his head. Oversize earphones covered both sides of his head, and tinted glasses with gold aviators framed his eyes. He looked the part of a pilot, she thought, admiring the sure, easy way his hands rested on the controls. Men were very sexy when they were doing something they loved and were good at, she mused; Fiske was sexy, she admitted to herself, feeling her face grow warm. Hastily she looked down at her hands clenched in her lap and tried to think about other things besides how surprisingly glad she was to see him again.

She had not expected to find him waiting at the curb, leaning against a shiny, dark blue BMW, when she left the house that morning. They had spoken briefly the night before when, tired but satisfied with her work, she had called him to say she was ready to leave town the next morning. He had sounded preoccupied when he told her a car would be waiting for her at seven and with luck she would be on the island by ten thirty Saturday morning.

"You're sure you can take the time to do this? Fly me to the island?" she asked now, worrying again that she was an imposition.

He shook his head. "No. I can't. We're really on our way to Wall Street." Caddy couldn't restrain an involuntary chuckle, and he smiled. "You asked me that question at least twice in the car and the answer's still the same: no, I can't spare the time from work, but I want to go up to Kincade and you're the bonus. I'm going to try and move this vote thing along a little this weekend. I've asked some friends to meet me there tonight."

Caddy's heart leapt at the knowledge that, he, too, had been looking forward to seeing her. A bonus, he had called her, and she filed the word away in her mind to think about later. "It won't really happen, will it? Selling Kincade, I mean."

"Not if I have anything to say about it, it won't. It's a lot of money though, and people can behave very strangely when large sums are involved."

She thought of what the cost of maintaining those big houses must be, and they were only second homes for the islanders. The money that was spent in one summer by any of the islanders could keep her family for more than a year.

"What's that big sigh for?"

"Just thinking how different Kincade is from any place I've ever been."

"You're a lake person, aren't you?"

So he had remembered her referring to lakes when she came out of the ocean, she noted with pleasure. But she only nodded. For a moment she was confused, not knowing whether she wanted to talk to him about herself or not. Suddenly, even though they were just making conversation, it seemed as if a lot of other things were going on between them.

"What lakes?" he persisted without looking at her.

"Eaglesmere, up in the Poconos," she replied briefly.

"Pennsylvania?" he encouraged her.

"Yes. My parents' publisher used to lend us a cottage up there every August." She relaxed. Now that she had offered a piece of information, she was committed to the conversation.

"I've heard about Eaglesmere. Big brown cottages around a big brown lake?"

"We never had one of the big houses right around the lake, just one of the old servants' cottages behind them." She faltered, trying to find a way to explain that the big houses at Eaglesmere would fit easily inside the houses on Kincade. She wondered what he would think of the Wilcoxes' little row house in Philadelphia, or the way her family all had to use the same bathroom, or how without the generosity of her parents' publisher there wouldn't have been any vacations at all. She looked at Fiske openly, thinking soberly how different their lives were, how totally different their upbringing. There really wasn't any common ground for them to meet on, when she stopped to think about it. She looked out of the window without seeing anything.

Fiske raised his voice as he throttled up on the engine. "And you liked it there?"

"It was wonderful. My brother and I would spend all day by the lake. He'd fish and I'd read. We both learned how to swim there. It was"—she searched for the right word—"uncomplicated," she finished, pleased with the definition.

"Uncomplicated." He whistled. "I could use a little uncomplicated right about now."

Curious, she asked, "Why?"

"It's a continuing effort to keep things going on the

island. A very complicated effort," he stressed the last phrase emphatically.

She knotted her brow. "It all looks so casual, as if it took care of itself."

"Hardly. There are the three roads to maintain, the ferry to keep up, the telephone lines are constantly having to be repaired, and there's the insurance. The harbor has to be dredged out every spring."

She mused for a moment, considering what he had told her. "And the houses themselves. There's winter damage, and paint . . ."

". . . and digging out the wells every spring and replacing the generators. It never stops. The Manor needs a new roof, which means we have to get a barge to bring over the shingles and tar paper, then we have a roofer come over and put the damn thing on, and then we have to get another barge to cart the old roof away."

"I can't imagine what that must cost," she murmured faintly, thinking what it had cost to put new linoleum on the tiny kitchen floor in Philadelphia.

"A lot." He shrugged. "Most of the older generation sees Kincade as something more than a place to go every summer. For them it's still the way it was when it was founded: a haven from civilization. But some of the younger generation don't feel quite so ethical about it. They're all caught up in their careers, or their social lives, or whatever."

"And you?" She really wanted to know.

"It defines me," he answered simply.

He didn't continue, as if his answer was all the explanation she needed. Oddly enough, she understood perfectly what he meant, and she nodded her head slowly in agreement. She could empathize with his bond to the island, as if what happened to him off-island was the sum of what he had learned on Kincade; she had felt a whisper of that possibility herself. She knew he was looking at her and turned her head away so he wouldn't see her blush.

"Watch the road," she admonished.

"Do you always boss the driver around? It seems to me I remember being told to watch the road the last time you were in my passenger seat." He banked the plane skillfully again and they headed out over the water.

She shook her head and didn't answer. All of a sudden she was very conscious of how alone together they were. She was acutely aware of his hands as he touched first one control and then another. Only a few inches separated their arms, and for one fleeting second she almost leaned closer so they could actually touch. She inhaled shakily as a feeling in her chest, like an extra heartbeat, came and went. Somehow, she felt more completely alone with him than she had on the deserted beach, and she found the sensation not at all unpleasant.

On either side of the plane, clusters of fluffy white clouds loomed up; ahead of them more clouds moved across their path. As the plane was engulfed by the billowing, white mass, it bumped gently and she ducked instinctively, as if the cloud were a solid wall and they were going to hit it. Feeling foolish, she straightened up hastily and looked over at Fiske, hoping he hadn't noticed, but his lips were twitching and she knew he was trying not to laugh.

"All right, all right," she said crossly. Her fear of flying was nothing compared to the relief she felt that the physical intensity that had momentarily engulfed her had subsided. "I'm sorry."

"Wait," he promised.

"Do I have a choice?"

"Not unless you've got wings," he replied promptly.

The clouds began to thin and she could see sunlight ahead. The plane had leveled out and they were flying smoothly in a straight line. Cautiously, she relaxed. It really wasn't so bad, she thought judiciously; maybe she could even get used to it.

"Look." He pointed ahead.

They were flying out of the clouds. On their right, the Long Island coast had become almost a sliver, beyond which the dark Atlantic Ocean stretched endlessly. In the distance to their far left, Connecticut was only an expanse of green, and straight ahead, an island rose out of the sound. Suddenly, she felt as if she, not the plane, were flying; sitting in the cockpit she had nothing but the window between her and the air through which they were flying. She felt as if she were soaring and she held her breath, not wanting the moment to pass. In what seemed like only seconds they had flown over the island and she looked at Fiske, wondering why they hadn't landed.

"We're the next one. That's Fishers down below."

"Is it as nice as Kincade?"

"Nope. Lots of big houses, a club, and a lot of socializing."

"You have big houses and socializing too."

"Not as much as Fishers, though, thank God."

He pulled a lever and pushed some buttons and the plane slowed perceptibly. She sat up straight, clutched her seat belt, and looked anxiously out of the window, down at the water.

"Easy does it. We're just beginning our descent. Look ahead, there's Kincade."

She nodded her head. She didn't trust herself to speak. All the pleasure she had been experiencing at flying vanished as he banked the plane and it looked as if the water was rising to meet them.

"I'm sorry we couldn't stay up there longer. You liked it, didn't you?" He turned the control and looked out over the left wing. The plane was tilting now, and the island was beneath them. His voice was matter-of-fact as he explained what he was doing; it had a very soothing effect on her, and despite her fright she managed to look down at the island. It looked too small to land on. "I'm going to circle the windmill and come back in over the northern end. Then we'll put down at International, taxi for a little bit, and we'll be home. Here we go."

She could sense he was looking at her, and she tried to unclench her hands so he would think she was unafraid.

"You can close your eyes, if you like. I'll tell you when it's all over." His voice was gentle.

Despite her panic, she laughed. He laughed too, and by the time they stopped laughing, the little plane had taxied bumpily to the end of the grassy runway and come to a halt. Fiske pulled off his earphones and glasses. His grin had faded and he was watching her intently. She wanted to tell him that she knew it had probably taken more effort for him to talk her down than to land the plane, and that he had made her feel very safe, but the shyness he seemed to induce in her made her hesitant. He seemed so sure of himself; he probably thought she was foolish to be afraid of flying.

"There's Nelson." She pointed excitedly to a battered vintage wooden station wagon parked next to the wind sock. Nelson was standing by the front fender and, surprised at the warmth she felt, she waved at him as if they were the best of friends who had known each other forever. Fiske leaned across her and opened the passenger door.

"Am I supposed to jump?" She looked down at the muddy grass.

"There's a ladder behind you. Drop it down and hook the top on the bottom of the door. It's small, but it'll get you off."

She followed his instructions, and when the five-rung ladder was in place she reached back for her canvas bags. Nelson had reached the foot of the ladder and was holding it steady, a wide smile of welcome on his face as he waited for her to descend.

Fiske leaned over her again and called down, "Uncle Nelson, I've brought your package safe and sound."

"Good work, my boy. I can't thank you enough. Caddy, my dear, welcome back."

She could smell the lightweight tweed jacket Fiske wore. It smelled of rain and the pipe he occasionally smoked and something else she couldn't quite identify; perhaps it was the scent of his shirt or the Shetland sweater he wore. His shoulder brushed hers. His face was so close she could have breathed on it, and suddenly she wanted to move her head forward and touch her forehead to the warmth of his cheek. Once again, she found him disturbingly attractive and she tried to breathe shallowly, hoping he wouldn't notice, but he turned his head at that same moment and looked right into her eyes with the same look of recognition she had seen there before. She could see his pupils darken and she knew he had felt something stir between them too.

"Come on, boy. We've got to get moving."

Nelson's command shattered the fragile moment. She turned her head, Fiske sank back into his seat, and

she began to lower her luggage into Nelson's impatiently waiting hands. When all the pieces were down,
she half-rose and turned, letting her legs find the ladder's middle rung; her hands grasped the sides of the
doorway and her head was level with the open cockpit.
She looked across at Fiske. His hands were fastened
on the idle controls and he was staring straight ahead.

"Thank you," she said, making an effort to keep her
voice neutral. She wanted to let him know by the tone
of her voice that they were still simply friendly ac-
quaintances, bound by the circumstances. She was going to ignore what she had just felt and she wanted him
to do the same. She was on Kincade to work, not to
have a summer flirtation with one of the islanders.

"You're welcome." His voice matched hers. He
turned his head and grinned at her.

She was relieved and then contradictorily perplexed.
She wondered if, after all, the moment *had* only been
in her imagination. "I really liked the middle part. It's
just the takeoff and landing that frighten me. I know
it's silly. You're a great driver."

He pretended to look pained. "Pilot. Pilot. Ace pilot, actually."

"Then I owe you a long, white silk scarf to wear
when you fly—as a thank you for bringing me up."

"No thank you needed. It was my pleasure. I'm going down again tomorrow about four, if you want a
ride back to New York."

He began pulling himself toward the door and she
backed down the ladder until she felt the ground beneath her feet. Nelson surprised her by kissing her
roundly on the cheek, and she surprised herself by
kissing him back just as warmly.

"Don't count on it, Fiske," Nelson said, picking up
two bags and heading for the station wagon. "I'm go-

ing to keep her longer than that. I've counted almost three hundred kites in the last two days. I want her to photograph as much as she can."

She and Fiske each picked up one of the two remaining bags and followed him.

"How's she supposed to get back to town from New London?" Fiske asked, ignoring Caddy completely.

"I'm right here, you know," she said indignantly, throwing her bag into the back of the old wagon, "and I can get myself back down perfectly well. They have trains up here, don't they? I mean, there's civilization back on the mainland, isn't there?"

"Little firebrand, isn't she?" Nelson said delightedly.

"I had a hell of a time with her on the way up, scratching and biting all the way." Fiske shook his head sorrowfully.

She giggled and felt surprised at herself. She couldn't remember the last time she had been teased or, in fact, the last time she had giggled. All the tiredness from her five nights and days of immersion in her work disappeared, and the relief she felt from having finally resolved her feelings about her relationship with Ward welled up in its place. She felt at peace, almost lighthearted. She drew a deep breath and smiled broadly at the two men.

"Welcome to Kincade," Fiske and Nelson intoned solemnly in unison.

"Welcome to Kincade," she answered happily.

CHAPTER 11

Almost four hours after landing on the island Caddy trudged up the middle road from the great marsh, on her way home to the Loverings. Nelson had crawled around with her for the first hour and a half, pointing out the new nests the kites were building and showing her where she could conceal herself to photograph.

The afternoon had not gone well. The fine weather had turned gray and most of the birds had been elusive. She had crouched beneath a low scrub pine, the Wellingtons that Eliza had insisted she wear her only protection against the cold, muddy water. A sharp wind had sprung up, blowing ripples along the canals and swaying the trees with its force. A branch had scraped her forehead, and she lost her lens cap somewhere in the reeds. She had prevailed upon Nelson to leave her and return home. She was worried at the way he still looked pale from his recent illness; the chill he had caught in the marsh had turned into a lingering case of bronchitis. Admitting he and Eliza were in the habit of late-afternoon naps, he had departed, still giving her instructions over his shoulder as he climbed slowly up the incline. Despite her determination to take as many shots as she could of the kites in their daily patterns, the cold had driven her away from the damp marsh at least two hours earlier than she had intended.

She looked at her watch. It was only four o'clock, still too early to go back to the Loverings; they were probably still napping. A flight of small terns circled over her head, and she wondered in amazement that she had been giddy with pleasure only a short time ago while now she was so tired and cramped with cold. She heard a car's engine and looked down the road, hoping it was Fiske coming to check on her, but the sound faded and grew fainter. She assumed it was one of the Northrups going home. She halted, considering her options: She could wait or walk home. Or, she thought, she could go to the Northrups' and ask Josie for a ride. After a minute during which her equipment got heavier and heavier, she decided Josie probably wouldn't mind having her arrive on her doorstep a second time. Her step quickened and she started walking toward where she had heard the car. She'd like to see Josie again; not to mention the fact that she could certainly use the drink she was pretty sure she'd be offered and the cheerful warmth of that comfortable house.

The wind was increasing, the mist had turned into a steady drizzle, and she kept her head down as she hurried to the turnoff to the Hall and plunged down the muddy, rutted road to the back of the house. She came around the corner to the back door where she had entered the first time, and halted in surprise. Next to the Northrups' Land-Rover was Fiske's Jeep, and pulled up on the grass were two others she had never seen before. The Northrups must be entertaining.

She huddled inside her anorak indecisively, wondering if she should go in anyway or turn around and leave. The cold rain made up her mind for her, and she opened the door and tentatively called, "Hello?" but nobody answered. Hearing voices from the living room, she pulled off her muddy boots, hung her drenched jacket on a wooden peg by the kitchen door, and walked through the house to the living room.

"Hello," she said hesitantly, feeling like an intruder.

Eight surprised faces looked back at her from the circle of bodies sprawled around the fireplace. A fire burned briskly on the hearth and she could smell hot rum.

"I got caught in the rain," she apologized, conscious of the muddy scratch on her face and her wet clothes. "I didn't want to disturb the Loverings so I thought I'd . . ." her voice trailed off uncertainly.

"Caddy, how nice. Come in and meet everyone." Josie rose smoothly with a polite smile on her face.

The men straggled to their feet. Outside of Fiske, who was quietly standing behind the others, a half-smile on his face as his eyes met hers, she knew none of the six looking at her expectantly. Josie took her around the circle, introducing her first to her husband, Jonno, his brother, Randy, and Randy's wife, Deane, and finally to Ford and Bill Ludlow, who rose from their seats on either side of Ford's wife, Claire. Only Fiske was left after the introductions were complete, and when they reached him he put out his hand and held hers without letting go. She was very conscious of the pressure of his fingers curled firmly over hers.

"Ah, the noted photographer," he said formally. "Looking very fetching after an afternoon in Kincade's own Great Marsh. Is the scratch something new?"

"I had a fight with a branch and lost," she answered, taking back her hand and rubbing her forehead.

"Here. Sit by the fire. You look frozen."

He pulled a low chair forward and pushed her down gently. She held her head up, but inside she felt uncomfortable and out of place. The feeling lingered well after Josie handed her a mug of steaming buttered rum, which she drank slowly, warming her hands on the mug gratefully.

The others had resumed their seats and were talking quietly among themselves, but the conversation soon lagged and an awkward silence fell over the room. This was more than a social occasion; she had probably walked in on an attempt by Fiske to band the islanders together. More than ever she wished she had walked the entire distance back to the Loverings. She put her mug down on the hearth next to her chair, preparing to make her apologies and leave, as if she were unaware of what was going on in the room.

"Finished already? Want another one?" Fiske asked.

"No. I feel much better. I should leave . . ."

"You caught us in the middle of a council of war, Caddy," Josie said, frowning at her husband, who looked as if he was about to silence her. "It's all right, Jonno. Caddy knows what's going on."

"The point is," a tall, thin man said, "she's not supposed to."

"Bill." The streaked-blond girl who had been introduced to Caddy as Bill's sister-in-law, Claire Ludlow, chided him softly. "Don't be rude."

"I'm not being rude. This is a discussion for ourselves—we shouldn't be sharing it with someone who doesn't own property here." Caddy wished she could just vanish into thin air. She knew she was blushing and her shoulders tensed, preparing to rise and make a hasty retreat.

"I'm sure she's as nice as she is pretty," Bill's portly brother Ford said in a pompous manner, "but she works for a magazine, and we don't want any publicity, do we?" He smiled insincerely at Caddy. "I'm sure you understand."

"I'll vouch for her." Fiske's voice was quiet but very firm. She looked up. He was leaning against the mantel, apparently absorbed in cleaning his pipe.

The room was quiet again, as if the assembled group was thinking over his words.

"She's known about our own little land war for some time, Ford, and she hasn't told anyone. She's not likely to repeat anything heard here. Would you, Caddy?" Josie moved around the circle, filling up the mugs again; her husband shrugged his shoulders and reached for a fistful of potato chips.

"No. I wouldn't." Caddy shook her head. "But I understand and I'll be glad to leave. I don't want to interrupt you."

Randy Northrup banged his mug on the coffee table and they all laughed. "Let's get on with it. If Fiske says it's okay, that's good enough for me."

Josie held the pot over his head threateningly. "I say okay, too, and I've got the rum."

"Just what I said: Let's get on with it." Randy held up his oversize mug and she filled it to the brim.

"If you drink all that, you're going to be too plowed

to be of any use to anyone," Josie retorted over her shoulder, moving on to Fiske. He put his hand over his cup and shook his head, and she returned to her seat next to her husband, putting the empty pot on the floor next to her. Leaning her head against Jonno's shoulder, she extended her legs on top of the coffee table with a comfortable sigh.

Fiske cleared his throat, and eight pairs of eyes swiveled in his direction. "You all know why we're here today—to talk about Asher's offer—and I want to thank you all for making the effort to get here. I know it wasn't easy for you to arrange on such short notice, especially when the season hasn't started and there's only one ferry running." Someone groaned and the others laughed.

"When I got back from London I spent a couple of weeks of vacation up here. It was the first I'd really focused on how serious some of the islanders are about selling out. I sure don't want it to happen and it occurred to me, you guys might feel the same way. What the hell, we grew up here together. If there's going to be a fight, and it looks like there will be, it seems to me the younger generation ought to get together and present a united front." Caddy coughed on purpose, a low sound, but Fiske immediately looked at her. She intercepted his look and raised her eyebrows, trying to let him know she wanted to leave, but he shook his head almost imperceptibly and turned his attention back to the group. She was torn between wanting to stay and hear everything and feeling as if she oughtn't be there at all. If Fiske and Josie think it's all right, I guess it is, she decided, leaning back, prepared to be an interested observer.

Deane Northrup interrupted him. Her pretty face was deeply tanned from a recent Florida vacation with their three children, and her dark hair was fastened with red clips. "You're assuming the younger generation wants to stay." She looked directly at the Ludlows. "Maybe some of us want to sell."

"That's part of why we're here," Fiske acknowledged. "I'm hoping we can get those who want to stay organized into a unit, and then go on and try to convince anybody who's on the fence that it would be a mistake to sell."

"Hear, hear." Jonno had his arm around his wife, but he raised his mug in a toast to the issue. "Good idea, even if it's yours, Spencer."

"Maybe Deane's right. Perhaps some people would rather sell. It's a lot of money." Ford studiously avoided their eyes. His wife looked uncomfortable.

"What the hell are you talking about, Ford?" Bill Ludlow leaned around his sister-in-law to look at his brother. "Name me one person our age on the island who would choose to have more money than they've already got rather than being able to come back to Kincade year after year. Christ. I'm probably the only one here who's struggling along in the magic world of the theater, and I'd eat sawdust before I'd give up the island."

Caddy inched her chair along the wall, away from the blazing fire and out of the circle. Now she could watch the group in the circle and try and match names with faces. She was looking at Fiske when Bill spoke. An expression of surprise crossed his face and she wondered why.

Ford responded to his brother angrily. "It's not that easy. You're single and no one expects you to assume the role of head of household." He made a sweeping gesture that encompassed the rest of the group. "It's different for us. We've got kids to educate and their futures to think of." And all that costs a lot of money, Caddy thought soberly, remembering how she had had to depend on scholarships for her own education.

"My God. You can't be serious. Are you even considering this guy's offer?" Bill's voice shook with outrage.

"Dad wants to sell. I thought he might have told you."

At this point Caddy began to feel as if she were watching a play, one where the characters spoke their lines and moved across the stage set of the Northrups' living room. She sat entranced as the drama unfolded.

Claire had her head lowered and was studiously examining her rings. The room had fallen quiet as the others watched Bill. The lanky set designer rose agitatedly to his feet and walked over to Fiske.

"Have you heard anything about this?" he asked, looking for reassurance.

"Yes," Fiske admitted. "He came to see Dad and they had a hell of a row. They haven't spoken since."

"Why didn't Dad tell me about all this?" Bill asked the room at large. No one looked at each other and his face paled as the realization hit him.

"You're kidding." His voice was full of pain and disgust. He turned away and walked slowly to the window, looking out at the driving rain with his fists jammed into his pockets.

"Will." Ford spoke his brother's childhood name softly. He rose and went to the window and put his arm around Bill's shoulder. They looked at each other soberly for a moment, reading each other's thoughts, and then, simultaneously, they broke into laughter.

"Will someone please tell me what's going on?" Deane asked plaintively.

"Commercial break, honey. Don't let it worry your pretty head." Randy squeezed his wife's knee.

Jonno disentangled himself from his wife and disappeared into the kitchen. Claire rose and, without a backward glance at the two Ludlow men who were talking quietly in a corner of the room, headed for the bathroom. Josie and Fiske stared at each other soberly.

"How am I doing?" he asked her.

"Okay."

"Think this is going to fly?"

"Keep on punching."

Caddy wondered if Jonno was aware of the deep bond between his wife and Fiske and if it ever bothered him. Probably not, she decided, looking at the other woman. Josie had the serene and satisfied look of a well-loved woman happy in her marriage. Caddy looked up at Fiske and found him looking down at her, a quizzical expression in his eyes. For the second time that day, she blushed. She was sure he knew exactly what she was thinking about.

Jonno reentered the room carrying a large bowl of apples and with a new bag of potato chips under his arm. Barbara Davidson's freckled face smiled tentatively around his shoulder at the room.

"Hi, Josie. Sorry I'm late."

"Babs." Josie motioned to the seat next to her that Jonno had vacated and gave her a hug when she sat down. Not in the least offended, her husband plumped down next to Deane and offered her the bowl of apples.

"Sorry we're late. We missed the ferry. Hank got one of the Cleary boys to run us over."

"Where is our Hank?" Josie craned her neck to see if Barbara's husband was coming through the doorway.

"He stopped off to see Rufus." As Barbara reached over for an apple and bit into it, she spotted Caddy. She stopped mid-bite in surprise. "Caddy. What are you doing here?"

All the heads swiveled in Caddy's direction as if they had forgotten she was in their midst. She felt as if she was being dragged into the middle of their play, and instinctively she leaned toward Fiske's reassuring bulk.

"Photographing. Nelson found three hundred more kites," Fiske replied for her absently. Relieved, Caddy leaned further back into the shadows in an attempt to resume her self-appointed role as audience.

"My God," Barbara said in awe. "He must be ecstatic."

Caddy merely smiled across the room.

"Why is Hank with Rufus?" Fiske asked curiously.

"I don't know. They had some business together. He said he'd be along."

Everybody had resumed a seat around the fireplace. Caddy examined them, one by one. Jonno had thrown another huge log on the fire, and dancing flames cast bright light over the serious faces watching the interplay between the two Spencers. Caddy looked at Fiske, conscious of the way the firelight played on the planes of his cheeks and his forehead. He looked very much in command, and she thought he must be a very good manager of people. She could well understand why his firm had made him their youngest department head. He fingered his pipe automatically and, with an echo of the desire it had evoked, she recalled the scent of smoke on his jacket when he leaned over her in the airplane. When she lowered her gaze, she saw that, as on the plane, her hands were clenched.

Resolutely, Caddy looked up, waiting to see what would happen next. Fiske looked at her questioningly, as if he wanted to make sure she was all right, and she smiled her reassurance. The clock on the mantel read five thirty. She knew the Loverings would be awake and looking for her to arrive, but she didn't want to leave until she knew Fiske had accomplished his goal. She had understood and been in sympathy with his desire to fight off the developer, but now she found she cared more deeply than she could ever have imagined about Kincade remaining a pristine island. With surprise, she realized she was begining to love the island.

Fiske rapped on the mantel with the stem of his pipe for attention. When all conversation had stopped, he asked, "Where does this leave us? I'd like to think we have the nucleus of a fighting wedge here, but maybe we ought to see. Shall we take a vote?"

"You know we're in," Jonno yawned, stretching his arms wide above his head. Josie nodded in agreement.

"And us." Randy held up his wife's arm as though she were a victorious prizefighter.

Not looking at his brother, Bill Ludlow raised his hand.

All eyes were fastened on Claire and Ford. They looked at each other wordlessly, obviously communicating in some sort of marital shorthand. Finally, Claire smiled ruefully at her husband and Ford, still looking at his wife, said, "We're in."

A small cheer went up from the rest of the group. Caddy couldn't believe the relief that flooded through her at this sign that the group was unanimous. She stretched out her legs in front of her with pleasure. Jonno disappeared and came back with two bottles of wine and a tray of glasses, and Bill reached over and wrung his brother's hand. Fiske was grinning broadly.

"What's the occasion?" The voice was followed by

the appearance in the doorway of a slightly portly man in his early forties wearing a tweed jacket and a starched shirt. A Union Club necktie was carefully knotted under his collar, and a foulard silk handkerchief peeked out of his breast pocket.

"Ah. Look who's washed ashore." Randy clapped.

"Hank. How nice." Josie smiled pleasantly and kissed him on the cheek. "You're just in time for wine."

"Did I miss something?" With a grin, he looked to his wife for help. He shook the men's hands, kissed the women, and stared at Caddy. "And who do we have here?"

"I'm Catherine Wilcox." She didn't like the way he was looking at her, as if she should find him attractive. She didn't, and she made her voice purposefully cool.

"Ah, yes. The photographer from *Nature's World.* Welcome to Kincade." The group groaned in unison and Caddy had to smile when he affected elaborate surprise. Another character in her play, she thought.

Everyone had a full glass of wine when Jonno, still standing and looking straight at Hank, said, "We were about to have a toast." He raised his glass. "To the Flying Wedge." He drained his glass. The others raised their glasses and murmured, "The Flying Wedge."

"I'll drink to that," Hank said. "What is it?"

"Kincade's younger generation's answer to Bruce Asher. We don't want to sell, and we're going to do what we can to stop him."

"It's a lot of money," Hank commented ruefully. He drank deeply. "But what the hell, it's only money."

"I don't know how Asher got to all the islanders the way he did, but we don't intend to let him get any further," Fiske informed his brother-in-law.

"What the hell are we going to do?" Hank rocked

back on his heels, a slight smile on his face. "How can we compete with Asher's offer?" There was something about Hank's smile, a commiserating quality, that made Caddy faintly uneasy. She looked around the room; no one else had seemed to notice. It must be her imagination again.

"Apples and oranges, old boy. We don't have to compete. We just have to make sure we don't sell," Randy announced.

"Not ourselves, and not anyone else, right?" Hank agreed blandly. He smiled down at his wife. He strolled over and stood next to the end of the sofa where Barbara was sitting. He put one hand on her shoulder and patted it gently. "We're here to stay, aren't we, darling?"

"Of course. I love Kincade. You do too, and so do the children."

"Of course we do," he smiled. "We all love Kincade." He raised his glass and finished his wine, putting the empty glass down on the end table. Again, Caddy thought there was something that didn't ring quite true about Hank, something a bit insincere. She shivered. For some reason she didn't trust him. She jumped as the little clock rang the hour.

"My God." Ten heads swiveled in her direction. She rose quickly in alarm, looking across the room at Josie. "I forgot all about the Loverings. They'll be worried about me. I've got to get back to the house."

"I'll drive you," Josie answered immediately.

"I'll call Eliza and let her know you're on your way." Jonno headed for the hall.

"No. I'll take her. I'll be right back," Fiske said calmly.

He threaded his way through his friends. Josie was standing by the door and when Caddy reached her after the group had given her a surprisingly warm good-bye, Josie amazed her by reaching out both hands to her with a warm smile. "Come back soon, Caddy. Next time we'll have time to talk."

Flushing, Caddy felt the quick pleasure of being accepted. She was tempted to linger, but Fiske put his hand on her elbow and propelled her out the door and into his Jeep.

"It went well, didn't it?" she asked as he navigated the Jeep through the rain up the steep incline to the road. The Jeep smelled of gasoline and tarpaulins. Sleepily, she sniffed, and smiled to herself: the aroma of Fiske's pipe tobacco was there too.

"It isn't over yet," he answered soberly.

"But they're going to work together. Isn't that what you wanted?"

"Not everybody. But you're right, it's a start. I sent somebody up from the firm to dig into the deeds, just to see that they're all in order. They are, of course, but while he was in New London the clerk in the registrar's office told him Asher had already filed an application to rezone the land for commercial and high-rise use. He's allowed to begin filing for variances if he's got a pending sale. What my guy hasn't found out yet is what sort of documentation Asher was able to present to prove he has a pending deal. I've got two associates working on it now and we'll find out, but it was a hell of a surprise. Somebody on Kincade has agreed to sell land to Asher."

"But don't you all have to agree before there can be any sale to an outsider? I mean, one person can't just sell their land all alone, right?" She felt vaguely frightened, and the very fact that she could react with fright made her understand just how involved she had become in the fate of the island.

"Right. It means there's been some misrepresentation somewhere. It's going to kick up a hell of a mess. Whoever agreed to sell their land had to have told Asher they could get him the rest of the island."

Caddy thought hard, trying to remember something she had read somewhere. "Doesn't the state or the county—or whoever issues variances and permits—have to let the applications be a matter of public record?"

"Yes. We should know sometime soon." He pulled the Jeep to a halt in front of the Loverings, but he didn't turn off the engine.

"Aren't you going to come in and say hello?" Caddy wasn't sure if she wanted him to come in or not, but she was reluctant to say good-bye.

"Not tonight." Idly, he turned the windshield wipers off and on again. The rain was coming down in sheets, pounding on the roof of the Jeep, and enclosing them in a pool of silence within.

"I like your friends," Caddy said slowly, watching the rain strike the window and thinking back over the afternoon.

He shifted in his seat so his back was against the door and he was facing her. "So do I. We've got a lot of history together. Josie likes you, you know."

She smiled. "And I like her."

"Funny, I like you too." He stretched his arm along the back of his seat. His fingertips brushed her across her back and closed on her shoulder.

Alarmed, she looked across at him. In the dim light it was hard to read the expression in his eyes. She remembered the feel of his body as he leaned across her in the plane, and her heart began to pound. She was glad it was dark so he couldn't see the blush she could feel rising up her throat. He lowered his head toward her, as if he was going to kiss her, a faint smile on his lips. *No,* she thought in confusion. *No.* She leaned away toward the door.

Instead of kissing her, however, his smile faded and then, slowly, as if reluctant to have her leave, he leaned across and opened the door for her. A gust of wind blew in some rain and Caddy pulled the hood of her anorak up over her head. Still confused and vaguely disappointed, she climbed down and stood in the downpour.

"Caddy." Fiske rolled down the window and stuck his head out; he had to yell over the sound of the rain. "I'll be over for breakfast. Don't leave without me."

She waved, but it was too late. The Jeep was already disappearing up the hill. Her thoughts were still in a turmoil—wondering why he hadn't wanted to kiss her after all and what it would have felt like if he had—when she reached the front door, and it seemed perfectly natural to find Eliza waiting to welcome her with open arms.

CHAPTER 12

"And then I spent four more days in the marsh, but Thad, I'm sure the work I did there was the best I've ever done."

Caddy pounded the pillow into shape and rolled over on her side, the better to look at her brother, who was propped up in his bed. She liked the way he had let his dark-blond hair grow nearly to his shoulders; it made him look a little like a rock star, as long as you didn't notice how thin his limbs were. His most vivid feature were his eyes, she thought. They were almond-shaped and a deeper hazel color than hers, almost black, and when he looked at her, as he was doing now, his gaze was riveting. It was late and they had been talking for hours, but neither of them wanted to go to sleep. From the street below she could hear the sound of a car start up and drive away. It was a sound that always made her think of Philadelphia: wheels bumping over the cobblestones.

The Wilcox house was a mud-colored father-son-and-holy-ghost, so named because originally it had only three rooms, one on top of the other. Over the years an extension had been added and a fourth floor, but it still had only three bedrooms and one bathroom for all four of them. The largest room, which should have been the parlor, was devoted to their parents' library and work room. The dining room had become the room where the family had their meals and read and where the one tiny television they owned sat almost unnoticed in a corner. Books were everywhere: on the staircase, in the bathroom, over the sink, and on every windowsill. Caddy had a little bedroom on the top floor, next to the attic, but she seldom slept in it, preferring to make a nest for herself on the old couch in Thad's room.

"But what happened about the vote?" Thad's eyes were bright with interest. She had told him everything that had happened to her on the island, trying to bring it alive for him so that he, too, could see the rolling hills and the shining ocean and the large houses poised like seven sentinels, each guarding its own particular piece of land. She had even told him all the secrets she had heard, describing the islanders in detail and lining up for him who wanted to sell and who did not.

"It hasn't happened yet. Fiske says there may never be a vote. He says he thinks there has been an egregious misrepresentation made by Asher to someone on the island, but he can't find out who it is."

"Who do you think it is?" He ran his fingers through his hair. Caddy smiled to herself: The gesture was practically an effeminate one, but when Thad did it it reminded her poignantly that long hair was Thad's way of attempting to look like normal young men his age, guys who went to concerts and played guitars with each other in their college dormitories. She laughed at him and threw her pillow across the room, and he promptly pulled an elastic band from beneath his pillow and fastened his hair into a ponytail.

"No one has been able to find out who actually agreed to sell their land to Asher, but I have an idea Fiske thinks it's his father's best friend, Clifford Ludlow."

"Byzantine, Cad."

"Good word."

"So's *egregious*. What's it mean?"

They looked at each other and laughed. "Look it up," they chorused in unison. Ever since they had been old enough to read, both their parents had insisted they use the dictionary themselves to look up the meaning of words, with the result that, as adults, they both had a wide and varied vocabulary.

"What's he like?"

"Clifford Ludlow?" she asked.

"No. Fiske Spencer. Do you like him? I kind of think you do." Thad wiggled his eyebrows. Caddy wished she had a camera ready; he looked like a Pan when he did that, his upper torso that of a handsome man while the lower half was hidden beneath the covers.

She thought about Fiske for a moment and found herself slowly nodding her head. "I do. He's straightforward and he works hard." And I like the way he smiles at me, and the way he smells, she thought guiltily.

"Funny?"

"He likes to tease, but it's not mean, it's just . . . I don't know, nice. I like his eyes," she added slowly, thinking about the way his eyes changed color when he looked at her, the way they had become determined when he was talking to the group, and the way they had bored right into her just before she had thought he was going to kiss her.

"What about his mother and father, and his sister—do you like them too?"

"I'm not sure about his father. I don't think he has much use for me. His mother is nice though. I like her. She used to be a concert pianist, and she loves to garden." Caddy pictured the herbaceous border and wondered if she would ever see it bloom. "I'm not sure about his sister; she hasn't been particularly welcoming to me, but that's okay. She and Fiske are very close, I can sense that."

"Like we are."

"Yup." She looked at him: wasn't his face thinner than the last time she had been down? She loved him deeply and it hurt her to see him pale from being housebound. His life had been filled with too much suffering, yet he rarely complained. She didn't think she could have been as brave if their positions were reversed and she was the one with multiple sclerosis.

"Did you write the new story down?" she inquired softly. She felt the small knot of worry ease when his face lit up with eagerness and delight.

"Yes. It took a hell of a long time, but it's on paper. You're going to love it, Cad. At least I hope you will." He looked suddenly uncertain.

"You know I will. I want you to write the others down too, all of them. I have an idea about your Max stories."

"What?" he demanded.

"Wait and see." She pulled her hair over her eyes and peered at him mysteriously.

"Listen, Caddy. If you're thinking of showing them to somebody, don't. I don't want anybody else to read them," he stated firmly. His eyes narrowed and he looked determined. Only his hand, which pleated a corner of the light blanket that covered his knees, let her know how uncomfortable he was about the prospect.

"Not even if it's someone I trust?" She thought of Josie's serene face and her warm, friendly manner. She knew Thad would love Josie if only he could meet her.

"No, God damn it. I'd feel like a fool having someone I don't know passing judgment on them. You and I like them, and that's enough."

"Okay, okay. I won't." She felt deeply disappointed, but she wouldn't argue with him. Arguing only made him more tired, and when he was tired his symptoms were worse.

After a moment when Thad looked as if he might pleat the entire blanket, he asked casually, "Who's the person you trust? Fiske?"

"It's Josie Northrup. She's an editor in Boston, and I kind of thought she might take a look at them and tell us if they're good enough to publish." She pulled herself up and sat on the edge of his bed, holding his thin hand between hers. "They're great stories, Thad. Please let me show a couple to her."

He shook his head, but she persisted. "I was going to do it without telling you, but that wouldn't be right. I won't if you say no, but I wish you'd think about it."

"No one will like them. They wouldn't understand." His voice was adamant.

"Children would. They'd understand all the adventures and silliness, just the way we do." She leaned over and yanked gently on his ponytail. "Do let me try, Thad. I'd only send them to Josie, no one else, I promise."

"Maybe."

She leaned back against the foot of the bed as if she didn't really care, but secretly she was pleased. If he was even considering it there was a good chance he'd agree, and she was certain his tales were good enough to be published. Already she was spinning fantasies where he had a career of his own that he could pursue, one that would give him an outlet for all his pent-up energies while largely confined to his bed and his wheelchair. Satisfied with her night's work, she turned the conversation to other topics.

"I didn't tell you what happened with Ward."

Thad grimaced. He had met Ward several times when Caddy had been in college, and he hadn't liked him. He called him "Prime Time Ward" and said he was like one of those plastic masters of ceremonies on television quiz shows. "Tell me. It better be good." He frowned again, as if he had been struck by an unpleasant thought. "You're not going to marry him, are you? I wouldn't mind if you got married, but not to that jerk."

"Thad. That's awful. No, I'm not going to marry him, quite the opposite. I think he really wanted me only to be a proper little politician's wife. He wanted me to give up the job on Kincade just to go to a dinner with him. It made me realize I didn't really want to marry him at all. He's the one who ended it though," she finished slowly.

"I never liked him anyway." He threw a small pillow into the air. It fell to the floor and they both ignored it —Thad because he couldn't reach it, and Caddy because she didn't want to remind him that she could.

She feigned hurt feelings. "Well, I like that. Here I am, the only man in my life has ended a relationship of over three years, and all you can do is gloat. What about my stressed-out psyche? What about my acute anxiety and underlying depression? What about the fact that I've chosen to be an old spinster living alone with her cat?"

His face filled with quick concern. "You do feel badly, don't you? I'm sorry then, Cad. Have you told the Aged P's?"

She smiled at their childhood name for their parents, which they had borrowed from the Dickens novel they read aloud to each other one winter.

James Wilcox was tall and reedy, his parchment-like skin stretched taut over his high cheekbones, and Louisa was short and frowsy, but together they were a formidable pair, much respected in academic circles. They never argued with each other, or disciplined their children, or minded the lack of money. Thad used to say their parents could eat the same food night after night and never notice, and Caddy was pretty sure he was right. They smiled at each other.

"The aged P's will probably never notice Ward's gone," Thad pointed out.

"Much less think it's worth worrying about."

"As long as you're happy, dear," Thad said in a falsetto that was meant to sound like their mother. He assumed his normal, deep voice. "Are you going to tell them?"

"Not yet," she said. "Tomorrow. I wanted to tell you first."

"Poor Cad. Don't be unhappy." He dropped his head back on the pillow.

She was filled with compunction; she could see he was getting tired. The nurse's aide who took care of him had told her he should be asleep by ten, and it was after midnight. She should have paid more attention to the time. Straightening his covers, she kissed him lightly on the forehead.

"Never mind. I'll be all right." She turned off the bedside lamp and fumbled her way back to the couch.

"Do you want to talk about it?" His voice drifted sleepily across the space between them.

"Not tonight. Not really."

"I can listen, you know." She could tell he was making a valiant effort to stay awake, and she smiled in the dark.

"I know, Thad. You always do. Go to sleep now; we'll talk more tomorrow and you'll read me the story."

"Night, Cad."

"Night, bro."

She listened until his regular breathing told her he was asleep and then, quietly so as not to wake him, she slipped out from beneath the blanket and tiptoed to the door. With one last look at the still figure, she left the room and closed the door gently behind her. She stood on the tiny landing, looking up at the narrow stairs to her own room, but she was too wide awake to sleep. The house was chilly and she shivered. A door opened on the landing below and a faint light showed up the stairs. She heard her mother descending down to the main floor and she followed the sound.

"Caddy. You startled me." Louisa Wilcox had one hand on the door to the library. Her white hair stuck up in a halo around her head and her other hand clutched a shawl around her shoulders. All of a sudden she looked very old and very small to Caddy.

"I couldn't sleep and I thought I'd make a cup of tea. Want one?"

Louisa looked up and down the short hall dubiously as if searching for an answer; Caddy's heart sank a little. Clearly her mother longed to go into the library. Caddy was unsurprised. She was used to finding one or both of her parents reading at the long partner's desk when she came home late, and it seemed perfectly natural now to find Louisa preparing to go to work in the small hours of the morning. Without waiting for an answer she went into the old-fashioned kitchen, made two cups of strong China tea, and returned to the library, a box of crackers under her arm.

"You're up late." She put the cup of tea on the table next to her mother's open book and took a seat across from her. The table was surprisingly neat, the only spot in the room that didn't have stacks of pamphlets and notebooks piled in untidy heaps. Bookcases rose from floor to ceiling on three sides of the room; only the windows had prevented her father from installing shelves on the fourth side.

"I just wanted to finish . . ." Louisa's voice trailed off as she looked yearningly at the open book. Once again, Caddy refused to take the hint.

"Mother." She leaned forward, trying to capture Louisa's attention. "Ward and I have broken up."

Louisa looked up and smiled a sweet smile. When she smiled, Caddy thought, it was clear to see Louisa had once been a very pretty woman. Her skin was soft and still unlined, and her eyes, dark and almond-shaped like Thad's, lit up when she smiled. "You did? Well, I'm surprised," Louisa said vaguely. "I thought you were fond of Ward."

"I am, or I thought I was." Caddy realized she was holding her breath, wondering if her mother would finally talk to her about love. They had never discussed the subject before and, indeed, all Caddy's education about sex had come from a book Louisa left in her room when she was thirteen.

But Louisa merely asked, "I'm sure you know best, dear, but are you sure that's what you want?" One hand was still holding the page of her open book flat in readiness.

"I'm sure, but it's been difficult. I feel . . ." She faltered and stopped. She wanted to pour out her heart to her mother, but she didn't know how. She wanted to tell Louisa how confusing it had been to care enough for Ward to share the intimacy of his bed and yet not love him enough to marry him. She wanted to tell her mother how hard she worked, how much she loved what she did, and perhaps even validate the way she seemed to be sacrificing everything to her career. She longed to ask Louisa if she thought her daughter would ever be able to love anyone and be loved on equal terms in return, if she thought Caddy was capable of the same kind of commitment Louisa seemed to have made so easily to James. She even found herself wanting to tell her mother about Fiske, and that bothered her as much as anything. Why would she want to talk about Fiske to Louisa? Miserably, she twisted her teacup.

"Your decision doesn't seem to have made you very happy, Catherine. We rather thought you enjoyed all that New York café society," her mother said mildly, eyeing the rotating teacup.

"It wasn't my decision. It was Ward's. I did find his kind of life in New York exciting at first, but it wasn't enough. He wanted me to give up my work."

"Ward wanted you to do that?" Louisa was clearly horrified. She looked around the library as if she couldn't imagine ever being separated from her own work.

"He said I could take pictures as a hobby." She clenched her hands into fists and burst out, "How could I have imagined I was in love and been so wrong? I spent almost three years with him and I didn't know him at all. If I could be so wrong with him, I could be wrong with anyone." It felt good to finally say the things that had been bottled up inside her since that awful lunch with Ward.

"You know, dear, I've always rather thought you were a romantic."

Caddy turned her head away in skepticism. Louisa couldn't know her at all if she was calling her a romantic.

"No. Hear me out." Louisa folded her hands on the table and lectured her daughter in a gentle voice. "A romantic in the best sense of the word. Even though you're steadfast about your profession, you're still a dreamer and an idealist. You wanted someone—a knight in shining armor, perhaps—in your life, and you thought Ward was the one. You're not the first person who's made that mistake. You really mustn't let it make you bitter."

Caddy sat back, amazed, watching her mother serenely sip her tea. Louisa had never spoken to her this way. For the first time she realized her mother truly cared about her in the way she had always longed for; that, indeed, beneath the air of vagueness was a maternal heart. She leaned forward eagerly, ready at last to open the floodgates of her thoughts, but the moment had passed.

Louisa, having said what she had to say, was smoothing the pages of her book, her mind obviously wandering back to her research. She nodded her head gently but dismissively as she said, "I'm sure you'll know the right thing to do. You always know best, dear. You always take care of everything so well."

She smiled her sweet smile again and bent her head, unable to resist the lure of her book any longer.

Disappointment welled up inside Caddy and she sighed. Her mother hadn't really changed a bit. Their conversation was ended for the night. She hadn't come to Philadelphia expecting to confide in her mother, she'd really come to see Thad. It was meeting Louisa unexpectedly in the middle of the night that had created a false sense of intimacy. Her mother had always treated her as an adult, responsible for her own decisions, and this time, despite her startling evaluation of her daughter, was no exception. It should have come as no surprise to Caddy that her mother treated her as an independent, self-sufficient adult: that was how she had been raised, and that was what she had become.

She closed the library door behind her and started up the drafty staircase. The patterned runner on the stairs was worn thin and she avoided the holes by habit; the entire house was worn thin, she thought as she reached the top floor. Living on their salaries as they did, her parents had no money left over for the luxuries of fresh paint and paper or even enough heat, and she sprinted for her bed. When Caddy was younger, one of their books had been adapted as a textbook, and for a brief, halcyon period they all had new clothes and James had even invested in a sensible secondhand car. But that was long ago, and now their modest salaries were stretched as thin as the rug, supporting themselves and their son.

The light from the street filtered through her louvered window and she thought about the houses of her friends when she was growing up, filled with warmth and flowers and comfort; the larger homes of

Ward's friends, with their servants and enormous rooms filled with chattering guests; and she thought about Kincade. The islanders pretended to live such Spartan lives, but it was all a game to them; none of them could imagine what Spartan really meant. Well, she knew, all right. It meant wearing hand-me-down clothes, doing all the housework yourself, going through school on scholarship, and always worrying if there would be enough money for Thad to have the care he needed. It meant never having a vacation unless a kind friend invited you somewhere, never being able to enter a restaurant unless you were the guest, never having any money at all for special treats. It meant sometimes making decisions you might not make if you didn't have to earn every penny you spent.

Despite it all, she knew she and Thad were very lucky. She had loved him from the moment she saw his tiny red face when Louisa and James brought him home from the hospital. They had laid the infant in her arms and she had held him, knowing even then that he was something so special that nothing could ever come between them. He had opened his eyes and looked at her as if he understood. She had hovered over him and tended him, delighting in his funny little ways when he was a toddler. They had been each other's best friend growing up, and they still were. She pumped her pillow into a more comfortable shape. And we always will be, she thought fiercely. I won't let him die. She could hear a church bell ring twice. As she drifted off to sleep, the shadowy figure of a man crept into her dreams and she thought it was Ward, but when the figure turned, it was Fiske's face and Fiske's eyes she saw.

CHAPTER 13

James Wilcox spooned honey over his breakfast granola, added a dollop of sour cream, and proceeded to eat his creation with relish. Caddy was aware of Thad looking at her with a straight face and dancing eyes. Their father ate on, oblivious to the amusement he was affording his children. Louisa spooned her oatmeal sedately, a closed book on the table next to her dish and a dreamy look on her face as she contemplated her husband. Overhead they could hear the footsteps of Thad's nurse's aide as she made his bed and ran the water for his daily bath. It was eight o'clock in the morning, and for the first time in months the Wilcox family was gathered around the old dining room table in the back parlor together, sharing a meal. Caddy checked her watch surreptitiously: She really needed to be on the ten o'clock Amtrak back to New York.

"You've just arrived, Catherine," her father said. "Surely you can spare your family more than one night."

She looked at him guiltily. She knew she should stay longer, but finding Thad in good spirits if not in good health had reassured her, and she was anxious to return to her darkroom to finish cropping the final kite series. Thad had his head lowered, trying to hide his disappointment.

"I meant to stay longer, but I just couldn't finish before I left. It's a big assignment for me, Father, and I want to do it right. You understand, don't you?"

"Harrumph." He finished his tea and looked at his wife.

"James." She smiled.

"I suppose so. If I knew you were going to fly in and out like some bird of passage I wouldn't have gone to the Athenaeum last night."

"Sure you wouldn't." Thad smiled his mother's sweet smile at his gruff father, while the other two looked amused.

James was Secretary of the Acquisitions Committee at the Philadelphia Athenaeum, and he never had let anybody or anything interfere with one of the meetings he chaired when the prestigious private library was deciding what books and manuscripts to acquire for its collection. Now he smiled wryly in acknowledgment of their insight and folded his napkin neatly and inserted it into the heavy silver napkin ring with his initials on it. Louisa slipped her napkin into a smaller silver ring of her own and rose when her husband did. She looked at her husband, waiting for him to speak. Thad and Caddy watched him too. This was always a favorite moment of theirs, when their parents were anxious to escape to their work but didn't know how to do it without making it obvious that they preferred the company of each other in the solitude of their study to that of anyone, including their two children. Their children knew they were loved, but they were perfectly used to being forgotten for long stretches while their parents chased on paper the aboriginal tribe that might make them famous, but would never make them wealthy.

"Well, then." He beamed down at his offspring. They waited, not daring to look at each other.

"Well, then. We'll wish you a safe journey back to Gotham, Catherine, and Thad, we'll see you at supper." He looked at his wife as if he thought he'd done rather a good job of it, and she nodded briskly. He bent down as if to kiss his daughter on the forehead, but she forestalled him by rising and putting both arms around his neck.

"I'll be back soon," she promised. Undemonstrative as her father was, she loved him dearly and she always felt at moments like this, when she hugged him, that he actually rather enjoyed it.

"Fine, fine." He patted her and extricated himself, but he smiled slightly.

She turned to her mother, who was looking at her anxiously. Caddy knew how little Louisa liked such demonstrations of affection, so she contented herself with kissing her mother on the cheek.

"You'll call me if you need anything, won't you?" she asked Louisa.

"Yes, dear. Of course. We always do, you know that." Her mother was already turning away when she paused, obviously struck by a fleeting thought. "You won't be unhappy, will you? Without that young man?"

"No, Mother. I'll be fine." Caddy gave Louisa the only answer she ever wanted to hear and was rewarded by a smile of relief. The senior Wilcoxes disappeared into the library, and soon the low murmur of their voices could be heard as they consulted with one another.

"*Are* you fine, Cad?"

She turned back and looked at her brother fondly, all remembrance of her broken night's sleep gone from her mind. "I'm okay, Thaddeus. Don't you worry."

"You're always taking care of us, sending money and checking in with my nurse to see if I'm okay. Who takes care of you?" he grumbled, pushing a piece of toast around his plate with a fork. "We're all like a bunch of leeches, feeding off you."

"That's gross. It's a little early in the morning for leeches, isn't it?" She slipped back into her chair and poured herself another cup of coffee, leaning her elbows on the table while she drank it.

He looked vaguely perturbed, as if struck by a new thought he didn't much like. "Well, who does?"

She racked her brain for a way to reassure him so that he wouldn't worry about her. She was never free of the worry that she might precipitate the stress that made his disease accelerate, and she wanted to avoid that at all costs.

"Eddie," she teased. "Agatha. Max the Balloonist."

"Cad," he warned, and she turned serious.

"I really am okay, Thad. I promise. I don't need to be taken care of, I'm used to doing for myself and I like it this way. I'd probably make anybody's life hell if they tried to take care of me and tell me what to do." She thought of the way Ward had promised he would take care of her, as if that were the one thing she had been waiting to hear, and she shivered.

"But I don't mind."

"You're different," she said tenderly. "You're sweet like Louisa and smart like James. Me, I'm going to grow old and be a battle-ax, just like Agatha."

"Cad." He was outraged. "You won't do that. You'd hate being married three times."

She smiled wryly; anyone else would have seen her father in her at that moment. "I'm not sure I'd like being married at all. Sooner or later it always seems to come down to living somebody else's life."

The phone rang, and they both looked toward where the sound was coming from. It emanated from a small table by the door, covered with an untidy heap of university bulletins. She hurried to it, groping around for the instrument she knew was buried underneath.

"Catherine." The peremptory voice Agatha assumed whenever she had to use the telephone issued from the receiver.

"Aunt Agatha. Is anything wrong?" She turned so she could watch the expression on Thad's face; sure enough, he grimaced when he heard her say the name of her caller. Some years ago, when the MS was less advanced, James had taken his son for a visit to Gramercy Square. It had been a disaster from the moment Agatha had looked at the frail boy and sniffed, plunging into a determined lecture on how all illness was simply a question of mind over matter and look at her, almost eighty and never an unwell day in her life. Thad, fresh from a stay in Children's Hospital on Bainbridge Street, had taken a very un-Thad-like violent dislike to her, and nothing Caddy had been able to do had ever changed his mind.

"What could possibly be wrong? Really, Catherine,

you must stop assuming all the woes of the world are yours to fix. Now," she continued briskly without waiting for a response, "that young man of yours has been on the phone again."

"Ward called me?" She was mystified. His letter had left no questions unanswered. He couldn't be calling her.

"No," Agatha said scornfully. "The charming young man who visited here. He flew you up to that island you're always disappearing to, God knows why."

She pictured Fiske's teasing smile, his square jaw, the easy way he moved. "Fiske Spencer? Why would he call?"

Thad grinned, but she ignored him.

"He and Nelson Lovering wanted you to lunch with them. Since I knew you wouldn't be home in time, I've invited them here for cocktails," Agatha finished with satisfaction.

"You've done what?" Caddy felt suddenly breathless.

"You heard me perfectly well. I've invited them for cocktails. This evening." Her aunt's voice was smug and Caddy could picture her, Eddie asleep on the foot of her bed, while she drank her morning chocolate in the high canopied bed she had brought back with her from Paris forty years ago.

"Why tonight? You know I have work to do." Averting her eyes from Thad's penetrating stare, Caddy toyed with the telephone cord, her heart beating as she remembered how Fiske had appeared in her dream the night before.

"Nonsense. You can do that another time. You work too hard anyway, child. Besides, I want to meet this Nelson Lovering. I've never known an ornithologist— it might be interesting."

Despite herself, Caddy started to laugh. "You mean he's single, don't you?" she accused her aunt. "You're outrageous."

"So they tell me." Agatha sounded pleased. "Don't be late."

Caddy shook the receiver, but true to form, her aunt had already disconnected. She replaced the telephone in its hiding place and looked at her brother.

"What's wrong? You look funny."

"Your Aunt Agatha has invited Fiske Spencer and his uncle Nelson Lovering for drinks tonight in New York."

"Poor Uncle Nelson. He's in for it."

"It sounds as if they wanted to pay a call and she maneuvered them into cocktails. I wonder why they accepted." She frowned in puzzlement.

He laughed gleefully. "Nelson's not married, right? She's probably shopping for husband number four. I think you've got the outline of a disaster, here, Cad. You and Aunt Agatha and Eddie all waiting for Fiske and Uncle Nelson, gin and marzipan at the ready. I can see it now: Nelson walks in, drooling Eddie nips him in the ankle, he falls into Agatha's lap, and they live happily ever after. End of scene."

"God." She looked at him in awe. "How awful. Fiske barely survived the one time he met her—I can't believe he's coming back. What do you suppose they want?"

"Dalliance, Cad. Dalliance. It's obvious: Nelson is using you to get to your fabulously beautiful and seductive aunt."

"Stop it, bro. He doesn't even know her, and besides, I never met a man less interested in women in my life. He belongs to his birds, heart and soul."

"He's gay?" Thad straightened up and asked with interest.

"Don't jump to conclusions, Thad. Not everyone who stays single is gay."

"Then if it isn't a romantic interlude, it must be business. Maybe they want you to photograph more kites."

"It couldn't be—that's all done. If there are more of them, I don't want to know about it."

"Hell, I don't know. You'll find out when you get there."

They were quiet for a moment, each pondering the strange phone call, and then they looked at each other and shrugged.

"You'll call me after they leave tonight, won't you, Cad? It has the makings of a hilarious story worthy of Max."

"Easy for you to say, you don't have to be there."

His voice was wistful. "I wish I could."

"I know."

All the amusement left his face, and he looked so wretched that she said impulsively, "You could, you know."

"Come to New York? How?" His eyes lit up, but his voice was cautious, as if he didn't dare hope.

"Not this time, because I have to leave almost right away, but soon. I could rent a car and drive you up. Agatha would love to have you, even though you acted like such a jerk the last time. We could do stuff—go to the theater and the galleries." *And you could have a better life,* she thought, determined to make it happen.

He turned his head away so she wouldn't see the disappointment that had replaced the hope in his eyes. "I don't think I could do all that. Go to the theater and everything."

"Sure you could. We could get one of those folding wheelchairs and you could speed around the galleries like crazy. Oh, Thad. Let's do it. We'll have the best time." In her eagerness she leaned too far across the table and the rest of her coffee spilled on the table-cloth.

"Nice, Cad," he scoffed.

She ignored the spill. "Say yes," she commanded.

"I don't know . . ."

"You want to, don't you?"

"Yes."

She felt a surge of excitement and she hurried to solidify his agreement. "Then it's a done deal. As soon as I get this story off to Dave in final layout, you're coming to New York and that's that." She rose quickly, before he could protest, and fled from the room, taking the stairs two at a time to collect her suitcase and rush for the train. Before she left the house she looked in on him again, but hearing the low murmur of voices as he talked with his nurse's aide, she contented herself with a shouted farewell and a promise to call him later that night from New York.

By the time she reached Gramercy Square almost four hours later, she was tired and irritable. Thirtieth Street Station in Philadelphia had been crowded and dirty, the train had been too noisy to read Thad's story with any concentration, and she had been unable to find a cab to take her downtown to the house. Lugging her suitcase into the subway, she had torn the low heel off her boot and wound up limping the last four blocks across town. The house was quiet when she arrived, which meant Agatha must be having her nap, and she hauled her suitcase up the three flights of stairs and dumped it in the middle of her room with a sigh of relief.

She looked around in appreciation. Every time she returned to her little set of rooms it seemed more like her home than the house in Philadelphia; the way the light touched the prints she had hung and the few pieces of furniture she had collected pleased her very much. She looked at her watch. It was only a little after two o'clock, which meant she had the rest of the afternoon to work uninterrupted. Whistling softly in the way she did when she was content, she changed quickly into her work clothes and disappeared into the darkroom.

Four hours later, freshly showered and wearing a short linen skirt and her best silk top, she descended to the parlor. Her shining hair hung loosely down her back, gold hoops were fastened in her ears, and she had splashed herself liberally with her one bottle of Chanel bought at a duty-free shop the last time she returned to the country from a shoot in South America.

"Lovely, my dear." Agatha beamed in approval. "It's about time you got out of those pants you insist on wearing. You look like a lady—and a very beautiful one at that."

She kissed her aunt affectionately. "You're the beautiful one, Aunt. Where did you get that shawl?"

"It is nice, isn't it?" Agatha preened. The gold and silver threads of the shawl glimmered in the early evening light. Diamonds glittered at her ears, and it looked as if she had added even more rings to the ones she usually wore. Her lips were carefully outlined in a magenta red and her eyes shadowed with dark blue mascara. Caddy knew she should look like a monster, but she thought her aunt magnificent: Only Agatha could have carried off such a dramatic getup with noblesse. The front doorbell rang at that moment, and with an imperious gesture she motioned to Caddy to admit their guests.

"Hello." Fiske had obviously been going to say something else, but his eyes darkened. He halted abruptly and stared at her. She was very conscious that her pulse was racing and her heart was beating rapidly. Surreptitiously, she took a deep breath and smiled up at him.

Nelson, who had been standing behind his nephew, pushed past him impatiently so that he could bestow an enthusiastic kiss on each of Caddy's cheeks. He presented her with a large bunch of violets. "Here, my dear. A touch of Kincade for you. Eliza sends her love." He walked by her into the hall and looked up at the moldings and the skylight set in the roof far above. "Splendid. You don't see many houses like this anymore. Untouched, I see. Splendid." He looked into the stiff front parlor and chuckled. "I grew up in a room like this. Wonderful. It could be eighty years ago." He rubbed his hands in anticipation. "Where's our hostess? I'm looking forward to meeting her. Eliza says we know her family."

Nelson was standing in the doorway to the parlor, still admiring the proportions of the long room. Caddy stared at his back with amazement. She could barely recognize him as the grizzled, unkempt figure who had led her through the marshes. He was wearing an old suit, but it was clearly a tailor-made one; his shirt was freshly starched, he wore a jaunty bow tie, and there was a bright blue bachelor's button in his lapel. His shoes were gleaming and his hair had been newly barbered; even his beard was neatly trimmed. He looked like a boulevardier bent on an evening of gaiety, and she thought of Thad's dark suggestion that perhaps he was looking for a romantic dalliance; all of a sudden it didn't seem so impossible. She choked back a laugh and turned to Fiske to share her amusement with him, but he was still looking at her with a puzzled expression on his face.

"What's wrong?" she asked lightly.

"Nothing. I was just thinking," he responded slowly. His gaze didn't waver and she felt herself beginning to blush.

"You think too much, my boy," Nelson boomed. "You should try not to be so serious. All work and no play, you know."

"Come on. Agatha's waiting. She's been looking forward to having you both here." Caddy led them down the hall and threw open the door. Eddie was waiting. He disregarded the older man entirely and headed straight for Fiske's ankles.

"Why me?" Fiske asked plaintively. He sidled sideways and glared down at the dog.

"He likes you, young man. That's a compliment. Eddie doesn't like many people."

"Then I'm honored." He held Agatha's proffered hand in his and smiled down at her.

Caddy was amused, knowing Agatha wasn't about to flirt with Fiske when there was a new man in the room. "And *you* must be Nelson Lovering. Welcome," Agatha said with a roguish smile to that gentleman. She offered Nelson her hand, and to Caddy's sheer delight, Nelson bent over it with a smooth bow. Agatha patted the cushion next to her. "Sit by me. Caddy will serve the drinks. She knows just how I like them made." Without looking at her niece, she made another gesture, which sent Caddy hastening to the drinks table.

She had mixed the gin and splash of vermouth and was carefully stirring it in an iced pitcher when she thought it was safe to risk a look at Fiske. He was standing near her, watching her work, his expression a mixture of glee and triumph.

"What's so funny?" she asked. "You look like you swallowed a canary."

"Notice anything missing?"

She looked around the room. Agatha and Nelson were talking together like old friends, their heads close together. There was no sign of Eddie.

"What did you do with him?"

Fiske nodded his head significantly at the door. She could hear a faint sound, but it seemed to be coming from further away than the other side of the closed door. She felt a bubble of laughter rise up inside her. Her lips twitched with amusement as she raised her eyebrows in a query.

"In the cupboard in the hall," he whispered, taking the tray containing the four martini glasses she had carefully filled.

"He'll suffocate." She tried to sound severe, but failed miserably. Her eyes were dancing as she looked at him.

"Pity." He winked at her before he turned and offered the tray to Agatha with a perfectly straight face.

The next fifteen minutes passed in pleasant conversation. Agatha flirted outrageously with Nelson as they discovered a wealth of people they knew in common. Fiske asked Caddy about her trip to Philadelphia and listened with interest to her plan to ask Josie to read Thad's latest story.

"You don't think she'd mind, do you?" she asked earnestly, finding she really wanted his opinion.

"Not at all," he reassured her. "She loves discovering a new talent. I agree with you: If there's anything in his stories, she'll know right away. She'll be able to tell you how to go about getting them published."

"It would be wonderful for him."

"Nice for you, too, to know he'd have a way to help support himself. Everybody should have a preoccupation they love." He finished the last of his martini and looked into his empty glass.

"Catherine. I think we could use another drink, if you don't mind." Agatha coyly covered Nelson's hand with her own pudgy one.

"I'll do it." Fiske rose promptly.

"No. No. Catherine knows just how I like them," Agatha insisted firmly. Obediently, he sat back down.

"Five parts gin, practically no vermouth, and a lot of ice," Caddy whispered to Fiske as she left her seat for the drinks table.

Nelson raised his voice, addressing her as she swiftly poured the gin into a crystal pitcher and began stirring in the ice. "Don't you make mine too strong, young lady. I have a proposition for you and I want to keep a clear head."

"What is it?" She poured the chilled mixture into the glasses and carried the tray back to the group. She was conscious of Fiske watching her as she offered the tray to each person in turn. When she paused in front of him she looked at the tray, not his face, but she was acutely aware of his hand as he removed his glass.

Agatha adjusted her shawl over one shoulder and gave a sidelong glance to see if Nelson was watching her, but he had focused his attention on Caddy. Fiske drank his martini imperturbably, observing his uncle with amusement.

"Otis Ross. Ever hear of him?" Nelson beamed with excitement.

"Of course, the famous journalist." What could Nelson have to do with someone so famous, she wondered.

"And naturalist, my dear. One of the best. He's head of programming now at Republic Television, and his wildlife series won an Emmy last year for best natural history documentary. I want you to meet him. I've told him all about you."

"That's nice of you—I'd love to meet him. I watched the entire science series they did season before last and it was wonderful, but I don't know why he would want to meet me." She was excited and curious, but felt a bit wary at being foisted on someone so important.

"He's an old friend. Well, not old, he's thirty years younger than I am, but we've known each other for over a decade. Actually, I've done a little consulting for him now and again," Nelson added modestly.

"What Uncle Nelson means is, Ross comes to him for advice whenever he can. Ross would love to get Uncle Nelson to moderate one of his series, but Nelson won't play," Fiske informed Caddy. He grinned at his uncle, who flapped his hand as if he were trying to brush something away.

"Never mind that." Nelson edged forward eagerly in his seat and looked intently at Caddy, his brilliant blue eyes snapping with excitement.

She loved his enthusiasm and found herself wondering if she would be as full of élan when she reached that age. She hoped so. She leaned forward herself in order to hear him better.

"He's going to do a new kind of documentary on Africa along the lines of the Civil War piece that young Kenneth Burns did for PBS a few years ago. He wants to do an exhaustive study of endangered species, and he plans on using old photographs of the ones that have already disappeared. He'll put their stories together with shots of species presently endangered to show how quickly a life form can vanish."

"It sounds fascinating, but what could I add to that? You're talking about television and I'm a still photographer."

"That's the beauty of it." Nelson gave a tiny jump in his seat, and Fiske chuckled. "He's going to present it in stills with lots of narrative voice-over, rather than action, because he feels it will lend a new kind of credibility to the story."

"But will it?" She thought it sounded very ambitious and perhaps a little arty. Would the viewers, used to live film of wildlife, be held by a series of still shots?

"Of course. Think of *Civil War*. There were no live people, no moving pictures of action. Just old photographs and film of places without people."

"You could do that," Fiske said calmly, helping himself to a handful of dubious-looking almonds piled in a silver dish.

"What would I photograph?" She honestly couldn't see what role she could play in the project.

"Anything you like." Nelson roared triumphantly. "Otis is head of programming now; he doesn't direct the series himself anymore. He's looking for a director to take over the whole show."

"Nelson, you're crazy. I don't have any experience directing." She began to wonder if perhaps he had spent too much time out of the real world on his secluded island.

"Listen to the man, Catherine. You're jumping to conclusions. You must try to be open-minded." Agatha finished her drink and looked reflectively across the room at the gin bottle. This time it was Fiske who rose and gathered up the empty glasses.

"You could. I know you could. I didn't even have to tell Otis about you; he knew who you were."

"He did?" She was amazed. Her work had been appearing in wildlife publications for years, and she had won the Audubon award, but why would anyone but the editors know who she was? She was flattered to think she had been recognized by a naturalist as renowned as Otis Ross. Maybe Nelson wasn't so crazy after all. She was tense with excitement, and she sipped from the glass Fiske put into her hand without really noticing.

"He was interested. He was interested." Nelson sat back with a sigh of satisfaction as if he had accomplished his mission.

"He was?" she repeated dumbly.

"Do you hear an echo?" Fiske asked Agatha with raised eyebrows.

"I don't know about an echo, young man, but I know an opportunity when I hear one. Say thank you, Catherine," she admonished her niece.

"Thank you," Caddy said faintly, still looking at Nelson in disbelief.

"I take it that means Uncle Nelson has your permission to arrange an interview between you and Otis Ross?" Fiske smiled at her. Fiske managing things again, bringing us to the point, she thought in the midst of her confusion.

"I will, I mean he does—oh, I don't know what I mean. What will I say to Mr. Ross? Should I take my work for him to see? Does he want to talk to the editors at *Nature's World* and *Audubon*? Or *National Geographic*? Should I send him my book?" Her words tumbled out as she tried to think of all the things she could do to get the job. Agatha was right, but it was more than an opportunity. It was the chance of a lifetime for her, and she wanted to do everything she could to make sure Otis Ross chose her.

"Then that's it. I'll call tomorrow and set things in motion." Nelson looked at his nephew in satisfaction.

"Well done, Uncle." Without looking at Nelson, Fiske set his empty glass down on the little marble-topped table. His gaze was fixed on Caddy as he rose, and when he spoke again, his words were for her alone. "We've overstayed our welcome, I'm afraid."

She felt drawn to her feet by the intensity of his look. Unconsciously she put one hand on his arm in her earnestness to make him understand the enormity of what had just been presented to her. "How can you say that, when Nelson has opened a door that may change my life?"

His hand quickly covered hers and his voice was gentle when he answered, "I know. I didn't mean that. I meant, I think we should go while we still can. Neither of us is used to martinis." He smiled a crooked smile. "You won't let it change your life too much, will you?"

She turned toward the door. Behind her, Agatha had risen and accepted the arm Nelson offered her with a courtly bow. "It's all a dream, really. It may never happen," Caddy said in a low voice.

Fiske touched her shoulder. "It will. If you make it happen."

They had reached the door, and she looked up at him as if he had the answer to a question she hadn't even thought to ask. He bent his head down to hers, their eyes locked, and she held her breath, waiting to hear what he was going to say. Whatever that was was forever halted by her aunt's formidable voice demanding furiously, "Where's Eddie?"

CHAPTER 14

Caddy felt euphoric. Even the insistent blare of an irate taxi as she crossed Fifth Avenue couldn't alter her elation. She reached the sidewalk, smiled sweetly at a Lebanese street vendor selling leather handbags, and paused in front of one of Tiffany's windows. Inside, a mound of eggshells was topped with a huge yellow diamond, and she decided happily that it looked rather silly. Looking around, she wondered what to do. She should buy herself something special so she would always remember today, and then she laughed at herself; as if she could ever forget the day she became Otis Ross's newest director.

Otis had interviewed her more than once. Their first conversation had ranged over so many topics and

places they had both been that they had never really
gotten around to discussing the project. Their second
meeting the following day had taken place in the
drafty Republic Television studios on West Fifty-sixth
Street, when she showed him her work and he spoke in
detail about his plans. She had been flattered that he
knew so much about her at that meeting; obviously he
had done a lot of research on her credentials. Their
third meeting had been largely a discussion of just that
—her credentials, including the work she had done
with Kodak and Rollei digital cameras, feeding her
results into the computers she was able to access
through an acquaintance who taught at the School of
Visual Arts. Both of them had agreed that the new
computer tools provided a breakthrough technique en-
abling a photojournalist to have control over every
facet of a picture, allowing the photographer to capture shifting scenes in a way they had never been de-
fined to the human eye before. They found themselves
united in their belief that digital cameras would en-
hance the truthfulness of the project and should be a
major tool of the series.

Caddy had liked Otis Ross right away. Tall, with
silver hair and tanned skin, he spoke with a deep
southern resonance that lent a gentle authority to his
words. He had seemed to understand without much
explanation how she approached her work, letting her
subjects lead her, and she sensed he approved. They
had discussed her lack of production experience, and
she told him about the work she had done early in her
career as a production assistant for CNN before she
decided to limit herself to still photography. She was
honest when she told him she knew production wasn't
her strength, but he had told her he was looking for
vision, not mechanical expertise. The vision he wanted

was creative, innovative, unafraid; she countered by
promising him she didn't know enough to be scared
and had been relieved when he laughed.

Their third meeting had been their final one, and
then she had waited. For forty-eight hours she heard
nothing. Uncertain about her qualifications to begin
with, she had grown almost despondent, sure her experience could never measure up to that of the other
candidates for the complex project Ross envisioned.
She stayed close to home, finishing up all her free-
lance work, polishing the final galleys of the latest textbook, and turning aside any offers of projects for the
moment. She had cleaned out her darkroom, scrub-
bing the walls and floor until they appeared as if they'd
never been touched before; she had meticulously organized her files, paid all her bills, and cleaned out her
drawers. Then she had sat down and written Josie a
long letter of explanation and inquiry, folded it into a
mailer with Thad's story, and sent it off to Boston. But
Otis still didn't call.

She had picked up the phone several times to call
Nelson to ask if he had heard of Otis reaching a decision, only to restrain herself, not wanting Nelson to
think she was asking him to intercede on her behalf
any more than he already had. She had almost given
up hope and, according to Agatha, was becoming un-
bearable to live with, when the phone rang and it was
Otis, offering her the job. It would take two years of
her life from beginning to completion, she would have
all the resources of the station behind her, and she
would be paid more handsomely than she could ever
have imagined.

Hanging up the receiver after her heartfelt accep-
tance and thanks for the opportunity he was granting
her, she had danced around her room and out onto the

terrace. She had wanted to scream with the sheer joy of being young and alive with two solid years of work ahead that she knew she'd love and that would pay her more money than she'd ever earned before. The terrace had been too small to contain her elation. Pausing only to call Thad and ecstatically share her joyful news with him, she had fled into the street to work off her almost manic energy with a fast-paced walk that had brought her all the way to the corner of Fifty-seventh Street and Fifth Avenue.

Now, her energy somewhat dissipated, she hesitated. A walk around the south end of Central Park might be nice, but a cup of coffee and something to eat would be better. Deciding against the café in the Trump Tower, she headed over to the AT&T building on Madison Avenue where she remembered seeing a news shop and gourmet takeout. It was a lovely day; she would buy a paper and a croissant and sit at one of the small tables outside next to the arcade. Twenty minutes later she drained her coffee cup and sat back, the unread newspaper on the wrought-iron table next to her plate.

It seemed as if all of New York had chosen to cross Madison and Fifty-sixth Street as they enjoyed the fine weather, and she watched the faces of the pedestrians, enjoying their expressions and wishing she had her camera with her. One family of French tourists passed her table, talking volubly while the grandfather of the family lagged behind, eyeing the pretty girls. He winked at her and she winked back. Unable to resist the temptation, she hurried back to the newsstand and bought a disposable Japanese camera, unwrapping it as she returned to the table to wait for the next intriguing face to appear. Two small children with a woeful-looking large dog were next and she snapped their picture; then came a tall Jamaican with his hair in dreadlocks; and next was an elderly couple, hand in hand, their faces filled with serenity. She had the camera to her eye, focusing on a mounted policeman, when a limousine drew up to the building, blocking her view. The car door opened and Hank Davidson emerged, followed by a figure she recognized instantly from his pictures in the news media as the developer Bruce Asher. The two men stood together on the pavement, talking seriously to each other. Asher had one hand on Hank's shoulder and they were smiling at each other in apparent agreement. She exhaled in an audible gasp: This *had* to be about Kincade. Automatically, she took their picture. They shook hands and she quickly snapped three more shots. Asher entered the building, and Hank walked uptown and disappeared into the crowd crossing Fifty-seventh Street.

She was incredulous. It seemed impossible that Barbara's husband could be the one who was secretly negotiating with Bruce Asher. She knew immediately that what she had witnessed was important, but she felt dumbstruck, unable to accept that she had truly seen the two men together, that it wasn't some trick of her imagination. She looked down at her camera and then at the empty sidewalk where the men had stood. They had looked like two old friends, or two business partners at the close of a good deal; they certainly knew each other more than slightly. If Hank and Asher were in any kind of cahoots, and their parting had certainly had that appearance, she had to let Fiske know without losing a minute. She fumbled in her pocket for some loose change and, holding tightly to the evidence locked in her camera, headed for the nearest telephone.

* * *

"Tell me the whole story, right from the start." Fiske put his hand under her elbow and propelled her through the noontime crowds wandering around the South Street Seaport. His face was drawn and he didn't smile at her.

When she had given his secretary her name he had come on the line immediately, but as soon as she blurted out that she'd seen Asher and Hank together, he had ordered her to jump in a cab, saying he would meet her on the corner of Water Street where it dead-ended into the Seaport. He had been waiting, ready to pay the driver when her cab arrived. Caddy felt breathless from the surprise of what she had seen, the fast ride down the FDR Drive to the Seaport, and finding herself unexpectedly walking next to Fiske in the middle of the day. His hand tightened on her elbow, and he pulled her closer to him as they were surrounded by a crowd of noisy schoolchildren on a class trip.

"Wait," he said, looking around. "Let's get out of this mob before you tell me. Let's go into Sweets—we can talk there."

He caught her hand and pulled her into the small doorway off the cobblestoned street and up the narrow stairway to the second floor. Her hand was still in his as the brusque waiter led them to the end table, next to the window.

After he ordered two glasses of wine and the waiter had departed, Fiske leaned forward, his elbows on the table. "Now tell me exactly what you saw."

She drew a deep breath, conscious that he was relying on her to paint an accurate picture of what she had seen, that he trusted her judgment. Despite the gravity of the situation, she felt warmed by his confidence. By the time she finished her story they had finished their wine and were halfway through the platters of soft-shell crabs the waiter had put in front of them. The restaurant had emptied of the brokers who lunched there regularly, and the tables around them were empty.

"Jesus. Hank." Fiske looked devastated. He pushed away his half-full platter, his forehead furrowed in a deep frown of concentration. She was overwhelmed by a desire to reach out and smooth away the lines.

"I can't prove it, but I'm absolutely convinced in my own mind that they were doing business together and they both were pleased about whatever agreement they had reached." Caddy considered her own words and nodded her head; she was still convinced.

He cleared his throat as if something was stuck in it, but she sensed it was more of an attempt to keep his voice steady. "I never even considered that Hank wasn't with us. I counted on him."

She concentrated on the only time she had met Hank, at the Northrups', and remembered the faint sense of something lacking in his apparent sincerity. "Why would he ever be interested in selling? He and your sister have their own house on Kincade; their kids love it there."

"I know. I know." He looked so drawn and worried that she wanted to grasp his hand in comfort. "It's got to be money."

She leaned forward, pushing her wineglass across the table until it was parallel with his. The backs of their hands brushed each other briefly. She waited.

Fiske spoke slowly, as if he was trying to organize the facts he had in some sort of logical order. "He's a bond trader. The bond market's gone to hell. I ran into Carter Williams at the University Club—he's a partner at Hank's firm—and he intimated they were going to fold their bond operation entirely and stick to straight retail trading. Hank said Carter had it all wrong, but now I wonder."

"But don't Babs and Hank have enough . . ." She hesitated, searching for a polite way to mention the fact that they seemed to be wealthy.

"I would have thought so," he answered her question as if she had spoken out loud.

"Is there anything else Hank and Asher could have been talking about except Kincade?" she asked anxiously.

"It's hard to imagine. It's possible, of course, but if Hank had legitimate business dealings with Asher, I think Babs would have mentioned it to me—or to Dad. If she knew."

"I'm sorry I had to be the one to see them," she apologized softly.

He looked up and smiled; she was pleased to see the lines vanish. "Thank God it *was* you. No one else would have had a camera or known what to do with one. Anyone else from the island would have gone off the deep end and started a bigger flap than we have going already."

She was absurdly pleased at his praise. "Because of Hank?"

"I don't want him tarred and feathered until I have a chance to—"

"—protect Babs."

"Exactly."

Caddy could feel the communion between them like a cord stretching across the table. "What will you do?"

"Have the pictures developed this afternoon. Confront Hank with them and ask for an explanation. See what he says."

"Very lawyer-like." She nodded approvingly.

"It may mean nothing . . ."

"But then again it may mean he's the one working behind the scenes to amass enough land for a sale."

"Right." He stared at her bleakly.

"And then?" she prodded gently. Somehow she had to erase that stricken look from his eyes.

"Delay the vote somehow—until the end of summer if I can. Kincade would find it hard to be on the same side with one of their own who used private information and lied about it."

"Can you do that? Delay the vote."

"I think so." Even though his answer was mild, Fiske's voice was flat and his eyes were steely. She could sense he was already planning ahead.

"The camera." They spoke at the same time and laughed.

"Do you want it?" She pushed it across the small wooden table like a gift.

"What do I do with it?" He turned it over in his hands and read the instructions printed on the side.

"Get it developed. Or I will," she offered. "Any camera store will do it for you."

"We'll drop it off after lunch." He put it on the table between them and looked at her directly, focusing all his attention on her face. She blushed.

"It looks like you're having lunch with a bag lady." They made quite a contrast, she thought. She looked ruefully down at her jeans and sneakers and belatedly attempted to straighten her sweatshirt and smooth down the stray hair that had escaped her French braid. He was dressed in a tailored gray double-breasted suit and a serious foulard tie; his black leather shoes were highly polished, and gold cuff links nestled in the starched cuffs of his white shirt. There was something very magnetic about the way he wore his clothes. I feel as if I'm being drawn into him, bit by bit, she thought breathlessly.

He eyed her speculatively. "You could never look like a bag lady. Not on your worst day."

Feeling herself begin to blush again, she retreated hastily behind the dessert menu. She wondered what there was about him that seemed to make her feel like an embarrassed teenager.

The waiter removed their half-eaten lunch and brought them coffee in large china cups. The sun had moved behind a building and the room was dusky; they were the only customers left. They drank in companionable silence, looking at each other.

His eyes crinkled at the corners in the way she had noticed they did when he was pleased. He said gently, "This reminds me of the first time you came to Kincade."

"In the kitchen," she agreed, smiling back.

"Two dazers over coffee."

"I feel a little dazed now. It's been quite a day." She pushed her cup away. "With all the excitement I forgot to tell you: I got the job."

"Otis Ross?"

"Yes."

His face creased in a wide, congratulatory grin. "My God, that's fantastic. Good for you. Good for you *and* congratulations. Why didn't you tell me before?"

"I forgot. Silly, isn't it? This whole thing just swept it away for a while. But, thank you, I *do* feel terrific. It's beyond my wildest dreams, and I owe it all to Nelson— I'll never be able to thank him enough." She took a deep breath. "And . . . I feel a little nervous. I mean, I know I can do the series, but it's a whole new world, working in television."

"You'll be sensational. I'm proud of you."

She was flustered by his unquestioning conviction in her abilities; she couldn't believe how much his confidence in her meant. Too, there was another quality in his voice that told her he wasn't just referring to her new job. "You asked me at Aunt Agatha's not to let it change my life, but it will, because it's going to take every hour of my time for two years. I've had to kill myself to finish the jobs I'm doing for the *National Geographic* by August. Even so, I can't wait. He wants me to begin right away."

"Will you be staying in New York?" He toyed with his glass casually, but his voice was intent.

"Yes," she answered quickly. "Yes. There's one long period when I'll have to be in Africa, filming, but the rest of it's largely editing here in town and researching at the Smithsonian in Washington."

"Good."

He seemed terribly relieved. No, she was putting too much meaning into his words and his expressions, finding him altogether too attractive. She liked the way his eyes smiled into hers and the way his hair grew back from his forehead. He had an air of quiet authority about him that attracted her more and more, whether he was flying a plane, wading through the marsh with her, or, as he was now, looking at her across the table, wearing a Savile Row suit with the confidence of a man used to only the best. She tried to remember Ward's face in her mind, but Fiske's kept getting in the way. Her breath came a little more quickly, she felt too warm, and she knew, without any reservation at all, that she wanted him to kiss her.

The waiter appeared with their check and they both looked up in surprise. It was nearly three o'clock; they had been lingering over their lunch for almost two hours.

Out on the cobblestone street again, he looked down at her and said in a tone that would brook no opposition, "We'll do this again."

"I'd like that." The fresh sea breeze coming from the harbor blew a lock of her hair into her eyes. Before she could brush it back he reached out and gently tucked it behind her ear. She stayed motionless. His hand lingered at the side of her head momentarily. She held her breath, her eyes locked with his, afraid he would kiss her, more afraid that he would not. Bringing up his other hand, he held her head lightly between his palms and, drawing her nearer, turned her face up to his. He studied her face for a long moment before he leaned down and kissed her firmly on the mouth. The warmth she had felt in the restaurant rose up again with dizzying force and, unable to resist, she opened her mouth to him as she returned his kiss with equal fervor.

"I've been wanting to do that for some time now." Fiske's voice was husky.

"Please. Don't," she whispered. Her forehead still rested against his cheek.

He moved his hands to her shoulders and let them linger there briefly and then, as if he were reluctant to let her go, released her. "Why not? Is it me?" he asked, his face expressionless.

"No. I don't know . . . I just can't start . . . please don't ask me." She couldn't look at him. Her heart was pounding, and she felt as if she were shattering into small pieces. She had to regain her control. Around them, people passing by looked at them curiously, but Caddy barely noticed. They were too absorbed in each other. She felt the sting of tears.

"There isn't anyone else, is there?"

She stared down at the cobblestones and shook her

head numbly. How could she possibly explain, after kissing him so passionately?

He bent his head close to hers. "Then you'll let me call you, won't you, Caddy? I promise not to kiss you again unless you want me to." It wasn't really a question at all, she thought.

"You don't understand—" She raised her head defiantly and looked him straight in the eyes.

"I think I do," he interrupted. His face was thoughtful. "You think anything that interferes with your career is bad, and right now I threaten to fall into that category."

"I don't want—" she started to explain, but he put one finger gently across her lips.

"You're wrong, you know, I'm not going to interfere with your career. I won't argue with you though," he said, trailing his finger across the line of her jaw. "But I *am* going to call you and you *will* see me again."

She was unable to resist returning his smile. He looked so much the lawyer, not at all the man who had just kissed her in the middle of a crowd. She knew she should probably force herself to tell him she didn't want to see him again, but instead, she found herself nodding her head. Apparently satisfied with her reluctant response, he turned her around gently. Slowly they walked back the way they had come, carefully not looking at each other, but their shoulders and hands brushed against each other from time to time as they made their way out of the Seaport.

CHAPTER 15

The lights dimmed in Avery Fisher Hall. On the podium Andre Previn raised his baton, and the Philharmonic Orchestra began to play the haunting adagio movement of Elgar's Concerto for Cello and Orchestra. Seated next to Fiske, with her shoulder touching his, Caddy felt breathless. It seemed she had been breathless every day for the past few weeks, ever since she and Fiske had cautiously started to see each other. The excitement she felt had nothing to do with the music. Each time she saw Fiske she felt expectant, as if something exhilarating was about to happen. Just being with him was exhilaration enough, she thought. Up on the stage the orchestra played on and the house was hushed, attentive to the music, but for Caddy the music was an intricate, melodic background for her thoughts. She counted the times she and Fiske had seen each other since the day he kissed her at the South Street Seaport: six. This is the sixth time we've met since he kissed me. Since I kissed him back, she reminded herself with a secret smile. Only six times, but the telephone calls make it seem like we've been together more.

"Are you busy?" Fiske had asked at the beginning of that first phone call.

Her heart had begun to pound at the sound of his voice. "No," she had lied, ignoring the piles of research already heaped in neat stacks across her work table. She was flustered. Even though he had told her he would call, somehow she hadn't thought he really would. She pushed her chair away from the table and stared out over her terrace without seeing the pots of flowers or the dark sky beyond. It was ten o'clock and she had been working steadily for hours.

"I thought you'd like to know I got the camera developed." He sounded very businesslike. She could hear a bell ring at his end of the line and something in the distance that sounded like a vacuum cleaner.

"That's good," she replied cautiously.

"The pictures are fine. Not fine, but clear."

She remembered the Frenchman who winked at her. "All of them?"

"All of them. Even the dog. I've got him in front of me now." She felt a quiver of pleasure. She wanted to tell him about the odd way the dog walked, and how the children tugged him along on a long purple leash, but she hesitated. Wasn't she encouraging him even if she just talked to him on the phone?

Instead, she asked lamely, "Where are you?" What

an inane question. Her cheeks felt warm and, embarrassed, she frowned into the receiver.

"At the office, working right along with the cleaning woman. She writes the reports and I vacuum; it works for us." There was a hint of amusement in his voice that made her frown harder. He was laughing at her. She didn't say anything.

After a brief silence he asked politely, "Are you still there?"

"Yes."

"I've got to go to Cincinnati tomorrow on business, and I'd like to show you the pictures. I haven't eaten and, if memory serves, there's a place called Pete's near you. I could eat and you could watch. Or you could eat too," he added as if it were an unusual idea.

She couldn't help smiling. "Kind of you."

"I'm all heart." But she felt as if she was the one who was all heart. He was much too attractive, far too distracting, and she didn't want to start anything with him.

"Yes," she accepted quickly. Where had that come from? She had meant to say no.

"I'll swing by in about twenty minutes."

"I'll be on the front stoop."

The night they sat in Pete's until it closed had been their first date. They talked about everything and anything, from poetry to fishing, while other customers came and went until only the bartender and one tired waiter were left. They never looked at the pictures. She remembered how, even though his clothes had been rumpled and his tie a little askew, he still looked elegant; how his eyes had looked into hers as if he was trying to read her thoughts; how she had been unable to keep from reaching out her hand at one point to touch his, and how he had taken her hand in his as if it was the most natural thing in the world. At the door to her house he had stood beneath the fanlight and looked down at her, his eyes dark and unfathomable.

"Good night, Caddy Wilcox," he had said quietly.

"Don't you mean good morning?" Her heart had been pounding so hard she had been foolishly afraid he could hear it, and so she had leaned fractionally away from him.

"Good morning, then." Much to her disappointment, he hadn't kissed her then. She thought perhaps he interpreted her moving away as a desire on her part not to be kissed, and she was torn, knowing what she wanted him to do and relieved he hadn't. She wouldn't see him again, she resolved, climbing the dimly lit stairs to her apartment; he disturbed her equilibrium far too much.

As the adagio movement of the Elgar came to an end, she turned her head and looked at Fiske. He was looking at her, a smile at the corners of his mouth, and the look in his eyes she had come to know meant he wanted to put his arms around her. The allegro movement began, he looked toward the stage, and she sighed to herself. Because she *had* seen him again after that night at Pete's; she had seen him twice between his return from Cincinnati and before he left again for a two-week trip crisscrossing the country to meet all the firm's largest corporate clients. While he was away she had grown to anticipate the calls he made to her at the end of the day from wherever he was. Indeed, she found she planned her evenings so she was sure to be home.

"What did you do today?" he would ask.

"Work. What did you do?" she would reply, her feet already up on the other chair as she settled in for what usually turned out to be an hour-long conversation.

"Work. But tell me about yours."

"I've found the production head I want. I've offered him the job and he's thinking it over."

"Good job. What else?"

"The Smithsonian has unearthed a cache of photographs from Teddy Roosevelt's last African expedition. I may go down."

"I came through Washington on my way west. It's hotter than hell there already."

"What clients do you have in Washington?" she asked curiously.

"A large lobbying firm that sometimes goes over the line. They're a good outfit, but overly zealous in courting the legislature."

"And you keep them out of the slammer." Ward had dealt with lobbyists too. Loud men who drank too much and bragged about who they knew.

"Hell, no. We try not to have clients who skirt the law, Cad. We spend a lot of time mapping out their campaigns with them just to avoid that sort of thing."

She smiled with pleasure. Cad. He had called her Cad. No one but her family had ever thought to call her by that nickname.

"I may be back by Friday. Will you still be in New York? I had my secretary get theater tickets, just in case."

A prickle of alarm ran across her shoulder blades. She had never agreed to see him that weekend; he simply assumed she would. Just like Ward. Consciously, she put some distance in her voice. "I'm not sure where I'll be," she replied evenly.

"Fine. If I'm back in town, if you're free, and if we both want to, perhaps we'll go to the theater." Again, that same hint of amusement in his voice that infuriated her.

"Perhaps," she allowed. They had become friends, hadn't they? And friends could have dinner with each other and even go to the theater occasionally.

"If not, I could visit Agatha and Eddie," he said in a deliberative voice, as if that were a real option.

"Eddie hasn't forgotten you. He's waiting for you," she threatened darkly, but she couldn't help smiling.

"Then save me. Come to the theater."

"If we're both here."

They had both been in New York that Friday night, and they had gone to the theater, but this time, before Fiske turned away from her at her doorway, he had put his arms around her and kissed her so thoroughly that even now, sitting in the darkened concert hall, Caddy felt a frisson of passion just remembering the sensation of Fiske's lips on hers. Next to her, Fiske recrossed his legs; the tip of his shoe touched hers. The final allegro movement was half over, but even though she tried to concentrate, her concentration kept dissolving into a reprise of the last time they had seen each other, the night Fiske took her to a small restaurant in the West Village. There, behind the square, utilitarian dining room, they found a candlelit garden with a violinist who was playing to a handful of tables.

"All right with you?" Fiske asked, looking around. Immediately, a portly waiter wrapped in a pristine apron showed them to the one remaining table next to a trellis of roses.

"Very all right." It was enchanting. If she looked directly up, she could see a few stars and a sliver of moon. She felt as if they had escaped through a looking glass to a secret place. "How did you know about this spot?" She bit her lip, sorry she had asked. What if he came here with all his dates?

Fiske looked around with satisfaction, as if he had

created the entire setting himself. "I read about it. I've been saving it." Now the evening was perfect: He hadn't been here with anyone else.

"I'm starving," she announced.

"So am I." But he put the menu to one side and, rising, held out his hand.

She felt her hands begin to shake; at last she knew what was meant when people said their knees were weak. She couldn't dance with him. She didn't dare be so close to him. She rose and moved into his arms.

He led her around the tiny floor and she followed him easily. It's as if we've danced like this a million times before. We fit. Her body tensed. We can't fit. He moved his hand down her back until it was just below her waist. Unable to resist, she relaxed and gave in to the sweet, haunting sound of the violin music.

"I've been waiting for this," he murmured softly into her hair.

She couldn't answer. She turned her head so it was resting on his shoulder. She could feel the curve of his lips as he smiled and, even though he couldn't see her face, she smiled in response.

The music floated to a halt. He held her to him briefly and then led her back to the table. I'm like a lamb being led to the slaughter, she thought dreamily. This isn't in my plan.

The music rose to a final crescendo, and Caddy blinked twice. The dance floor disappeared and was replaced by the Philharmonic stage. She could feel Fiske looking at her, and she smiled. On the podium, Andre Previn lowered his arm and turned, bowing to the cheering audience in Avery Fisher Hall before leaving the stage. Caddy and Fiske rose too, clapping wildly for the dramatic performance. They were still clapping when the conductor reentered to take yet another bow, and they remained with the rest of the audience, applauding the performance until the Philharmonic Orchestra began to leave with their instruments and it became clear there would be no more bows.

"Thank you for that," she said over her shoulder as they inched their way up the packed aisle to the door.

They reached the plaza. All three houses of Lincoln Center were letting out at the same time. The Chagall murals glowed from within the Metropolitan Opera House where the Paris Opera had just performed *Tosca;* across from Symphony Hall, the audience streamed out of the New York State Theater chattering about the Alvin Ailey ballet they had just witnessed; in the middle of the plaza, the tiered fountain was lit and flowing with cascades of water. Inside, Caddy felt a cascade of happiness.

"There's nothing like Lincoln Center, is there? I always feel like I'm in the center of the world when I come here and all three houses are lit up. It awes me to think of so many people gathered together to worship the absolute best of the performing arts," she said dreamily.

"Nothing in the world." He caught her hand in his and drew it through his arm, holding her firmly to his side as he elbowed through the throng. Reaching the street, he paused. "Feel like a drink?" A chauffeur stood next to a black sedan, holding the rear door open for them. He nodded deferentially to Fiske.

"All right." She concentrated on not showing her surprise. The car wasn't a company car at all. Just like the plane, it was Fiske's.

"My place?"

Once again, that prickle of alarm attacked her. This time it was stronger and lasted longer. If she went to

Fiske's apartment, surely she was signaling him she was ready to take their friendship to a more intimate level. She closed her mind to her own defense system and took a deep breath. She nodded. As soon as she had done so, she felt her throat constrict and she wished desperately she could retract her assent.

The limousine sped quietly through the busy city, plunged through the leafy darkness of Central Park, and before she was quite ready, pulled up in front of a massive building with a discreet entrance on Park Avenue. They walked sedately through the marble lobby. Mirrored walls reflected back the image of a tall, urbane man dressed in evening clothes next to a pale woman with lustrous eyes wearing a black evening dress. She thought they looked like actors imitating the royal couple of England making a public appearance. She nodded regally to the elevator operator and entered the mahogany cab. Still staring straight ahead, they stood side by side with only their shoulders touching while they were taken swiftly to the penthouse floor. She took a deep breath, unable to decide whether she was excited or just plain scared.

When the door had closed behind them and they were alone, Fiske grinned and made a low bow, waving her in front of him into the apartment.

As they walked slowly down a wide, dimly lit hall hung with oil paintings on both walls, she looked around curiously. Her steps slowed. She became aware of vast rooms leading off the hall: first a long, formal drawing room; then a formal dining room with a massive dining room table with more chairs around it than she could count; a shadowy book-lined library with stairs leading up to a balcony; several closed doors leading to rooms she could only imagine; and at least two smaller halls leading to what she supposed were the bedrooms. When they reached the end of the hall and Fiske's hand was on the knob of yet another door, she looked back. The hall stretched down what seemed a huge distance to the arched entrance, and she realized that his apartment was the entire top floor of the building. Spencer. Of course. She felt like a fool for not realizing it sooner: Fiske wasn't just any Spencer, and this wasn't simply any apartment. Her surroundings were too vast, too hushed, its furnishings too *important*—the word leapt to her mind. She was in the home of the Spencer family, the same Spencer family that was the equal of any Rockefeller or Whitney in the country, the family that was so wealthy it had created its own foundation, which rivaled that of the Ford family.

She followed him hesitantly into what must have been a sitting room and came to a halt. With his back to her, Fiske was busy at a small bar set into the wall, opening a bottle of champagne. It was lucky he couldn't see her face, because she felt sure she must look as stricken as she felt. She felt as if Fiske had played a huge practical joke on her. All along, despite the fact that she had first seen him on Kincade, she had thought of him as a hard-working attorney, successful certainly, but never the possessor of this kind of enormous wealth. How could she have not known? She felt as if she hadn't been very bright; she should have known.

Two sides of the room had been rebuilt to include glass walls that overlooked a wide terrace planted with a virtual forest of trees and bushes. Beyond, the panorama of the New York skyline glittered like a string of diamonds. On the third wall, a large Matisse canvas glowed softly, and on the fourth, two small Corot landscapes hung on either side of the fireplace. Over the mantel, what could only be a Sargent portrait of a child who vaguely resembled Douglas stared down at her. Why had Fiske brought her here without preparing her better for the opulence she would encounter? Hadn't it occurred to him she couldn't help but be aware of the enormous differences in their backgrounds?

Fiske turned and saw her looking up at the portrait. "Do you like it? It's my great-grandfather, Old Gunning Spencer. It came with the territory. When Babs got married, Mom and Dad bought another floor in the building and I took this over, portrait and all." He handed her a crystal flute and toasted her with his eyes before he sipped the chilled champagne.

She accepted the glass, but she couldn't meet his eyes, and she didn't drink.

Fiske turned and looked up at the portrait. In an offhand manner, he laughed easily. "My great-grandfather was a genuine robber baron. He made a fortune in railroads, mostly on the backs of illegal immigrants, and then made himself respectable by buying art."

"And Kincade?" She thought about the Spencer's unpretentious life-style on the island, and then she pictured the large houses there.

"He started out trying to out-Newport Newport, but my great-grandmother didn't like it there, so he bought a share of Kincade. Apparently, my great-grandmother tried to get him to go to the south of France, but he refused."

"The south of France," Caddy repeated quietly.

"Ever been there?"

"No, I haven't." There hadn't been any scholarships to the south of France, nor any money in the Wilcox family to travel abroad.

Fiske's face lit up with enthusiasm. "We'll go together. In the fall, when the tourists have gone. I'll book rooms in Mougins. You'll love it."

Again, that feeling of alarm, but now it was more than a prickle, it was a stab somewhere in her middle. For a moment Fiske had sounded just like Ward, dictating their plans and assuming she would drop everything for a whim of his. "A little premature, aren't you?" she countered stiffly.

Something that might have been irritation crossed his face briefly. "Wouldn't you like to go to France?"

She nodded and stared straight at him, keeping her voice level with an effort. "Of course. And Spain, and Greece, and Morocco. Who wouldn't? I plan to do all that someday, when I have time."

There was a brief pause while he seemed to consider her rejoinder. He raised one eyebrow. "Sorry. I seem to have jumped the gun." He smiled so disarmingly that she had to smile back. As usual, just when it seemed he was going to say or do something she couldn't accept, he pulled back with such smoothness that she was left wondering if she was glad or sorry he had. It was safer to talk about Kincade.

"What about the other original families on the island?" she asked faintly. This was impossible.

"Like my great-grandfather. Most of them made their fortunes before the turn of the century. Not everybody wanted to storm Europe or build marble palaces—ergo, Kincade." He shrugged, as if it was very unimportant. He turned and walked over to the terrace.

The door was open and a faint smell of roses was in the air. Of course, she thought distractedly, he wouldn't need to lock the door; there probably was a staff of people tucked away in the recesses of the apartment, waiting to serve Fiske.

"Why didn't you ever talk about your family before? About all this? It seems we've talked about everything else these past few weeks," she said to his back. She put the untasted champagne down on a carefully polished mahogany table and walked across the room, past his still figure, to the railing of the penthouse. The breeze rustled the leaves of a tall larch tree next to her, and she reached out a hand to reassure herself it was a real tree growing forty floors above the city. The rough bark convinced her, and she sighed. Why had everything altered somehow? She no longer felt quite as comfortable with Fiske as she had before this evening.

Speaking slowly, Fiske watched her face carefully to gauge the effect of what he said next. "Caddy, you mustn't let yourself be overwhelmed by my family's wealth. It's just the way we are. We take it for granted and do our best to try and spend the money wisely. My father built a highly successful company of his own and is an artist in his own right. You know about Ma's career as a pianist; they both give more money away than they spend."

He looked at her, searching for some understanding in her face, but finding none continued rather stiffly, "You're rather defensive, you know."

"If by defensive you mean that I've earned my own way and it means a lot to me, then, yes, I'm defensive. I'm proud of what I've accomplished." She felt strong when she said that out loud, and the feeling was a good one.

"Well, so you should be." There he went again, disarming her with sincerity.

She looked up. He seemed to loom over her. His wealth seemed somehow to give him an overwhelming magnitude that made him almost incomprehensible. He was no longer just a disturbing presence that had unexpectedly entered her life, but a whole separate, imposing entity. And on top of that he had a way of taking over, like telling her she would go to France with him, that frightened her. Despite the breeze on the terrace she felt the return of the claustrophobia that sometimes overtook her in moments of extreme tension.

Fiske reached out and held her by the shoulders. He shook her gently. "We're being too serious. After all, we laugh at the same things, we like the same things, we understand each other, don't we?" He leaned down, as if to kiss her.

Despite the way she felt weak when he was so close to her, she forced herself to draw away fractionally. "I'm not sure we really do. You even look different here."

His face flushed, and he released her shoulders. "You're not making sense. I'm the same person I was when we walked in the front door."

"But you must have sensed how I'd feel or you would have told me sooner," she insisted. She took another step away from him. "We don't know each other very well," she repeated helplessly.

"Is it me, is it the Spencer family, or is it really still Ward?" he asked quietly. Perhaps she had been wrong to tell him everything about her relationship with Ward, even that Ward had been her only lover, but it had seemed so natural after he had related the outlines of his affair with Dierdre in England.

"Oh, no. Not that. He was important to me, but it's truly over and I have no regrets." She sank down on the side of a wrought-iron chaise and looked out over the city. Why did she feel so forlorn? She spoke slowly and reflectively, almost to herself rather than to him. "I never knew Ward as well as I thought I did. I be-

lieved he was idealistic and he wasn't; he was all form
and no substance. I found out all sorts of things about
him that made me feel shallow and sorry he was my
lover, but then it was too late, we were already lovers. I
don't want that to happen again."

Fiske paced a few steps up the terrace and then
returned. She could feel him standing over her. When
she looked up the expression on his face almost frightened her, it was so somber.

"You can't avoid having feelings because you've had
one less than perfect relationship, Caddy. It's just part
of life."

She should have known: He didn't understand at all.
"I know what I want out of life, and that's not it," she
countered coolly.

Abruptly, Fiske uttered a short, harsh laugh, but his
eyes were angry. "We're not talking about 'life,' Caddy.
All I did was bring you home for a drink and talk about
going to France together, for Christ's sake. You seem
to want all the T's crossed and the I's dotted. You can't
always know everything about a person going in—you
have to take some chances." She felt something curl
up inside her, something painful.

"I know that. I certainly took enough of them to get
where I am in my career." With her gaze she raked the
entire length of the penthouse terrace and the vast
apartment behind them. How had everything gone so
wrong so quickly? How could she make him take her
reservations seriously? "If I couldn't even conceive of
your living like this, couldn't even imagine it, what else
don't I know about you?"

"You mean am I an ax murderer? I'm not." He set
his jaw and glared at her.

"That's not what I mean and you know it."

"I don't know what the hell you *do* mean. The only

conclusion I can draw is that you simply don't want to see me anymore. Is that right?" He had reverted to his attorney's voice and his questions weren't really questions at all, but rather points of evidence he was using to present conclusions to an absent jury.

Caddy sat, frozen. She hated the way he was talking to her, but she didn't interrupt. All at once she realized she would have to stop seeing him, give up the intimate telephone conversations she had grown to love. She couldn't risk her hard-won career on a wealthy man-about-town who might want to turn her life upside down and then leave her or, worse from her point of view, want her to enter his cushioned world and annex herself to him. The shock of seeing him in his family home, surrounded by the trappings of his vast wealth and talking so carelessly about jaunting off to the south of France, had made it all crystal clear to her.

"I've thought a lot about you, about whether we could have a relationship. But frankly it didn't occur to me you would take all this so dramatically." He waited for an answer and, when she didn't provide one, turned and left the terrace, his steps ringing on the flagstone.

Stricken at the turn of events, she watched him out of the corner of her eye. He was pouring himself another glass of champagne. The light glinted on his signet ring, and in his evening clothes he looked as if he had stepped down from one of the portraits of his robber-baron ancestor. She bitterly regretted coming to his apartment, and sweeping over her was a flood of anger at herself for allowing her attraction to him to betray her. Nothing good could come of it. She rose and followed him into the room.

"I think I'd better leave now," she said coolly.

"As you wish. It's your decision. The car is waiting downstairs," he answered, matching coldness with coldness. He studied the label on the champagne bottle and replaced it in the silver bucket with a small, angry crash.

Half expecting him to call her back and unsure how she would react if he did, Caddy straightened her shoulders and walked toward the door. But Fiske never said a word. As she made her way down the long hall toward the elevator, she wondered miserably how she could have so misjudged Fiske. She had let herself be drawn in by his charm, almost trusting that they might possibly have a real relationship, but she didn't know him at all. The silence behind her was louder than any explosion, and, afraid she was going to cry, she quickened her step.

CHAPTER 16

Fiske watched intently as the ferry entered the harbor and drew slowly closer to the dock. It had been almost a month since he had seen Caddy, four long weeks when he had kept himself from calling her. The faces on the boat were distinguishable now, and he searched the crowd for one particular face but couldn't find it. Was it possible she had decided at the last minute not to come after all? He took an uneasy step backward. After all, why should he care if she was on the boat or not? After all, she was the one who had stormed out of his apartment, making it perfectly clear she wanted nothing to do with him. It wasn't like him to let a woman get under his skin. Nevertheless, he glared at the *Kincade*, willing the slow-moving, over-loaded little craft to move faster.

It had been Josie's idea to invite Thad Wilcox for the long Fourth of July weekend, along with Caddy to travel with him. It should have been her responsibility to meet the boat, but at the last minute one of the twins had had a minor accident and Josie had stayed home to make sure he was truly all right. Fiske wondered what Caddy would do when she saw who was meeting the boat, what she would say to him. His mood lightened and his lips twitched with amusement. He was the last-minute substitution, found when no one else was available. Even though he had made up his mind four weeks ago that he wasn't going to try to change her mind if she was so adamant in her poor opinion of him, it entertained him to imagine how she would handle the situation.

The *Kincade* was packed with islanders returning for the long weekend, and there wasn't an inch of free space on the deck. Small children wriggling their bodies through the railing were saved from imminent drowning by the firm grasp of their nannies; older children disregarded their parents' commands to come down immediately and continued to sit cross-legged on the roof of the small pilot's cabin; husbands and wives smiled at each other, reunited with each other by their return to the island they had come from far and wide to reach. On the dock, the families that had been there since Memorial Day waited for their friends and guests; among them, wives waiting for their husbands searched the faces of the passengers, waving in relief when they saw the one they searched for. A sense of expectancy and celebration flowed from the dock across the water to the boat and back again. The ferry reversed its engines and nosed carefully into its mooring. Captain Hardy blew the whistle three times, and a cheer went up from the throng.

Fiske's pulse began to beat more rapidly, but he waited by the Jeep, feigning indifference. Where was she? He had parked the Jeep as close as possible to where the *Kincade* would dock so Thad wouldn't have to walk too far. The gate was down now and passengers swarmed off the boat, eager to begin the weekend; two teenagers jumped from the roof of the cabin directly into the water, and Captain Hardy paused in his work to give them a tongue-lashing. His summer hand grinned sympathetically at the unrepentant swimmers while he off-loaded the inevitable boxes and crates of food. Everywhere, island dogs chased each other, and their barks mingled with the cheerful conversation of the crowd as it headed up the dock to claim wagons or take possession of family cars.

"Hey, Fiske. Racing tomorrow?" Ford Ludlow, his city jacket slung over his shoulder, paused for a moment. His tanned offspring waited politely, holding a tugging black Labrador firmly in place at the other end of a long lead.

"You bet. You?"

"Going to try. Heard the island meeting's been postponed again, this time to Labor Day. Everything on track?" He looked a little worried.

"Hope so. We're trying. You've got your troops in line, haven't you?" As he looked over the heads of the last stragglers, his heart leapt, and he never heard the other man's answer. Caddy was walking very slowly toward him as if she had all the time in the world. Next to her, a tall, pale young man hauled himself along with the aid of two metal crutches fastened just below his elbows; despite his obvious struggle to cope with the uneven planking of the dock, a grin lit his face as if he was already having the time of his life. Reminding himself sternly that Caddy had made it clear she wasn't interested in him, Fiske began to walk rapidly down the incline. Moments later, he was face to face with her. She stared at him expressionlessly; he only nodded.

"You must be Thad. Welcome to Kincade." He shook hands with her brother. As he uttered the traditional welcome, he smiled, liking what he saw. Thad was too thin and too pale, but there was humor and resolve in the lines of his face and intelligence in his eyes.

"Hello, Fiske," Caddy greeted him coolly. She was as reserved and self-contained as she had been the last time he had met her on this dock, the first time she ever came to the island. The same urge to coax a smile from her rose up in him, but this time he ignored it.

"Hello."

"Where's Josie? I thought she was going to meet us."

"Domestic crisis. She's waiting for you at the house." He frowned, wishing he had turned Josie down. It had seemed like an amusing trick, turning up to meet Caddy, but now it didn't strike him as a bit funny.

Thad carefully balanced himself and unhooked one of the crutches; he held out his hand to Fiske, and his handshake was solid and friendly. "Cad's told me all about Kincade. I feel like I've been here before."

He wondered if she had talked to Thad about him when she talked about Kincade. Probably not. He smiled at Thad. "Lots of people feel like that. The island does that to you. That, or it sends you running for the next ferry back. Here, let me take that." He reached for the folded wheelchair Caddy was dragging behind her.

Respecting Thad's need to manage his own passage, Fiske didn't offer to help as they approached the Jeep. He stowed the luggage in the back and held the door, waiting while Thad hoisted himself up into the passenger's seat.

"I've never ridden in a Jeep before. This is great."

Fiske was struck by a sudden thought. "Would you like to drive?"

"I don't have a license. Actually, I don't drive at all." Fiske pretended not to hear the defensiveness in Thad's voice.

"No one cares if you don't have a license here. Driving's no big deal. I'll teach you."

"Would you really?" Thad turned awkwardly in his seat.

"Why not?"

Fiske got behind the wheel and started the engine. He felt absurdly happy. Driving up the hill to the middle road, he slowed to a sedate fifteen miles an hour after they had made the turn and pointed out the roof of the Manor peeking through the trees as they drove by the Spencers' road. Driving toward the Northrups', he carried on a conversation with Thad, pointing out landmarks, but he watched Caddy in the rearview mirror. Her head was turned away as she looked out the window, and he couldn't see the expression on her face. Was she angry? Indifferent? Posing? She needed a good shaking. "Josie's looking forward to meeting you," he said to Thad instead.

"She's cool."

"That she is. She likes your writing."

"It's weird."

"That she likes it?"

"Yeah. And that she thinks it can be published. Jeez, I almost croaked when she called. Cad said she had written her and mailed her a couple of stories, but I never thought she'd just go ahead and call me." For a fleeting second, Thad looked almost frightened.

"She's a good editor. She told me one of your stories was the best she'd read in years." Fiske was glad he could honestly reassure Thad; Josie had been as excited about Thad's stories as he had ever seen her.

"God. And inviting me up here."

"She told me you have a book in you. Did she tell you that?"

"Yeah," Thad muttered. He looked anxious again.

"We're going to have to be careful to see she doesn't get a fat head. She thinks she's invented the wheel by discovering you." Fiske turned the wheel and steered the Jeep around a bend.

Thad laughed. "Cad says I'm the one who will probably get too big for my own good. Who the hell would think anyone would pay me money for some stories I made up for my sister? What a joke." Fiske looked in the rearview mirror; Caddy wasn't smiling.

"Will we see the marsh?" Thad shifted in his seat, trying to see out both sides of the Jeep at the same time.

"We can." He accelerated slightly. Caddy still didn't turn her head. "Followed by wine at Josie's." Thad made a sound of approval, but Caddy remained motionless.

That morning he had brought two cases of wine with him in the plane along with a box of food as an offering to Josie, which he had dropped off at the Northrup house on his way home from International. Even though it had been her idea to invite Thad for the weekend and she was excited to meet Thad, he knew she had a full house and would welcome extra provisions. He had been right: She had helped him put the cartons on the kitchen counter with satisfaction, reading the label on one of the wine bottles with approval.

"You didn't need to do this, but I'm glad you did."

"Seemed like little enough."

She handed him some small packages from the carton. "Here, put these in the refrigerator. How are your parents?"

"All this stuff with Caddy's snapshots has taken a big toll on the old man. Ma's good and worried; he locks himself up in the studio and won't talk to her. That's never happened before." He frowned, thinking about how old his father suddenly looked.

"What did Hank say when you told him?"

"I tried to meet with him in New York, but he made excuses. I had to tell him on the telephone he'd been spotted with Asher, and he tried to convince me it was legitimate business that had nothing to do with Kincade."

"Did you buy it?"

"No. Not at all. I sent an associate up to nose around New London again. There's no trail involving Hank, but there is some indication that Asher is going to file a signed presale contract as evidence to gain approval for the variances."

"Shit. You're kidding." For the first time since the issue had come out into the open, Josie looked seriously worried. She put the bottles of wine she was holding down on the table gently and looked at them, as if they held the weapons they needed to halt Asher.

"Nope. I felt I had to tell Dad everything I know for sure and most of what I suspect: that Hank has been working secretly to convince the islanders to sell on Asher's behalf. If that's true, and I think it is, Hank's undoubtedly looking at some big money from Asher for services rendered. The old man was disgusted at first and then devastated that a son-in-law of his could sink so low."

"Your poor mother. Does Babs know?"

"I told her about the pictures. She looked as if I'd slapped her in the face and then she got mad as hell at me, blaming me for persecuting her husband. I feel like hell. I don't want to hurt her, but sooner or later she was bound to find out and I guess it's marginally better if she hears it from me. I don't know, it's a mess."

"What are we going to do now?"

"Delay the vote until Labor Day. Buy time. Try and find a way out of this. Dad and I can get the vote postponed, but we don't know if we can fight all that money. He's going to talk to Rufus. I'm going to lean on Jonno to help divide up the island and pay each landowner a call."

"This weekend?"

"The sooner the better."

"There goes Fourth of July." She sighed, adding hastily, "Not that it doesn't have to be done. I'll help."

"You've got all your family up, plus Thad and Caddy. That's enough. We'll take care of it."

Josie began stacking the bottles in a large half-full wine rack. "God. What a freaky coincidence that Caddy actually saw them and managed to get photographs."

Fiske opened the door to the refrigerator abruptly and stared inside. It was heaped with salads and casseroles ready for the weekend, but he shut the door as if it were empty.

"Can't find anything to eat? We've got enough food for an army in there."

"Not really hungry."

"Love will do that," Josie offered.

"I didn't say I was in love," he muttered.

"Looks like it to me." She leaned against the counter with her arms folded and eyed him speculatively. "You've got all the signs—gaunt eyes, hollow cheeks, rapid weight loss, no appetite."

Fiske picked up a towel to swat her and she ducked. "I'm the picture of health. You've got it all wrong."

"Somehow, I don't think so."

"Give it over, Josie. You're being a pain in the ass. You know I'm not the marrying kind."

"Marrying? I was talking about love. You must be in worse shape than I thought."

He felt restless. He paced around the kitchen, picking up things and putting them down again. Josie didn't move. He knew she was watching him; he could see the teasing smile on her face out of the corner of his eye. He leaned over the kitchen sink and looked down at the marshes between the house and the ocean; the tide was coming in, and ribbons of silver water crept up the hummocks and stands of eel grass.

When he didn't answer her, Josie prodded him gently. "You know, I thought you were going to marry that girl in London." Josie's voice was carefully noncommittal; she could have been asking a question or making a statement.

He made a wry face. "Dierdre? The subject never came up, although I did get the feeling from time to time she wouldn't have minded marrying me, along with the Spencer money, of course." He tried to picture Dierdre's face, but all he could conjure up was a dim, faintly laughing outline.

"I like Caddy. Would I have liked Dierdre?" He knew Josie was keeping her hands busy to allow him the freedom to speak intimately, and he was grateful to her.

"No. You wouldn't have liked her." He was sure about that.

"Did you?"

Had he liked Dierdre? She had been wildly exciting, sensually inventive, always amusing and gay, but she had also been devious, ruthless, and frequently cruel.

"No. I don't think I did. She was fun. We knew the same people."

"But you didn't love her?"

"Not enough to marry her. You know me, Josie." He felt his chest constrict in momentary panic. He leaned forward again, inspecting the barn behind the house. "Did you know you have barn swallows?" he asked, trying to change the subject.

"Screw the birds. We're talking about something serious here." Holding a potato in one hand and the paring knife in the other, Josie turned and leaned one hip against the counter. Punctuating the air with the knife for emphasis, she lectured, "Listen, Fiske, you can't go on like this, going from woman to woman. It's a bad habit you've fallen into. One of these days you're going to meet someone you love enough to marry, but you won't be able to recognize it because you're so used to having one relationship after another."

"Ah. The C word—commitment." He gave up all pretense of looking out the window and faced her squarely. Caddy's image rose up in his mind unbidden. He could see every curve and every plane of her cheek, the arch of her eyebrows, her full lips. He shook his head, sternly willing her away. "I'm fine as I am, Josie. I've got work I love, family I care about, good friends, and on top of that, Dad wants me to take over the foundation this year." I keep saying I'm fine, he thought, but if I'm in such good shape, why the hell do I feel so out of kilter?

Startled, Josie raised her eyebrows. The Spencer Foundation was one of the most influential in the country, with headquarters in a modern glass building on West Fifty-seventh Street. It gave away millions of dollars annually to worthy causes, besides supporting a prestigious think tank.

He nodded. "He says he wants to spend all his time on his painting and it's my turn to make the decisions. He and Aunt Hetty will stay on the board, of course, as will Mother and Babs."

"Is that okay with you?"

"Do I have a choice?" He smiled tiredly. The fear that had been nagging at him grew suddenly larger: His entire life would be spent attending to Spencer family business, slipping his feet into the shoes of leader of the family until that was all there was. For the first time it seemed a very sterile future.

"No, I guess you really don't," she replied gently.

He shrugged. "Listen, Josie, you've got to stop trying to marry me off. Just because you and Jonno think you've invented the wheel doesn't mean everybody else has to follow in your footsteps. I don't need to be married to feel complete, and I certainly don't want to get married just because I'm a Spencer and supposed to continue the dynasty."

"What about just plain marrying for love? I saw the way you were looking at her at the house."

"Who? Claire?" He looked innocent.

"No. Caddy. You know what? I think you're too stubborn and set in your ways to know you're falling in love with her." She looked at him speculatively. "Maybe *fallen* is a better word. If you have, you'd better do something about it. She's special."

"I know," he said quietly. He shook his head, trying to dispel the memory of holding Caddy in his arms the first time he kissed her.

"Well?"

"I don't know. You're talking marriage and I'm . . ." His voice trailed off and he stared at her without seeing her. In her place he saw Caddy, laughing up at him with the light shining on her long hair.

"You're what?"

He focused on her and answered in a deceptively mild voice that fooled neither one of them, "I don't know, Jose. Leave it alone, will you?"

"Fiske. Watch the road," Caddy called.

He swerved the Jeep sharply. Startled, he realized his mind had been locked on the morning's conversation with Josie, and he had been driving without paying attention; he barely avoided hitting a young fawn. The surprised deer dove so swiftly into the woods at the side of the road that only a few faintly quivering ferns marked his flight. Gaining the center of the road again, he looked at her almost coolly in the rearview mirror, his mind still far away. This time she met his stare with a puzzled look of her own.

"Are we almost there?" Thad asked abruptly.

"Yup." He steered the Jeep into a U-turn, turned off the engine, and sat back in his seat. On the passenger side of the car, the great marsh stretched away to the horizon. He watched Thad's face as he spotted first one bird and then another, saw the look of incredulity dawn on his face as the marsh came alive for him. Instinctively, Fiske half-turned in the seat to share the moment with Caddy, but she, too, was leaning forward, looking at the marsh as if she had never seen it before. She was in profile, her bottom lip caught between her teeth, her eyes shining with delight as she watched the

birds fly up from their nests, forage for food, and return to feed their young. He watched her for a moment, enjoying her pleasure, before he turned his eyes
resolutely away.

Without turning his head Thad asked, "Do you
think there's any way I could actually go into the
marsh?" His voice was studiously indifferent as if he
didn't want Fiske to know how deeply he wanted to
make the attempt.

Fiske wasn't fooled. He studied the back of the thin
neck next to him and thought about logistics, the problem of Thad's crutches, the difficulty of getting him
into a small craft.

"Sure. Why not? I've got an aluminum rowboat we
could bring out at high tide. We've done it before."

"Really?" Thad grinned. "When?"

Fiske turned the key in the ignition. "Maybe tomorrow. Depends on what Josie has planned for you." He
started up the hill, pulling the wheel tightly to the left
and back onto the road. Shifting down into third he
continued, "Do we want to stop off and see the Loverings on the way?"

Caddy's head and shoulders appeared over the back
of the seats so she could make herself heard better
over the roar of the engine. "I don't think so, I want to
get Thad to Josie's."

"Cool it, Cad."

"You were up late last night, we've been traveling all
day—"

"Another time," Fiske interjected hastily. He
stepped on the gas and they headed for the turn that
would take them directly to the Hall.

Fiske shot a sidelong glance at Thad, thinking how
fine it was that Josie had liked the boy's stories right
away. He corrected himself hastily: man, not boy. It

was hard to think of Thad as a man; his illness seemed to have cloaked him in a permanent air of boyishness. He thought of the folded wheelchair in the back of the Jeep and wondered if he would have been as cheerful if he had had his freedom taken away before he'd a chance to use it. If Josie was right, and she usually was about things like this, then Thad was about to find his freedom after all. The idea pleased him.

He checked his watch as he slowed for the turn. Thad was looking slightly apprehensive, but Fiske elected not to embarrass him with an attempt at reassurance, knowing full well how Josie would sweep him into her generous orbit and make him hers. He wanted to speak privately with Caddy, but at the same time, glancing at her in the rearview mirror, he wasn't sure he wanted to be alone with her. She looked remote and pensive, wearing that now-familiar air of reserve like a protective cloak to keep him at a distance. Briefly, he wondered again what she was thinking about, but didn't ask. He decided he was just as glad if she had drawn away into her own thoughts; he was unsure if he wanted to know what they were.

He pulled up in front of the house, the screen door opened, and Josie followed by the twins spilled out to welcome their weekend guests. Thad let himself down from the passenger seat to the ground with only his canes for help. No matter what, Fiske was going to try to enjoy himself this weekend. Fourth of July on Kincade was traditionally a time of parties and homecoming, and he was going to put himself right in the center of it all. He would dance at Kincade House tomorrow night as he had never danced before, outsail every challenger, savor every moment. He climbed down from the Jeep and tossed young Ian Northrup up in the air; the dogs circled them trying to effect a rescue,

and Josie laughed. Behind her, Caddy and Thad
waited next to the door. Thad's face was in bright sunlight and he was laughing at the antics of the twins, but
Caddy had stepped back into the shadows and Fiske
couldn't see her face. He studied her curiously, trying
to figure out what she was thinking, but as before he
refrained from asking. He had never met a woman
who was repelled by the Spencer money, or a woman
who thought what she was doing was more important
than the possibility of a romance with the heir to the
Spencer fortune. And yet she had opened herself up to
him on the beach, she had yielded her body to him on
the dance floor, and she had confided some of her
deepest feelings to him in their late-night telephone
conversations. He felt a pang: he missed those conversations more than he wanted to admit to himself.
Busying himself unloading the Jeep, he reminded himself firmly that he had no intention of allowing anyone,
especially a woman who so infuriatingly divided everything into either black or white, to take over his life.
Josie was wrong: he definitely wasn't in love with
Caddy.

CHAPTER 17

Japanese lanterns glowed from the branches of the ancient oak trees leading up to Kincade House. In the field right next to the house, trestle tables covered in red, white, and blue tablecloths were set out in three long lines. Perpendicular to them, a buffet table holding empty chafing dishes and plates stood ready for the annual island supper. At the end of the driveway the road widened into a gravel circle with a fountain of a dolphin spewing water from its mouth, and behind the fountain, a two-story stone-and-brick house stretched out overlooking the sea, its wide Dutch door opened hospitably for the arriving guests.

As she followed Josie and Jonno Northrup up the shallow front steps, Caddy paused in the doorway and listened to the sounds of laughter coming from the side of the house. Thad was somewhere in that group with the Northrup twins. Perhaps she should go around and check on him before she let herself be swept into the adult party. She hesitated.

Jonno tugged at her elbow. He whispered in her ear, "Come on, Caddy. Stick close, here comes Rufus." A thin, courtly-looking white-haired octogenarian was bearing down on them.

"The patriarch of Kincade," Josie added out of the corner of her mouth. With a bright, social smile, she moved forward and kissed their host on both cheeks. Fiske may be inside, Caddy thought. I have to think of something to say to him this time, even if it's just to thank him for being so kind to Thad. Her heart began to pound in the alarming way it did whenever she thought about Fiske.

"My dear, you look radiant." Rufus patted Josie's arm genially.

"Uncle Rufus, may I introduce our houseguest Caddy Wilcox? Caddy, this is Rufus Kincade, our host." Caddy shook hands politely and murmured her thanks for being included in the party.

"He's also lord of the manor house, keeper of island traditions, horseman extraordinaire," Jonno elaborated as he took his turn shaking Rufus's hand.

"Not riding as much these days, I'm afraid. Getting old."

Josie held her hands up in mock disagreement. "Not you, Uncle Rufus. Caddy, this man rides all over the island deciding which woods need to be thinned or which roads dug out. He lays down the law and the rest of us fall into line." In the distance Caddy saw a tall figure crossing the hall, heading for the terrace. For an instant she thought it was Fiske, but he disappeared so quickly she couldn't be sure. Now her heartbeat was positively irregular.

"The Kincades were the first family to settle here, Miss Wilcox, but you probably have heard all about that." Rufus smiled down at Caddy. He held her hand a fraction too long and stood a little too near. Despite the smile of welcome on his face, his voice was slightly vague when he asked, "Have you been on Kincade long?"

Jonno answered for her. "Just a few days. She photographed the marsh for Nelson Lovering, but this weekend she and her brother are our guests."

"And a very beautiful guest, indeed." Rufus put his hand beneath her elbow and absentmindedly squeezed her arm. He moved her away from the Northrups and toward the bar, where a clean-cut young bartender, imported from the mainland with the rest of the help, handed her the gin and tonic she requested. Rufus accepted a dark brown drink in a short glass; the bartender obviously knew him. She sipped cautiously. The drink was strong and the afternoon was hot. Trying not to appear too obvious, she searched the room with her eyes: no Fiske. The windows were thrown open to catch the sea breeze, and she could hear the shouts of the younger generation as they played croquet on the lawn or hide-and-seek in the boxwood maze.

"Have you met these people?" Rufus waved his glass around affably, apparently not noticing that some of the liquid spilled out onto his jacket. Outside of Jonno and Josie, the only familiar faces in the room were Claire Ludlow, Deane Northrup, and Bill Ludlow, who was attempting to spear a large shrimp from a heaped platter with a small toothpick.

"Only one or two, I'm afraid. I've only been on the island to work, you know." She felt acutely conscious of the fact she was being quietly looked over by the other guests.

"Then you must allow me the pleasure of introducing you." He looked around hesitantly, as if unsure what to do with her, but his face cleared with satisfaction as his gaze lit on a man and a woman standing near the open window. The large room was filling up now. With relief she saw Douglas and Dorothy enter with Eliza and Nelson Lovering, the men dressed in neat blazers and the women in flowery silk dresses.

"I know Eliza Lovering," she offered quickly, hoping she could make a getaway to a familiar presence.

"Never mind them. I want you to meet the Dwights. Bess and Arthur. Lovely people. Lovely." He grasped her arm again and propelled her across the room, landing her neatly in front of a short, stocky couple dressed alike in white slacks and blue blazers; the man wore a red ascot and the woman had a long red scarf knotted around her neck. "Here we are," he crowed. "This is a friend of the Northrups', and these are the Dwights, Bess and my dear friend Arthur." A fleeting expression of irritation crossed his face and he shook his head. "I'm sorry, my dear, I seem to have forgotten your name. Silly of me."

Her face was beginning to feel stiff from smiling politely. These must be the people Nelson had called fools. "I'm Catherine Wilcox. Caddy." They looked like a pair of Kewpie dolls in their Fourth of July red, white, and blue. She sneaked a quick look around the room before turning back to the couple. She had a wild desire to giggle. Actually, everybody in the room was wearing either red, white, or blue, or a combination of all three; it must be an island custom. It was fortunate that the dress she'd brought for the occasion was a white linen halter neck with a full, swinging skirt that stopped just above her knees. She tried not to remember how carefully she had dressed or how she had been unable to think about anything but Fiske as she pulled the soft material over her head.

Arthur was talking to Rufus; he didn't look at Caddy. "Ah, yes, the photographer," he said with a drawl.

Bess was a little kinder. "You remember, darling. Uncle Nelson brought Miss Wilcox over to photograph the marsh. All those birds." She smiled so insincerely that Caddy had difficulty holding back a snort of laughter.

"I know perfectly well who she is. Ward Abernathy told me all about her," her husband said testily. "I still don't know why we bothered with all this record-keeping business. After all, if . . ." Of course, Caddy thought, these were the people Ward had told her he knew.

"Darling," his wife warned.

"I know, I know." He drank deeply from his glass and glared around the room, rocking back and forth on his heels. He seemed like a pompous little man, and Caddy decided she didn't like him.

Rufus finished his drink and looked around as if another would appear by magic; it was clear he'd made an early start and was way ahead of his guests. "Always liked Fourth of July. Been doing it this way ever since I was a boy. Races, dancing, everybody together. Wish Rufe was here. Do you know my son?" he asked Caddy owlishly.

She shook her head in answer to his question. He was either quite drunk or senile. She wondered if he'd last the evening.

"For Christ's sake, don't get started on Rufe."

"Such a dear boy. I've never understood why he lives in Madagascar," Bess trilled.

"Something about birds," Rufus said as he looked off into space.

"For Christ's sake, Rufe will come home when he's good and ready. He's got more sense than the rest of us anyway," Arthur announced with all the authority of someone who's positive he knows everything.

"Studies them. The birds," Rufus continued as if he hadn't been interrupted.

Arthur raised his voice slightly. "After all, who needs all this old-fashioned ritual? Here we are, on a perfectly good weekend, all lumped together to celebrate a holiday that doesn't matter a damn anyway. Not that it isn't decent of you to give the party every year, Rufus, but all this tradition is something I won't miss a bit." Arthur's face was getting red, and beads of perspiration dotted his shiny forehead. His wife looked pained and put one hand on his arm to quiet him.

"Are you moving?" Caddy asked with feigned innocence. It was impossible to resist an impish desire to put him on the spot.

"No, no," Bess interrupted hastily. "That's just Arthur. He really loves these gatherings."

"Thought you did, my boy. Fine old custom. Wouldn't miss it for worlds. Wish Rufe was here though." Rufus looked around the room with a return of the same vacant expression he had worn earlier, and Caddy wondered if he was so far gone he was looking for his son in the crowd. She didn't have time to wonder long because, spotting the bar, he left them abruptly and headed for another drink, moving amazingly quickly for an eighty-year-old man.

Left alone with the two women, Arthur stared at

Caddy as if he saw something slightly distasteful. "So you're from New York," he drawled. "A working girl on her own. Ward tells me you've had a book published." He made it sound as if she had some kind of disease.

"Yes," she said levelly. "You must let me have my publisher send you a copy." She fervently hoped he would refuse; apparently Ward hadn't bothered to mention it was only a textbook on photography. She was pleased to see a flicker of surprised respect in his eyes. Without waiting for his answer, she said good-bye as sweetly as she could manage and eased back into the cocktail party.

Where had Eliza gone? She shouldered her way into the crowd, but her progress was halted by Jonno's long arm reaching out to draw her into a close-knit group standing in a circle with their heads together. In the circle with Jonno were Randy and Deane Northrup, Claire, Ford, and Bill Ludlow, and, watching her quietly, Fiske. His eyes were dark, his face expressionless as he looked at her, and suddenly her knees felt weak.

"Managing okay? The Dwights didn't eat you alive?" Jonno asked.

"I'm fine." Her voice cracked just the least bit and, nervously, she cleared her throat. She should have stayed home as she'd wanted to, not let Josie and Jonno talk her into coming to the party.

"How are you, Mata Hari?" Ford toasted her with his glass, but he wasn't smiling.

"Don't be snotty, Ford," Claire snapped at her husband. "It's not her fault she happened to be standing there with a camera."

"I'm dying to see the pictures. I think you're so brave—I'd never have had the courage to do it."

Deane took one of the combs out of her hair and reinserted it.

No one was smiling. Caddy looked longingly at the door to the terrace. She took a tentative step backward.

"The son of a bitch," Bill swore bitterly.

"This will kill Babs," Deane said softly.

There was a general stirring of agreement, broken when Ford said sternly, "It's a damn shame, but we can't let Babs get in the way here—for all we know, she's involved too."

"Easy, Ford," Fiske said in a low, cautionary tone of voice. His face was still expressionless, but his eyes had narrowed threateningly. He feels about Babs the way I feel about Thad, Caddy thought immediately; it's impossible for him to think Babs would jeopardize Kincade, and that's how I would feel if I was in his place and they were talking about Thad.

Ford nodded. "All right, forget Babs, but we still should find out just how deeply involved Davidson is in this sale."

"Pretty fucking deep, I think." Bill looked at his brother, who nodded.

"Are we all going to confront Davidson? Or just let Fiske handle him?" Jonno asked. He was wearing bright red plaid slacks and a white blazer.

"Confront him? I'd like to beat the shit out of him," Bill snapped.

"What's this we, white man?" Randy asked Jonno in mock horror. "I don't want to get decked."

"I'll get it out of him." Instinctively, Ford squared his shoulders, preparing to do his duty.

Fiske's voice was still quiet, but some of the tension had left his face. "I told you: He denied to me that the pictures mean anything at all. He said he was working on a land acquisition in the Berkshires with Asher. If that's the tack he's taking, he won't admit to knowing anything about selling Kincade land."

"Did you believe him?" Jonno asked angrily. The noise level had reached a high pitch and the temperature in the room had risen as the sun, sinking slowly into the ocean, shone directly into the room. They were all standing so close to each other that Caddy could feel the tension between them. She could see the tautness in their faces as they instinctively turned to Fiske for leadership.

"No, I did not." The tone of his voice told them he was still reluctant to discuss his brother-in-law. She relived the moment when, seeing a dramatic shot, she had automatically taken the picture; for a second she wished fervently she had turned her back when she spotted Hank with Asher. Because of her, Fiske had been forced to face a betrayal that came from his own family. She looked down at her empty glass, unable to watch.

"Then what the hell do we do now?" Randy asked. One hand held his glass while the other was clenched into a fist.

"You all know we're going to canvass the island tomorrow and Monday; we've talked about it already. I think we should save our speculation about Hank until we've had a chance to get some hard confirmation. I'd hate to be wrong," said Fiske.

"Speak of the devil," said Jonno. Nine heads swiveled toward the door. Smiling broadly, Hank was shaking hands with Arthur Dwight; as Caddy watched with the others, he kissed Bess on the cheek.

"He doesn't look as if there's a thing wrong, does he?" Claire turned to her husband. "He looks like the cat who swallowed the canary."

"You're right, he does. I wonder if he thinks we're all just going to lie down for him to make a bundle off our land." Ford looked to his brother for an opinion, but Bill was staring across the room at Hank with a murderous look on his face.

"I'm going to kill the son of a bitch," he said in a flat, ugly voice.

Ford grabbed his arm. "No. You can't. Calm down, Bill."

Bill wrenched his arm away. For a second the brothers glared at each other. Caddy held her breath. Around them, people were beginning to look at the group curiously. She stole a look at Fiske, but he was looking down into his glass, his expression carefully noncommittal. Before she could turn her gaze away, he raised his head and looked directly at her, and as she felt her skin begin to turn warm, he nodded just once as if to reassure her she had been right to take the pictures.

With an exclamation of disgust, Bill allowed himself to be pulled back. Silently, the small group sipped at their drinks and looked uneasily at each other. A gong rang out and, with a murmur of forced laughter and relief, they began to move with the crowd out onto the side lawn where the buffet table, now piled high with platters of food, was waiting. Caddy didn't know quite what to do. The Northrups and the Ludlows were already on the terrace, but she hung back, looking for Thad.

"He's over there, under the trees," Fiske said quietly from behind her. Sure enough, Thad was seated next to Josie at a table with a crowd of teenagers. He was smiling.

"Thank you," she replied. She took a step forward. Although their bodies weren't touching, she imagined she could feel the length of his body behind her. She should thank him more completely for his kindness to Thad. She took a deep breath and turned, but all she could see was his back as he edged his way through the crowd. She looked disconsolately out over the scene below.

A line had already formed at both ends of the serving table. The younger islanders, in what was apparently a tradition, began to serve the older guests, who had established themselves in the best seats. Mainlanders, hired for the occasion, passed up and down the aisle between the tables, offering wine or cranberry juice. A mountainous chef who answered to the name of Tiny, his spotless white toque slightly askew, beamed from behind the buffet table. His creation, a towering dessert edifice of red, white, and blue pastries and cream, sat in the middle of the table; he accepted the congratulations of the guests as his due.

The sun had disappeared by the time everybody was seated. The scene was illuminated by flickering candles on each table, a circle of flares on the lawn, and delicately colored Japanese lanterns strung from tree to tree. The lanterns' soft glow lent a fairy-tale quality to the evening. Above them, the stars were beginning to come out, and behind the trees a half-moon was making its slow ascent. Caddy, having made sure Thad was all right, took an empty seat between Jonno and Barbara. On Barbara's other side, Randy waved for a waiter to bring more wine. When he arrived, an open bottle in each hand, Randy relieved him of his burden and began to refill the glasses of everybody sitting around him. Across from Caddy, Deane was eating shrimp as fast as she could, while on her right Ford watched her incredulously. On Deane's other side, diagonally across from Caddy, Fiske was seated next to a pretty blonde on his left who Caddy had never seen before. As she watched out of the corner of her eye, Fiske whispered something into the girl's ear and a peal of laughter rang out from both of them. Caddy felt a frisson of jealousy, a shudder so unexpected she nearly gasped.

"Ah. The return of the luscious La Peck." Jonno tossed an empty clamshell into a rapidly filling bucket of shells and lobster claws in the middle of the table.

"Who's La Peck?" Caddy whispered to Jonno. Next to her, Barbara pushed away her uneaten lobster and reached for the bottle of wine.

"Cindy Peck. She lives in Paris with her mother and father, but spends her summers with her grandparents at the Mill. She's had her eye on Fiske ever since she was a little girl. . . . Looks like she's grown up pretty nicely, I'd say."

Acutely conscious of the sandy-colored head bent so intimately to the blond one, Caddy savagely ripped a claw from her lobster and cracked it open. She hated blond hair, she hated Paris, she hated Cindy Peck. She wanted to be the one sitting next to Fiske, with her shoulder touching his as he made her laugh. Abruptly, she halted what she was doing: She must be insane. After all, wasn't she the one who had walked away from Fiske? Why should it matter who he flirted with? She stabbed at an elusive piece of lobster meat, despising herself for the way she couldn't keep him out of her mind. She wanted to cry. Suddenly, the claw went flying in one direction and the lobster cracker in another, as something fell heavily against her.

It was Barbara. Her eyes were closed and her head sagged forward as she slipped sideways in her chair. Randy Northrup half-rose from his chair as he reached out both hands in an attempt to steady Barbara's limp body.

"She's drunk. She must have been at it all afternoon," he said in a low undertone. "Help me get her back to the house before everybody notices."

Quickly, Caddy looked over at Fiske. He should be the one to help his sister. But Fiske had his body half-turned toward the Peck girl, his arm draped intimately over the back of her chair. "Shouldn't you tell Fiske?" she whispered, feeling spiteful.

"I don't want to cause a scene. You get on one side and we'll walk her over to the trees by the drive. Maybe the shadows will hide us." He grasped Barbara's upper arm firmly. "Up we go, baby. Time for bed."

Barbara was lifted by the pressure of his grasp. She swayed for a moment. Her eyes opened and she stared vacantly ahead at nothing. "Tha's fine. Bed."

Her eyes began to close and her knees began to sag again, but by this time Caddy rose swiftly and put her arm around the other woman's waist. Barbara was a lot heavier than she looked. Three abreast, they made their way as fast as Barbara's weight would allow to the safety of the dark driveway and up the smooth grass bordering it to the house. Entering the front hall, Randy eyed the staircase dubiously. "I don't think we can make that," he said. There was no way; Caddy's arms felt like lead as it was.

"The drawing room?"

"Have to be—she's about to go. We'll put her on one of the couches." He shifted Barbara's weight to get a better grip around her waist. Caddy stepped back, allowing him to maneuver. Barbara's head was thrown back at an odd angle, her eyes were entirely closed; she hadn't waited to pass out. Randy dragged her across the rug and arranged her none too gently on an overstuffed sofa. He straightened and took a step back, looking down at his handiwork with an expression of distaste. "Let her sleep it off."

"Has this happened before?" I hate this, Caddy thought. She looks so pathetic. Barbara was sleeping peacefully, her mouth slightly opened. She moaned once and rolled over on her side.

"Once or twice. Josie wondered if she was developing a drinking problem, but the rest of us just thought she couldn't hold her liquor."

Caddy wrinkled her nose. The smell of liquor filled the room. "Which is it?"

"Who knows? Both, maybe. We don't see much of her in the winter, but she's been hitting it pretty heavily so far this summer."

Hesitantly, Caddy asked, "Does Fiske know?"

"If he suspects, he hasn't said anything to me."

Angrily, Caddy remembered Fiske's head bent close to Cindy Peck's, the two of them oblivious to the rest of the people at the table. "Do you think he saw us when we left?"

"Nope. If he had, he'd have taken care of it. I probably should have told him and let him handle her, but I didn't want to draw attention to her. She's going to feel more than a hangover when she wakes up." He straightened his tie and smoothed back his hair.

"You mean remorse?" She knew she would want to die of embarrassment if anyone saw her that drunk.

"Big time. If she even remembers it." He yawned. "I don't think there's anything else we can do here. Let's wander back to the party." Strains of music could be heard coming from the side terrace where a small orchestra was tuning up. As they listened, the musicians swung into the refrain from "Mountain Greenery." He smiled a pleased smile. "Listen to that. It's dance time."

Caddy felt vaguely uncomfortable. "You know," she said slowly, "I think I'll sit here for a while, in case she wakes up."

"Honey, she's out for the count."

"I wonder. If it were me, I'd hate to wake up and not know what had happened."

He grinned. "Why do I think you'd never get drunk in public and pass out in the middle of your lobster?"

She shrugged. He was right, but just because she never had didn't mean she couldn't imagine what it might feel like. She patted him on the arm and motioned him out of the room. To her surprise, he bent down and kissed her lightly on the cheek before he saluted her and went off in search of a dancing partner.

Caddy could hear the sounds of laughter mingled with the swelling music as she wandered around the room, picking up small objects and examining them closely before she returned them carefully to the exact spot she had removed them from.

The portraits on the walls of Kincade House had different faces than the ones in Fiske's apartment, but the similarities were striking. She chuckled to herself as she imagined a small factory tucked away somewhere on the eastern seaboard with an assembly line that turned out oil paintings of austere ancestors in ornate gold frames. Trailing one finger lightly over an inlaid mahogany table, she wandered over to the French doors that were opened onto the croquet lawn; beyond it the moon cast its shadow on the water. The excited laughter of a group of children chasing fireflies mingled with the sounds of the music.

Leaning her head against the door, she let the murmur of the party outside flow over her. It was hard to disapprove of the people of Kincade even if they had more money than she had ever thought possible. Most of them were so talented and enthusiastic about their preoccupations, unlike Ward's friends who seemed to be only interested in knowing people who could advance their careers. And yet many of the people of Kincade were powerful in their own right, more powerful than Ward's friends, but they used their resources quietly and wisely to help those less privileged than themselves. She found she preferred the feeling of family and tradition, the easy affection and camaraderie that flowed between the generations on Kincade. She liked the way that, no matter what their problems or their disagreements, they remained intensely loyal to each other.

Raised in the tradition of academia, the only social gatherings that she could remember from her childhood were modest receptions following a lecture or a string quartet, where everyone stood around stiffly drinking cheap sherry while they anxiously awaited the opportunity to make their escape. She took a deep breath, drinking in the scene in front of her with pleasure.

If only Fiske's face didn't keep reappearing in her thoughts. Nothing less than the desire to help Thad visit Josie could have brought her to a place where she was bound to meet him again. She closed her eyes, remembering how she had searched the crowd at the pier, looking for Josie but hoping to see Fiske. And when, like a small miracle, he was there in front of her, she had been so confused by her own joy she hadn't said a word to him. It was probably just as well, since Fiske had become so engrossed in Cindy Peck. He really wasn't that different from Ward, she reflected, feeling suddenly disconsolate. Like Ward, he didn't really care about anybody's feelings but his own.

She wished she hadn't made such an issue about his apartment, because it wasn't the magnitude of his wealth that really bothered her. It was the way he seemed to assume she would feel the way he did about it; that and everything else, she thought with a frown. She really had been pretty stiff-necked, but she was damned if she was going to find herself falling for another Ward. After all, it might not be so bad having a great deal of money if one used it as well as the Spencers did. She tapped her fingers pensively against the door jamb in time to the dance music. She couldn't seem to go for very long without thinking about Fiske. Despite her protests and her resolution to the contrary, he seemed to have hollowed a place for himself in her mind, if not her life. She sighed. It probably didn't make any difference, since she had been so stubborn and it appeared that Fiske had quickly found another interest in Cindy Peck. All of a sudden she felt intensely lonely.

Turning her back on the romantic view, she resolutely made her way over to where Barbara was stirring restlessly on the couch. She sat in a wing-backed chair and studied the prone figure worriedly. Barbara was thrashing about on the couch, her fists clenched and her eyes squeezed tightly shut. Suddenly, her eyes flew open and she stared fixedly at the ceiling.

"Where am I?" she asked in a perfectly sober voice.

"In the drawing room inside Kincade House."

"How did I get here?"

"Randy and I brought you."

"Did anyone else see us?"

"I don't know," Caddy answered honestly. Thank

heavens, she could leave now. She leaned forward, preparing to rise.

Barbara struggled gingerly to a seated position. She put one hand to her head. "God, I feel awful." The look she gave Caddy was almost hostile. "Why are you here?"

Caddy chose her words carefully. "I thought I'd stay with you for a while. I was about to go." She stood up.

"Why would you stay with me?" Barbara muttered.

"Actually, I was glad to have a few minutes away from the party. It's a little overwhelming seeing everybody from the island congregated in one place." She wondered what Barbara would say if she told the truth: She had stayed because Barbara looked so pitiful she hadn't the heart to leave her alone.

Barbara grimaced wryly and quickly closed her eyes as if the effort had been too much. "Not to mention the fact that my brother seemed to be all wound up in Cindy Peck," she jibed sarcastically.

"That's not it at all," Caddy countered hotly. Embarrassed, she wondered, Does everything I feel show on my face?

Barbara leaned her head tiredly back against the couch, too unwell to argue the issue. "Don't worry, it doesn't mean anything. That's just Fiske's way."

"What Fiske does is his own business." Caddy was pleased at the detachment in her voice.

Barbara opened her eyes wide and really looked at Caddy for the first time. She smiled kindly. For a moment she looked just like her mother. "Your secret is safe with me."

Caddy blushed. Trying to cover her confusion, she asked hastily, "Do you want to go back to the party?"

"No," Barbara whispered harshly. "I don't want to go back to the party."

"Would you like to go back to your house? I could get Rand—"

As if she hadn't heard a word Caddy said, Barbara continued feverishly; her words erupted in a spurt as if the dam of her self-control had been finally and irrevocably breached. "I don't want to go back to the cottage and I don't want to go back to New York. I don't want to see anybody, I don't want to have to talk to anybody, and above all I don't want to see all the commiseration in their eyes as they think to themselves, 'There goes poor Barbara Davidson, whose husband is the shit that's selling out the island.' " She clamped her mouth shut and turned her head away. Caddy was appalled by the naked honesty of the other woman's confession.

Slowly, she lowered herself back down into her chair. She couldn't leave now, not when Barbara had just made such a devastating admission. "I'm sorry," she whispered, feeling very inadequate in the face of the other woman's anguish.

When Barbara finally spoke again, her voice was dreary, as if she was profoundly exhausted. "Everybody thinks that Rufus Kincade drinks too much all of the time and that's why he seems to lose it sometimes. But that's not the whole story. He's actually getting senile."

"Barbara," Caddy said in her normal voice, trying to halt the flow of words, but Barbara kept on talking. I don't think she even heard me, Caddy thought. I'm not the person she should be telling; she'll hate herself later.

Barbara turned her wedding ring around and around her finger. "Hank found it out by accident months ago when he stopped in for a visit and Rufus thought Hank was his son and spent the entire afternoon reminiscing about events that happened over forty years ago. Hank played along with it, pretending to be Rufus, Jr. You know, Rufus is truly alone except for the servants that live in the house, and they're paid to do what he tells them to do. Besides, they're nearly as old as he is. With his son in Madagascar, there isn't any other family member to check up on him."

Was Barbara still drunk or was she just using the person nearest to her as the receptacle for her staggering disclosure? Caddy wasn't quite sure. She saw tears streaming down Barbara's face, but her eyes were focused and determined. The latter, Caddy decided. It's because she can't keep it locked up inside anymore, and I happen to be the one who is here. She thought for a moment. "Didn't anybody guess? What about the other islanders? Nelson? Somebody?"

"After his wife died, Rufus retreated more and more. Except for the Fourth of July celebration, he became almost a recluse. Oh, we'd see him riding around on his horse looking over the island property, but he rarely stopped to speak. We got used to him that way."

"Didn't any of the servants speak to anyone on the island about his failing mind?"

"They love him. Besides, they didn't want to lose their jobs, which they would if he were put in an institution. They tried to take care of him without anyone finding out. Hank began to take advantage of that, dropping in on a regular basis, just to visit. The confusion about whether Hank was his son continued, and Hank played on the old man's dementia, pretending he was young Rufus. One day he just put a piece of paper in front of Rufus and Rufus signed it, thinking it was a codicil to his newly drafted will. But it wasn't that at all; the document Hank had him sign was really an agreement to sell his land to Bruce Asher."

"Jesus." Caddy was horrified. "Doesn't Rufus have any idea what he's done?"

"Hank thinks Rufus has early Alzheimer's. Rufus fades in and out of the real world, and when he's with us he doesn't remember what he did when he was gone."

"Oh God, that's dreadful. I can't stand it." She was torn between not wanting to leave Barbara alone and feeling she should run out of the room and spread the alarm.

"It's more than dreadful: It's illegal. Oh, Hank," Barbara whispered. She closed her eyes again. Tears slipped down her cheeks, but she didn't bother to brush them away.

Pity welled up inside Caddy. She felt the depth of Barbara's pain, but was helpless to comfort her. All of Barbara's dreams had vanished for her; all her careful evasions, constructed to protect her husband, had come to nothing in the end. And now she had to face the fact that the man she loved was a common thief, who wouldn't even hesitate to steal from his own wife. "I'm so sorry," she whispered inadequately.

Opening her eyes, Barbara begged, "You won't tell anyone, will you? Oh, God. You were right. I shouldn't have told you. I'm so sorry." Pale and drawn, she looked far older than her years.

Caddy leaned forward. With all the conviction she could muster, she said honestly, "Don't be sorry. You had to tell someone."

Like a small child, Barbara pleaded, "You won't tell, will you?"

"Somebody has to know, Barbara. This could be the end of Kincade. You just can't keep what Hank's doing to yourself, even if he is your husband." Even as she said the words, Caddy could feel how disingenuous they sounded. Someone like Barbara would never let her husband down, no matter what. She thought frantically. "What about your brother?"

"Fiske? Especially not him. I know he's found out Hank's involved because of the pictures, but he doesn't know how bad it really is. I have to be the one to tell him." Barely managing to keep her voice level, she added resolutely, "I won't let this go on. I can't. It goes against everything I am." She drew a shaky breath and confided, "You see, I've loved Hank so much. I couldn't believe he would do this to us . . . to me."

Caddy nodded her head. She could understand that. "Does anyone else know what you've told me?"

Barbara smiled wearily. "No. No one else. You were just in the wrong place at the wrong time. Promise me this is just between the two of us?"

Caddy thought hard, wondering where her loyalties lay. How could she not tell Nelson? Or fail to give Fiske the ammunition he needed to halt the sale of the island? Despite her repeated resolutions to keep herself aloof from Kincade, she had grown to love the island, and yes, to love Nelson and Eliza too. She thought of Dorothy in her garden, Josie opening doors for Thad, and then there was Fiske.

"I can't," she whispered.

"Please," Barbara beseeched. "I know I don't have any claim on you or any right to ask, but please let me handle this myself." For better or worse, the pain in the other woman's eyes swayed Caddy, and she reluctantly agreed.

"All right. I promise . . . for now anyway. I won't say anything to anyone, but you have to promise me something in return."

"Anything. What?"

"You'll tell Fiske about Rufus before the end of the

weekend. Before Monday night. Will you promise me that?"

"Yes."

"Then that's what we'll do. And I *am* glad I was here." For a moment Caddy wondered if Barbara had heard her; she was gazing blankly into space, as if she were alone in the large, shadowy room. Finally, she mustered a smile and looked directly at Caddy.

"Funny, I'm glad you were here too; it feels better to have said it all out loud. I have a lot to think about though."

"Shall I stay?" She was oddly reluctant to leave the other woman alone. And besides, how could she go back to the table and pretend nothing had happened?

"No, but thanks. I think I'd like to sit here by myself for a while. I have to start untangling it in my own mind sometime. You go on back."

"I hate to leave you."

"It's all right, really."

Reluctantly, Caddy agreed. She wished there was something she could do, but she could see Barbara needed time by herself. She rose and slowly circum-navigated the couch on her way to the door. As she went by, she felt a gentle touch on her arm.

"Thank you," Barbara whispered softly.

She was overcome by the bare misery on Barbara's face; she didn't trust her voice not to break if she replied. All she could do was simply nod her head and leave the melancholy woman sitting alone in the half-darkened room.

Disoriented from the somber hour she had just spent, she stood on the threshold of the front door, trying to get her bearings. She was almost blinded by the twinkling lights. A sense of unreality overcame her as the gleeful sounds of the party reached her; she had actually forgotten the party while listening to Barbara's unhappy disclosures.

To her left, where the terrace widened and wrapped around the end of the house, the orchestra was playing to a dance floor filled with swirling figures. Small girls swung around with their fathers; brothers and sisters practiced intricate steps together; husbands and wives held each other close while they swayed to the music. The tables on the lawn had been broken down into smaller tables and rearranged nearer to the terrace, where the elder members of the community sat watching the dancing; occasionally one would succumb to temptation and be led smiling to the floor by a grandchild, where they would box step carefully around the outskirts of the terrace. The buffet table had disappeared, replaced by a discreet bar. A white-jacketed waiter perspired as he tried to keep up with the orders while, at the same time, keeping a watchful eye on the teenagers trying to filch beer from a large tin tub piled high with cans on ice. Smaller children, torn between exhaustion and exhilaration at being up so late, raced around the lawn; their shrill laughter and excited shouts mingled with the beat of the music. Over the entire scene, a starry sky spread its canopy across the heavens like a tent.

Leaning back against the house, she looked around for a familiar face. Josie was dancing with Nelson; the silver-haired man swung Josie around as if he were a boy of twenty. Her skirt flared around her knees, she threw back her head and laughed, and Nelson looked positively smug with his success as a dancer. Claire and Ford were holding each other close, their arms around each other, their eyes closed; Deane and Jonno were doing a slow, hip-swiveling, serious twist; Douglas and

Dorothy moved adroitly through the dancers, their polished steps perfectly synchronized to each other.

At the tables, Eliza sat listening serenely to Thad, whose wheelchair was pulled close to her. His face was alive with interest and his arms gesticulated wildly as he told her some tale or other. Caddy hoped it was a Max story; Eliza would like that. She looked around for Andy Gleason. If Thad became overtired tonight, he would be too exhausted to enjoy himself tomorrow. It was probably time to have Thad driven back to the Northrups', but there was no Andy immediately in sight. Her gaze raked back and forth over the people on the lawn and on the terrace, searching for him. Finally, he emerged from a dark shadow beneath the trees and, pleased, she watched him head straight for Thad, bend down, and speak to him. Thad shook his head, but Andy persisted, and finally Thad nodded reluctantly. Andy had his hand on the back of the wheelchair and it looked as if he was about to turn it around when Eliza leaned forward and must have negotiated for more time, because Andy smiled and nodded his head as he looked at his watch. He tapped Thad on the shoulder before he elbowed his way to the bar and began helping the beleaguered bartender.

Caddy leaned back against the wall again, allowing the scene in front of her to soothe the distress that wouldn't go away after the hour spent with Barbara. The music floated through the cool, rose-scented air, and the candles and flares made patterns on the ground. She wished she had her camera.

"May I have this dance?" She jumped nervously. Fiske loomed out of the darkness to her right.

His face was in shadow, but she could see the outline of his tall figure. Instinctively, she opened her mouth to warn him about Hank. She yearned to give him the answer to all his problems, but her promise to his sister kept her silent.

"No, thanks. I don't think I'll dance tonight." She didn't sound very convincing, even to herself. How could she relax in his arms when something so critical stood between them?

"Yes, you will."

She felt him grip her hand firmly. She resisted only halfheartedly when he led her purposefully along the terrace to the edge of the dance floor and turned back to face her. She glanced up, but when she saw his face so close to hers, she looked down hastily. He didn't speak. Instead, he pulled her to him, circling her waist with his other arm and holding her securely against his body. He began to dance, and she followed. Like the night at the restaurant, she seemed to know instinctively where he was leading and how he wanted her to follow. They didn't speak as they circled the dance floor, reversing at the other side to dance back the way they had come, but his arms tightened around her when any other couple got too close, and his head was turned so his mouth touched her hair. She closed her eyes, feeling inexplicably close to tears.

She tried to remember that this was the man who threatened to interfere with her career, who made plans for her without asking, who made her lose her temper and not even know why, and, worst of all, who could so easily ignore her when Cindy Peck was sitting next to him. They really had nothing in common except Kincade.

But she couldn't feel angry at him anymore, only tired and confused. It would be so natural to turn her head; her lips would meet his and he would kiss her the way he had in New York. She stiffened in his arms. If he knew what she was hiding from him—when he learned she hadn't told him about Hank—he would think she was dishonest and he would probably never forgive her. She shifted slightly, attempting to pull back in his arms, but his grasp tightened so she could barely move her upper body. When he steered them toward the rear of the flagstone veranda to where it wound around the front of the house, she had to follow. She closed her eyes, powerless to withstand the immediacy of his body. He danced them easily around the corner, leaving the other couples bunched together in front of the orchestra. Only the strains of the music followed them, until they were alone on the starlit terrace. The music halted and so did they, but his arm remained around her waist and his hand held hers, as if they were still dancing. She stood in the circle of his arms, her heart pounding.

He lifted her chin with his finger and brought her face to where he could see it. "That wasn't so bad, was it?" he asked very quietly.

She shook her head. More than anything else, she wanted him to kiss her; she was unaccountably disappointed when he didn't. With a gesture as gentle as the tone of his voice, he let her go. Calmly, he sat sideways on the terrace wall and pulled a pipe out of his pocket, looking perfectly prepared to stay. Unsure what to do with herself, she watched him out of the corner of her eye as he busied himself with a Zippo lighter, bending over to shield his pipe from the sea breeze as he tried to light it. A burst of laughter floated from the dance floor, and Caddy wondered what had happened to Cindy Peck. Not that she cared, but she was undoubtedly fooling herself; Fiske had probably asked her to dance only because he was being polite, not because he cared even a little bit about having his arms around her. Unconsciously, she sighed out loud and lowered herself to a seat on the wall.

"Tired?"

"Some," she admitted.

"Having a good time?" Fiske sounded amused.

"Yes."

"As I remember, you were more of a conversationalist the last time I saw you in New York."

Her throat closed up and she was unable to respond. She shook her head slightly. She leaned over and picked some geranium leaves from a plant in a clay pot; crushing them together, she held them to her nose, luxuriating in the spicy, pungent odor. She held out her hand. Fiske bent his head and inhaled deeply, smiling as he straightened up. She held up her hand, and the breeze took the leaves and blew them away into the night.

"Still mad at me?" he asked quietly.

"No." Her heart began to race. She wasn't mad at him, she didn't know what she was.

"Want to talk about it?"

"No. Not now."

"When?" His voice was so low she could barely hear him.

Confused and unsure of herself, she looked at him intently. "Fiske, I—"

He held up one hand to forestall her. "Don't. I take it back. I don't think I'd like what you were about to say, would I?" His face was stern, his pipe forgotten on the wall.

All she could do was shake her head.

After a moment of silence, when all that could be heard was the music and the sound of the night crickets, Fiske began to talk. He looked out over the ocean as he spoke, as if he were merely ruminating aloud.

She listened intently, knowing instinctively he was telling her something important. "This is my favorite party here. Fourth of July, when all the families come back. At first some people look different, the ones you haven't seen since the summer before, but then they click into place, a little older, perhaps a little grayer, but still the friends you've known all your life. Even though some of us live in the same cities in the winter, we rarely see each other. Oh, the kids often go to the same schools, or the wives serve on some of the same boards, and the men play squash and golf with each other occasionally, but oddly enough we keep our distance socially. It's as if we're so close in the summers, know so much about each other, that we need the time away in the winter." He ran his fingers through his hair absentmindedly. "There's not one of them I wouldn't go the distance for. When I'm old, I want to be here, watching the younger generations grow up, just as we did."

"You're lucky to know that," she said in a low voice. Undeceived by the lightness of his tone, she was sobered by the depth of his love for Kincade. "Outside of my mother and father, and Thad and Agatha, I don't have many friends. I envy you this"—helplessly, she searched for the exact word she wanted—"this *belonging,*" she finished in a passionate burst.

The sound of the waves lapping at the shore mingled with the orchestra, the moon was low on the water, and the scent of boxwood fused with the smell coming from the honeysuckle vine growing up the rear of the house. She stared out over the water, blinking back the tears. She could sense Fiske rise. She felt him stand behind her, his light touch as he put both hands on her shoulders. She shook her head, unable to speak. Her mind was a confused whirl.

"You belong here. You have from the moment you set foot on the island," he blurted out softly.

She moved her shoulders, his hands fell away, and she rose, facing him. She knew this was the moment when she should return to the party. If she stayed, she didn't trust herself to resist him. He was very close to her, she could hear him breathe. She looked up into his eyes, suddenly finding it difficult to breathe.

"Fiske, don't . . . I can't . . ." Her entire body ached with longing for him. She dug her nails into the palms of her hands. If she gave in to him now, she was lost forever and everything she stood for, had worked so hard for, would be crushed and vanish beneath the powerful force he exerted over her.

"You can." He pulled her to him and covered her lips with his. His arms held her tight against him and wouldn't let her go. She struggled briefly before she found herself returning his kiss. It was like returning to a perfect place, like returning home. Her arms stole around his neck, and when he buried his head in her hair, she didn't move except to turn her head into his shoulder.

His voice was husky when he whispered, "I want you, Caddy."

Lost in his arms, his words brought her to her senses. A wave of repugnance swept over her. She didn't want to open her eyes. She could feel how much he wanted her, feel it with every fiber of her body that ached because she wanted him, too, but the difference between them was that only a short space of time ago she had seen him look at Cindy Peck with the same desire.

"Caddy?"

She wrenched herself away. "No."

He held her by the arm, not letting her escape entirely. "Why not, for God's sake? Why?"

She wanted to hit him. "It could never work. We're too different," she replied hollowly.

"Our differences, as you call them, have nothing to do with the way I feel about you," he retorted almost angrily.

She couldn't bring herself to accuse him outright of being a philanderer, which is what she was almost certain he was. Filled with pain and chagrin, she tried to wrench her arm away. "I can't give up—"

But his lips covered hers, hard and insistent, silencing her words. This time she dug her nails into the palms of her hands and forced herself not to respond.

"I'm not asking you to give up anything in your life —only to add something wonderful." He shook her slightly to make his point, and it brought her to her senses.

She had almost lost herself in his arms. If she let that happen she would lose everything: her independence, her career, all hope of giving Thad a life of his own. She'd be like any other foolish woman who gave up everything for an affair that would distract her from her goals. She pulled her arm from his grip and backed away down the terrace. "No," she whispered, as if he were the very devil come to tempt her by taking her heart from her. "No," she repeated. The tears that had been close to the surface finally began to stream down her face, and she turned and fled from him.

"Caddy," he called, but she only ran faster, ignoring his call.

As she reached the corner, the sky overhead blazed with shooting stars and colored pinwheels as the Fourth of July fireworks began.

CHAPTER 18

After a stunned moment, Fiske ran after Caddy, but when he got to the corner of the terrace she had disappeared. Ignoring the fireworks, he threaded his way through the rapt crowd, trying to find her slim figure in the dark. The faces around him were all turned toward the heavens as the skies filled and emptied and filled again with brilliant patterns of light and color. Frustrated, he crisscrossed the lawns until, in the illumination from the final crescendo, he found her, only to watch her disappear into the Loverings' station wagon along with Andy and her brother.

Baffled and thwarted, he watched as the taillights vanished down the driveway. Anger boiled up inside him. In the dark, someone bumped into him and he barely restrained himself from lashing out. How could she have run away from him again, as if he were some kind of monster? Hadn't he told her he wanted her? Couldn't she see how much he cared about her? Enough to search for her and find her even after she had made it clear she wanted no part of him. Anger turned to confusion and, head down, he walked slowly back to the remains of the party. It was hard to believe he had begun the evening with such pleasure, because any joy he had felt had evaporated. Now he felt like hell.

He raised his head and looked around. He found he was standing in front of the bar. With a grim smile, he ordered a vodka and tonic and then, methodically and without any humor, proceeded to get very drunk.

Sometime much later he was vaguely aware of Jonno and Josie dropping him off at the Manor. Their laughter as they teased him about trying to outdo their youthful escapades came to him as if from a great distance and was lost in the darkness when he decided that a walk was what he needed. He was vaguely conscious of finding himself in the boat house, staring out over the lapping water of the sound. He must have dozed off there, because when he awoke in the darkness he set out to walk, anywhere, just to clear his head. He talked to himself sternly as his long strides carried him over the roads and fields to the beach: He was too old to let an intractable girl upset him; no woman was worth it.

But Caddy wasn't just any woman, he admitted to himself. She had gotten under his skin. From the first moment he saw her he had sensed on some primal level that she was different from all the other women he had flirted with, made love to, or fancied himself in love with. He respected her commitment to her profession, which matched his own, but beyond that there was something in her eyes, a kind of delicacy mingled with grave composure, that seemed to pierce his soul. He'd tried to ignore the powerful attraction she held for him, but he hadn't been able to fool himself. Every time he saw her he felt lured and beguiled into a deeper place in his emotions than he had ever ventured before. His steps slowed and he frowned and halted, staring at the house without seeing it.

He couldn't disguise how he felt any longer: just as Josie had diagnosed, he was in love with Catherine Wilcox. Against all reason and without wishing it, he had astounded himself by falling in love, and this time he knew without a doubt it was the real thing. He wanted to spend the rest of his life with her. And she? His frown deepened. She had shown him in every way possible way that she was so stubbornly resolved to be on her own that there was absolutely no room for him in her life.

He looked around the garden in frustration. His eyes darkened with determination. He couldn't be wrong about something he felt was so completely right. She was the misguided one, confusing resolve with stubbornness. He felt the first glimmer of amusement since Caddy had run away from him. She couldn't have returned his kiss the way she did if she didn't care as much as he; her body had betrayed her. He wondered if she knew it. His spirits rose fractionally and he squared his shoulders resolutely. For a moment he felt as grimly determined as he had when he decided to fight Asher for Kincade, but this time, he thought with a tired grin, what he was going to fight for was of far greater magnitude.

He strode rapidly up the incline to the veranda, his head down and his hands stuffed into his pockets. The sun was trying to break through the dense fog that layered over the island. In his mother's garden only the bare outlines of the flower beds were visible, making rectangular designs on the lawn. In front of him the Manor loomed gray and silent in the pale, early morning light; one faint light, in his parents' bedroom, glimmered through the fog. He looked at his watch. It was five thirty in the morning.

"Fiske." His mother was standing in the doorway in her bathrobe and bare feet. "What are you doing there?"

"I couldn't sleep so I went for a walk on the beach. What are *you* doing up at this hour?"

"I can't find your father. I just woke up and he wasn't in bed." She looked faintly worried.

"The studio," Fiske said reassuringly. Sometimes his father woke up early and started painting just as the sun rose. But this morning, he realized suddenly, the fog had not lifted and there was no sun. Smiling at her to conceal his own mounting concern, he turned and walked across the lawn toward the shed. There was no light coming from beneath the door. He wiped the beads of dew from the window with his hand and peered inside.

He could see the back of his father's motionless figure seated on a low stool in front of his easel. He rapped on the windowpane to attract his attention, but his father didn't turn. His mother had followed him and was standing right behind him. Worried now, he shielded her from the window so she couldn't see inside. He was engulfed by a sense of danger and he could feel his heart beat faster. "I think he's fallen asleep. I'll go in and wake him up," he lied gently. "You go back up to the house."

She took an uncertain step backward, but made no

move to return to the house. "Are you sure he's all right?"

"Yes, I'm sure." Carefully he walked around to the door and turned the knob. The door gave way easily in his hand and swung open. "Dad," he said quietly, hoping against hope that there would be a response. When Douglas didn't answer, Fiske forced himself to walk forward and look down at the figure slumped against the easel. His father's eyes were closed and he looked as if he were merely sleeping. His body had fallen forward with his head resting against the canvas; next to his outstretched hand, his palette and brushes were untouched, as if he had been sitting there waiting patiently for the darkness to fade in order to begin painting. Fiske felt numb. He reached out one hand and felt for Douglas's pulse. He was unsurprised to find none. Somehow he had known the second he saw the unnatural stillness of his father's body that he was dead.

Automatically, he bent down carefully and put one arm around Douglas's back and the other beneath his knees and lifted him in his arms. Without turning, he held his burden and said quietly to his mother, "I'm going to carry him up to the house now. I want you to turn around without looking and walk in front of me." He shivered as he heard her low, pained moan pierce the silence, like a wounded animal, but when he turned around she was standing with her back to him. Her shoulders heaved as she began to cry. Wanting to go to her but unable to move, he waited until, slowly, she retreated up the path to the house.

Barely holding back his own tears, Fiske shifted his father so his head was cradled against his shoulder. He followed his mother with steady, measured steps, staring straight ahead until the small procession reached the library. Tenderly, he laid his father on the sofa and placed his arms next to his sides. Fiske straightened, then looked down for a moment. Even though Douglas was dead, he had an unaccountable urge to try and make him comfortable. Reaching back down, he slipped a pillow beneath his father's head and drew a folded blanket from the bottom of the sofa up over his body, tucking it beneath his chin.

Satisfied that he had done all he could do for the moment, he turned and held out his arms and drew his mother close to him. Wordlessly they clung to each other as her sobs increased. He held her, soothing her with his hands on her back until the worst of her uncontrollable spasms abated. When she tried to pull away he guided her to her chair in front of the fireplace and lowered her, keeping his body between her and Douglas's still form as a shield.

"You don't have to keep protecting me," she managed to say between her sobs. "I'm not a child. I know he's dead. I knew it the moment I saw your face when you looked in the shed window."

Fiske knelt beside her and held both her hands firmly in his, as if by the very act of touching her he could ease her pain. He didn't dare think about Douglas being dead; he couldn't give in to his own grief when he knew so much would depend on Dorothy and Barbara being able to rely on him.

Barbara. Someone would have to tell her. All the details that surround a sudden death flooded his mind as he crouched by his mother: all the relatives to be told, the islanders, Douglas's friends in New York and around the world; there would have to be a service, the attorneys to be contacted, the newspapers and the foundation to be notified. For all his modesty, Douglas Spencer was the head of one of the wealthiest, most influential families in the country, and his death would be a very public affair. Thinking about how he had to be strong for Dorothy and handle the details and arrangements, he experienced a shock that was almost physical as he realized that, with his father's death, he had become the head of the Spencer family.

He squeezed Dorothy's hands and released them, rising slowly and unsteadily to his feet. He looked down at her blankly, his mind racing in several directions at once as he swiftly prioritized what had to be done first. His mother's voice speaking softly brought him back to the immediacy of the room and its occupants.

"Darling. I want you to leave me alone with your father for a few minutes. To say good-bye before anyone else knows. Will you do that?" When Fiske nodded, she continued in an even voice, "Then I'm going to tell Grace. She can sit with him while I dress. She loved him dearly, you know." Dorothy's voice quavered, but she steadied it resolutely.

Watching his mother gain control over herself and knowing the effort it must have taken, Fiske felt his own eyes mist, admiring her courage in a way he never had before. He held out his hand. She clung to it while she rose stiffly and stood facing him.

"I want you to be the one to tell your sister. I want you to tell her and bring her to me. Will you do that?" she asked for the second time. Again, he nodded. "Good. Then we'll be all right. The three of us will stay here with Dad until you make the arrangements for us all to return to New York." She reached up and pulled her son's head down and kissed him gently on the forehead.

Fiske nodded. He bit his lip, not trusting himself to speak. If he spoke he knew he would break down entirely, and there was no time for that now. He hugged her to him fiercely, putting all his love for her into his embrace.

"I know, darling. I love you too. I'm better now, I promise. You go to Barbara." She shoved him gently toward the door.

Reluctantly, he acceded to her wish and left the room, still trying to find the right words to say to her. Dorothy was unaware of his presence. She had knelt on the floor next to the sofa, and she was holding her husband's hand. Her face was close to his and she was smiling slightly through her tears, as if Douglas had just confided an enormous, secret joke to her that only the two of them could possibly understand. Silently, Fiske pulled the door closed and left them alone.

Shivering slightly, he stood on the veranda, blinking in the sunlight that had banished the fog. Everything looked so normal, as if it were any other day. The breeze rustled through the tops of the trees, Dorothy's garden was alive with brilliant color, and somewhere a dog was barking. It seemed inconceivable that his father wouldn't come out of the door behind him, slap him on the back with one of his jokes, and try and wheedle Fiske into sailing around the point with him on such a fine morning. He looked at his watch in disbelief: only an hour had passed since he had walked over this same grass to the house, hoping not to waken anyone as he climbed to his room.

Wearily, he reached in his pocket for the keys to the Jeep and, not finding them, decided to walk through the woods to the cottage. He dreaded telling Barbara. She and Douglas had that relationship fathers and daughters enjoy if they're fortunate, when each is a confidant and admirer of the other. Their communication had been filled with a kind of verbal shorthand they had developed over the years, which not even

Barbara's marriage or the birth of her two children had ever changed. She would be devastated. He slowed his steps, troubled by the memory of how he had last seen her the night before, bleary and hung over, leaving the party alone.

A pheasant flew up out of a thicket of raspberry bushes, startling him with its flapping wings; there must be a hen and chicks somewhere nearby it was protecting. He moved along the narrow path, pushing aside an occasional branch that had grown out over the trail, making a mental note to tell the gardener it was time to clear the walkways that crisscrossed the property. He halted, appalled he could even think about such a mundane thing at a time like this; his mind must be playing tricks on him, trying to convince him it was a normal day. His eyes scanned the view through the trees to the water. Three small boats were heading north, probably trying to get to the fishing grounds before the tourists arrived from the mainland in their large party boats.

Anxious to get to his sister now, he hurried through the remaining forest until it dwindled to a few trees on the edge of a large meadow not unlike that of the senior Ludlows, but no modern house was planted in the middle of the shining field. Instead, an antique Victorian house with sparkling white-painted gingerbread decoration and a patterned, peaked slate roof sat demurely beneath a towering weeping willow tree. A light burned in the window of the extension, where Barbara and Hank had installed a new kitchen with wide glass windows and a potbellied stove for heat on chilly autumn mornings. Someone was awake; he only hoped it was Barbara and not her husband. His footsteps left a dark trail on the dewy grass as he approached the house quietly. The solitary figure sitting at the kitchen table jumped when he tapped on the glass window of the back door.

"Fiske. What are you doing here so early?" Barbara swung the door open to let him in. She was wrapped in an old flannel bathrobe, her hair still damp from the shower, and she held a chipped coffee mug in her hand. She looked tired but composed, as if she had spent the time she should have been sleeping coming to some sort of a resolution that left her calm and at peace with herself.

He tried to smile, but failed miserably. "Babs . . . it's Dad."

"Is he sick? Do we need a doctor? What's wrong?" She rubbed one bare foot against her other ankle and looked up at him anxiously.

He fought to keep his voice even. "I think it was probably a heart attack. He's—"

"He's all right, isn't he?" she interrupted, her voice thin with fear.

"No, honey, he's not all right. He's dead."

"Dead?" she breathed incredulously. "He can't be."

Fiske removed the mug from her hand and put it on the windowsill, while at the same time putting his other arm around her so he could pull her against his shoulder. "It must have been very sudden and very quick. He was just sitting at his easel, as if he was waiting for the sun to rise. He looks like he's asleep, Babbo."

"But he's dead," she said dully, her words muffled by his jacket.

"Yes."

She twisted like a caged bird trying to free itself. He held her lightly, ready to let her go if that was what she wanted, but just as she tried to take a step away she collapsed, her body doubled over in pain and her fists clenched as she began to weep. He guided her to the window bench and sat down with her, keeping his arms around her shoulders so he could hold her while she cried. He had no idea how much time passed before her sobs turned to whimpers and she leaned against him in exhaustion, her swollen eyes closed and cheeks wet with tears. He had to keep himself strong for her, but inside he felt as if he was breaking apart.

"I can't stand it," she whispered. "Oh, God. I can't stand it. I was just waiting until it was late enough to go over to the studio and see him. He can't be dead when I need to talk to him."

"You can talk to me, Babs. It won't be the same, I know, but I'll try and listen."

"Oh, Fiske. You're so damn *good.*" She rose unsteadily and wandered over to the stove, looking down at it as if she had forgotten it was there. Finally, she reached for the coffeepot, shook it, and, finding it empty, automatically filled it with water and spooned coffee into the top. She remained standing, watching the dark liquid drip down into the pot. Fiske watched her warily, wondering if he should put her to bed; she was so pale she looked as if she might faint at any moment. Uneasily, he rose, prepared to catch her if she fell, but to his surprise she turned and asked matter-of-factly, "You want coffee, don't you?"

"Sure." He didn't, but he thought she needed something to do to keep herself steady, and he accepted the mug she offered with a faint smile he hoped was reassuring.

"Mom sent you, didn't she?"

"Yes. But I would have come anyway." He sipped the scalding hot brew and tried not to grimace. It was much too strong.

"What do we do now?" She sat back down at the

table and leaned forward, cradling her mug between her hands as if she needed the warmth to keep away a chill. "I guess I go up to the house, right?"

He slid into a chair opposite her and leaned forward with his own mug so their heads were closer together. "Mom's getting dressed now. Grace is with her. I'll take you back when you're ready, and we'll start making calls."

She turned her head away as if she didn't dare look at him when she asked, "Where is he?"

"I carried him into the library. I'll call the mainland and we'll all fly down to New York with him as soon as we can get transport."

"Mom. How is she? How did you . . ."

"She woke up and he wasn't in bed. She was looking for him when she ran into me coming home. We both went down to the shed and I went in and found him."

"God. How horrible. You must have died."

"Close to it," he conceded wearily, rubbing his eyes as if he was trying to erase the image of that still figure slumped over his easel.

"Did you carry him up by yourself?"

"Yup."

"Christ. How awful."

"Not so bad, really. I didn't even think about it. I just wanted to get him in the house, as if he'd be safe there. Silly, I guess."

"Not so silly, darling." The first glimmer of a wan smile crossed her face fleetingly. "You're a nice guy."

"Maybe." How could he possibly explain the way he felt? It was as if the shape of the world had changed in an instant. He turned his mug, watching the damp circles it made on the tabletop. "Everything is suddenly different now, Babs. It really hasn't sunk in."

"God. You're head of the foundation now. Head of

the family too. Does that mean I come to you when I want to do something the trustees won't like?"

"Did you go to Dad?"

"Of course."

"Then I guess so. It's too soon to know what it'll be like, Babbo. We'll have to take it a step at a time. I'll do my best."

"I know you will. Poor Fiske." She reached out her hand and covered his, squeezing it gently. "I love you."

"I know."

Suddenly the floorboards creaked as someone descended the back stairs. They looked up, startled, as Hank appeared on the bottom landing, fully dressed despite the early hour and looking the picture of a country squire. Involuntarily, Fiske's lips twitched in a grimace of amusement. Hank was probably pleased to find his brother-in-law unshaven, still dressed in the same clothes he'd worn the night before: they were crumpled, covered with grass stains and sand from his nocturnal wanderings. Fiske controlled himself quickly. But when he looked carefully at his sister to see if she'd noticed his smile, she was staring at him with a perfectly serious face. To his surprise, her eyes were filled with an amusement that equaled his own. It vanished, however, as she looked coldly at her husband.

"What are you doing here so early?" Hank poured himself a cup of coffee and drank it standing at the stove. He eyed Fiske apprehensively, as if wondering if it had to do with him.

"Douglas died early this morning," Fiske responded almost politely. The last thing he wanted was to have to talk to Hank or be forced to listen to his insincere condolences. He realized soberly that this was only the beginning of the long and painful public process of telling people of his father's death. The few private moments he and his sister had shared would be their last until all the panoply of burial was over. He braced himself. Barbara was still staring at her husband with distaste, as if he were a stranger who had wandered uninvited into her kitchen.

"How awful. How did it happen? How's Dorothy?" Hank made no move to touch his wife, nor did he look at her. Despite his questions of concern there was something calculating in the way his eyes shifted back and forth.

"We're not sure, probably a heart attack. She's okay, thank you," Fiske answered briefly, looking from him to his sister, trying to assess the mood between them.

"You may as well know, Fiske," Barbara announced flatly. "We're getting a divorce. Hank was just on his way back to the mainland." Fiske was stunned.

"Of course I won't go now," Hank interjected.

"Of course you will," his wife replied coldly. "There's no reason for you to stay. You never liked my father to begin with, so don't act hypocritical now."

"Babs." Fiske rose to his feet. He looked down at Barbara. Her arms were folded and she was staring up at him almost defiantly; there was no repentance in her eyes for excluding Hank from the family at a time when he would be most expected to be at her side.

"It's over, Fiske. That's what I was going to talk to Daddy about today." Her voice faltered and she turned her head with a quick motion of pain. "Now he'll never know, thank God. He would have hated a divorce in the family."

"I still think I should stay, for the sake of the children, if nothing else," Hank said easily, as if they were discussing a cocktail party.

Fiske drew a deep breath. All of a sudden he felt

profoundly exhausted as the long, sleepless night and
the events of the morning finally caught up with him.
Looking at his sister, he made a quick decision. "No,"
he said firmly. "I don't know what's happened between
you, but if Babs doesn't want you here now, then you'd
better leave as you planned." Barbara turned her head
away again, but not before he saw the look of relief
and appreciation in her eyes. He stared steadily at
Hank until the other man, averting his glance, put
down his cup and strode to the door, slamming it behind him as he left. The glass rattled in its frame.
Shortly, they heard the car start and the crunch of tires
on gravel as it left the property.

"Thanks," Barbara said softly.

"My pleasure." He managed a smile. They looked at
each other, enjoying a wry moment of communion.
"Do you want to tell me what that was all about?"

"Not now. There's no time. I have to go to
Mommy."

"I know you do. So do I and we will, but first I want
to know what's going on here."

Softly, she began to sob again. "You sound just like
Daddy."

"Come on, Babs, you'll feel better if you tell me."

"We're getting a divorce." She wiped her eyes on
the edge of a dish towel.

"You told me that. Why?"

"Rufus Kincade is senile. Hank found out. He got
Rufus to sign papers illegally selling his land to Asher.
That's all."

"That's *all*? What the hell are you talking about?"
Fiske was shaken and furious. The idea that Hank
could take advantage of someone's tragic descent into
senile dementia was so abhorrent and repugnant to
him, he felt almost ill.

"I've known for a while, but I pretended to myself it was all right, that he was just acting like the rest of you guys. You know, you're all always talking about 'doing deals.' I let myself believe no one would get hurt, that Hank was just doing a deal, making money for us. It was so important to him. It wasn't enough that there's all the Spencer money. He had to be bigger than the family, more of—I don't know—a robber baron on his own. He *needed* it, and I loved him so much I thought if it made him happy then it would be all right in the end."

Fiske couldn't speak. Rage filled him that one of their own, a Spencer by marriage and an islander by adoption, could steal land from Rufus, could actually attempt to bring about the end of Kincade merely for his own personal aggrandizement. The thought was unspeakable to him. All he could do was bow his head so Barbara wouldn't see his fury. Why hadn't his sister told him? He raised his head and looked wordlessly at her.

"I know," she said dully. "It's horrible. I should have stopped him. It's my fault. I pretended it wasn't happening, hoping it wouldn't work or it would all go away, but when it didn't all I could do was get drunk. God. What a mess I am."

"No, you're not, honey." Pity replaced his anger. "Love does funny things, I guess."

"*You* would never have let something like that happen in the name of love though."

"Maybe. Who knows?"

But Fiske was sure, given a similar situation, he wouldn't have been able to compromise his principles, and he knew Barbara was well aware of that side of him. The room was very quiet as they each were lost in their own thoughts. Outside, the shrill, early morning sounds of the birds rising signaled it was getting later. He didn't know what to say to comfort Barbara. She began to speak in a low monotone, and he let her words drift over him until Caddy's name leapt out at him. He raised his head abruptly and focused intently on each word his sister said.

". . . after she left, I just sat there in the dark, alone with myself. I finally faced the fact that Hank simply wasn't worth loving, that I'd been a fool. It isn't just that he was ready to throw away Kincade—that was awful enough—but he didn't care that he was doing it illegally. Telling Caddy made me really see him for what he is: a crook."

Fighting his exhaustion, Fiske tried to make sense of what he was being told. "Caddy knew about this last night? She never said a word." He simply couldn't take it in that she had known something so important to the salvation of Kincade and hadn't told him.

"I begged her not to. I don't know why, but I felt I could trust her." She pushed back her chair and rose. "I'll get dressed and get the kids up. Will you wait and walk back with us? I'll tell them about Daddy as we walk."

"I'll help." He stood up and tried to stretch, but his muscles felt like lead. Barbara had trusted Caddy, an outsider, a woman she barely knew and had initially been prepared to dislike. He shook his head. He couldn't think about the significance of that now.

"That's what I figured." For the first time a real smile lit her pale face. She turned with a swift motion, as if she couldn't let another minute lapse without going to her mother, and quickly ran up the back stairs. He could hear her low voice murmuring to Allison and Jared as she woke them and the children's bare feet padding on the board floors as they left their beds.

Restlessly, he walked outside, needing to get out of the house into the clean, fresh air. He turned his face up to the sun, enjoying the feeling of warmth. The scent of hay growing in the field next to the house was sweet and fresh, but so ordinary, as if it were any other morning, that it added to his feeling of detachment, as if he were not really here at all.

Opening his eyes, he looked around blankly. The trees were too green, the sky too blue for a morning when his father had died; everything should be somber, black and white to reflect the enormity of the tragedy. He began to pace up and down the driveway.

Somewhere, behind his grief for his father, the knowledge began to take shape that his own life would never be the same. Now it was his turn to head the family, to keep the traditions and lead them for the next decades until, like his father and his father before him, it would be time to turn those responsibilities over to the next generation. His face was bleak and his hands clenched behind his back as he walked, his head down, deep in thought.

Despite his mother waiting for him at the Manor, his sister and her children clattering down the stairs to join him, and the knowledge that there were able, handpicked advisers to assist him in New York, he faced the fact that the burden of guiding the Spencer fortune and the Spencer Foundation would ultimately fall on his shoulders. A vision of the future stretched ahead of him, an unending series of decisions to be made for the good of the family and the people and institutions who relied on the Spencers for support. The back door slammed, and turning to face the children, he was stopped by the look of fear on Barbara's face.

"What's wrong?" he asked sharply.

"What's wrong with you? You look ten years older than you did a few minutes ago. What's happened?"

He thought about telling her, and then he reined in his thoughts. He couldn't add to her grief and worry; it was his job to help and protect her. Smiling gently, he held out his hand to her children and allowed his father's mantle to fall firmly around his shoulders.

CHAPTER 19

Caddy slipped into a pew at the rear of St. James Church, a program clutched in her hand. Overhead, two large fans spun slowly in a vain attempt to cool the hot interior of the dimly lit sanctuary. Every pew was filled. Black-suited vestry members quietly inserted the latecomers into the few remaining seats in the rear and side pews. The organ was playing a Brahms sonata, softly accompanied by a sweet, piercing flute. The altar was banked with flowers, as if all of Dorothy's garden had been picked up and set down again in the front of the church, and over it all the scent of candles and musky incense hovered. At the back of the church the flower-draped casket waited, guarded by eight pall-bearers, all friends and colleagues of Douglas. She recognized Clifford Ludlow and Nelson standing on one side, their faces pale and drawn, looking strangely formal in their dark suits and sober ties as they waited for the signal to proceed down the aisle.

She wasn't exactly sure why she had come to the funeral; it wasn't as if she knew Douglas very well. She wasn't a member of his family, and she certainly hadn't lived on Kincade all her life. Right up until this morning, when she had returned on the shuttle from Washington, she hadn't been sure if she should attend the services, but when she thought of Fiske and Dorothy and Barbara having to go through the complicated and painful business of burying their father and husband, she had known she wanted to be there too. Even if they never knew she had been in the church, she wanted in some small way to show how badly she felt for them and how truly sorry she was for them that Douglas had died. But she hadn't even spoken to Fiske since his father died, she thought miserably.

She bent her head and tried to pray. Despite the fact that James and Louisa rarely attended church and professed to believe in a holistic deity of their own invention, she had been sent to St. Peter's Church School for the first six years of her education and, forced to attend weekly services, had found surprising beauty and comfort in the Episcopalian ritual presented so matter-of-factly in the two-hundred-year-old church. She still attended church occasionally, but her faith, she reminded herself ruefully, was frail, and the only prayer she could remember was the Twenty-third Psalm. She said it softly to herself twice, lingering over the words "Surely goodness and mercy will follow me all the days of my life," hoping fervently it would be true for Dorothy and Fiske and Barbara. Little as she had known Douglas, she could sense the void he would leave in their lives, and she prayed they would be able to find comfort in each other without his presence.

The music ended and she looked up. The family, led by the white-robed rector, was entering from a small door in the front of the church on the right. Dorothy, her head held high and her face serene, walked next to the rector to the front pew, followed by a stern-faced Fiske and a tearful Barbara. The rest of the family, including a woman who was obviously Douglas's sister, and Grace Byrne straggled in behind, filling up the two pews left empty for them behind the immediate family. As the coffin, drawn by the pallbearers, started down the center aisle, the congregation rose and the rector began to intone, "I am the resurrection and the life, he who believeth in me shall have life everlasting . . ." Caddy's eyes misted with tears.

The minister had seated himself and the organist was playing a Chopin étude she had heard Dorothy play one evening at Kincade. Caddy remembered the firelight shining on Douglas's face as he watched his wife with love in his eyes, and she looked at her lap, feeling the tears rise again and wondering why she was so affected by the loss of a man she hardly knew. Automatically she rose with the rest of the congregation and sat when they did, following the service in the prayer book with the help of the program. Near the end of the program was printed the word *Eulogy,* and she looked at the rector, expecting him to ascend to the pulpit.

Instead, Fiske rose from his seat at the end of the pew, mounted three shallow steps to the chancery, and turned to face the congregation.

Her heart began to beat faster. She hadn't seen him since the night of the Fourth of July picnic when she had fled into the darkness, away from the overwhelming power of her attraction to him, afraid of her own feelings. Her first drowsy thought upon awakening the following morning had been of Fiske and the feel of his lips on hers. Not even Jonno's sober face as he made breakfast for the boys while he told her of Douglas's death or Josie's hurried departure for the Manor had totally erased the remembrance of his arms enfolding her. She held her breath, waiting for Fiske to address the hushed mourners, admiring his courage.

"My mother and sister join me in thanking you for being with us today. Dad wasn't overly fond of large crowds, but I think he would have been secretly very gratified to know so many of you wanted to share this moment with his family. To those of you who knew him well, he was more, much more, than the head of the Spencer family and the Foundation. He was an artist of note, an accomplished raconteur who enjoyed nothing more than telling or hearing a good story, a constant husband, devoted father, and loyal friend, a wicked squash player, and a devious sailor. He preferred to live a private life, inasmuch as that was possible, doing good without any fanfare or publicity, trying to make the world a better, safer place. His courage and wisdom were a constant example to all of us, especially to Barbara and myself; his support the bedrock on which we relied throughout our lives. We will miss him." Fiske's voice became harsh with grief and, abruptly, he stopped speaking. It was evident he was fighting for control, and the sight tore at Caddy. Tears spilled over and trailed down her cheeks.

She lowered her head, not wanting to intrude by so much as a fleeting glance on Fiske's struggle as he tried to regain his composure. She hardly heard him as he said a few more brief words and regained his seat next to his mother. The music started again, the pallbearers wheeled the coffin back down the aisle, and this time the rector led the recession followed by Dorothy leaning on Fiske's arm. Barbara, the tears streaming down her face, was close behind, holding her children's hands; there was no sign of Hank. The church emptied slowly behind the entourage, giving the family time to leave in the row of black limousines lined up on Madison Avenue. Overcome with the sadness of the occasion and the lines of grief in Fiske's face as he passed her, staring straight ahead at the coffin as if he couldn't bear to take his gaze away, Caddy slipped out of her pew, behind the side pews and out the side door to the street. The heat hit her like a wall; in a second, her dress was damp with humidity and she shifted her bag from her shoulder to her hand, looking for a taxi.

The funeral hearse rounded the corner, followed by the cortege. As the first limousine passed her, she found herself looking straight into Fiske's eyes. He was holding on to a strap and leaning slightly forward, facing his mother and sister who were clinging to each other on the backseat. His eyes widened when he saw her and he moved, as if to call to her. Involuntarily she took a step forward to go to him, but the car had already moved on and she stood alone on the pavement, watching as the rest of the limousines slowly followed.

"Caddy?" Josie and Jonno Northrup were exiting the church with a small knot of people. Josie wore a slim black linen summer suit; her long blond hair was swept up into a sleek chignon, and she had a leather attaché case slung over her shoulder. Jonno steered his wife toward Caddy with one arm under her elbow; in his other hand he carried a small overnight case and a furled umbrella. The three kissed like old friends in

the way people often do when they meet each other in
an unfamiliar setting.

Shifting his case to his other hand, Jonno put his
arm around Caddy as they walked toward the corner.
"Tough, very tough," he said glumly.

Caddy nodded slowly. "But Dorothy . . . she
looked so calm, almost peaceful."

"He was just too young," Josie almost wailed. "It's
not right."

"Fiske is really knocked out. I don't think it ever
occurred to him Douglas would die so soon. God
knows how I would feel if Dad . . ." His voice trailed
off and he looked worriedly at his wife.

"Don't worry, darling. He's fine," Josie said emphatically.

"So was Douglas." Jonno looked around, trying to
reassure himself by locating his own parents among
the departing mourners.

"Don't do this to yourself, darling. You can't start
fussing over Dad. He'd hate it. It's bad enough we've
all lost Douglas. He was one of a kind." Obviously
trying to change the subject, she turned to Caddy and
asked briskly, "Are you coming to the cemetery?"

"No, I don't belong there. Are you?"

"Yes. Jonno's not, he's got to get back."

They had reached the intersection and Caddy saw
that the crowd in front of the church was breaking up.
Other cars, their headlights on to form part of the
cortege, were picking up passengers, some people
were scouting for cabs, and the rest were dwindling
slowly down the street until they disappeared into the
noontime throng of pedestrians. She waved at Eliza
and Nelson, who were standing uncertainly on the
church steps looking very sad and old; their shoulders
were touching as if they needed each other's comfort.

Josie sighed. "Poor Nelson. He's taken this very hard. Maybe I'll ride out in their car and keep them company."

Jonno looked at his watch. "Good idea." He smiled briefly at Caddy. "I'm taking the shuttle back to Boston. Josie's going to go to the cemetery and come back and spend the night in the city." He handed his wife the overnight case and kissed her cheek. "You'll be okay, won't you? You'll call me tonight?"

"I'm fine. I'll call." She adjusted his tie and patted it carefully. "Don't worry. Don't let the kids eat junk. Get some sleep."

"Romantic, aren't we?" He kissed Caddy's cheek, patted Josie's rear end, and loped off to find a cab.

"Actually, you are."

"What? Romantic? Don't be silly." Josie's eyes were soft as she watched Jonno gallantly give up his cab to an older couple and head farther north to look for another one.

"You girls want to ride with us?" Nelson pointed to one of the black cars at the end of the line. "That's ours. There's plenty of room."

"I'm not going, but thank you." Caddy returned Eliza's kiss and helped her into the backseat, watching until she had settled herself comfortably.

Eliza leaned forward in distress. "Are you sure? We'd love to take you."

"No. Really."

Nelson looked very hot and tired; his face was gray beneath his tan and his eyes were sorrowful, but his voice was vigorous as he insisted, "Nonsense. Come with us. This has been a terrible shock. It would make Eliza happy if you did."

She kissed him. "No, I can't. But thanks, it's nice of you."

"When will we see you? When are you coming up?"
He looked as distressed as his sister.

"I don't know. My work is finished there."

"You could just come and visit us, be our guest."

She shook her head. "I've got so much work to do.
I've been buried down in Washington at the Smithsonian for a week culling through their photographic
archives. I just got back early this morning. Now I've
got to bury myself in the Museum of Natural History
searching out color plates. Between the research and
trying to get into the field, I probably won't have my
head above water until after Labor Day."

"Come to us then," he urged. "If I'd known this job
was going to take you away for so long, I never would
have told you about it."

"I have you to thank for it all. I'll never be able to
tell you what you've done for me."

"Pshaw. We've been over that ground already.
You're the man for the job and that's all there is to it.
But it doesn't have to mean we don't see you anymore.
When you've returned to Kincade once, you'll return
for the rest of your life, don't forget that." Caddy's
heart swelled with pleasure and gratitude: Nelson understood how deeply she had come to love Kincade,
but more than that, he had accepted her into his island
world.

She smiled at him with all the affection she felt. "I
won't forget. I promise. It's just that after the research
here is over, I'm scheduled to go to Africa with Otis in
early October, so I can't see when it will happen. But I
promise I'll come back one day when I can." Her eyes
misted with tears and she hugged him fiercely.

"Whoa, young lady. Don't get ideas." He was smiling as he chided her. Eliza tapped on the inside of the
window, beckoning him to join her out of the heat.

"I'll go with you, Uncle Nelson. Thanks. Caddy, are you sure you won't join us?" Josie raised her eyebrows and looked searchingly at Caddy.

"I'm sure. I almost didn't come to the funeral. I didn't know if I should . . . I mean . . ."

"Fiske will be glad you did."

"How can you be so certain?" Caddy turned slightly, pretending to watch the traffic.

"Because I am. He's certain too, and I'm not just talking about all this." Josie made a gesture that encompassed the church, the mourners, and the waiting cars. "He cares deeply about you—"

"No, he doesn't," Caddy interrupted positively.

"What are you girls talking about?" Nelson interrupted plaintively. He took a fresh white handkerchief out of his pocket and wiped his forehead. The sun beating down on the pavement sent up waves of heat from the cement and made it feel twenty degrees hotter than it was. When they didn't answer, he kissed Caddy again and gratefully joined his sister in the air-conditioned backseat of the car. The chauffeur closed the door and waited patiently for Josie to finish her conversation and join them.

Josie laughed gently. "You'd best come up and stay with us. Bring Thad. Now that he's going to be a published author I can write off your eggs and bacon on my income taxes. Author entertainment, you know." She raised her eyebrows again.

"No. I don't think so, but thanks for asking."

"Why? Afraid?"

"Afraid of what?"

"Afraid you'll find out you're in love with Fiske and have to do something about it?" She was grinning. Caddy wanted to flee from Josie's grin and the panic that was rising up within her.

"You've got it all wrong, Josie. Don't tease me about it."

Josie's smile faded and she looked entirely serious as she said flatly, "I'm *not* teasing. You're as much in love with him as he is with you. You're both just too damn stubborn to do anything about it. If you aren't careful, you're going to miss the greatest ride life has to offer."

"He doesn't love me. He just wants to have an affair with me. There's worlds of difference between the two. Besides, I—" Caddy's voice was low. Her heart was pounding and, despite the appalling heat, she shivered.

"He loves you." Josie interjected firmly.

"Time to leave, Josie." Nelson had rolled down the window and Eliza's thin voice came from the rear seat of the car. Ahead of them the cars were beginning to move slowly; the first had already turned the corner in the same direction the hearse had taken.

Josie leaned forward and kissed Caddy. As she turned to walk around the front of the limousine to where the driver was holding open the front door, she called back, "Don't be a fool, Cad. It's too important."

The car door slammed, the chauffeur sprinted around to the driver's seat, and moments later the car edged away from the curb with Nelson and Eliza waving back at her from the rear window. Soon the sidewalk was empty and the street filled with honking taxis and trucks. Behind her the doors to St. James were closed as if there had not been over three hundred mourning people within its walls only a short while ago. Aimlessly, she began to walk down Madison Avenue in the direction of her office and the work there, but her thoughts kept returning to Kincade; the night Fiske held her in his arms and told her he wanted her, and the desolate look in his eyes when he passed her in the car carrying him to his father's burial. How was it possible that one look of desolation could cancel out all the distrust she had felt about his intentions or make her forget all over again that she had no place in her life for him? Now she was confused. Tears stung her eyes. All she wanted to do was put her arms around Fiske and offer him comfort.

Struck by an idea, she halted in the middle of the sidewalk. Of course. She would call on the Spencers, a visit of condolence to tell them how very sorry she was. They were sure to stay in town for a few days; she could go to their apartment. And perhaps, once she was there, she could find some way of letting Fiske know that, despite the fact she was only another woman in his life, she wanted them to be friends, good friends. She nodded slowly to herself. She *did* want to see Dorothy and Barbara, and even though it meant returning to that mausoleum of an apartment, she could do that, if that would make peace with Fiske.

CHAPTER 20

A wave of late afternoon heat hit Caddy as she exited the taxi cab and walked hastily into the cool, dim interior of the lobby.

"Mrs. Spencer, please," she said steadily to the waiting doorman.

"Who shall I say is calling, ma'am?"

"Catherine Wilcox."

"Very good."

With his back to her, the doorman spoke discreetly into a small house telephone. Caddy pushed back her hair nervously with one hand and straightened her belt with the other. Now that she was actually here, she wished she hadn't come at all. Perhaps the Spencers wouldn't want to see her; if they did, what could she say? How could anything she might say possibly compare with the dignitaries from all over the world who had come to the funeral to honor the modest head of the Spencer family? She remembered sitting in the back of the church and noticing two senators and at least one foreign head of state in the front pews. It had only made her more aware of the huge difference between her background and Fiske's; not even the obituary—which took up three columns of *The New York Times*—detailing the history of the rise of the Spencer family to the very private position of power they held in the country had prepared her for the multitude of famous faces she had seen among the mourners. What on earth was she doing here? Extending her condolences to Dorothy and Barbara and seeing Fiske, she answered her own question firmly.

The doorman turned and nodded. With a pleasant smile he pointed toward the elevator where an elderly, uniformed operator was waiting. Her heels clicked across the lobby, but she looked neither to the right nor left, not wanting to see her reflection in the mirrored walls, not wanting to be reminded of the night Fiske had brought her to this building.

"Spencer," she murmured.

"Yes, ma'am." The doors closed silently and the elevator rose swiftly. Caddy's nervousness increased as they passed floor after floor. When they finally halted, she felt as if she'd left her stomach down in the lobby. She looked at the wide entrance in surprise.

"Where are we?"

"The Spencer apartment, ma'am. The penthouse floor."

"But I wanted Mrs. Spencer's apartment," Caddy protested.

"Mrs. Spencer is visiting Mr. Fiske Spencer." Caddy

felt rooted to the floor of the elevator. It hadn't occurred to her Dorothy Spencer would be anywhere but her own apartment in the same building. Conscious that the elevator operator was looking at her curiously, she walked hesitantly forward and nodded briefly to the maid who was waiting in the arch that led to the long main hall. Unable to speak because her throat suddenly felt as if it had closed forever, she followed obediently where she was led, right to the sitting room where Fiske had brought her and where they had argued.

"Caddy, my dear." Dorothy Spencer, dressed entirely in black and carrying a small handbag, ignored the hand Caddy dumbly proffered and put both her arms around her. Her smile was as sweet as ever, but her eyes were devastated. Caddy's eyes filled with tears of nervousness and sorrow.

"I hope you don't mind my calling," she whispered.

"I'm glad you did. Nelson told us you were at the funeral. It was so kind of you to come." She held Caddy away from her and smiled.

"I'm sorry for you." Try as she might, Caddy was unable to say anything more elaborate, but she put all the sincerity she felt into those five words.

Still holding Caddy by the arm, Mrs. Spencer turned. "Look, Fiske. Look who's here, Caddy Wilcox."

Caddy had been so focused on controlling her own tenseness when speaking to Dorothy Spencer that she hadn't looked further. Now she saw that she, Dorothy, and Fiske were the only people in the room. She stepped back hastily. "I'm sorry. Perhaps I shouldn't have come. I thought . . ."

"We were receiving? But we are, my dear. You just missed my sister and her family. Her children are leaving today, but she's going to stay on with me for a while." Dorothy slipped her handbag over her shoulder. She smiled slightly, a tired, worn smile. "As a matter of fact, you caught me just as I was going to slip away for a few minutes. Babs is coming back shortly, and she and Fiske will be here for our callers. I'm very much afraid I need a nap."

"Of course you do," Caddy agreed. Quickly she added, "I'll go out with you." She just couldn't remain in the room alone with Fiske. Speaking to him with others present was one thing—it had seemed like a fine idea even while she was getting dressed to come up here—but now that she was face to face with him, without the presence of strangers to act as a buffer, she was terrified. What on earth had given her the idea she could be so bold?

"No, dear, you stay. Fiske will want to talk to you, I'm sure." With a sweet smile and an affectionate pat, Dorothy left the room. Caddy's heart sank. From the stern expression on Fiske's face, it didn't look as if he wanted anything to do with her, much less talk to her. His eyes were wary and the smile he offered her was reserved, as if she were someone he knew very slightly.

Caddy squared her shoulders and drew a deep breath. Despite the cool breeze wafting in from the terrace, she was perspiring and she could feel her dress sticking to the middle of her back. "Fiske, I'm sorry about your father," she began lamely.

"Thank you. It was nice of you to drop by." Not a muscle moved in his face. He looked so unapproachable that her heart sank even further. This was impossible. She would say a few words of condolence and make her escape.

"Your eulogy was perfect."

"I'm glad you thought so." He was getting more formidable by the moment.

"I had hoped to see Barbara too. Will you tell her how sorry I am and that I'm thinking of her?"

He nodded once. "Of course. Thank you."

There was no point in lingering. Fiske obviously had no intention of prolonging their pitiful conversation. She looked him directly in the eyes. "Then I'll leave now. I just wanted you all to know how badly I felt for you." She thought about trying to shake his hand, but her nerve failed. All she could do was smile politely. "Tell Barbara I'll write to her. Good-bye, Fiske," she said softly. She turned.

"Wait."

She spun around. "What?"

"About Barbara . . ." He looked at her as if he was calculating a set of numbers in his head.

"Yes?" At least he was talking to her; he hadn't let her walk away without saying something personal to her. Suddenly she wondered if, given Douglas's death, Barbara had managed to tell Fiske about Hank and Rufus.

"Babs told me you stayed with her at the dance when she passed out. Thank you for that. It was kind of you." Having said that, he closed his mouth firmly as if he had said all he had to say to her and their accounts were squared.

"It was nothing," Caddy assured him. But it *had* been something, something tremendously important, and she yearned to tell him the entire story. But she couldn't; she had given Barbara her promise. Her shoulders sagged.

For the first time since she had seen him standing across the room, Fiske smiled with a hint of the old Fiske, the Fiske who had made her care for him de-

CHAPTER 22

The remnants of their breakfast lay forgotten on the table at the other end of the deck while Caddy and Josie sunned themselves in the early September sun. Through half-closed eyes, Caddy drowsily followed the progress of two low-flying gulls soaring over the wetlands. The sun felt hot on her skin, and she closed her eyes completely and turned her face up toward it. For the first time in weeks she felt completely relaxed.

"This is nice," she murmured without turning her head. The women were stretched out side by side on chaise longues, their mugs of coffee on the deck beside them.

"Blessedly quiet," Josie replied lazily. A cormorant shrilled stridently and both women chuckled.

"May it last forever." Caddy opened her eyes as the import of her idle words hit her. She sat up and looked over at Josie. "Will it? Last forever?"

Without opening her eyes, Josie grinned. "I think so."

"Captain Hardy told me Rufus Kincade, young Rufus Kincade, was home." As much as she was longing to know exactly what had transpired on the island, she was reluctant to appear too pushy.

"Like Lochinvar from the West, riding out of the sunset. Except in this case it was Madagascar. Jonno says he got a power of attorney signed before he even dropped his suitcase, but whatever he got, it's taken care of Asher."

Caddy was puzzled. "Even if young Rufus protected the Kincade family land, Asher could still make a run on the island, couldn't he?"

"Not when the Flying Wedge started tossing words like *coercion* and *litigation* around. None of us has heard from him since."

"God. That's wonderful. Just wonderful." With a sigh of pleasure, Caddy leaned back and closed her eyes again. She felt a surge of delight. Now the Great Marsh, the swooping kites, and the bayberry bushes that cradled their nests were safe.

A boisterous roar of laughter came from the far end of the deck. Caddy turned her head and fastened on its source. With the help of their elder brother, the twins, Ian and Randy, had laboriously moved their blocks outside in order to construct one of their huge forts against the side of the house; Thad, standing in the middle of the fort, directed the three young Northrups in their efforts.

Josie chuckled and said in a low voice, "Look at

them. They think Thad hung the moon. They'd follow him anywhere."

"I never knew he was so good with children," Caddy responded almost humbly. "He's had only a few friends his own age because of his illness, and there just haven't been any kids around, little ones, I mean. He's got a real touch, hasn't he?"

"It's better than that. He really likes them and he treats them as if he and they were the same age; they love him for it. He's never too busy or too tired to play with the boys, and he tells them endless stories. They'll remember this time as long as they live. You know, 'That summer the famous author spent with us, and now his stories are read all over the world.' "

She looked at Josie curiously. "You keep saying that, that he'll be famous. Do you really believe it?"

"You never know in this business, but he's got something very special and the publicity department is wild about his work and his personal story. He creates a world on the page that's more than just imagination, it's a whole morality play—and that's the stuff of the best children's writers. Like Grimm, and Sendak." She leaned back and stretched her arms wide, grinning with satisfaction. "And I discovered him. He's going to be really big and put us all on the map, I just know it."

Caddy looked at her brother with an expression that was almost reverential. He was crouched behind the walls of the fort, his thin hair sticking up and his face alight with delight as he marshaled a force of tin soldiers to defend the ramparts, looking for all the world as if he were a careless seven-year-old himself instead of a twenty-two-year-old veteran of more hospital stays than she could remember.

Josie straightened up and looked very practical. "He doesn't need an agent now, but he will. I'm going to

give him a list of the good ones to talk to, and he
should have a lawyer look over the contract we're
drawing up for him. It's for the first book, which we're
putting together now, with an option to buy the second. There are bound to be many more; I've heard
him telling the boys enough new stories, different ones
without Max, to know that for sure. He'll get some
money on signing the contract, some more when the
finished manuscript is accepted, and the rest when the
book is published."

"I'll help him find an agent—" Caddy started, but
stopped in surprise at the vehemence with which she
was interrupted.

"You'll do no such thing." Josie grinned in apology
even as she continued firmly, "Thad is perfectly capable of handling his own affairs. Underneath all that
natural sweetness and imagination is a very practical
mind. There's no reason why he shouldn't be allowed
to make his own choices."

"Sorry," she said slowly. "I can't get used to the
change."

Josie patted her arm affectionately. "I'm not sure
it's really a change, honey. More like Thad coming into
his own, perhaps. You took such good care of him, he
never needed to ask for anything or make his own way.
It's good for him to do for himself. It gives him confidence and independence, and that's got to be good for
his health, don't you think?"

"That sounds like a nice way of saying I smothered
him," Caddy responded with a sad half-smile as she
watched Thad rise up out of the fort and roar at the
twins in mock ferocity. The twins squirmed with pleasure and giggled delightedly at his antics while Mikey,
bolder than his brothers, crept around to Thad's rear
and pounced on his back. Without a break in his roar-

ing, Thad reached behind and, balancing himself carefully, slowly pulled Mikey up to his shoulders, holding the little boy's legs securely in front so he wouldn't fall. He had never looked happier.

"No way. He might not be here if you hadn't taken such good care of him," Josie said gently.

Caddy felt a little rueful. She had learned a lot about herself and her family lately. "That's probably not quite true. I guess Mother and Daddy aren't quite as helpless as I made them out to be. After all, they do teach their classes and forage for food occasionally, and they go to the symphony like normal people, even if Louisa takes a book along just in case." Overcome by the picture of her mother dressed in her ancient black evening dress carrying a large, black leather tote bag to hide the book she couldn't bear to leave behind, Caddy began to laugh helplessly. Thad gently shook off his companions and wandered over to hear the joke. His eyes lit with humor when Caddy told him what had started her off.

"You mustn't think we don't love them," Thad assured Josie.

"On the contrary, I think you two adore your parents. You both couldn't be as nice as you are or talk about them with such delight if you didn't. I can't wait to meet them."

Thad and Caddy exchanged amused glances. "You have to come to Philadelphia to get the full flavor," Thad said.

"I will. I will," Josie promised. She stretched again and yawned widely, then rose from her chair. Looking over at the dishes on the table, she made a face. "I think I'll live dangerously and just leave these. They'll keep. I promised myself a morning on the beach with the boys." She put two fingers in her mouth and whis-

tled loudly. Moments later, surrounded by three small
blond heads and a leaping dog, she set off in the direction of the water, her own head bent to better hear the
excited conversation of her sons.

Left to themselves, Caddy began stacking the dirty
dishes on top of each other, and Thad slumped in a
chair. He watched her collect the empty coffee mugs.
She paused, the mugs still in her hand, to look out over
the shallow marsh.

"Happy?" he asked shyly.

"Very. These past two days have been idyllic. No
ringing telephones, no fax machines, no people wanting me to make decisions. I love it." She sighed with
pleasure and sat down at the table, glad to have a few
moments alone with her brother. All the confusion of
getting her project off the ground must have worn her
down more than she had realized. It seemed all she
had done since her arrival on Kincade was laze around
the house. She would rouse herself to nibble at her
meals or sleepily enjoy the antics of the children, only
to steal away happily to her deck chair where she
would find her eyelids growing heavy, her book left
unread, as she sank into a sweet doze in the late afternoon sun.

"I'm proud of you, Cad," Thad said. "You did just
what you said you would: make it big in the big time."

"You make me sound like a rock star," she laughed.
"I was in the right place at the right time with a lucky
connection. You're the one who's making it big. People
will be reading your books long after the rest of us are
gone. I'm the one who's proud."

"Seems funny. Josie thinks people will want to read
about Max," he mused. "He was just something I
made up for us, to make you laugh. I never thought
anyone else would be interested. It's funny, isn't it,

how things work out? You come to Kincade, meet Josie and Nelson, and the next thing we know I'm publishing a book and you're putting together a series for public television."

"Serendipity."

"I'll say. We're lucky, aren't we, Cad?"

She had her face turned up to the sun, her eyes were closed, and there was a smile hovering on her lips. At his words, her face broke into a smile, her eyes flew open, and she grinned broadly at him. "Lucky, and thanks to the parents, kind of talented, I think."

He looked around nervously and rapped on the wooden table. "Don't brag. It's bad luck."

She laughed out loud. "I wouldn't to anyone else but you. You're right, we're lucky."

"Josie says I have to have an agent. Will you help me pick one?"

She looked at him and her heart swelled with love at the serious expression on his face. She remembered Josie's admonition. Reaching over, she grasped his hand in hers. "Darling, I would if I thought you needed me, but you and I both know you can manage perfectly well without me. I know you'll make the right choice. I'll always be around to talk things over with you, and I want you to think seriously about spending more time with me in New York, but you're going to want to make your own life."

He puzzled over this quietly for a moment. "You mean move away from home?"

"Maybe," she admitted. "I don't know. You'll figure it out—and I'll always be there to listen when you do."

He reflected for another moment, reached a decision, and announced, "I don't think I would ever want to be away from our house in Philadelphia all the time. I like it there. It's quiet and it's easy to think up stories in my room, and besides, they're used to me in Philadelphia."

"That's true," she agreed swiftly. He was probably thinking about his doctors and the hated hospital where, despite his loathing for the place, they knew him and took such good care of him. Because he always hated talking about his disease, she added quickly, "See? You've made a decision already. You know what you want. You'll be just fine."

"Anyone home?" Thad and Caddy looked at each other in surprise. They had been so engrossed in their conversation that neither one had heard the sound of the engine. Caddy peered cautiously over the railing, wondering who was calling so early in the morning.

"Nelson!" she called down with pleasure as she spotted his silvery hair. "We're up here. On the deck."

"I have eyes. I can see for myself. What's the matter? Gotten so high and mighty you don't come and see your old friends? Eliza's been asking for you." He stood, arms akimbo, at the bottom of the wooden steps leading down from the deck and glared up at her.

Quickly, she ran down the steps and put her arms around his shoulders and kissed his cheek. "I'm so sorry," she said remorsefully. "I got off the ferry and fell asleep and never woke up. I'm the biggest slug you've ever known."

"Otis still working you too hard?" he asked gleefully. "He's a powerhouse of energy. How's it going?"

She sat down on a step, prepared to answer all his questions, and wrapped her arms around her bare knees. The sun was shining directly into her eyes, making her squint as she looked up at him. "He's not working me too hard. I'm working me night and day, that's the trouble. There's so much to do, so much I want to do. Every time I think I've got all the photographs I could ever want or need, we discover a new source, and off I go to investigate."

"Doing it all alone, are you?"

"Not at all. I've hired a staff, I'll have you know, and they're wonderful. They work as hard as I do, but we want it to be perfect, so we never stop."

"No such thing as perfection, my girl. Aren't you old enough to know that by now?" He looked up, over her head, to where Thad was beginning his laborious descent. Managing stairs had always been problematic for Thad, but neither of them moved to offer him assistance. Caddy was touched that Nelson understood her brother preferred to manage on his own. Nelson's voice was gentle as he called, "Good morning, lad. Ready to go?"

"Where are you guys going?" she asked Nelson curiously.

"We take a walk some days. Some days he drives. Sometimes we visit Eliza and check on her cooking. Today I've got something a little special planned: I've brought the canoe and I'm going to take him right into the Great Marsh."

"Can I come?" she asked eagerly.

"Certainly not. This is something we've been planning on; no women allowed." He spoke sternly, but the light in his eyes was anything but stern as he looked from brother to sister. "You can come another time, if you're good."

"Chauvinist." She sniffed and rose with a dignity that was only a little marred by the brevity of her shorts. She joined Nelson on the ground and waited for Thad; together, the three of them walked the remaining distance to Nelson's shiny new red Jeep. Struck by a thought, she turned to Nelson and asked accusingly, "I thought you said you'd never have one of these things yourself. You said the old station wagon would last another twenty years. I thought you were the one who gave me all that song and dance about walking everywhere."

"Never mind. Never mind." Testily, he tried to brush her off. "Eliza's not as young as she used to be, you know. We need the Jeep for her."

"Fraud."

He had climbed behind the driver's seat and was waiting patiently for Thad to settle himself next to him in the front. Leaning out the window, he winked. "Pretty racy though, isn't it?"

"*Racy* doesn't do it justice." She eyed the fire-engine red color and commented blandly, "Everybody sure must know when you're coming down the road."

"Gives them time to get the hell out of the way." With a cheerful wave, he drove away. She watched their heads through the rear window and chuckled as Nelson hit a pothole without slowing down, making them both bump up and down in their seats. When the sound of the engine had died away, she finally turned and ran back up to the deck, briskly collected the dishes, and took them through the house to the kitchen where she washed and stacked them neatly on the shelves. Giving a final look around the kitchen to make sure she had left nothing for Josie to have to clean on her return, she pulled an old Shetland sweater from a peg in the hall and slipped out the back door and away from the house. Finally, a few hours alone when she could take a long, rambling walk by herself around the almost deserted island.

From his vantage point in the passenger seat, Fiske saw a bright red Jeep driving too fast in the distance ahead of them on the lower road.

"Who's driving a new red Jeep?" he asked, not really caring.

"Nelson." Her hands fixed firmly on the steering wheel, Eliza peered straight ahead, as if there was some danger of the road disappearing or the station wagon suddenly taking off on its own. Despite the black mood that hung over him, Fiske smiled. Eliza hated to drive.

"Nelson? A new Jeep?"

"It's really mine. I'm just letting him use it this morning," Eliza replied primly.

At that, Fiske laughed aloud involuntarily.

Eliza looked at him and then quickly back at the road as if it might have changed in the instant she took her eyes from it. "That's better," she commented.

"What's better?" he asked politely. He was too tired to make conversation, even with Eliza.

"You laughing. You should do it more." She slowed for a curve and concentrated on turning the wheel. At this rate we'll never get there, Fiske thought. He reached his arm out the open window and let the branches of a clump of laurels brush against his fingers. They felt cool and smooth, comforting somehow. He brought his arm back in the window. Nothing was really very comforting these days.

"Thanks for picking me up, Eliza."

"I'm glad to do it, my dear. We haven't seen much of you since Douglas died. We miss you," she told him simply. His eyes misted and he cleared his throat. He was suddenly very tired, more tired than he could ever remember feeling.

"There's been a lot to do. Dad's papers, attorneys, the Foundation . . ." His voice trailed off. Hour after hour of poring over columns of figures, listening to people tell him what had to be done, phone calls from seemingly every person in the world who suddenly needed money from the new head of the Spencer family, and, through it all, attempting to find time to pick up the reins of the Spencer Foundation, to add his own vision of what it might be to the existing structure.

"Your mother told me you'd taken a leave of absence from your job. That must be a help."

"Not really." At least at his job he knew what he was doing, and the results were part of a group effort with a measurable bottom line. Now, he alone held sobering responsibility for the family fortune and for the Foundation that affected the well-being of so many people's lives.

"I know, dear," Eliza said gently.

And somehow he felt she did. He reached over and put his hand on her shoulder; still peering intently ahead, she smiled and nodded. All of a sudden he felt better. Just being on Kincade, among the people he loved more than anyone else, gave him a sense of well-being he desperately needed. He frowned. Perhaps not everyone.

With no other preamble he asked abruptly, "If I tell you I'd like to walk the rest of the way, will you be cross with me?" He had an overwhelming urge to feel the ground beneath his feet, to walk through the woods to the house.

Eliza drew the station wagon promptly to a halt. Carefully she turned off the engine and made sure the gear was in neutral. Then she turned slightly so she could look directly at him. "I think that's a fine idea. A walk will do you good."

Fiske leaned over and kissed her soft cheek. "You're a doll, Eliza." He reached for the door handle.

"Fiske?"

"Yes?"

"Before you get out I want to tell you something."
He waited.

"Nelson and I both admire the way you handled all
the nonsense, as Nelson calls it, this summer."

"You mean Asher? I didn't do much. Most of us felt
the same way."

Eliza patted his hand firmly. "No, dear. You were
the one who kept a level head, who saw to it that
nobody lost their temper and said things they might
later regret. No matter what you say, we know you
were the one who thought up the idea of having a
charter. And it's a good idea, one that should have
been thought of years ago. We're very proud of you,
and Douglas would be too. I just want you to know
that." She smiled so tenderly, Fiske was afraid he was
going to choke up.

"Not such a big deal, just making sure anyone who
wants to sell their land has to offer it to the rest of the
island first. Not a big deal at all." For the second time
he found he had to clear his throat.

"But it is a big deal, to use your words, and *you* were
the one who thought it up and who got everyone to
agree. Now no one can sell Kincade land without our
all knowing. Thank you, dear boy, thank you. Now, go
take your walk. Do you need a ride back to your
plane?" she asked briskly. How like Eliza, to finish so
prosaically.

"No, but thanks. Mother doesn't know I'm coming. I
just felt an urge to check in on her. She can run me
back after lunch." He looked at his watch. "Or tea," he
smiled ruefully. With a final peck on her cheek he was
out of the car, with his suit jacket slung over his shoulder.

Walking rapidly, he skirted a stand of tall sea grass,
ducked beneath the low branches of a clump of pine

trees at the far side of the field, and emerged on a narrow sand path that wandered the entire length of the island. He was breathing heavily and perspiration ran down his back. I'm acting like I'm being chased, he thought with bleak amusement. Taking a deep breath, he looked around. He was in the middle of the island's small forest, where the deer hid their young and the badgers lived. The light filtered through the trees and touched the leaves of the thicket beneath their branches. He smiled to himself. Somewhere near here, the summer he was eight, he and the Northrups had built a tree house high in a copper beech, a secret place they had never told another soul about. I bet I could find it if I had time, he thought reflectively. He shook his head at the idea and started in the direction of his mother's house. His necktie was too tight and he pulled it off. A muffled sound of laughter startled him, and he halted. The sound seemed to come from the left. He listened intently, but all he could hear was the soft air rustling through the leaves. Eliza was right; I'm tired, my imagination is playing tricks on me. He took a few steps and heard the laughter again. My God, he thought with rising excitement, it's coming from the old tree house; someone's there. Dropping his jacket on the path, he looked around once to get his bearings and entered the woods, peering upward once he got behind the first tree. There it was: the copper beech. And in it, almost completely hidden from view except from someone who knew where to look, was the tree house, intact after all these years. He wanted to laugh out loud. Carefully, hoping to surprise whoever was there, he inched slowly forward until he was beneath the tree. He looked up. He could see the boards that made the floor of the tree house, a small sneakered foot, and on the other side, where they couldn't see him, the blond head of the eldest Northrup boy. Jonno must have told his kids, he thought with outrage. A scuffling overhead made him draw back. He thought for a moment. No. Jonno would never tell. The boys must have discovered it themselves. They probably stumbled on it by accident and, having found it, claimed it as their own, to use and hide away from the grown-ups. Carefully, he withdrew without letting the boys know he had found them. They were still children and it was their turn to make-believe they could run away to a secret place where no adult could find them, to hold fast to the illusion they were alone.

What does that make me? he wondered as he picked up his coat. An old man? God knows I feel old. He kicked a stone ahead of him on the sandy path as he walked. No, not old, he conceded to himself, but definitely grown up, responsible, dependable, and the solver of problems, great and small. How was it possible that he could believe so utterly that what he was doing was worthwhile and at the same time be left feeling so—he struggled for a word—lonesome. He halted abruptly. Lonesome? Yes, God damn it, despite the people who surrounded him day and night as he felt his way into the role of foundation head, he did feel solitary.

He looked ahead to where the path broke out into the edge of another field, the field that backed up to his mother's property. The path was barely wide enough for two people to walk abreast, and fiercely, achingly, he wished he had a companion to walk next to him, a companion with a thin face and large grave eyes who somehow had made him feel complete.

CHAPTER 23

Choosing the lower road that paralleled the ocean, Caddy walked steadily for almost an hour, admiring the way the sun glinted on pools of still water hidden among the gently waving sea grasses that lined both sides of the road. The rushes were already showing brown tops that would turn into seeds for next summer's growth. Among them, drab, white-rumped plovers shrilled to each other as they gathered together in preparation for the annual fall migration to South America. With one last, lingering look at the blue Atlantic, she turned inland toward the middle road, carefully picking her way through the undergrowth of fern and bracken that threatened to scratch her bare legs. The sun was warm on her back, but the

air was cool and invigorating, with just a touch of
briskness that heralded the change of seasons. Arriving at the main road, she headed for the north end of
the island and the windmill.

The poplars and elms in the woods on either side of
the road were showing tinges of brilliant ruby and scarlet, and a few leaves had already dropped from their
branches, creating a dusty carpet beneath her feet. Despite the heat of the day, intimations of fall were everywhere around her. Ahead, tall, spidery lindens stood
like sentinels on one side of the road, and across from
them a dead pine tree was covered with a blanket of
snowy-white clematis in full bloom. A deep, musical
barking interrupted the deep quiet of the landscape;
she looked up just in time to see a long string of Canadian geese heading purposefully off-island, in perfect
vee formation, their black heads a startling contrast to
their pale breasts. She contemplated them, wondering
if they were the same flock she had seen arriving the
first day she had been on the island.

Bending down, she picked up a long branch,
stripped it of its smaller twigs, and continued on her
way, using the branch as a staff. She passed clumps of
purple wild cabbages growing beneath a spreading willow tree, a thicket of gnarled yew where a tanager with
jet-black wings perched on a branch preening its flam-
ing scarlet head and breast, and finally, a hedge of
silvery Russian olive, which made her come to an
abrupt halt. She had arrived at the entrance to Manor
House. Standing on her tiptoes, she peered over the
hedge toward the house. From a distance the Manor
looked empty, the windows on the ground floor shut-
tered and the front door closed. She deliberated for a
moment. She had no desire to run into any of the
Spencers, but she really would like to see Dorothy's

gardens one more time. She thought Josie had mentioned the family was all in New York, and deciding to take the risk she walked slowly down the road to the house, prepared to turn around and quickly retrace her steps at the first sign of habitation. Cautiously she walked across the lawn, and hearing no human sound, her confidence grew as she rounded the far corner of the veranda to the garden.

She caught her breath at the glory of the colors spread out before her. Chrysanthemums of every size and hue filled the beds nearest the house. Dahlias—orange and white, shocking pink, and bright yellow—edged the borders; golden marigolds, the largest she had ever seen, were planted in a streak like the brilliance of sunlight at one side. The borders were crowded with bright blue spikes of weatherglass, low candytuft, tall lilac larkspur, creamy white everlasting. Between them and behind them all, the family of asters glowed: ruby red, mauve, pale pink, and cherry red. Saving the best for the last, she finally edged around the corner of the farthest bed from the house to where the herb garden lay that she had helped Dorothy plant in the spring.

"I heard steps coming across the lawn; I hoped it was you. I've been wondering if you would come and see the fruits of your labors." The gentle voice came from beneath a large straw hat. Dorothy was kneeling on her scrap of rug in the middle of the far bed surrounded by tall spires of lavender. Her back was to Caddy, but as she spoke, she turned and smiled. Her smile was warm, but even so, Caddy was shocked by the sadness in the older woman's eyes and how much she had aged in the past two months.

"I'm sorry," she said contritely. "I didn't mean to trespass. From the road it looked as if the house was empty. I couldn't resist coming to see the garden once more." She must have been unsuccessful in keeping her dismay at the other woman's appearance out of her voice, because Dorothy smiled gently before turning away again to resume her digging.

"Sit," she invited. "Talk to me while I dig up these bulbs. I keep saying I won't do this anymore, but every year I do."

Caddy walked carefully to the little path between the beds and stooped down, touching a small pile of brown bulbs heaped in Dorothy's gardening basket. "What are these?"

"Iris bulbs. They have to be taken out of the ground before the first frost so they don't get frozen. I keep them up in the attic and put them back in the spring. It's a nuisance, but the flowers they produce are so heartbreakingly lovely each year I can't resist doing it for one more season." She leaned back on her heels and wiped her forehead. Despite the warm sun she was wearing an old cardigan sweater with leather patches at the elbows, much too large for her. Caddy thought she remembered Douglas wearing that same sweater the evening they had all sat around the fire and listened to Dorothy play Chopin.

"I'm sorry," she said, not quite sure if she was referring to the fact that Dorothy was pulling up bulbs all by herself, or that Douglas had died, or that Dorothy missed Douglas so deeply she wore his old clothes for comfort.

Dorothy smiled again; this time she looked up, right into Caddy's eyes. "Come and help me, if you feel like it. There's enough work for two."

Caddy sank to her knees and began to weed around the border, using her bare fingers to pull up tenacious clumps of grass clippings that had rooted among the flowers. Dorothy handed her a gardening fork and a pair of gloves, which she accepted in silence, pulling on the gloves and attacking the grass with the fork. She wanted to say something more about Douglas, something personal, but adequate words didn't come and all she could do was lower her head and work steadily on. A small pile of discarded weeds had grown beside her on the lawn before Dorothy leaned back, stuck her trowel upright in the earth, and looking around, sighed with pleasure.

"There," she said. "All done."

Caddy looked at the overgrown bed dubiously. "It looks like it still needs a lot of work to me."

"The bulbs are all up—that's all I'm concerned about today. The gardeners have done what they could, keeping the yew trimmed and the main beds weeded, but I lost control of this patch weeks ago when . . ." Her voice trailed off and she looked over Caddy's head toward the shed.

"It must be so hard for you. I'm so sorry," Caddy interjected quickly, suddenly able to say the words that had eluded her earlier.

Dorothy put one hand on Caddy's shoulder to steady herself. Slowly, she pulled herself to her feet. She grunted softly from having been in a kneeling position so long and said matter-of-factly, "I know you are, dear, and I truly appreciated your calling on us and writing at the time. We all did. Barbara told me how kind you had been to her the night before her father died; it meant a great deal to her. She hasn't had an easy time of it, poor child."

"I heard from Captain Hardy on the way over that she was here on the island, but Josie said she thought you both had gone back to town. Is Barbara in the house?"

"No. She stayed with me for a while, closing up the Manor, but she had to get back to the children. They need her more than I do right now." She settled herself on a small twig bench nestled between the herb beds and pulled off her gardening gloves. Caddy moved over to the grass in front of the bench and sat facing her, her long legs in the sun and her face shadowed by an extended branch of the willow tree above them.

Hesitantly, she asked, "Is—"

"Hank is gone." Dorothy answered the unspoken question briefly. A fleeting expression of distaste crossed her face as she continued. "He's moved to Palm Beach and is doing something or other in real estate there. This has been extraordinarily difficult for Barbara, losing both her husband and her father at the same time." She fished around in the pocket of her sweater and, with an expression of pleasure, pulled out a bent and wrinkled cigarette. "Ah. I thought there might be one left." She lit the cigarette with an equally wrinkled pack of matches she pulled out of the other pocket and inhaled deeply, blowing the smoke up toward the sky.

Caddy was amused. "I didn't know you smoked."

"I don't," Dorothy replied calmly. "I haven't for over twenty-five years. I found an old pack in the tool-shed that one of the gardeners must have left, and I've been smoking them up, one a day, since I got here. Don't tell Barbara—she'd have a fit. So would her brother."

Caddy took a deep breath. Here was the opening she had been looking for ever since she had encountered Dorothy, the chance to talk about Fiske. Now that it was offered to her, she was unsure how to pro-

ceed. "How is he?" She lowered her head, wondering
if she sounded as foolish as she felt.

"Fine. Well, perhaps not fine, but managing beautifully."

"Losing his father must have been hard on him."

"They were very close." Dorothy inhaled one last
time, stubbed her cigarette out in the grass, and put
the butt tidily away in her sweater pocket. "Surprisingly close, actually. They're such different personali-
ties, really."

She was surprised. "Different?"

"Yes. Douglas should have been an artist right from
the start. He had enormous talent and the kind of
temperament that comes with that kind of gift: icono-
clastic, single-minded, even selfish. Because of the
Spencer money, he forced himself to be what he wasn't
—managerial, even-minded, a planner and a leader.
Only when he grew older did he allow himself the
luxury of turning over the terrible burden of managing
the fortune and giving it away to others so he could be
free to paint. Fiske is different. He goes after what he
wants—he would never wait a lifetime for something
he wanted to do." But he didn't come after me, Caddy
thought sadly. He didn't want me that much, because if
he had, he never would have let me push him away.
She stiffened and resolutely pushed all thought of her
relationship with Fiske from her mind.

"Won't he follow in his father's footsteps?" She was
genuinely puzzled. Her impression of Douglas had
been of a somewhat irascible man, and yet his wife was
firmly drawing a picture of him as a free-spirited artist.
She must have missed something, somehow.

"Of course he will, but it will be because that's what
he wants to do, not because he has to sacrifice anything to do it."

"You make Fiske sound very hard," she said in a small voice.

Dorothy was silent for a moment, considering Caddy's statement as if it were a new idea. "I don't mean to," she said finally. "I meant he was dedicated. He'd sacrifice himself in a minute for me or Barbara, the family, or anyone he truly loved, but in this instance he's thought it all through and he sees his responsibilities as an adventure, not a burden. He's fortunate that what he has to do and what he wants to do are one and the same, that's all. His father wasn't that lucky." She looked around the garden as if she was taking a long drink from a cup for the last time. "I'll miss this."

"Are you going down today?"

"Today or tomorrow, I haven't made up my mind. The Ludlows want me to dine with them and, now that we're all speaking again, I think I may. The four of us always had dinner together the last night of the season. I don't want that to stop."

"You must be glad the question of the island being sold is all over and done with. Even as an outsider, it was easy to see how hard it was on everyone. I couldn't help caring myself."

Dorothy rose and collected her gardening tools, Caddy picked up the basket, and the two women began to slowly wend their way on the grass paths through the flower beds toward the house. When Dorothy finally spoke, it was as if she was saying aloud for the first time something she had been privately thinking about for weeks.

"There was a time, just before Douglas died, before we knew about Hank and poor Rufus, when I thought we—the islanders—were going to be divided forever. If Clifford and Douglas, who had known each other all their lives, grown up on the island and into manhood together, could fall out, then there was no hope for the rest of us. Even when the whole sad story came out— when we knew that Hank had obtained Rufus's signature illegally and after Bruce Asher had been convinced to withdraw—the tensions were still so strong between us all. It was Fiske who changed all that." As if by consensus, they stopped, turned their backs to the house, and stood looking out over the trees to the water. Softly, almost ruminatively, Dorothy continued thinking out loud. "He showed such compassion and forbearance for even the most intractable owners, the ones—and there were a few—who still wanted to find another buyer and sell, that I saw my son as I never had before."

"Did you go to the annual meeting?"

"I did. I hadn't meant to, but at the last moment I was sure that Douglas would have wanted me to attend and I did. The room was packed; everyone who owns a piece of Kincade was there with all their families, even the children. I don't think there's ever been a time in my memory when no one was absent. We always use the old workers' quarters at the Homestead for the annual meeting; it's the only place large enough to hold us all. First young Rufus spoke, telling us quite simply that his father wasn't well and apologizing for his part in it all."

"His part?"

"Not being here to notice that his father was going downhill. Letting Hank take advantage of him in the despicable way he did."

"Was Rufus there?"

"In the rear, sitting with a paid companion. It's confirmed now: He has Alzheimer's." Dorothy linked her arm with Caddy's, and they turned and resumed their slow walk to the house. The breeze from the water rustled the mottled vine leaves overhead as they left the gardens and walked through an arbor at the side of the lawn. "He looked so sweet, almost like a young boy again."

"There weren't any fights though, were there?"

"No," Dorothy admitted. "But there might have been had it not been for Fiske. We have no officers or anything of that sort, but he led the rest of the meeting quite naturally because he'd been the one to deal with Asher in the end. He let everyone speak who wanted to, but somehow or other he managed not to let them run on too long or get too heated. He had gotten together with some of the others and drawn up a charter—a simple document, really—for everyone to sign agreeing to offer their land first to the other islanders should they want to sell. By the time he was through discussing it, it was signed by all the owners. Not one person thought it was an unfair or poor idea."

"Well, it's not—a poor idea. It's a very good one," Caddy said defensively.

Dorothy eyed her speculatively and chuckled to herself. "Of course it is, but up here the smallest change can mean a Byzantine set of arguments. This one went through without a hitch."

"Nelson must have been pleased. It means it won't be easy to break up the land, doesn't it?"

"Of course. If the young ones feel they can't keep up, somehow or other the rest of us will find a buyer within our families."

Caddy sighed. "It must be wonderful to be able to be so sure of that."

"That's the personal reward of being more fortunate than most, my dear. The other side of it is that a great fortune brings with it great responsibilities. One always has to be conscious of that. There never is a time when one isn't aware that doing for others is a sobering burden." She looked sideways at Caddy, as if to gauge the effect of her words.

Intercepting the look, Caddy stopped and faced her squarely. Drawing a deep breath, she asked, "Why are you telling me this?"

"Because of Fiske," Dorothy admitted finally. "He doesn't confide in me about his affairs of the heart, but I would be a fool if I didn't notice how he feels about you. He's a very proud man, my dear—some have even said arrogant, but I know him too well to believe that —and he cares about you. You must know."

Miserably, she shook her head. "I'm not sure about a lot of things right now."

They had reached the veranda. Dorothy reached out and took the basket from Caddy and set it down on the steps. "You mustn't be so hard on yourself. You know, I don't believe you are quite as uncertain as you think," she commented quietly. She looked up at the sky and back at Caddy. "I would invite you in, my dear, but I'm tired now and I'm going to lie down for a rest. If I don't see you before I leave, will you promise me you'll come visit me in New York? I feel as if we're old friends now, and I don't want to lose you."

Caddy felt a lump in her throat. She nodded, not trusting her voice. She stood very still as Dorothy reached out one hand and gently touched her cheek, bent across and kissed her lightly, and turning, disappeared into the darkened house.

Left alone, Caddy retraced her steps to the road. Blinking back the tears as she rounded the curve from the drive to the hill, she failed to see the tall man walking toward her until he was right in front of her.

"Lost?" Fiske asked quietly.

Her heart began to pound. She could feel her face flush. She shook her head. "What are you doing here?"

"I live here. What are you doing?"

"Visiting your mother."

"How is she? My mother, I mean."

"Fine. She didn't say you were here."

"She doesn't know. I came up to bring her back to New York."

"In the middle of the week?"

"She is my mother after all." Despite herself, Caddy laughed. "That's better. It's good to see you again, Caddy."

She shifted from foot to foot, took a deep breath, and in a low voice he had to stoop to hear, said, "You didn't seem particularly pleased to see me the last time we met." She looked up quickly, confused by her own gaucherie. "I'm sorry, it was right after—"

"—my father died. And you're wrong: I was glad to see you, I just—"

"—was giving me a little of my own back. I'm sorry about all that too," she told him softly. They smiled at each other ruefully.

"We seem to be stepping on each other's lines," he said.

"Friends?" she asked hopefully.

"Perhaps," he replied enigmatically.

She studied his face for a moment. He was thin and drawn, as if he hadn't been eating regularly or getting enough sleep. There were lines on either side of his mouth that hadn't been there the last time she saw him. He looked older, and her heart ached for him. Impulsively she told him, "You know, I saw you driving away from the funeral. I wished I had spoken to you then, before you got into the car, but you left so quickly and you didn't see me."

He looked down at her soberly, and her heart began to pound even harder as she saw the dawn of a slow, intimate smile in his eyes. "But I did see you. You were standing on the sidewalk outside the church and I thought you were a mirage, all fresh and clean in your summer dress. I wanted to jump out of the car and . . ."

"And what?"

"Nothing," he ended abruptly.

"Has it been . . . it must be difficult for you, taking his place." Mentally, she cursed herself for stammering.

"Harder than I would have thought possible. He was one of a kind."

She nodded sympathetically. At a loss for words, she looked up as a boisterous horde of dark, glossy mallards flew low over the house toward the Great Marsh. Behind the main group a few stragglers uttered strident honks as they struggled to keep up. Fiske watched them too, his head turning in unison with hers as they watched the flight path of the quacking birds. Even when the mallards disappeared over the treetops, neither of them spoke. She should leave now. Listlessly, she swung her homemade staff and took a step away from Fiske toward the main road. But she couldn't leave without telling him what had been on her mind ever since the night of the dance. She turned impulsively back and found him still watching her.

"I'm sorry I ran away from you at the dance. It was rude," she blurted.

"I shouldn't have taken it for granted that you felt the same way as I did," he responded gently.

Miserably, she noticed that he spoke in the past

tense. All her fears were confirmed: If he had thought he loved her once, he no longer did. She raised her eyes and looked directly at him. His eyes were expressionless, and despite the stubborn set of his mouth, she thought he looked as if he was holding something back within him only by the tightest control. Her heart leapt with hope. Perhaps he hadn't lost all of his feelings for her after all. She smiled tentatively, but his eyes remained expressionless.

She turned her head away and reached out, plucking aimlessly at the hedge. She felt a warmth that had nothing to do with the September sun. He was very still, watching her intently. The only sound was the wind soughing softly through the trees and the far-off hum of an engine fading into the distance somewhere on the main road. She gave a small cry of pain, holding up her hand: In her mindless ripping at the hedge, a jagged branch had torn at the skin and there was a thin line of oozing blood. Forlornly, she inspected the damage. In the most natural fashion Fiske reached out and took her hand and kissed it. Her head was lowered as she stared fascinated at their two hands, watched him reach into his pocket for a handkerchief and carefully wrap it over the tiny wound.

"You know," he said conversationally, "I've been thinking a lot lately and I've come to the conclusion that if two people love each other, no matter what the other issues are, they ought to snatch at the possibility of happiness and hang on to it for dear life. I don't think we get more than one chance, do you?" He still had possession of her hand, holding it lightly as if he had absentmindedly forgotten to release it. He leaned down and kissed her lips gently, persuasively, and very firmly.

Staring at their two hands she responded shakily,

"You make it sound like a moral obligation." He kissed her again. This time, she kissed him back.

His voice was very soft, as if he was afraid of frightening a butterfly poised for flight. "Whatever it is, Caddy, I love you. I'm not quite sure how or why, but I've known from the start that you were going to belong to me, just the way I belong to you."

Startled, she looked up at him. The love blazing from his eyes swept over her like a tidal wave, but this time she didn't run away, meeting his look with one of her own in which she let her whole heart shine without reservation. With a choked sound that could have been triumph or laughter, he enfolded her in his arms, and for a long time all she could hear was the beating of his heart.

If you're looking for romance,
adventure, excitement and
suspense be sure to read these
outstanding romances
from Dell.

❖

Antoinette Stockenberg
☐ **EMILY'S GHOST**   21002-X $4.99
☐ **BELOVED**   21330-4 $4.99
☐ **EMBERS**   21673-7 $4.99

Carol Marsh
☐ **IN HER OWN LIGHT**   21362-2 $4.99
☐ **THE SILVER LINK**   21624-9 $4.99
☐ **MORNINGS OF GOLD**   21627-3 $4.99

Jill Gregory
☐ **CHERISHED**   20620-0 $4.99
☐ **DAISIES IN THE WIND**   21618-4 $5.50
☐ **FOREVER AFTER**   21512-9 $4.99
☐ **WHEN THE HEART BECKONS**   21857-8 $5.50

Meryl Sawyer
☐ **NEVER KISS A STRANGER**   20682-0 $4.99
☐ **PROMISE ME ANYTHING**   21464-5 $4.99